The Awakening of Meena Rawat

Anoop Judge

Black Rose Writing | Texas

The author grants the final approval for this literary material.

First printing

ISBN: 978-1-68433-706-4
PUBLISHED BY BLACK ROSE WRITING
www.blackrosewriting.com

Printed in the United States of America
Suggested Retail Price (SRP) $19.95

The Awakening of Meena Rawat is printed in Sabon

*As a planet-friendly publisher, Black Rose Writing does its best to eliminate
unnecessary waste to reduce paper usage and energy costs, while never
compromising the reading experience. As a result, the final word count vs. page count
may not meet common expectations.

This book is for my mom, lnderjit Ahuja,
who gave me the gift of life and of storytelling.

And for Tony:
Friend, love, partner.
For Amaraj & Ghena:
My heart and soul.

The
Awakening of
Meena Rawat

PROLOGUE

India, 1996

"*Aai*, please don't leave me."

My mother lies motionless in the back of an ambulance. I begin to reach out, to touch the hairy arm of the paramedic sitting on a cracked vinyl bench that runs parallel to the stretcher bed where she lies. To draw his attention to her. Only a foot of room lies between the stretcher and the bench.

At the base of the stretcher is another seat where I sit facing my mother's head. I massage her ankles, which are bluish-black and puffy. Tears wet my cheeks. "Please help my *Aai*," I beg.

The man jumps back violently, pushing himself away from my outstretched hand. His face puckers like a well-sucked mango seed. "How dare you try to touch me," he roars. "Filthy *Chamar*." In the closed van, his words ricochet like bullets.

Aai inhales painfully as if drawing her last breath. Panic swirls like boiling milk in my belly. I kneel, hands clutched together in entreaty. Desperate, though careful not to touch him, I fall prostrate to the rubber-covered floor. My nostrils quiver as I smell the nauseating scent of blood and dried urine. With my hands clasped, I stretch my arms out in front of me and raise my eyes pitifully as the ambulance rattles over uneven streets. All I can see are the tips of his reinforced, black lace-up boots. This is the first of two things about this man that are forever burned into my memory. Hard boots built for a tough job. The other is the way his gaze slithers away from me—careful to avoid eye contact—as if he might catch something.

His jaw tightens when I look up at him again, but he continues to contemplate the view outside the window. Even though I am only ten, I can tell he is bored and disinterested, and merely seeing out another shift. He feels nothing for us . . . not for me and not for my *Aai*. Because 'nothing' is exactly what we are to him.

"Let her die," he says viciously. "She's a sweeper. A bloody *Chamar*. There are always more of you, like rats. And who needs more rats?" He shrugs as he shifts his unblinking stare back to the window.

I struggle to my feet, listing to keep my balance. My *Aai*'s glassy eyes stare at the roof of the ambulance, but they seem far away—far from this man, this existence. I whimper like a hurt dog as tears roll down my face.

The van shakes as we ride over another bump through the potholed streets of my village, jostling my *Aai*, who lets out another gasp of pain. Her ragged breathing rips my ears, and her chest convulses up and down. I foolishly clasp my hands in a moment of hope as if the heaving chest is proof of a resurgent life force within her.

Aai grasps weakly at her chest, and then her hand falls away. Her eyes and her mouth fly open again. She looks shocked by death. She looks like my *Aai* no longer.

I muffle my cries, but empty sobs leak into the tight, hostile space in the back of the ambulance.

She is dead. My *Aai* is dead.

1
MEENA

California, Fall 2014

A lock of hair catches on my dry lips and I shove it out of the way before rolling over and burrowing back into my duvet. Even before my eyes open, I sense that Bhavesh is awake. The sound of his impatient voice floats from the kitchen next to Maya's bedroom, where he's making a business call. I have been falling asleep in Maya's room almost every night, waking up cramped and tired in my eight-year-old daughter's bed. I could get up and make my way back to our marital bed during the night, but I almost never do. I am not sure how I feel about that. Good, I suppose. But worried, too.

Sunshine slices through the break in the curtains, sending a beam of white light onto the carpet next to the bed where I lie and wonder what my husband's next outburst will be. Last week's was about the lack of a clean, starched shirt.

Women are not fit for independence. The words he had yelled at me then echo in my mind. It is one of his favorite lines from the Hindu scriptures.

Hearing him on the telephone fills my mouth with a bitter taste as I pick up on his precise enunciation of every word. Someone is getting an earful from him—probably one of his vendors in India, late with a shipment.

"You *bewakoof!*" he bellows after a repetitive litany of instructions to pick up, package and send motor parts for his business (*now, repeat* the same process for Tata Hitachi, you imbecile!) Across the years I have heard this over and over again, and each time Bhavesh sounds more enraged as his life has grown ever more dissatisfying to him.

I clap my hands over my ears. I am sorry for whomever Bhavesh is talking to, making them feel like a second-rate employee. I know that feeling all too well.

Great, I think, anxiety moving like a current through my body. That means Bhavesh will probably be in a foul mood. I should have woken up earlier and come down before him.

I shiver slightly as the memory of my ten-year-old self echoes in my twenty-eight-year-old mind, a shape that lingers on the edge of sleep. Every rut in the road that cursed van had run over, every pain-filled sound my dying mother had made, the floor that stank of sweat and death—all of it still twists inside me. It had only been because of the largesse of the local *zamindar*—in whose home my mother had worked as a sweeper, cleaning their toilets for over twenty years—that *Aai* had been fortunate enough to receive any medical attention at all. For all the good it had done her to die in the back of that van subjected to the hostility and indifference of a man paid to save her life. A familiar sickening feeling boils inside me.

The little girl I was then—pale, squalid-looking, with rough braids hanging across my face—had not understood. It was all I had ever known. The caste system had been outlawed in India for many years, yet was still being practiced. I grit my teeth, wishing I could go back to being my ten-year-old self and right the injustice that had happened in the back of that van. I should have screamed at the medic to do his job, or I should have reported him for his unlawful behavior.

With a forceful shake of my head, I bring myself back to the present and my sleeping daughter beside me.

"Wake up, Maya. You'll be late for school." I shake her roughly when she doesn't respond.

"Mom!" Maya cries, protectively grabbing her shoulder as she awakens and turns to look at me, bleary-eyed. My lovely daughter's expression droops into a pout, enormous tears in her soft brown eyes.

I reach out to her, stung with guilt. "I'm so sorry, sweetie. Mommy had a bad dream, and she's grumpy this morning. She shouldn't take it out on you."

I put my arms around her and slowly rock her. "Don't cry, *pyaari beti*." Remorse lodges itself in my throat.

"It's okay, Mommy," Maya replies. "I forgive you." A mischievous smile finds its way onto her face. "I forgive you, as long as you get me a puppy."

I cannot help but laugh. My daughter is learning subtlety and manipulation. "We've spoken of this," I scold, pulling back the covers to encourage her out of bed.

"Maybe I'll ask Daddy," Maya says cheerily, grabbing her bright pink *Dora The Explorer* pillow and pressing her nose into it.

I keep my face expressionless. "Not this morning, huh?"

Maya shrugs, her train of thought sliding seamlessly to another topic in the way only a child's can. "What shall I wear to school today?" she asks, climbing out of bed.

We pick an outfit together, chatting back and forth to get the right balance of cuteness, style, and warmth. It takes about fifteen minutes, and then we trudge downstairs, both of us reasonably pleased with the outcome.

Bhavesh has finished his telephone conversation and stands by the counter spreading margarine on his morning toast. The scowl he wears before noticing his daughter gives me a clear warning of his mood.

"Daddy!" shrieks Maya, causing him to break into a wide smile. She runs to his outstretched arms, and he gathers her up. With that even-toothed smile and his way with his daughter, most women would find Bhavesh attractive—an *excellent catch* is what they would say.

Seeing me hovering behind our daughter, Bhavesh frowns. I turn away, barely meeting his eye, and lay out the fixings for Maya's breakfast, hoping to avoid conversation for as long as possible. Maya has perched herself in front of the family computer and is happily engrossed in images of puppies.

"You're going to be late dropping her off," he says to my back. His tone is curt, like he was on the phone.

"Yes, we got behind this morning." I speak carefully, not turning around to reply. The back of my throat itches terribly. I do not think my head can take the strain of explaining myself to him right now.

I need not have worried. By the time I finish with Maya's breakfast, Bhavesh has left the kitchen. I hear him stalking around the lounge section of the open-plan living space, then the family room. I relax, unclasping my hands from their tight hold on the milk carton.

Then he appears back in the kitchen. He is all nervous energy, presumably still agitated after the phone call to his vendor. It must have been serious. My shoulders hunch, as if bracing against an icy wind, but Bhavesh is rooted in his thoughts and has forgotten me. He turns and heads towards the front of the house to his office.

"Maya, come have your breakfast!" I call quickly. Sometimes I feel like I'm drowning, and I long to escape into cold air. "We have to be quick, honey."

Ten minutes later, with the dishes still in the sink, clothes not yet in the wash, and a dirty towel lying in the corner of the bathroom, I tug at the front door and pull it open with a *whoosh*. Most days, I make sure I complete the little tasks, so that Bhavesh does not snipe at me. Yet lately, I have purposefully left them undone. It is my minor rebellion against his hypocrisy, I guess. One need only look into the bombsite he calls an *office* to see that.

Now on our own, Maya and I chat cheerfully, fingers entwined, as we head to our car parked on the tree-lined street of our California-perfect, suburban neighborhood. Maya's little backpack bounces on her shoulder as the cool morning breeze brushes our faces.

Much of the time, my daughter fills my mind. Some of my thoughts are trivial, like how glad I am that I won the battle to make Maya wear a sweater on such an unusually crisp morning. At other times, I fill my thoughts with love and thanks for the pleasure my daughter brings me. She is the only genuine joy in my life. Despite my best efforts, those are not my thoughts today.

I glance upwards. The sunshine has disappeared and given way to a rough gray sky, places dark and angry but with the potential for a powerful, cleansing rain. Dull, depressing, miserable; the type of sky that makes it difficult to keep a lid on the memories of my former life—

memories that constantly spill out and intrude upon this other life I have made for myself.

These days my memories are more insistent than ever and I must work hard if I am to suppress them. But that is impossible when they seep into my carefully constructed reality.

2
MEENA

India, 1996
Kalanpur, Uttar Pradesh

The cooling winds that often blow in from the Arabian Sea are still, and the temperature has crept up into the nineties. Monsoon season is still almost five months away, so there is none of the terrible humidity that accompanies the sweltering heat in this region of northern India.

Even so, my skin burns as I climb, faltering and nervous, beside my Gopi *Mama*—my uncle—all the way up the steep hill leading to the orphanage's flaking blue gate. By the time we reach the top, my uncle is uncharacteristically sweaty and I am feeling light-headed. We have covered some distance today and both pant with exhaustion.

The tumbled-down building at the top of the hill is made of featureless gray stone. Vine-covered walls rise two stories to a steeply pitched roof, and black iron bars cross narrow, deep-set windows. The glass in some windows is broken out and the holes are stuffed with rags to keep out the cold.

Even from a distance it looks grim and forbidding. It reminds me of the *bhoot bangla* story about a haunted house that *Aai* used to tell me when she wanted me to hurry up and drink my milkless chai on the days the rent money was due. Up close, however, it is depressingly real. A dilapidated sign hangs over the main gate, proclaiming in faded letters, "Grace Mercy Children's Home."

The gate opens as we come near, a *chowkidar* springing to attention as a gleaming white ambassador car appears from within. The driver, dressed in a white uniform and cap, blares his horn at us in obvious displeasure.

My Gopi *Mama* leaps out of the way, pushing me before him. Had he not been so quick, the car would have hit us. His tattered white *dhoti* skims the side of the front tire, which is now smudged with brake dust on top of the dirt from our journey.

"*Arre, Arre,* Meena," he growls, pinching my ear. "Come on now, child. Don't keep the good nuns waiting."

I shrink at his fury, not yet old enough to distinguish between anger and misdirected guilt. Hanging my head, bone-tired after the long morning's walk, I wonder who was in the car. Had they been coming, like me, or going? Will I have to be in this terrifying place forever?

If my Gopi *Mama* had been unhappy about being burdened after my mother died, my aunt—a big woman filling a dark sari like a mound of rising dough and a severe coif—was furious. "What are we, a charity?" I overheard her berating my uncle one afternoon. They had sent me on an errand to the market but I had returned after a few minutes, having forgotten to take a bag.

Hesitating numbly outside the door, I had overheard them. "Should we take in every child whose parents can't be bothered to look after them? It is okay for your useless dead sister now, isn't it? She doesn't have to worry about money or food anymore."

The ground seemed to sway beneath my feet, and I had to hold on to the wall. She made it sound as if my *Aai* had died on purpose, too lazy to look after her own child any longer. I knew enough not to show my hatred and to be as careful and helpful as I could. Yet they are still taking their first opportunity to get rid of me.

Gopi *Mama* reaches the gate and raps the heavy, bronzed knocker that reverberates into the dusty front yard. The *chowkidar* pokes his head out with a disapproving expression.

"What do you want?" he barks.

"I'm Gopi Prasad," my uncle says, cupping his palms together, thumbs against the chest, his head bowed slightly. "I've come to see the nuns of Grace Mercy about my niece."

He points a finger at me, making me feel conspicuous in my tatty clothes. Shame rises like bile as I look down at my sweaty and dirt-stained blue chemise and at the holes visible in the elbows of my blue cardigan. Fidgeting awkwardly, I try to hide my bare feet, which are sore and blistered.

The *chowkidar's* gaze is swift and scrutinizing; I shrink inwardly, clutching a red, embroidered cloth bag to my chest. The bag is my prized possession, a gift from my mother, purchased from the weekly *Mangal* Bazaar just before she died.

The *chowkidar* slowly slides open the heavy, wrought-iron gate. It shrieks loudly in protest, making my ears ring as it opens on a small dusty courtyard. My uncle and I follow him through the courtyard and into the main building, which is cold and dark despite the warmth and brightness of the day. The floor—a mixture of wood, damaged tiles, and ice-cold stone—stings the soles of my feet, while the sweat from my long, hot walk chills me.

The building is hushed, its sounds muted as if the place is under some spell. A large muscular woman appears, her face grim and unsmiling. She wears rimless glasses and on her head perches a white cap with the brim turned up all around, like the little paper boats that children in our village make. She ushers us into an even darker room, which is bare except for a solid, plain desk with two worn-looking leather chairs in front of it. The walls, like those in the unlit hallway, are a dull, ugly white. On one wall there is a brightly colored picture of Jesus Christ and on the other, behind the desk, a cross of dark wood. A visible stain runs through some of the cross, and, judging by the stain that runs up the wall behind the cross and into a larger stain in the ceiling, I think the roof must have had a significant leak in the recent past.

"I'm the mother superior. This is the little girl, yes?" she asks my uncle in a commanding tone. The nun wears a simple white habit, faded and worn but spotless, and a heavy crucifix around her thin, wattled neck. Her face is wrinkled like a dried date and her voice is cold and austere. My heart seizes at the thought of being left with her as she shuffles to an equally worn leather captain's chair behind the desk. A wooden clock on the wall behind us ticks away the sound of it like a crow pecking the remains of a dead tree stump.

"Yes, yes, Sistah. She is alone, poor child. Her mother . . . Sistah, gone to Heaven, *na*." Gopi Prasad shakes his head with pity, a bit too vigorously. I have never heard him like this before. Is it because of her immense authority, or because of his desperation to be rid of me?

"You do know we have no other *Dalit* children here? Meena will be the only one." The mother superior eyes my uncle cautiously.

Gopi *Mama's* fingers are so tightly laced in his lap that his knuckles have turned white. "Yes, Sistah," he replies meekly. "I have nowhere else to go, Sistah."

A maidservant with squinty eyes, dressed in a raggedy, jade green sari just like the kind my *Aai* used to wear, scurries in with a steaming cup of tea on a chipped ceramic tray.

"Tell Sister Gina I want to see her," the mother superior tells her with a nod. The maidservant places the tray before her and leaves.

A few moments later, a nun with a round, cheerful face and sparkling eyes scampers in. She looks young and disordered beside the mother superior. Flushed, she breaks into a broad smile when she spots me.

I panic at the sudden attention and hide behind Gopi *Mama*, sucking my thumb. Embarrassed, my uncle arches his back, trying to catch hold of me.

"Come now, Meena. Let's not be rude to the Sistah."

"It's all right," Sister Gina says after introducing herself. Her voice is calm and soothing. "You are just fine there, aren't you, Meena?"

At the sister's kind words and soft face, my shoulders slump under the weight of all that has happened—my mother's death, my unwelcome presence at my aunt and uncle's home, the journey, and this strange place. The only reply I can manage is a hiccup.

Sister Gina slips off her tightly laced black shoes, still smiling at me as her feet hop lightly on the ice-cold floor.

"Meena, look what I have for you." She squats down beside me.

In her hand are two sweets labeled *Cadbury Chocolate Éclairs*. The two purple and gold treasures tantalize me, catching the light in the tilt of Sister Gina's hands. I look up into Sister Gina's eyes and my fingers tentatively reach out, half-expecting these impossible prizes to be snatched away, or for my hand to pass right through hers, the sweets and the kind sister all an apparition.

"It's all right, Meena," Sister Gina says kindly, her gray eyes twinkling in the poor light. "They're yours."

"Thank you," I stutter, my voice stuck in my throat. I clutch the sweets tightly to my chest against my red cloth bag.

Sister Gina stands up and holds out a hand. I take it with a glance back at Gopi *Mama*, but he turns his face away as Sister Gina leads me from the office and into the corridor. Suddenly his voice calls after me, unconvincingly hearty, "I'll come back for you, Meena *beti.*"

The nun smiles down at me, sadness lacing her lips, and she tightens her grip on my hand.

3
Meena

Fall 2014
Fremont, California

The rules are with me always, and they are here with me now at the Fremont Hindu temple as the priest recites the scriptures in a low monotone. Dressed in only a loincloth, his face and body streaked with ash, the traditional red thread of a *Brahmin* runs over his shoulder and diagonally across his chest as he drones on. His face is dark and emotionless as he reads from the Holy Scriptures, though for all the expression in his voice, he could be reciting assembly instructions for flat-pack furniture.

This is my conduit to God, I think to myself wryly.

The Pandit of the village temple where my *Aai* and I lived recited the rules to us every morning as if sleeping might have wiped our memories clean. I could lose almost every other memory, but those are as clear to me today as they were back then, like they have become tied to my DNA. In a sense, they are, going all the way back to my ancestors.

Rule Number 1: An Untouchable cannot wear *chappals* unless they are in the Untouchable part of the village—that part of the village with the gutter at its center, where dung patties impressed with hand marks lay drying on mud walls in the midday sun.

Rule Number 2: Untouchable children must wear a green wristband to school. No one else wore a wristband, and the children who were not

Untouchables were *Brahmin* or *Kshatriya,* created from the head and the shoulder of God. Untouchables like me were created from the feet of God.

The Pandit in the temple in Kalanpur would bellow, "We are *Brahmins!* You are Untouchables!" The first a glorious exultation, the second a venomous accusation that caused spittle to spray out over the worshippers. I remember cowering in the back as he glared at us.

Consigned to the most degrading menial work and poverty, the fate of the Untouchables showed in our defeated faces and raggedy saris. No matter how much we might have washed before worship, my kind always seemed to carry the grime of our dirty existence.

I shudder at how my *Aai* was one of those wretched people—the vermin who scurried amongst the refuse of her superiors, better out of sight and out of mind, her presence spoiling the view.

And then Rule Number 3: Untouchable children cannot share the same bench as *Kshatriya* or *Brahmins.* I press my eyes shut and remember the first time I broke that rule.

• • •

Summer 1998
Grace Mercy Children's Home
The rain falls heavily, like a river emptying from the sky. I peer through the gray haze of monsoon rains from my seat by the schoolroom window, but I can barely make out the dark, formless shapes of the gigantic pipal trees on the side of the building.

My stomach is rumbling so loudly that the math equations on the page in front of me float in a blur. All I have eaten today is the gruel served up by Sister Gina before class. More watery than usual, the gray mess of oatmeal porridge was enriched with just a smattering of milk.

Some of the other twelve-year-old girls who whisper and giggle from behind their desks in the front of the class distract me from the window. My assigned seat sat at the perimeter of the classroom where I painstakingly planted myself in the wobbly old elbow chair with only three legs, its upholstered seat stained with grease marks. I slouch in my seat straining to hear, yet careful not to be obvious about it, as always.

"Look at him," says a girl in a high-pitched tone as she indicates the teacher. The girl has deep-set and tawny tiger-eyes, and the blackest hair I have ever seen. Her hair is lustrous and shiny, unlike mine, which always seems to be the color of the dust that litters the corners of the orphanage.

"See how he stands? I think he wants to make love to the chalkboard." Tiger-eyes-thick-black-hair sniggers with a hand to her mouth. The girl across from her, Rosy-plump-cheeks snorts. "Or his equations."

The first girl flips back her hair with a wicked grin. "'I want you x plus y.'"

I can barely stop myself from laughing. Mr. Mehta is new and comes from outside the orphanage to teach us. This is only our third lesson with him. Before the first one, the mother superior came to lecture us from the front of the class about how lucky we were to have a real math teacher. But all the rotund and very bearded man does is face the blackboard—his legs an extraordinary distance apart, his groin at the place where his equations are about to start landing—and then he babbles on and scribbles incomprehensible numbers and words. When the board is full, the chalk goes down and he turns to glare at us with beady eyes. It is so quiet you can hear a pin drop, and that marks the end of the lesson.

"I'm glad he's so small," says Tiger-eyes-thick-black-hair with a glint in her eyes.

"Why?" Rosy-plump-cheeks asks, glinting back.

"If he could reach the top of the chalkboard, the lesson would be longer."

I cannot stifle my laugh and both girls frown at me. Tiger-eyes-thick-black-hair flashes her fierce eyes in my direction and I quickly turn away, back to the monsoon rains and the dread of not having enough to eat in the ebb and flow of Grace Mercy's resources. In the last two years, food has always been the first thing to grow scarce, with caste determining how much we get. Sometimes, we get nothing at all. Sister Gina always tries to be fair, but usually she only handles breakfast, and not always that. Some days, breakfast doesn't even happen.

As always, I must wait for the other castes to get their food when we finally fill the dining hall, and I'm feverishly hopeful when I see the plates of the other girls before me. But by the time it is my turn to be served, they have run out of *rotis* and the *aloo subzi* is finished.

My face drops, hunger scraping vicious fingers inside my stomach. I stand at the kitchen door pleading with the kitchen-hand, Mahadev, until he cannot stand the sound of my voice anymore.

"*Chupp*, you *Chamar*," he shouts at me as he flings a couple of *rotis* and some mango-chili pickle in my direction.

I gaze longingly at the other girls sitting in rows throughout the mess hall. It is far too wet to go outside, and the thrumming of heavy raindrops on the roof drowns out the sound of chattering girls and boys. But I am forbidden to sit on the benches where they eat. As an Untouchable, I might pollute them and their food. I hunch by the wall nearest the exit and pick at my food carefully, so I do not drop it, wishing for a seat to make things easier.

When the girls finish, they file out, tittering and chatting. I take my chance, slinking noiselessly up to their bench at the back of the hall, and take a seat as inconspicuously as I can manage. I quickly unfold my *dupatta* and remove the *rotis,* tearing a corner and pushing it into my mouth. Ravenous, I tear off another piece.

"Ee-e-h, you bloody *Chamar,*" a familiar voice calls out. "What do you think you are doing?"

I spin around to see Mahadev striding towards me. He looks terrifying as he hurtles angrily in my direction. He is dressed as usual in a white *dhoti*, a long white shirt, and heavy black sandals. His clean-shaven face is dark-complexioned, and he wears a red *tikka* on his forehead.

"I . . . I have n-not done anything," I say, fear gripping me. Instinctively, my hand comes halfway up in a defensive motion. "I have not eaten any of the other girls' food, I swear." I lift up the *rotis.* "These are mine. Y-you gave them to me."

"Not done anything?" Mahadev repeats, his eyes bloodshot with fury. "You have polluted the bench, you dirty, filthy *Chamar*! Who is going to sit here now?"

"B-but why not?" I implore him, reaching out my hand. Accidentally, it brushes his as he looms menacingly over me.

"Do not touch me," he screams, jerking his hand away. He shakes with rage, veins popping in his forehead. "You shameless girl . . . you . . . *you* have the audacity to touch *me?*"

I shield my head with an arm as he waves his arms around.

"What is this?" he cries. "Will you strike me, too?"

"No, no!" I protest. "I wou—"

"—I will show you what it means to touch me—a *Kshatriya!* See how I touch you back."

With a quick scan of the eyes, checking that no one is around, Mahadev appears to forget his distaste for touching my kind and grabs my ear, twisting it sharply. The intense explosion of pain worsens when he yanks me up to my feet, my *rotis* and pickle falling to the floor. I swallow back bile, almost vomiting my little piece of *roti* back up. I cry out in agony.

"Even your shadow contaminates this bench," he says. I can smell his sour breath as he spits the words over me. "It's not fit for sitting on now; it will need to be chopped up for firewood. Are you happy with yourself, you filthy girl, wasting a good bench like this?"

He turns and leaves me there, throbbing and sick with shame. Tears falling down my face, I bend down and pick up the *roti,* not knowing when I will eat again.

• • •

I wipe the tears off my face with the back of a fierce hand. Since I am to be blamed for these sins I am unaware of—punished for them—it occurs to me for the first time in my young twelve-year-old life as I turn to leave the mess hall, that I might as well commit a sin or two of my own.

With purposeful strides, Mahadev emerges from the kitchen with a bowl of *aloo subzi* that he must have saved for himself. It looks like a generous portion. Noticing me lingering near the exit, he throws me a disdainful glare that seems to say "what are you still doing here?"

My stomach flutters as the idea forms inside my head. My subconscious immediately splits between the part of me that recoils at the idea and the other part of me, the one that dares me to stand up for myself, to stop being such a victim. To have my revenge against Mahadev.

"One of the Sisters was looking for you," I tell him.

"I was in the kitchen," Mahadev says. "Why didn't you tell her I was there?"

I look at the floor guiltily. "I didn't see where you went, I was still crying."

I watch two emotions cross his face, one after the other. The first is a flash of pleasure, most likely at the thought he had hurt me enough that I should have been crying. It is quickly followed by a burst of panic. "Which one?"

"What?"

"Which Sister, you imbecile!"

"Oh . . . um, I can't remember her name. She's not been with us long."

Mahadev looks back at the food he was about to eat and gives an irritated huff. "Nuns," he grumbles, "won't even let a man eat in peace."

He walks past me, intentionally barging me aside, almost knocking me down, and leaves the mess hall. I move quickly once he strides away, checking that the kitchen is empty, then I cross to his bowl of food and stare down into it. The aroma pulls at my stomach, which is still painfully empty. I cannot eat his food, though, as much as I want to. *That* will be noticed.

There are several *rotis* beside the bowl, and I turn my attention to these first. "Too unclean to touch you, am I?" I say under my breath and reach a hand down to rub it across the top *roti*.

I recoil in terror as soon as I have done it and I look around, half-expecting Mahadev to burst through the doors, this time ready to do more than twist my ear. Or perhaps one of the nuns or a student, or any one of so many people who could easily turn up and see me.

What am I doing? I think. *This is crazy!* And it is crazy, but there is something breathlessly thrilling about it. Before I know what I am doing a ball of phlegm is rolling around in my mouth and then falling into Mahadev's bowl of *aloo subzi.* "I pollute you," I say gleefully and stir it in a little with my finger, sucking off the evidence as I leave the mess hall.

4
Meena

Fall 2014
Fremont, California

On Tuesday morning, as I am driving to work, I switch on the radio to distract me from thoughts that stir in me like dead leaves.

"Next on Philosophy Talk," says the radio host, "Do you believe in Life After Death?"

I hike up the volume.

"Hello, everyone," continues the host. "Meet Bob Olsen, the author of *Answers After Life*. Bob, death is one of life's few certainties . . . or, is it?" I laugh inwardly, shaking my head. *How American.*

His voice grows deeper. "That may just be two sides of the same delusion. Heaven is God's carrot, and Hell is his stick. It's like what Nietzsche said about Jesus—he was so hungry for love that he had to invent hell, so he could send those who refused to love him there." The traffic light turns red and I drum my fingers on the steering wheel, thinking about the errands I have to run after work. *I need to go to the bank, the dry cleaners, and the Indian store for the Brooke Bond Taj Mahal tea that Bhavesh likes for his morning chai.*

"Heaven is the flip side—it's where you go if you've been a good little soul. What are your thoughts, Bob? What evidence have you found of life after death?"

Bob's voice comes on, high and nasal. "Hello, Jim. Thank you for having me on the show. The Catholic Church has long held that a just God without an afterlife is inconceivable, because it would mean that Hitler and Anne Frank had the same fate. I believe—"

I flip the indicator to turn right. A cloud moves across the sky in front of the morning sun, and a beam of light illuminates the plain wooden cross at the front of the church on Mission Street.

Fascinating though the arguments are, they are mostly based around a Judeo-Christian point of view, and I wish they would broaden the discussion. I swat at the radio button irritably and change to a music station to drown out the meaningless chatter.

As I turn onto the eastern edge of campus, marked by a poorly fenced, bumpy parking lot already full of compact and energy-efficient cars, I give a rueful nod. Too bad we don't look for an eternity beyond this life in heaven or hell like Christians do. As an Untouchable, my soul has likely spent a fair amount of time in the lowest level of the Underworld already. I pull into a spot—scowling ferociously as I brood—though my marriage to Bhavesh, a *Kshatriya,* hopefully has elevated me enough to avoid the same fate next time around.

Or has it?

Last week after visiting the temple, I removed the *mauli* and hid it from Bhavesh and Maya, but I could not shake my thoughts all week. I felt false, unworthy of being a *Kshatriya,* yet also a traitor to the *Dalit* caste. Surely there is no greater detriment to my own *karma* than to be this way—caught between castes, belonging nowhere. Climbing from my car and walking through the university grounds, I pull a face and inhale deeply, breathing in the crisp wintry air.

California State University East Bay has long, low buildings linked by glass walkways. On gray mornings like this it looks inviting, with its buttery light shining out across the parking lots. My bag looks out of place on an otherwise smart-but-insipidly-dressed East Indian university administrator, dressed as I am in a ruffled white blouse and black pantsuit bought from a discount department store years ago. The bag of red *chanderi* silk, my mother's gift, is embroidered with flattened silver wire and trimmed with bold applique and mirror work. Much mended by me and inevitably faded, I marvel that I am still able to use it almost eighteen years after my *Aai* bought it from that street market in Kalanpur. It's just a bag, but it has seen so much and crossed half the world to be where it is and what it still is—the only remnant of the mother I once had.

Climbing up the dank-smelling stairwell, I think about the project I am working on for the English Department, cataloging their collection of works by Chaucer and Shakespeare with automation software. I perk up as I remember. Today we will start indexing—something new to look forward to.

Scrabbling around for my keycard, I feel a sudden twinge in the small of my back. I lean backward for a moment and massage it. This job has been bad for my back, with a lot of days spent bent over in awkward positions. *But maybe this is just what I need to get promoted.* I slide my keycard and open the door to my office. *Then, they might move me out of the janitor's closet.*

My office is about six feet across and less than twelve feet deep; its grimy window is the only thing keeping it from being a closet. Bookshelves lining the left side encroach upon the meager space. My desk dominates the right side, which is the only place where it can fit. When not at my desk, I must tuck my chair all the way in, or else the room turns into a collision course.

My only personal item is a framed poster of *Durga Ma* killing the demon *Asura* hanging above my desk. "For inspiration and, you know, womanpower," I explain hastily when visitors to my little hovel ask about it.

'Where is it from?' and 'How old is it?' are innocent questions asked out of politeness or genuine interest, yet I always dread them and give hasty answers, which must seem to my colleagues the deflections they are. But how can I say that it was a gift from the only man I ever truly cared about? *No, not my husband. Yes, you're right, I should have gotten rid of it years ago, wicked wife that I am.*

For the next few hours I pound relentlessly at my computer, losing myself in a world of structure and organization. Although indexing the university's catalog records is a tedious job, occasional gems pop up to keep a thread of interest running through.

Leaning back in my chair, I raise my arms over my head and stretch. My stomach growls and I turn to look at the clock on my desk. *Wow, 12:10 already? I really have lost myself in work today. I was supposed to meet Tammy for lunch at noon.*

I grab my coat and my bag and rush from the office, pulling on my coat as I walk down the corridor while trying to send her a quick text. I groan, realizing how foolish I must look to passersby as I wrestle with the arms, taking four times as long to complete the action than if I had just stood still. I do not care, though; impatience is giving my feet wings. I run panting across the university grounds and I arrive at the cafeteria located at the east end of the campus babbling apologies, much to Tammy's amusement.

"Yeah, yeah," Tammy says with a grin. "If it were anyone else, it would sound like an excuse, but I know all about you and your thing for indexing."

I give her a grateful hug.

"Must be something I'm missing with it," Tammy continues, pressing two fingers to her forehead, "because it always seems a bit boring to me." At the table next to us, two young women, one wearing a burqa, are looking at a laptop together and talking passionately about a class on Islamic Studies.

"Indexing," she says with a dreamy expression on her face, letting the world roll seductively off her tongue. "Wow, when you say it like that, it sounds quite hot. Gotta get me some of that."

I chortle. In moments, I am comfortably ensconced in conversation. Aside from Maya, my lunches with Tammy are the most perfect thing in my life. Only the setting is wrong. We should be in a stylish coffee shop somewhere, curled up in couches with a roaring fire nearby. Instead, we are in the university canteen, a less than intimate place. For one thing, the metal chairs are not exactly something you could 'curl up in.' It is impossible to sit comfortably enough in them to stop my posterior from going numb halfway through lunch.

Some days we get off campus if we get going quickly enough. Discovering unknown places with Tammy is always exciting but expensive, so we cannot do it too often. I cringe at the thought of Bhavesh's black caterpillar eyebrows scrunching ferociously if he saw a credit card charge for lunch with Tammy of over twenty dollars. In my mind's eye I can hear him yelling, "Do I work all day so you can blow off twenty-thirty dollars on lunch?" Still, Bhavesh tolerates my friendship with Tammy because it happens at work and does not intrude on my time outside of it.

"You should come," Tammy says, giving me a big crinkle-eyed smile of hope. "What do you think?"

With a start, I realize that I have been so intent on enjoying our closeness I have not been listening to our conversation. I push the shrimp on my plate and try to cover. "Uh-huh . . . So, give me some details."

Tammy's round, friendly face narrows. "I did," she shrieks. I grab her hand and squeeze it gently. Tammy hates having to repeat herself. It reminds her of her ex-boyfriend who never listened when she talked to him.

After a beat, Tammy clears her throat then says, "The university's networking dinner with the Vice-Chancellor. All the department heads are going. You could come with me, Meena. It might mean more funding for your project and you could stay longer. Maybe forever."

Tammy clasps her hands—a teenager's gesture, not one of a professional woman in her early thirties. I give her an indulgent look.

"Not that I'm, like, biased in that direction or selfishly motivated," she continues with a wink. "Not like I might have some breakdown if I lost my lunch partner."

An unfamiliar rush of joy fills me, making my heart dissolve into honey. I do not want to lose my lunches with Tammy, either. Our camaraderie is such a welcome change from the monotonous interactions between me and Bhavesh, and it opens me up to university gossip, feuds between teachers, a new language, and a new life I have never experienced before.

I cherish our uncomplicated relationship, but I could never keep it going if I lost my job. Sadness squeezes around me like shrink-wrap. I cannot imagine a situation in which my husband would happily let me go off to meet my friend for drinks or dinner in the evening. Then again, the Vice-Chancellor's dinner is work, and more funding might even mean the university would take me on directly. That could mean more money—something that Bhavesh would likely be happy about.

A loud clatter of cutlery slices into my reverie as a kitchen hand accidentally drops the tray he is holding. Tammy swivels around, then turns back to me.

"Plus," Tammy says, her eyes shining blue like a peacock's neck, "the guest is some famous Indian corporate guy."

Coming from someone else, maybe it would be a little insulting, but I know my friend's heart. Her face is open, guileless.

"Oh, yeah," I say slowly. "I saw something. I'll . . . I'll have to see what's going on with Bhavesh and let you know."

Tammy's face drops. She puts down her fork and gives me a swift, searching look. "Maybe don't mention that you are coming with me," she says carefully.

"Why would you say that?" I shrug good-naturedly, implying that I think Tammy is being silly. The truth is, Bhavesh barely even acknowledged Tammy on the one occasion they met. I know that was intentional—after nine years of marriage, I am well aware that Bhavesh does not give much value to women, especially single women like Tammy.

I am struck by a sudden thought and I giggle so hard I keel over sideways. "I think it might be better to tell Bhavesh that you would chaperone me. Better I turn up to an event like that with a girlfriend than all alone and, you know . . . available." I blush.

Tammy simpers approvingly and flutters her eyelashes exaggeratedly. "I wouldn't trust me to chaperone anyone."

5
Meena

Fall 2014
Fremont, California

It is only mid-September, but in the fading glow of the sunset, our house appears gloomy when I return from work. Maya is taking an evening hip-hop dance class at school, so my little princess is not here to brighten up the place.

Her classmate Allison's mom will bring Maya home, thanks to a neat carpool system that has worked well for the past year. Thank you, *Bhagwan*. I drop the girls off at school in the morning, allowing Allison's mom to attend a step aerobics class. In return, she brings Maya back on Tuesday evenings. I cannot help but feel that I get the better end of the deal, gaining the extra time when I arrive home, while Allison's mom ends up doing exercise, of all things.

I love the ease of these friendly systems in the U.S. I wonder how much the countless moms who make these arrangements appreciate just how easy they are. In India it would be harder, with much more formality to it. Our families would need to first figure out if carpooling was even a proper arrangement to enter, since the relative castes would determine if one child's bottom was worthy of gracing another's car seat. Here it is just two moms helping each other out, because their children are in the same class and have chosen to be friends.

I do not have time to relax. Bhavesh will be home soon and will want his dinner fresh and hot, so I quickly begin the routine that transforms me from 'office worker' to 'homemaker mommy.'

I take a speed-shower, then swap the office clothes for jersey pajama pants and a loose, V-neck tee. Moments later, I am heating oil in the frying pan in the kitchen before emptying the contents of the pressure cooker into it. Maya is always hungry when she gets home and needs feeding before I roll out Bhavesh's *rotis*, lightly fried on a hot *tava* and served fresh while he sits at the head of the mahogany dinner table, reading the local newspaper, *The Argus*.

Chopped onions go into the pan next, followed by stewed tomatoes and thin slices of fresh ginger. After another minute, I add the contents of the pan to the bubbling kidney beans and happily stir the whole mess together. *My step aerobics*, I think wryly.

The aroma of ghee and cumin flavoring the curry always put me in a trance, bringing me back to my childhood. But no matter how much I try, my *rajma chawal* never smells as good as my *Aai's* did. The ringing of the doorbell interrupts my thoughts.

"Mommy, Mommy, guess what I learned from Ms. Tracy today!" Maya prances into the kitchen after we have waved off Allison and her mother.

"Come on, missy, let's get you to McDonald's and your chicken tenders," I overhear Allison's mom say as they hurry off. I try not to appear overly proud that my own daughter has a home-cooked meal waiting for her.

As I fill a large pot of water to boil, Maya is already performing, tapping, turning, and twirling as her fluffy pink tutu with sparkly sequins spreads out around her. Just as she has spun in a full circle, the doorbell goes again—this time, with a tone of impatience. My heart sinks.

Bhavesh comes pounding into the kitchen, the blazing kitchen light illuminating his five o'clock shadow. The astringent lime-patchouli odor of Old Spice mingled with body sweat wafts off him as he picks up Maya, spins her around in his arms, and fusses over her.

"Did you get your paycheck today?" Bhavesh shoots me a questioning look over her shoulder.

"Yes," I reply automatically. "I'm putting the rice on, but then I will get it for you."

"It is amazing, don't you think," he asks with an approving sidelong glance, "how even a *Dalit* can develop herself in a place like America? All you needed was the opportunity I gave you, and now you are earning money in an office job." He rubs his fingertips together. He looks not just satisfied, but proud of his pupil. "Amazing. You must feel grateful for that," he continues with his equivalent of what Americans call 'foreplay.'

My stomach muscles clench.

From the corner of my eye, I glimpse Maya's legs clad in shining pink disco tights stretched out in front of the T.V. as she flips the channels on the remote. While I remain completely still, she squeals in delight as she spies a yellow sponge dancing excitedly on the screen.

In the glare cast by the overhead fluorescent light, Bhavesh's eyes glint with relish. "How I made you pure and brought you to this place. In India you would be cleaning toilets, like your mother, but here you have an office job."

The tiny nicks in the lacquer along the bottom board of the oak cabinet behind his head hold my determined gaze. I will not point out that I was the one who got my job. It belongs to me. I made the application, put together a resume, and went to the interview and assessment session. If I stay silent this way, he is less likely to get stirred up like a nest full of hornets and spoil the peace of the evening.

• • •

Summer 1996
Kalanpur, Uttar Pradesh
I am nursing an injury on the other side of the village square from the water tap, a thorn having found its way into my foot. As we are not allowed to wear shoes in public—and we do not own them—the soles of my feet are like leather and horn hard. I always keep my eyes firmly fixed on the ground as I walk so I hardly ever hurt my feet on anything like a shard of glass or a sharp metal edge.

It must have been when I stepped into a puddle, felt mud squelch my toes and then a sharp prick as a thistle pierced the cracked rind of my foot.

"Ah, Ah, *Aai*," I scream as I hop on one foot.

My *Aai* crouches next to me. The tip of the thorn has broken off and become a small splinter, making it hard to dig out. I see a telltale furrow of worry on her face as she bends over me and tries to pull the thorn out. But the splinter has worked its way deeper into my foot, and my skin already looks angry and sore.

"Wait here, *pyaari beti*," she whispers. My mother often calls me her sweet girl, especially when she feels I need comfort. "I will fetch water from the tap so we can clean your poor foot."

I watch her cross the square, hugging her small tin bowl to her chest. She turns around and warns, "Meena, don't touch it. You'll push it deeper."

Once her back is to me, I return to poking my foot, squeezing harder until my eyes tear in pain. As the splinter shifts, I push my thumbnail across the skin repeatedly, hard and rough like sandpaper. A tiny black tip emerges from the center, surrounded by beads of blood, and I keep pinching, ignoring the tears rolling down my face, and then I am pulling the thing free. I stare in fascination at this tiny piece of a plant that caused so much pain.

"*Aai!*" I call out in a timid voice.

I rise and hobble across the square. The roofs of wealthy houses nearby are almost visible, their terracotta-colored Roman tiles adorning many of the larger houses in my village, like the one my mother cleans. But here at the center, in this poor village, only the temple has such a decorative, gabled roof. The surrounding hovels have grimy walls of rough concrete or stone, and the roofs are corrugated, made of sheet metal or plastic, parodying the Roman roofs less than a quarter of a mile away.

About halfway across the square, I spot my mother by the tap. A man dressed in a fine white *dhoti*, a long white shirt, and heavy black sandals towers over her. His clean-shaven face is dark-complexioned, and he wears a red *tikka* on his forehead. As I speed up my steps, straining to hear, the wide gold of his watch wristband and the rings on three fingers of each hand glint in the sun.

"If you touch this tap, *Chamar*," he says, his voice booming through the stale air, "then whom will it be fit for? Only other *Chamars*. That is selfish, wouldn't you say?" He looks no older than my *Aai* and speaks to her slowly, deliberately, as if she is too dim to understand.

"But my daughter," she says, her shoulders shrinking as she pleads with him. "She has hurt her foot and all I need is a little water to clean the wound."

"So what will it matter if your dirty daughter has some more dirt in her?" His cackle cuts through the hot, humid air.

"Maybe if you would get it for me," my mother begs, her hands clasped together in submission, "then I would not have to touch the tap."

"Harrumph," he roars, his mouth twisting to one side. "That sounds like I would be serving you," he continues, scowling fiercely.

Aai shakes her head, the strain of keeping her voice even showing in her tense knuckles. "It would be helping me."

"Well," the man says with a cruel grin, "perhaps if you asked properly. When *Chamars* want something, they should be on their knees, in their proper place."

My heart is hammering as he points to the ground.

"Go on, get on your knees."

It is near market time and throngs of market sellers and villagers fill the square, some drawing close to the drama unfolding in front of the communal tap. But the unshaven men in their faded *lungis* and soiled undershirts and the *Dalit* women dressed in cheap, synthetic saris in garish prints and silver nose-rings keep their faces averted, pretending they can neither see nor hear what is happening. My skin tingles with fear and embarrassment.

My mother hesitates for a moment, then sinks to her knees. "I just want to clean my daughter's wound," she mumbles, face to the ground.

"All right." The man shrugs and holds out his hand. *Aai* looks up to his outstretched hand, her eyes filling with gratitude. She lifts an arm to pass him the bowl. Quick as lightning, the man jerks his hand away.

"But," he says, in his slow, patronizing voice, "if I have to touch your filthy bowl, then what is the difference? I will still be polluted." He leans forward and spits on her. "Your touch pollutes everything. Now go away and do not come to the tap again. Get your water from a dirty puddle, like the rats."

My mother collapses into herself, and I want to run to her. I want to show her that the splinter is gone and there is no need for the water. But I turn around and scamper away, not wanting to draw attention to myself. My heart is like a madly bouncing ball, beating the breath out of my body. I will pretend I have not seen a thing.

. . .

Now, in front of Bhavesh, I try to keep my back straight. "There's this thing on at work," I say haltingly, then begin to clear the dishes. "It's a . . . dinner."

"You want to go?" Bhavesh responds absently as he looks away to continue reading his newspaper.

"Well . . . yes. It would be good." I say, keeping my voice even.

"But you cook dinner here each night; why go to work to have it?" Bhavesh looks up over the edge of the newspaper, meeting my eyes. I cannot tell if he is teasing or being serious.

I adjust my apron. "Really, it's for networking." I clear my throat. "I might get more funding for my department—maybe even a pay raise."

Oh, why did I have to jump into the money argument so soon? I castigate myself.

But, confusingly, Bhavesh plays along. "A pay raise, huh? See, it's just like I said. The things you can do here!"

"So, you think I should go?" I keep my voice suggestive.

Bhavesh slithers behind me as I continue to wash the dishes.

"I tell you what I think. I think you should go to bed early tonight; your husband has a need to pleasure himself." He leans in closer—his hot breath on my ear, which throbs in pain. "Just make sure you don't forget your place."

6
Meena

Fall 2014
Fremont, California

"Mommy, I've forgotten my lunch!" cries Maya, close to tears as she and I pull up to the school gates.

I park the car and run around, helping Maya hop out of the passenger seat. I reach down and brush her cheek. "Don't worry, my princess."

She puts her hand on a jutted hip and looks up at me with an outraged look on her face. "But I'll be so hungry. I'll be *starving!*"

I cringe. I can almost feel the crippling pain of my empty stomach in Gopi *Mama's* house when my aunt and uncle reluctantly took me in for a month when my *Aai* died. Gopi *Mama's* wife had me doing all the heavy tasks: scouring pots that blackened and broke my nails, fetching water from the communal tap, lighting coal fires that turned my eyes a stinging red. I did not complain for fear of going without dinner again, and I rarely cried for fear of half a dozen slaps. *Luckily my daughter will never know that.* I take a deep breath as I wave at another mom crossing the intersection.

One day, after a long walk home carrying a sloshing bucket of water in temperatures so hot the melted pitch of the road stuck to my *chappals*, I poured myself a tumbler of cold milk from a pitcher reserved for Gopi *Mama's* sons—mean, round-faced boys whose features I have forced myself to forget. I gulped great mouthfuls, spluttering milk everywhere when *Mami* suddenly appeared. A vein pulsed in her forehead when she caught me drinking the milk.

In one swift motion, *Mami* seized the tumbler I had put down and threw it at me. A heavy thud rang out followed by a metal clatter as the stainless-steel tumbler fell to the floor.

"You wretch; how dare you take our food! Before the end of the week, you'll be out of my house," she exploded, shaking her fists like maracas, "or my name isn't Shakuntala Devi." For hours I had curled myself into a ball, rocking back and forth as I wiped back hot tears, terrified of where I would be sent.

I rub my temples with my fingertips, trying to get rid of a headache forming at the back of my skull. I say nothing as I turn to Maya, who is chewing her lip with a worried look on her face as she gazes up at me.

I pat her head comfortingly. Why let her know how much suffering I went through?

I can hear the babble of children's voices as I adjust the pink ribbon holding Maya's glossy dark hair off her face. "I will get you something and bring it to the school office. Anything you like, my darling."

"Chocolate sprinkle donut!" exclaims Maya, a bright smile breaking through her distress like sunshine through monsoon clouds.

"*Almost* anything," I say, grinning back. "I meant a sandwich."

"Chocolate sandwich!" says Maya. She grins toothily and twirls away.

I put my arm around my daughter and steer her towards the school gate. "Shall I choose?"

Maya nods, clapping her hands in glee.

"I'll get you something nice, I promise." I lean down to give my daughter a kiss, then hurry off to a nearby deli. Finding a long queue, I check my watch and consider where else I could get Maya her lunch. But as the queue jerks forward, I quell my irritation and will my turn to come quickly.

Nearing the counter, I eye the case where various meats and fillings sit, ready to be packed into a freshly made sandwich. Further along the counter is a smaller cabinet stuffed with cakes and desserts. *But no tray of ladoos like those made by my Aai.* I sniff, involuntarily flooded by another memory as has been happening so often these days.

In *Aai's* small hut, Gopi *Mama* and I are sitting next to each other and relishing every ghee-laden crumb while my *Aai,* enjoying this unexpected visit from her younger brother, dimples as she watches us eat.

I wonder how much I can trust the memory or whether it is an idealization, remembering my mother in a romanticized haze. If I had been eating *ladoos,* I doubt I would have been paying much attention to her, except in the hope that she was preparing another tray.

But the memory is vivid, full of texture and smell. The *ladoos* were so warm and so fresh from being fried that they were still soft and formless. They collapsed in my hands, covering me in a delicious, gooey mess as the smell of homemade ghee and cardamom wafted through our one-room hut with its mud floor, mud walls and thatched roof. It felt cramped with the three of us sitting on the one bed that my *Aai* and I shared, but it did not matter as we enjoyed this rare moment together.

And again, I saw the image of my mother's contented smile, just like I imagine my own face to look when gazing upon Maya.

"Ma'am? *Ma'am* . . . ? Ma'am!"

The server looks impatiently at me, his shoulder-length black hair tied to the nape with a leather thong. Embarrassingly, a little dribble has escaped my lips. Trying to pull myself together, I wipe it and my memory away.

"Um . . . What cakes have you got?"

I ask him to hide my daughter's unhealthy lunch securely in a wrapper so she will not get into trouble at school. They are like hawks, I think. What is the harm in allowing children to have some illicit pleasure once in a while?

When I arrive back at the school gates, filled with pleasure at the image of Maya's face lighting up when she opens her lunch bag, the yard is still full of children playing. I hover by the entrance, hoping to catch sight of her before the bell rings. I spot her practicing dance steps led by her friend, Allison, who is demonstrating hip-hop moves to a group of girls. At home, I have seen Maya practicing one or two of them that girls her age probably shouldn't know. But now I fluff my hair indulgently.

Allison and her gaggle must have been watching MTV or some other show to help spice things up a little.

Just before the bell rings, Maya starts to show one of the girls how to do a sensuous move. A sob escapes my lips.

I have not been aware of how . . . *accepted* Maya is. Liked. Respected. How she dimples when they finish their performance and how the other girls congratulate her.

A sense of calm fills me, stilling the worry that I constantly carry like sweat from my pores.

. . .

Summer 2001
Grace Mercy Children's Home
Kalanpur, Uttar Pradesh
"Fire! Girls, get out of your beds!"

I instinctively pull my thin sack of a blanket over my head as the other girls in my dormitory stir with grunts and shouts—hardly unusual for an early morning at the orphanage. But the yelling outside continues as Roopa, the queen bee of our dormitory, demands, "What's going on?"

Roopa, a *Brahmin* and supposedly from a wealthy family, refuses to mix with anyone from a lower caste—especially not me, the sole *Dalit* in my dormitory. I cannot sit side-by-side with her in the classroom; instead, I am sent to a dirty mat on the floor or in a rickety chair at the perimeter of the room while the other girls are assigned a bench. In the dormitory that houses seven of us girls, her bed is the farthest from mine, which is at the very end of the row of beds lined up side by side.

How Roopa has ended up in the decrepit hole that is Grace Mercy Children's Home—how there was not someone with the means and will to take her in—is a constant source of speculation among the girls. If not family, at least there should have been someone who could have seen her as an investment—a future 'good match' for a wealthy *Kshatriya*, perhaps fetching a good dowry.

I sometimes wonder if her haughty disdain of us stems not from her noble birth, but because she is forced to be in an orphanage. Roopa treats the nuns like servants rather than what they are—the only thing that stands between life and death for all of us orphans. All the girls follow her like sheep except for me, after the way I saw my mother humiliated by her kind who confuses arrogance with worth.

From under my makeshift blanket, which barely warms me during the frosty nights of Kalanpur, the strident footsteps of Sister Gina resound as she bursts into the room. I smell smoke in the air.

"What are you doing, all of you? Get up and get out, now! Meena, get out from under those covers!"

I have not heard the softly spoken nun shout before, and this shocks me into action.

"Sorry, Sister," I call. I fall out of bed onto the icy floor before stumbling from the room behind the other girls, who are already way ahead of me.

A layer of thick black smoke hangs in the sparsely lit corridors. I cough as the smoke grows thicker until it is blinds me as I run faster through the maze towards the entrance of the orphanage. My heart pounds. Oh, *Bhagwan,* why are there no fire safety escape routes? The panicked shouts of the other girls pierce through the billowing smoke from up ahead.

"What's going on? Where do I turn?" My heart hammers in my throat as I stumble upon Sister Teresa struggling with Jamuna, a small, undernourished-looking girl with solemn eyes and two long braids looped up on either side of her face. She arrived at Grace Mercy earlier in the year, younger than I was on my arrival. Jamuna's eyes are stretched wide, her large black pupils dilated.

"She's mentally defective," Roopa has sneered more than once. But from the faraway look in Jamuna's eyes, the way she hardly interacts with anyone and the fact that she is never violent to anyone but herself, she is clearly affected by whatever she went through before she came to the orphanage. Sometimes she turns her face to the wall and screams at it. Other times she bangs her head or claws at herself until one of the nuns restrains her, and she cries out at night in such anguish that it makes me pull the covers over my head.

Once, as I moved soundlessly through the corridor back to the dormitory after dinner, I overheard Sister Teresa and Sister Gina whispering to each other as they perched on a windowsill carved into the tumble-down limestone wall, "I can't cope with her . . . How can we keep her safe? Maybe we can find somewhere better for her, where she can get some counseling or treatment."

But that was months ago, and she is still here. They must know as well as everyone else behind these walls that, for most of us, Grace Mercy is as good as it gets.

"Cover your faces and keep going," Sister Gina calls out, agitated. She helps Sister Teresa try to lift Jamuna, who has collapsed, shaking, in a heap on the stone floor. As we race onwards, the smoke thins near the front of the building where the mother superior stands, her face strained with worry. She motions us outside.

"Line up in groups with your dorm-mates," she booms, gesturing with her arms.

I make my way to the other six girls from the dormitory who are huddled together in the wintry night. A bitter wind whips across the courtyard, bringing flecks of icy rain with it. The girls look scared, their eyes vacant as they crowd together for warmth.

As the small courtyard fills up, I am forced to stand close to the girls so I do not become mixed in with the girls of another dormitory. Shivering uncontrollably, I clutch my thin nightgown close to my body and edge deeper into the courtyard's many shadows to use the other girls as a shelter from the wind.

Roopa turns and notices me. "What are you doing?" she asks indignantly.

"It's c-cold," I answer through chattering teeth.

"So what?" Roopa replies witheringly. "I don't care if you're dying, you filthy *Chamar*. Piss off."

I stare back, speechless.

"Mo-ove," Roopa says again, as if I am too thick to understand her.

A spark goes off inside me, setting alight a flame that flickers in the brutal wind. I keep staring intentionally while the other girls join her like a herd of sheep until all of them are shouting insults at me.

"I said, 'move,' you dumb runt. What's the matter? Are you too stupid to understand me?" Roopa's face is twisted and ugly as she moves toward me, deftly avoiding the cook, watch guard, maintenance crew and local villagers who have arrived, speeding past us into the building with empty buckets.

I keep staring calmly at her. Only inches from my face, Roopa screams at the top of her voice. "MOVE! MOVE! MOVE! MOVE! MOVE! MOVE!"

I flinch, but I do not shift my eyes from Roopa's flushed face. Her nostrils twitch as if she smells something unpleasant.

"Move! Move! Move! Move!" the other girls chant louder and louder.

Sister Gina suddenly wedges herself between us, her face furious. "What are you doing, you silly girls?"

The four sheep all look at the floor as Roopa defiantly meets the nun's gaze.

Sister Gina spins around to me. "What about you, Meena?" she asks in the softer tone she reserves for me. "If you have anything to say, you can tell me."

I shake my head, knowing what trouble I will be in if seen as a *chugalkhor*, a snitch.

One of the local villagers emerges from the orphanage and calls out, "It is okay. Only a pan fire. It did not spread far; we have already put it out."

Sister Gina's eyes narrow, and she shakes her head at me in quiet sympathy. The other nuns hustle us back into the building and out of the freezing wind.

I am sobbing, my shoulders hunched, when I arrive back in the dormitory, though I keep my face turned to hide my tears from the others. I miss my mother so much, shards of pain flood my body; my stomach feels as if I have swallowed razor blades. She would have hugged me tight, planted a dozen kisses on me, and held me close.

Once they are all back in their beds, the nuns gone and the lights out, Roopa's voice rings out in the darkness. "Shame it wasn't an actual fire, *Chamar*. I would have loved to see you burn."

I muffle my sobs beneath the rough blanket, the sound of giggles making me cringe in shame.

"You think you were funny tonight? You think you're a big, tough girl?" Roopa hisses.

I peep out from under my blanket. The veins on Roopa's neck bulge as her words cut like a knife through the close, hot dormitory air.

"Do you know that in the village I come from, on a full-moon night we make *Dalit* girls like you run naked and the *zamindar's* sons throw colored water at them? Then, when they stand shivering, their nipples pointed and hard, that's when they take their pick," Roopa swipes the back of her large hand across her lips in relish. "Bah, these nuns . . . They know nothing! You wait; I'm going to get you."

7

Meena

Fall 2014

Fremont, California

I flinch as Bhavesh slams the front door behind him with a loud bang.

"Why did you not buy bread? I told you we were almost out of bread. You know I like a sandwich when I come home."

I keep my mouth shut as usual, continuing to cook dinner, but I roll my eyes behind his back.

"The bowl you set the table with is chipped," he continues, growing more furious. "You need to be more careful when you wash up. I am always buying new bowls and plates because of your carelessness."

And so it goes on, with Bhavesh finding something else to grumble about every few minutes, intent on getting me to defend myself or to offer some excuse or explanation so he can really lay into me.

And all this because I would not give him a blowjob.

Why doesn't he just do what most men do and serve himself if he needs relief so badly?

I stifle a giggle. It is a wicked thought, beyond where my rebellious inner thoughts would usually go. I blame Tammy.

I had been feeling a little unwell when he presented himself to me two evenings earlier. I had forgotten to lock the shower door, and he had come home early. When I came out, wrapped in just a towel, I gasped at him sitting on the bed with his trousers down.

"Come here," he commanded in a low voice, his eyes glinting like steel. "I've had a hard day." He flicked his fingers against the straining bulge beneath his boxers. "You need to show me some support like a good wife should."

"I'm having a terrible migraine, Bhavesh and . . ." I stuttered, wringing my hands, "and Maya will be home soon. Please, can we do this tonight?"

He grabbed my wrist as I went to gather the gray sweats that I had laid on the bed. He started to push me down on my knees but then, unexpectedly, he let me go.

Nodding his head curtly, he waved his hand to dismiss me. I gathered my clothes with my heart in my throat and fled to the bathroom.

Meeting my husband's needs was a chore at the best of times, but thankfully, he mostly just wanted sex from me, and sex with Bhavesh did not require a great deal of participation, just the odd moan or a small cry or two near the end. Although I am not sure that is even necessary anymore; his rough hands are proof he does not care whether or not I enjoy it. In fact, it came as a relief when he said one night when I was particularly tired after a busy day, "Stop making those noises. You sound like a cheap whore."

Oral sex was a lot more unpleasant; it took more effort, and it was more about trying not to gag or vomit. And it was not like I ever got pleasured in return.

Bhavesh's moods being unpredictable as they are, it is probably for the best that I have decided against going to the Vice-Chancellor presentation dinner at the university tonight; there will undoubtedly be a scene and I will most likely end up staying home anyway, more upset than ever. No—instead, I will make a point of spending time with Maya once my daughter is home from her playdate.

I finish cooking and place dinner plates on the table. Typically, Bhavesh has wandered off just as I am about to serve—probably to his office to check his e-mails or to the garage to plug in the nightly charger on his energy-efficient car.

"Bhavesh," I call in my most placating voice before sitting down at the dining table. There are three ceramic plates neatly laid out with paper dinner napkins and utensils. Fragrant steam rises from a bowl of chicken curry layered with bay leaves and olive oil in the middle of the table. A bowl of basmati rice flavored with roasted cumin is next to it on a snow-white doily. I have also put out a green-and-cream container of Verka yogurt from the Indian store. "Dinner's on the table," I call louder.

I pile rice on his plate, ladle a spoonful of chicken curry over it, and then sit down to my meal. It is soothing, after a long day, to eat on my own, but after a minute or two, I call him again. When there is no answer, I sigh heavily. I know I should go get him, but I cannot muster the energy.

Another couple of minutes passes. Afraid that I will be blamed if he does not know dinner is ready, I cannot enjoy my food, so I rise to find him. Just then he appears—jaw set, eyes dark and angry. I shrink into myself.

"What's this?" he asks, scowling ferociously. "Dinner is ready?"

"Yes. I— I called . . ." I dab nervously at my mouth with a napkin.

Bhavesh spies my half-eaten meal. "But you have eaten most of yours."

"I was hungry," I reply, keeping my voice calm, quiet, and accommodating. "I called you, more than once."

Bhavesh leans over to pick up his plate of rice and chicken curry, then looks across the table, his eyes rock hard. "No *roti*, even. What sort of wife are you?" He clenches and unclenches his fist. "No *roti* and cold rice. How hard is it to come and find me?"

"It's not cold," I protest, rising from the table with my head bowed. "I can microwave it for you."

"I work all day to provide for you, you lazy *Dalit* bitch, and you can't even give me a hot meal and a fucking *roti*!" Bhavesh's fury erupts like hot lava, making my stomach twist in a knot. This is what he has been looking for all along—a reason to blow up at me.

"I'm sorry, Bhav—"

His bowl of food hits the wall and shatters with a loud crash. Thick brown curry and crumbling kernels of white rice splatter everywhere, followed by a ringing silence as if the entire house is in shock. For a moment he looks dazed, then he strides towards the front door.

"Maya will need picking up," he says brusquely, pausing briefly to pick up his car keys from the hallway bureau as he heads out.

Numbly, I remain frozen in place for several minutes. Through my fog, I think back to the way Bhavesh twisted my ear the week before. He had behaved like it was foreplay, but it had not felt like it.

Now, this. The force with which the bowl hit the wall shook me to the core. He had not just thrown it—he had *launched* it.

In slow motion, I move vaguely about the dining room before finally bending to pick up the pieces of the shattered bowl one by one. Then I fetch a cloth and begin cleaning the smeared mess on the wall. The paint is light, just a few shades off magnolia, and every single spatter is likely to stain. The task is impossible, but I stubbornly hold back a sob.

The wall clock in the lounge area chimes the hour. Seven o'clock. I stop, straighten my back, and toss the cloth aside. No tears tonight. I am going out.

I dress quickly so I am gone before Bhavesh and Maya come back. If I am glad of one thing it is that my daughter did not see this. Though, of course, it would not have happened had Maya been there. Bhavesh is a different person in front of his daughter: cheerful and indulgent, usually listening to her commands with a gentle grin. I hope he will make up a good lie when Maya sees the half-cleaned mess on the wall.

I do a passable job with my wardrobe selection—there is never much I need to dress up for—but there is no time for makeup. I am undecided as to whether I should leave a note, then grow annoyed at myself for being so 'domestic' right in the middle of my little rebellion. But I think about Maya and leave the note, anyway.

Hurrying out of the door, I turn and catch sight of myself in the mirror. *Actually,* I think to myself as I rush off, *I'll put on some lip gloss on the way.*

· · ·

Winter 2005
Grace Mercy Children's Home
Kalanpur, Uttar Pradesh
I peer at myself in the chipped mirror hanging above the dirty, cracked sink in the girls' lavatory, running a tongue over my newly glossed lips.

My mind shifts to three months earlier when my uncle and aunt had shown up at the orphanage without any notice.

They'd arrived in an old, beat-up, originally-white-now-yellow Maruti car, which my uncle later told me he had bought a month earlier. To my surprise, they had ushered me to the car and driven me into town.

After nearly eight years in the orphanage, with not a single visit from anyone, their arrival shocked me. It had been even stranger when they took me for a meal at *Haldiram's* restaurant. Sweet lassi, *papri chaat*, drizzled with yogurt and tamarind chutney spiked with julienned radish, black salt, and fat golden-brown *gulab jamun. Papri chaat! Gulab Jamun!* In all my life, I had never been offered these delicacies.

"*Dheere!*"

Mami wanted me to chew slowly. I slowed my eating, relishing every bite.

Then, they took me shopping for a sari at *Tulsi Creations* in the Santushti Shopping Complex, a murky maze of shops, restaurants and beauty parlors as cramped and teeming as an ant colony.

My aunt took the glossy pink lipstick I had picked out from the lipstick display at the New Fashion Beauty Parlor in Uttam Ganj. "Meena *beti,* you are smudging. This is how you do it," my aunt had said with a rare smile. She leaned in so close I could smell the Himalaya talcum powder that I remembered her applying to her face after her morning bath.

I shifted uncomfortably, looking into the small mirror that the girl behind the makeup counter had handed me.

"Apply the color first to your top lip. Then the bottom," *Mami* said, smacking her lips together to demonstrate. "And now, open your eyes wide so I can put on some kajal. Yes, there."

She stepped back a little and admired her handiwork. "Aaah, see how pretty you're looking."

I had slowly turned to the mirror on the opposite wall and gazed at my reflection, marveling at what a little lipstick and kohl liner had done to my heart-shaped face. The blue silk sari, like a brilliant sapphire, had a thin gold border that made my brown eyes gleam. For the first time in my eighteen years, I felt beautiful.

"Come in, come in," the mother superior had said as she brought us into her office on our return.

My aunt laid the parcels on the armchair in the corner of the room and waved me near her. The mother superior retreated through the door, closing it behind her.

"We have to make something of this hair," *Mami* muttered, twisting and pulling it back as I fidgeted in front of her. The hairs on the back of my neck stood up, unused as I was to the touch of another human being. She plaited my thick hair and twisted it into a bun at the nape of my neck. When she was done, Gopi *Mama* pulled out a camera.

For the first time that day, my aunt's customary hostility towards me returned as she lost her patience trying to 'get something usable.' I followed her instructions demurely, but my posture was deemed too stiff or I squirmed too much in front of the camera. She clearly did not realize I was unaccustomed to having my photo taken.

"Meena, turn your body sideways," she'd snapped. "No, no, more to the left." She clucked her tongue crossly. "Now, tilt your head down, girl. Sit straight, for God's sake!"

After Gopi *Mama* had taken a few pictures, my aunt grudgingly nodded her head. "I think this is the best we can do. Go on, Meena, take off the sari and blouse."

At my obvious dismay, she quickly added, not quite meeting my eyes, "You won't be able to keep them nice in this place. We'll keep them for you."

"Does that mean I will see you again soon?" I asked hopefully, clinging to the only family I had. I could barely stand my aunt and did not have much love for my uncle, who had turned into a complete stranger since he'd dropped me off at the orphanage. But without them, I would have no family at all—nothing to make me feel that one day I would get out of this place.

"I hope so," answered my aunt cryptically, vaguely waving her hand. My mouth formed the words to ask her what was going on, but she was busy swatting at a fly hovering near her face—no doubt attracted by her Himalayan-scented talcum powder—and the moment was gone.

Now, all these months later, I give my lips one last admiring look before going downstairs to meet Gopi *Mama* and my aunt who, once again, turned up unannounced this morning. I am summoned to the mother superior's office just before classes are to begin.

Without being told where we are going, I obediently get into the car and silently gaze out the window while my uncle drives us over potholed roads to the other side of Kalanpur. We pass through fields of grain, and through shop fronts of ironmongers, jewelers, and cigarette-*paan* vendors before finally struggling up a muddy, treacherous road to a well-kept, two-story brick house sitting at the end of a long, gravel driveway behind an iron gate.

Honking his horn and gesticulating wildly through the open window, Gopi *Mama* shouts at the *chowkidar*, "*Arre*, open the gate, man. We are late already."

The car rolls to a halt and I gingerly climb out of the back seat as my Aunt pulls me forward. A lanky man in a pale grey Safari suit approaches us, his underarms stained with sweat. His slicked back salt-and-pepper hair reeks of coconut oil, and his skin is the color of glossy ebony with deep pockmarks etched into his face. He fawns over my uncle and aunt, but the look he directs at me is sly and greedy. Later I will find out he is a well-known marriage-fixer.

The man leads us into a drawing room with large wicker chairs and a divan arranged in a semicircle. Two well-dressed men in suits and ties sit on the chairs across from two women who recline, dressed in *Banarasi* saris and heavy gold jewelry, on a green-and-cream patterned sofa. My aunt and uncle bow their heads and push me quickly upstairs without introducing me. My brow furrows after we enter a sparsely furnished bedroom with a small white bed where the clothes bought for me three months before are laid out.

"Put these on," says my aunt throwing me a sharp look before she slips out of the room. My uncle follows silently behind with a furtive look on his face.

I get dressed quickly, suspended in anxiety. Then I creep over to the window to gaze out over Kalanpur, marveling at the way the larger-than-life houses in this area gradually sink into the low shacks and the shanty houses of the slums.

At the orphanage, once we reached the age of sixteen, we could sometimes go out in the city unsupervised. I, of course, was always marked by a wristband as a *Dalit*. I had heard of *Dalit* girls being raped by upper-caste men in my village, and the one time I ventured out, I shrank into myself. But neither that nor the mark of a *Dalit* stopped upper-caste men from hurling lewd comments about my pubescent body and smacking their lips at me. A man wearing thick black leather boots followed me as I ran panting, my hair flying, over loose concrete and dog turds—all the way back to the safety of the orphanage's gates. After that, I never left the orphanage unaccompanied.

Dreading what might come next, I consider going downstairs or sticking my head into the corridor and calling for my aunt. By the door is a walnut dressing table with an oval mirror framed in gold. On the wooden surface lies a kajal—a deep black eyeliner pencil, a box of bright, pasty eye shadow ranging from dark brown to light blue, and the gold tube of glossy lipstick I had selected at the beauty parlor in Uttam Ganj. My aunt had said nothing about makeup, and though I do not really know what I am doing, I pick up the kajal and try my best to remember how my aunt had applied it around my eyes. My first attempt makes me look like a *junglee* boy in need of grooming, so I hurriedly wipe it off. After my third attempt, my kajal-lined eyes shine like coiled, black cobras.

The eye shadow I pick is pale bronze, just a few shades lighter than the color of my skin. I suddenly look beautiful, almost like a Bollywood movie actress (the nuns let us watch the weekly Hindi feature film on the T.V. in the dining hall on Saturday nights), the ones who know how to sing and dance and shimmy their shoulders and always get caught in the rain in plain sight of good-looking men. In awe, I sit in front of the mirror, preening in my beautiful blue sari, marveling at the slip-shiny feel of the silk against my skin.

The door jolts opens, making me jump, my heart leaping in my chest.

My aunt appears with an approving look on her face. "Ah, good," she says with a nod, "you have put your own makeup on." She inspects my face. "Well, I wouldn't say it was a *good* job, but we are pressed for time. He's waiting. I will do your hair and your *bindi*. You put on lip gloss." She opens the door handle. "I will be back in a few minutes."

Within a few minutes she returns and piles my hair into a bun, then hurriedly applies a sticker *bindi* on my forehead. She seems nervous. I wonder whom she meant by 'he.' She takes my elbow and frog-marches me downstairs.

Gopi *Mama* and the marriage-fixer circle me as my aunt pushes me toward the door leading to the kitchen. On the countertop, I notice there is a plastic tray bearing a teapot and some cups for tea. "Be nice to him," they whisper. "Don't talk too much." "Don't be too quiet." "Answer his questions." "Don't stand like that!"

My head spins as a handsome young man with an eye-catching smile strides confidently through the mesh screen door. His eyes widen appreciatively as our gazes meet, before I quickly look down, aflutter with shyness. I feel a tiny tremor in my stomach like a pebble dropping; only one person has ever looked at me like that, and he left.

"Meena," the man says, pulling a folded white handkerchief out of his pants pocket and wiping his forehead. He sounds nervous as he wraps his lips around my name. "I am Bhavesh."

8

Meena

Fall 2014

Hayward, California

"So, what made you change your mind?" Tammy asks as she plops herself down across from me at a small table by the window of the Revival Bar & Café. She looks flustered and slightly disordered in her rush to make it. But we have plenty of time; it is still an hour and a half until the start of the presentation back at the university.

"Well, how often do I get out, huh?" I muse, giving her a sidelong glance.

Tammy tilts her head to the side as she gazes fondly at me. "Like . . . *never.*"

I blush at my friend's bluntness, and a ripple of fear courses through my body. How will Bhavesh react when he finds me gone? I purse my lips as Tammy heads for the bar to get us a couple of beers. Might as well enjoy myself.

She hands me a beer and we raise our glasses in a toast. "When one of the girls who works with me mentioned the dinner, I didn't realize we even had a new Vice-Chancellor. I feel out of touch with what's going on, even though I'm there every single day."

"Yeah, that's why the dinner's a little earlier than it would be most years," Tammy replies, checking her phone and turning off the ringer. "I think he wants to 'make himself known.'" She looks thoughtful. "Did

I mention the Indian entrepreneur who's speaking tonight? His name escapes me." She sips her beer, and a faint trace of foam remains on her upper lip. She waves her hand in the air in a loopy gesture. "He's supposed to be very successful."

"I doubt they would invite unsuccessful ones," I joke.

Tammy chuckles. "Well, he must be a pretty big deal." She takes off her brown corduroy jacket and smooths the wild tangle of blond curls that have spilled around her shoulders. "Damn, I knew I should have had it cut."

Her bright blue eyes flit around the bar. "You can tell the new VC wants to impress. I reckon you want to move in on him tonight for that funding. He'll be saying yes to everything, especially if that speaker guy is close by."

I splutter on my beer. "Move in on him?" I have to raise my voice to be heard over the music.

Tammy winks. "Well, you know . . . whatever it takes. He's a lot younger than the last VC."

"You're wicked!" I clap a hand over my mouth.

I wish I were brave enough to own my sexuality like she does—to talk in such a free way about men and sex. Her suggestiveness always impresses me—it's clear that her womanhood belongs to her and not anyone else.

"Ah, but I think you could be badder, Meena," Tammy leans forward and cups my chin in her hand. "I see it in you." She pierces me with her blue gaze.

I wrinkle my nose, give my head an emphatic shake, and gesture towards the next table where the server has put down a platter of appetizers. "Right now, I think I need to order some of those onion rings."

I swirl my beer, watching the foam rise over the lip of the mug.

"So, what did 'hubby' think of you coming out tonight?" Tammy asks in feigned innocence, leaning back and folding her arms.

Tammy only met Bhavesh once for about twenty seconds when he came to get the house keys from me, having brilliantly left his own set in the cab he had taken from a meeting downtown. She and I were having lunch in the cafeteria, talking animatedly about a New York

Times article about the unequal pay in Hollywood—I had put my phone on silent—when Bhavesh strode in, impatient and brusque.

"Why didn't you answer your phone?" he had said belligerently, not caring that I was at lunch or that I was with Tammy. "Get me the spare keys." I could tell by Tammy's eye roll that she had found him disagreeable.

I grin mischievously. "Actually, he doesn't know."

Tammy's eyes widen. "You lied to him?"

"No," I say, turning a carefully composed face to her. Tammy looks intrigued, much to my delight.

Just when Tammy looks as if she is almost jumping out of her skin, I say serenely, "I went while he was picking up Maya . . ." I grin at Tammy's look of astonishment. "Don't look at me like that—I left him a note!"

Tammy claps her hands in delight. "No judgment here. Good for you." She gulps down her beer and signals to the server to get us another. "Keep them on their toes."

I know I probably should not drink another. But every time I relive the events of the evening and think about their possible consequences, I need a good swallow of something to wash away the taste of fear in my mouth.

One corner of Tammy's lip rises in merriment as she raises her glass. "To networking . . . and other adventures."

•　•　•

The eight-foot wall surrounding the garden of oleander at the rear of the two-story brick house affords enough privacy from the prying ears of my aunt and uncle and the people we have come to visit. I find out later that the short man and his wife, a plump woman with hair drawn back into a bun, are Bhavesh's distant relatives, and they have set up the match. I have only just met Bhavesh, this handsome man—a *Kshatriya,* from the warrior caste—and we are already meandering together through the garden. Though we are alone, I can sense his relatives observing us as they hover behind glass doors just a few feet away.

"Your photo was lovely," he says earnestly, beads of sweat lining his jaw. "Now that I see you, I know it was not a trick of the camera."

My face grows hot and I suppress a nervous giggle. Does he not know I am a *Dalit*? He could lose his caste just by drinking water served by me.

It is like I am in a dream, suddenly the star of the Bollywood musical that we watched on television months ago. Set hundreds of years in the past, it told the story of a young girl swept off her feet by a prince who fell in love with her. He did not care what others thought and risked everything—his crown, his station, his wealth—and she eventually became his princess and queen-to-be. But even she, a girl of lowly station, had not been as low as a *Dalit*.

A thought hangs on the tip of my tongue. But, if my aunt were to hear me utter the words, there would be no way to describe the trouble I would be in. I glance at the glass doors, then pointedly turn away from their prying.

"But do you not worry about my caste?" I ask in a low voice so the onlookers cannot hear. "I am a *Dalit*." I tingle with fear, knowing I should be entirely submissive, already five or six years older than most girls offered for an arranged marriage. Even were I not a *Dalit*, mine would still be considered a desperate situation.

"I do not care about caste," Bhavesh answers emphatically. Passion flickers in his eyes. "I . . ." He falters self-consciously. "I thought you were *Brahmin* when I saw your photo." His voice is slow, precise, and fills me with tenderness. "But why does that matter? I don't want to marry for position. I . . ."

"You're like me," I blurt, blushing harder. "You want to marry for love."

His lips quirk in a grin, and I feel my insides melting. How could this dream be true? The sunlight seems to whoosh through my head like a brisk breeze and I put away my thoughts about another dark-haired man with a sharp pointed nose who called me *jaan*.

• • •

The Vice-Chancellor dinner is all that I had hoped it would be—special, exquisite even, with free-flowing wine, decadent crabmeat and Swiss cheese dip and crackers. I am careful not to drink too much—just one glass of wine after the beers with Tammy in the bar—in case Bhavesh will smell it on me.

At first, I am so nervous about mixing with the other university staff that I hang back, hiding my lack of ease with idle conversation. But, champagne in hand, I soon relax, chatting amiably as though I have always attended parties like this. I learn that the assistant to the director likes to golf with his boyfriend on weekends and the tall woman who dresses like Nancy Reagan, forever breezing through hallways with a stack of student folders in her arms, dreams of becoming a fulltime author of children's books.

Gazing at myself in the bathroom mirror, I am delightfully aware of how easily conversation bubbles out of my mouth. I marvel that, all of a sudden, I feel *normal*, like I belong here amongst these learned, sophisticated people. I am not just the shy little homemaker who works solitarily at a university as if she does not deserve better, afraid of being caught by her husband, who demands she fraternize with him only, and who is used to being told that her focus should be only on work, because her 'real life' is with her husband and daughter.

I head quickly back upstairs to the conference hall in case Tammy feels neglected. I find her happily engaged in conversation, and I make my way past the other guests, who are gathered around, smiling and greeting each other excitedly, to join her.

"Look at you," Tammy says, as I appear at her side with a glass of soda water. She politely removes herself from an elderly Physics professor who seems to be moving in on her. "You are *owning* the room tonight."

I flush to the roots of my hair.

Tammy darts a glance at the retreating man with a wistful expression on her face. "I did not understand a word that man was saying, but there really is something sexy about tweed. Too bad he's not twenty years younger."

I nearly spit out my soda water at the piercing shriek that slices through the room. The Vice-Chancellor has arrived on the stage, microphone in hand, and he looks aghast at the audio/video technician who rushes to adjust the amp. Regaining his composure, the Vice-Chancellor leans forward and speaks warmly into the microphone. "Please find your seats."

He nods at his audience. "Evening, everyone. I am so pleased to see such a welcome turnout. I know it was short notice and earlier than you would usually expect."

The Vice-Chancellor is tall and thin, unlike his predecessor, who had a stocky figure and a barrel chest. As if to compensate, he sports an old man's buzz-cut that looks like it belongs in the sixties, and he fusses constantly with a tiny pair of round spectacles. His suit looks tailored, as if he'd stepped out of an Indian club in the times of the British Raj, like in the film *Lagaan*, which Maya and I watched one Saturday while Bhavesh worked on his income tax returns.

"My reason for arranging this dinner so early was that I couldn't wait to meet you all in a relaxed setting. But I also had another reason, and that reason is our guest speaker here this evening." He throws a quick look to the side of the stage.

"Our guest is a busy man, and I had the exceptional good fortune of running into him during the summer and spending an evening with him." I can smell Tammy's citrusy perfume. Someone in the audience coughs twice. "I felt that what he has to say is perfect for our students to hear, and I also felt that we—as an institution—would benefit as well."

The Vice-Chancellor takes a sip of water from a glass placed at his elbow. "This gentleman is the embodiment of success built from the ground up, of a business philosophy driven entirely by ability and not politics. Of morality, yes, but also of ruthlessness used in the right place and at the right time."

He gives a slight nod. "Don't let me waffle on any further. Ladies and gentlemen of California State University, I give you Fortune 500 entrepreneur Ram Nayak."

The room applauds as a man in a navy pin-striped suit, 5' 8" and athletically built, steps up to the podium. I feel myself falling, the room collapsing as if made of paper.

9
Meena

Winter 2002
Grace Mercy Children's Home

Ramu Nand Nayak suddenly appears in the front courtyard of Grace Mercy Children's Home just after I turn fifteen. Night has just fallen after another meager supper of roti and *daal* and I tiredly sweep the courtyard—an evening chore that has been delegated to me this week.

Ramu looks like he is about my age and he is accompanied by an official-looking adult who pushes him forward towards the boys' home. Although the orphanage takes in both boys and girls, we are only together during meals, classes and prayers. Otherwise, we live in separate buildings, connected by a single, well-watched corridor.

It is almost five years since I first passed through those same faded blue gates. I have changed a great deal—my face is rounder, I'm taller and my hair is longer, yet the gate surrounding the orphanage remains the same—blue, mismatched against the black railings, now layered in five more years of rust.

I barely notice the boys at the orphanage even though, at fifteen years old, I probably should. The nuns might have had something to do with this, but then again, that doesn't seem to stop many of the others. It is hard enough just keeping out of the way of the other girls, to slither undetected amongst them, for me to think about much else. Plus, Roopa has recently started noticing the boys more, and it would not do if she caught me talking to a member of the male species Roopa has decided is the flavor-of-the-week.

The new boy looks sad as he is brought across the front courtyard. This is normal for a new arrival—sadness and tragedy almost always precede induction into the orphanage. *It is the one thing that we at Grace Mercy have in common*, I reflect to myself, as I move towards the tangle of spiders' webs in the corners.

Our eyes meet in the growing darkness. Hoping nobody is watching, I give him a small nod. A glimmer of a smile sparks in his eyes as he disappears with the man inside the building. I pull at the webs with the mottled straw of the broom, unsure whether I will see him again. Some children spend only a night or two at Grace Mercy, or perhaps a week, and I have learned to keep my distance before I get too attached to them. These children are only here to wait for relatives to come and take them away—perhaps uncles and aunties traveling from across the country to collect them. At Grace Mercy these orphans are *khushkismat*: Lucky Ones.

But I cannot stop thinking about this sad boy, and I look around for him the next day. The boy is not at any of the tables at breakfast, or in my classes. By lunchtime, I have begun to think he might be another transient.

As I walk out and sit on my usual bench that afternoon, he appears with his lunch in hand.

"May I sit with you?" he asks shyly, pressing his lips together.

"Yes," I say quickly, moving to the side. He first places his lunch, then himself, beside me on the narrow bench. I glance down and then up at the boy, wondering if he knows that I am a *Dalit*. Does he know I have been contaminating this bench for many years? Will he care? He does not look like a *Dalit*; his clothes are too nice—unwrinkled and stain-free. Even his shoes are black and shiny, like they were just polished.

"My name is Meena," I say with trepidation.

"I am Ramu," he replies, unwrapping his *rotis*. His eyes remain down, as if to avoid looking at me.

After a few moments, I blurt, "Are you *khushkismat?*"

His head jerks up. He looks startled and confused. "Lucky?" A slightly hysterical tone creeps into his voice. "Why would I be lucky?"

I frown. "I thought maybe someone was coming for you," I remonstrate.

A pained expression crosses his face. He remains still as the seconds drag on, his *rotis* untouched on his lap.

"It's okay," I break through the silence, embarrassed about my insensitivity. I soften my voice, trying to comfort him. "It's not . . ." I stop myself saying it is not so bad at Grace Mercy; that would be a lie, probably an even bigger lie for him in his well-kept clothes than it was for a *Dalit* like me.

"The nuns are nice," I say instead. "Most of them."

Ramu continues to stare at his *roti*.

"Look," I say eventually, "there's something you should know, before you have an inauspicious start here."

He darts a sideways look at me.

"I'm *Dalit*," I say. "If you associate with me, the other children will shun you."

Ramu catches his breath, like he might burst into tears. He quickly regains his composure, picking up a *roti*.

"I know," he says clearly, lifting his chin. "A nun sent me out here to sit with you. I am *Dalit*, too."

I look him up and down in shock as he takes a small bite of his *roti* and begins to chew.

"I like to eat outside," he says casually through a mouthful of food.

My shock turns to relief under the turquoise blue sky dappled with clouds piling up like a bubble bath.

"You wait until the rainy season," I joke, "not so much fun then."

His eyebrows rise in surprise and he pulls at his sharp pointed nose, as if he imagines he would long be gone by then. Perhaps he is *kushkismat* after all.

· · ·

"I never came to an evening like this, to listen to some person I may or may not have heard of tell me about success." He winks, and just like that, the dark-skinned man with closely cropped black hair has endeared himself to his audience. "I imagine if I had, I would have thought, 'It's all right for him to say these things, conceited bastard'"

A small ripple of laughter runs through the hall, and multi-millionaire Ram Nayak, who used to be an orphan boy named Ramu, allows himself a small chuckle.

"Am I right? It's one thing for an experienced—I don't know—," he puts a finger on his chin, "computer programmer to tell you how to write code. But success in business is so ill-defined." Ramu scans the audience with genuine interest. "True, big success seems to strike as randomly as lightning. Sure, if you hold a big metal rod in the air, then this may improve your chances of being hit." He raises his hands slightly in the air. "But it's still no guarantee."

His accent is unmistakably Indian, yet more polished than I would have expected, as if success had applied spittle and a cloth.

"So," Ramu continues in a soft voice, "what right do I have to come up here and tell you how it's done? And, the truth is, I can't anyway. I don't have a magic wand, no great system. I could tell you lots of motivational lines about attitude and setting yourself manageable goals and all that . . . well," he grins sheepishly, "bullshit."

Surprised giggles erupt from the audience. He shrugs. "Sorry, but that's the word for it."

The glare of the overhead fluorescent light falls on his face and makes a pattern on his cheeks. "Actually, truth be told, it's not bullshit—not all of it. Attitude, motivation, organization . . . All these things have a place in the lives of a lot of really successful people. But, for me, it comes down to two really simple things." I feel a little jump in my stomach at his blinding grin. "Two and a half, let's say."

Ramu's face grows serious in his earnestness. "Really, this is it, good people. It's about how I want my life to be, and it's about how I want the world to be." He brings his hands together into a gentle clasp, almost in prayer. "And it's about how well I can make those two things line up."

•   •   •

During those first few weeks at Grace Mercy, Ramu does not always appear in the dining hall at meal times. But when he does, I beat him to the bench which in my mind has become 'ours' after being 'mine' alone for so long. I watch and wait in hope, absently nibbling my food.

And he does come. At first, he silently takes his place beside me, but he gradually opens up as if he senses I will not hurt him. He never talks much about himself, and he tells nothing detailed about his life before the orphanage, but he shares a wide range of opinions and idle chatter about almost everything else. "Kapil Dev has changed the image of the Indian cricket team." "Indian politicians like our last Prime Minister, Mr. Narasimha Rao, are to blame for the corruption scandals in the country." "Miss India runner-up Priyanka Chopra has won the Miss World title . . . Wow!"

Ramu is nearly a year older than me, so he has spent almost six more years of his life beyond the walls of Grace Mercy. I sit happily beside him, soothed by his voice and his company, cocooned in a world beyond the trials of Grace Mercy.

After a few months, Ramu arrives as I am finishing my lunch. He is carrying a dessert in a *Haldiram's* cardboard box, and he places it on my lap in front of me. I recognize it instantly, even though I have only eaten it twice before.

"*Gulab jamun,*" I say excitedly, my mouth watering as I look down at the round, brown ball made of cottage cheese and fried in sugar syrup. "Where did you get this?"

"Today I thought I was going to be *khushkismat,*" Ramu grins wryly.

I look at him blankly.

"My uncle came to visit me," he says breathlessly. He looks triumphant. "All the way from New Delhi."

"Cross country," I sigh longingly. Cross-country relatives usually come for one reason: to adopt an orphan.

My stomach clenches. "Is he going to adopt you?" I try to keep my voice as neutral as I can.

"No." Ramu looks at me quizzically.

"Then why come all this way?"

"To pay his respects. He could not make the funeral." Ramu has told me only that his parents died in a car accident. "And to tell me he will not adopt me." He does not look overly distressed when he tells of his Uncle's decision.

"I'm sorry, Ramu," I stutter, trying not to sound too relieved.

"It's okay," he says matter-of-factly. He smooths his thick black hair to the side. Suddenly I notice he has hair growing above his lip. His voice grows excited. "He has offered me a job. Well, a job interview, at least, when I turn eighteen."

I cut a slice off the *gulab jamun* with the tiny plastic spoon that was in the box and pop it into my mouth. The flavor of the rosewater-scented syrup almost brings tears to my eyes.

"What does your uncle do?" I ask, breaking off the sugary dough piece by piece, wanting it to last.

Ramu chuckles. "He is a wealthy man; he owns a leather factory."

My eyebrows rise in surprise. "He is not *Dalit*?"

"Yes, but other *Dalits* work in his factory. Even some non-*Dalits* work in the higher positions in his company."

I look at him in shock, pausing from my nibbling. "*For* him?" Ramu nods, watching me intently as I devour the dessert with pure delight.

"Wow," I say, truly impressed. I frown. "So, why didn't he adopt you? That's . . . mean."

Ramu pushes my hand away as I offer him a taste of the *gulab jamun,* indicating that I should finish it. "Maybe. He said that my time here would make me into more of a man than he ever could." He sighs. "Just words, probably. But I'll take him up on his offer when the time comes." He straightens his shoulders as he declares, "I'll be so good at my job that I will own the company one day."

Something in the way Ramu speaks—his eyes sparkling with determination, his lips curved into a knowing, secret smile—makes me want to believe him. I lift the dessert in his direction again, this time more forcefully, luxuriating in the whiff of rosewater that wafts up between us. "This is your *gulab jamun,* Ramu. You should eat it."

"But I don't want his food," Ramu says. "I want his job."

I look away, then back at him. "That's going to be in two years," I point out gently.

A look of uncertainty crosses his face. He pauses, then says in a rush of words, "I really wanted to go with him today." His eyes are downcast as he mumbles, "I'm sorry."

"Sorry?"

Ramu gives a small nod. He squeezes the bridge of his nose hard between his thumb and forefinger. I have noticed that is something he does when he is stressed.

I shake my head and I can feel my lips tremble. I lean my head on his shoulder for just a moment. "You don't have to be sorry. Here," I say, handing him the dessert. "Share it with me. You don't need to feel guilty about wanting to be wanted. Besides, you've known me for just a few weeks. You don't owe me anything." But when Ramu looks at me, I know that the most grown-up thing I have ever said is not exactly true. Even after only a few weeks, there is already a bond between us.

. . .

The stage is a sea broken only by two islands—a microphone stand and a table with a jug of water and a small water glass. Ram Nayak returns to the center of the stage after taking a sip of water, microphone in one hand, water glass in the other.

"When I was a seventeen-year-old boy, my life wasn't how I wanted it to be. Part of this had to do with things that nobody could really help. For instance," he hesitates, scanning his audience, then continues, "I lost my parents at sixteen and was placed in an orphanage. This was a very sad time for me, and the orphanage was not always the nicest place to be. Yet, in India," his expression is a mix of anger and sadness, "where I come from, in case you hadn't guessed, not every orphan finds their way to an orphanage. In this respect, I was lucky not to die on the street as many children do."

Ramu glides softly to the front of the stage and clears his throat, a casual, almost idle air about him. In his hand, he gently swirls the cup of water around like it is whiskey.

"My life as an orphan, although not ideal, was not really the problem. The problem was my caste—my place in society." He speaks slowly, his head thrust forward on his shoulders, and he nods slowly as he looks earnestly at the audience. I sink lower into my chair, not wanting to be seen.

"Now, some of you may know of the caste system—at least you may have heard of it—but let me just explain it briefly, so we are all on the same page.

My heart rate ratchets to deafening levels as I realize Ramu is going to reveal his origins as a *Dalit*. The whoosh of blood through my head is so powerful it makes me dizzy.

"The caste system, although outlawed for over sixty years, is a part of the Hindu belief system, which is the majority religion in India. Castes are based upon the idea of *karma* and of reincarnation, that souls are born forward from one life to the next, and that the *karma* of a previous life will affect our station in this one, then the next one, and so on."

He turns to beam at the crowd, his eyes bright. A winning, white-toothed smile—like Tom Cruise—different from the gap-toothed grin he had as a child. "A history lesson and a religious education lecture all in one speech. Bet you would have stayed home if you had known that was coming."

The laughter from the audience is polite, if slightly nervous, and Ram Nayak's high-wattage grin slides into something a little more roguish. "Stay with me. It's all relevant, I promise.

"There are three castes." He holds up three fingers to emphasize his point—the same long fingers I remember, only more tanned and wrinkled. "The *Brahmins* are the highest caste, the holy men, the leaders. The *Kshatriya* were traditionally the warrior caste and still hold a high position in society. The *Dalits* are the Untouchables, who get to do all the worst jobs. *Dalits* are considered unclean and must stay away from the other classes because they might pollute them."

I sit perfectly still in my seat. He leans forward to speak into the microphone. "Guess which caste I was born into?"

"A *Dalit*," a woman's voice calls out from the back after a moment of quiet.

Ram Nayak's face suddenly clouds over. "What gave me away?" he asks wryly, before the clouds break and the roguish look returns.

"I'm just kidding," he winks. "That's absolutely right; I am a *Dalit*. The lowest of the low. In much of India, particularly the rural parts, including where I grew up and in the orphanage, most people considered me worthless. Good for only unblocking latrines and sweeping streets.

Even now, there are plenty there who would shun me, despite my achievements."

He gives a little shrug. "Now, don't get me wrong, esteemed people of California State University. I don't tell you this story to make you feel sorry for me or to impress you with just how far I have risen from such humble beginnings against terrible odds. I tell you this story to illustrate my point as clearly as possible."

He drifts back to the table to place his glass down, gesturing animatedly with his hands.

"I did not like my life as an orphan *Dalit*. I wanted to be anything but *Dalit*. But I was never going to magically grow new parents, and in India, whatever caste you're in, you stay there forever. So, instead, I needed to change the world. Or, more precisely, the world immediately around me, to make that happen."

He steps forward to the front of the stage, his fathomless black eyes sparkling as his whole face lights up. "I started doing that at seventeen years old, and I'm still doing it now—being who I want to be. It's a work in progress, as I imagine it is for many of you here. *Always*."

Amazed by Ramu's control over the crowd, I glance covertly at Tammy, who sits in the chair next to me. Her expression is the sort that someone might make if they were watching an ice-cream sundae being made for them.

Ramu stands with his toes almost at the edge of the stage, an animated look on his face, looking out across the gathering, most of them clearly successful, accomplished people in their own right. "You see—and if you take anything away from my speech tonight, take this—changing the world is almost never a grand, sweeping move." He lowers his voice.

A small smile tugs at the corners of my mouth as I watch Ramu make the large hall feel like a chummy little club, with the entire audience listening intently to every word he utters.

"The first step I ever took on my journey was in convincing someone to invest in me and my future, to give his life savings so I could go to college. And believe me, at the time, it looked like a poor investment. And, although convincing him came down to one face-to-face meeting, I had spent months planning how I was going to say it—how I was going to sell myself to him, the only way a child with no previous sales experience can give the pitch of a lifetime."

He pauses, then his voice becomes louder.

"Changing the world, *your* world, is the same thing. It's about lots and lots of little changes all the time."

Someone in the audience lets out a cheer, making Ramu chuckle and give a thumbs-up sign.

"And maybe you will be a little disappointed to hear that—maybe you came here hoping to get some magic bullet for success. But if you stop and think about the implications of what I've just told you, then your mind should be a little blown by it. And you'll realize that you need to get up early tomorrow morning—I'm talking *really* early—and start working on it, because that's what it's going to take to get you there."

He coughs, looking slightly embarrassed, then beams. "I think I ended up giving one of those bullshit motivational speeches, anyway."

10
Meena

Fall 2014
Hayward, California

For the whole of Ram Nayak's speech I stay rapt, unable to pull my eyes from him. When he finishes and shakes the Vice-Chancellor's hand, waving and leaving the stage to a round of applause, I feel almost sick to my stomach, a bundle of nervous energy. I glance at Tammy, who appears oblivious to my distress.

"I like him," calls Tammy over the noise. "There goes a man who knows how to wear a suit."

I paste a smile on my face and continue clapping mechanically. I should go. Leave before he gets a chance to see me. Before he gets a chance to . . . see what I have become.

· · ·

Summer 2002
Grace Mercy Children's Home

Green is for *Dalit*. It has been a custom throughout much of Uttar Pradesh and other parts of India for many years, but the kind nuns always resisted such blatant displays of caste within Grace Mercy.

I do not know what changed, but the orphanage relies greatly upon the goodwill of the community in our part of Kalanpur. Most likely, someone whose patronage matters applied enough pressure. Sister Gina's voice is uneven, as if she has climbed up a long hill, when they tell us about the new rule during class. Defeat blends with shame in her eyes.

I stare past her at the blank blackboard, but I am not as devastated as Sister Gina is about the whole thing. I have stood apart for years without the help of a wristband. I am friendless among the other girls at the orphanage because everybody knows that I am an Untouchable. Yes, it is unfair, but since Ramu arrived at Grace Mercy a few months ago, all the little injustices and ordeals—being the last to get our share of sweet milky tea prepared on Friday mornings after the other kids are done eating (and, sometimes not at all); having to enter the Hindu temple not through the main entrance but through a door at the back, meant for beggars and *Dalits*; not being allowed to eat sitting next to a caste Hindu or to use the same utensils as they do—can be rendered ineffective with a few simple thoughts: *I'm going to see Ramu at lunch,* or *It's almost time for dinner; what shall we talk about tonight?*

Ramu scowls when we are given the green wristbands in class.

"Red is my favorite color," I joke as Ramu complains about them on our lunch bench. I imitate Princess Roopa once I am sure no one can hear me. "Red is so much more *me*. Red, I could have made work; it goes with my wardrobe. But green . . . oh, so last spring."

"It's not funny, Meena!" he hisses. "It's another way to control us, to put us down."

I draw back, shocked. He has never snapped at me before. "It's just a piece of green cord, Ramu," I say, laying a gentle hand on his arm.

Ramu's words stay with me, and for a day or two, I view the wristband with resentment. The dormitory is the one place where I am not required to wear it, and to stay out of trouble I keep it on until just before bed. I slip it off under the covers, not wanting to have the other girls witness my humiliation.

So, as usual, I removed it just before bed last night, but unbeknownst to me, the wristband fell from the corner of my cot onto the floor. In the morning, in a rush to get to breakfast on time and not seeing it as I dress, I forget about it—that is, until Roopa brings it to my attention.

By the age of sixteen, Roopa is no longer just mean and vicious; she has become subtle, as well. Instead of confronting me in front of all the nuns, she usually waits to pick on me in the dormitory. But after six years of it, I have become pretty much immune and, at some point, the nuns started paying special attention to our dormitory, especially Sister Gina—my guardian—who has literally been sent from God. Of course, it is not just about me. The girls in our dormitory are mostly of a certain age where 'misbehaving' now means sneaking off to meet boys in a manner that God most definitely would not approve of.

Roopa deals with this by making jokes about the nuns' obsession with watching over our night-time activities, having something to do with the fact that they were never going to have 'night-time activities' of their own. "Can you picture all those nuns over there fondling one another?" she chortles. Another time I heard her say laughing as hard as a hyena, "Sister Gina is such a pervert. She can't look at the near-naked body of Christ on the crucifix without getting dirty ideas in her mind."

How the girls in the dormitory loved that one—the brazenness of it, the lack of respect for a nun's authority. But the problem with moments like that, I notice, is that Roopa will need to outdo it. Being adored is all about constantly upping your game.

I walk quickly ahead of the other kids, returning to the dormitory before lunch to store books and schoolwork, taking the quickest way through the west corridor across Marigold Garden. The garden is beautiful in an otherwise dour and practical—and slowly decaying—orphanage. There are marigolds, roses, hibiscus, and even a little jasmine over against the building. Most of the children seem to ignore the garden, except one time when I came upon a girl and a boy who jumped apart when they saw me approaching the shrub of yellow marigolds.

Now, walking along the west corridor, I pass the steps to the abandoned bell tower and notice a boy skulking near the door that leads out to Marigold Garden. I look at him in surprise; the boys' dormitory is in the opposite direction. It is Buta, and I come to a standstill, a knot of panic in my stomach. Now the tallest and stockiest of the boys, he has been at Grace Mercy for almost as long as I have. Only since he turned sixteen about a year ago have I observed the hardness in his eyes and fear the sense of menace he carries with him. (I remember his birthday clearly because his grandmother brought *gulab jamun* to distribute to the rest of the class, but they did not give me one, not even a slice.) Some of the girls try to flirt with him, but he treats them with the same cold nonchalance as everything else. But this has not prevented Buta from being the focus of Roopa's attention for the last two weeks—something that makes me even more scared.

The corridor is too quiet. I realize I am alone. Then I catch sight of someone beyond the double doors at the end of the corridor that leads to the garden. The narrow gap between those doors lets in a draft that almost always blows down the west corridor. An eye appears.

Fear shoots up the length of my spine like a painful rod. Roopa and Buta's friend, Sanjay, appears from the direction of the bell tower steps. Behind them, at the other end of the west corridor, two more figures are turning some girls back the way they have come.

I keep my head down, absurdly hoping I can still make it to the garden and be on my way. I run as Roopa and Sanjay rush toward me from behind, but the only way to go is towards Buta. I am small, lithe and quick, but the corridor is too narrow to make my escape.

"Get her, Buta!" Roopa screeches. As Buta heads toward me from the side, I dodge away, but he fools me and I run straight into his grasp. I struggle, but his grip is like iron.

"What are you doing?" I shout, terrified. "Let me go!"

"Don't mess around, Buta," Roopa hisses. "Get her in!"

I spot the slightly ajar door of the janitor's closet that is set into the side of the corridor. I howl as Roopa pushes past and holds the closet door wide open for Buta to shove me through.

The janitor's closet is much larger than I had imagined—nearly half the size of the dormitory—with shelves, wooden racking, and even a dirty old porcelain sink.

Roopa faces me with a vicious grin on her face.

"Roopa, what are you doing?" I plead.

"Roopa," Sanjay shouts, pointing to the racking behind her, "the cloth!"

Roopa grabs a dirty rag from the shelf as Sanjay and Buta grab my arms.

"Get off!" I cry, flailing and kicking. I start coughing as they push me hard into the wall, winding me.

"Hold her still," Roopa cries.

"Roopa!" I scream. "Please let me go." Tears stream down my face. There is no pity in Roopa's eyes as she forces a cloth reeking of a toxic chemical into my mouth.

"Shut her up, Roopa," Buta complains. "You want Sister Gina to hear?"

Buta slaps me across the jaw with the back of his hand. Roopa, laughing gleefully, pinches my cheeks, her fingers digging into the hollows to force my mouth open enough for her to push the rag down my throat.

I gag, but I force myself not to throw up, so I will not choke and die right there on the stone floor. Buta slams my back into the wall again, causing my shoulder blade to explode with pain. I keep as still as I can, trying not to faint.

"Get her on the floor," Roopa commands, her voice grating, "where she belongs."

The boys knock me down and pin me to the floor, each with a hand on one shoulder. I lay there convulsing in panic, like a deer pinned by a tiger.

Above me, Roopa paces back and forth, looking too buzzed to stay still. "You did this to yourself, *Dalit*," she lectures.

I keep looking up at her, too scared to move.

"You see this?" she says, waving her bare arm at me. "I wear nothing on my arm, no green wristband. This is because no one can tell me what to wear. I know what I am. I am better than you, *Dalit*," she screeches, her tone full of self-righteous indignation.

"And you wear *your* wristband so that you never forget what *you* are. So that you remember your place at the feet of your betters. So, where is it?"

Buta grabs my wrist, his grip so vice-like that it feels as if he will crush it as he grins wickedly at me. Tears of pain rush from my eyes.

"You've forgotten your place," Sanjay says in his nasal voice, "so we must teach you."

Roopa's face lights up like a *diya* on Diwali. "What shall we do?" she asks excitedly, continuing her pacing.

I see Buta and Sanjay sharing a look without Roopa noticing. Then Buta releases my wrist and climbs to his feet.

"Hold her," he instructs Roopa, and she eagerly obeys, crouching down to take his place. Once she has me pinned, Roopa looks expectantly back up at Buta, waiting to see what he will do.

Terror rises, flooding my mind as Buta undoes his belt and pulls his trousers down.

"What are you doing, Buta?" Roopa says with sudden uncertainty.

"What does it look like I'm doing?" he replies gruffly. "I'm showing the *Chamar* her place."

"But—"

"Hush, girl," he replies, holding up a dismissive hand, "just hold her down."

I thrash and kick my legs, squealing in panic.

"I just . . ." Roopa protests. "We don't have to . . . There'll be other things we can do."

"Shut up, Roopa," Sanjay snaps. His eyes look hungry, feral.

"It's not like I'm ruining her chances of a good marriage. Come on, Roopa, this was all your idea."

She turns and looks back down at me for a moment, her grip on my shoulder loosening slightly. Our eyes lock, and I see something in hers that I have never seen before, not in Princess Roopa. Shame.

Then Roopa looks away, pushing down more forcefully on my shoulder.

Buta suddenly flies forward, the trousers around his ankles causing him to topple next to me, reaching out his hands just in time to save his face from meeting the floor. Ramu appears where Buta had been a moment before. He is much smaller than Buta, but he looms over the others like a giant. Sanjay tries to leap to his feet but Ramu, eyes filled with rage, kicks him before the boy is even halfway up. Sanjay lets out a shriek and topples backwards, arms shielding his head.

Ramu ignores Roopa, who cries out and scuttles away in panic. Reaching down, he pulls me to my feet before either of the other boys can recover. "Hurry," he says urgently.

I pull the rag from my mouth and fling it away as we run out of the room, my hand tightly clutching his.

11
Meena

Fall 2014
Hayward, California

"Come on, Meena," Tammy says, "don't get all shy on me. We need to talk to them."

I have been immobilized, pinned to my chair since Ram Nayak left the stage. "Oh, I don't know. It's just—"

"What? What are you going on about? You were doing fine earlier, with no help from me. Now we can double team the VC and see about getting your project that funding. We'll be like . . ."

"Like who?" I interrupt, my voice a thready whisper.

"I don't know . . . Thelma and Louise." Tammy laughs.

"Thelma and Louise?" I look at her, puzzled.

"I know, but I was trying to think of a stereotypical strong female duo, and that's all that came to mind. Kind of sad, if you think—"

"No, I mean, who are Thelma and Louise?"

"Really? You're kidding me." Tammy looks askance at me, bemused. "Well," she drawls, "I guess that makes sense. Sorry, sometimes I forget you weren't here for the nineties." She takes me by the arm. "We need a movie night some time. There are some things Susan Sarandon has to say which you need to hear, young lady.

Tammy tosses her hair. "Anyway, I digress. We need to charm the Vice-Chancellor while I'm still at my most charming. And I reckon we've got about ten minutes before that window closes."

"What happens then?" I ask, brow furrowed.

"Either 'Miserable-Drunk Tammy,' who cries about her bad luck with men, or 'No-Way-I'm-Going-Home-Alone-Tonight Tammy,' and . . . Well, I'm sure you can imagine why we don't want to still be here when *she* turns up."

Reluctantly, I follow my slightly wobbly friend from our chairs and toward the more crowded part of the room. People politely hover near the Vice-Chancellor and his guest, performing a slow, intricate dance that they hope will place them into the path of the VC's sedate—and oft-interrupted—stroll through the gathering.

"I told you we should have gotten over here earlier," Tammy grumbles. "We've got at least six groups to out-maneuver before we're even anywhere close." She shakes her head at the throng of people between us and the VC. "This won't do," she says. "They'll be at the door before we're anywhere close. It's time for action."

"No!" I protest, not really knowing what Tammy means, except that it doesn't sound good. "Let's not."

"What have you got to lose?" Tammy asks. "Your project will be over soon, then you'll never have to see all these boring assholes again, anyway." She chews on her nails, an old habit of hers. "Unless you do something now and change it." There is a truculent note in her voice as she says continues, "Dammit, I don't want to have to find a new lunch partner!"

"I think you're putting too much emphasis on one conversation." I give a slight shake of my head.

Tammy shushes me with a finger to her lips, then puts one hand around my waist and entwines her fingers with the other. "I could just make an appoi—" She pulls me into a dance of a string waltz, through the guests, as we twirl an erratic, yet purposeful path across the floor.

"Tammy," I protest, trying to stop myself from laughing as we stumble closer to the Vice-Chancellor and Ram Nayak, who are still mostly obscured in the middle of a small crowd, save for the very tip of the buzz cut atop the VC's head. "Tammy, come on, stop it."

"Look out!" cries an older woman dressed in a black pantsuit and patent black heels. She and her partner almost lose their drinks as we waltz into them.

"Tammy!" I raise my voice a little louder than I mean to, finally bringing my friend to a halt. Tammy tries to look sorry.

"Meena?" A man's soft voice breaks through. "Meena, is that you?"

. . .

Summer 2002

Grace Mercy Children's Home

I did not eat lunch—mentally, a part of me never wanted to face Roopa or Buta again—and Ramu was not at dinner. Passing close to Sister Gina's office on the way back to the dormitory after finishing my paltry dinner of two leathery rotis and *aloo-sabzi*, I notice the nun is tending to a cut above Ramu's eye.

"You!" Sister Gina calls with a dark expression on her face. I return to stand in the doorway of her office, which also doubles as the infirmary.

In the last year, Sister Gina has aged, beginning to look less like the youthful, charismatic woman she was when I first entered the orphanage, and paler and more drawn like the other nuns far beyond her in years.

"Do you know how this happened?" she asks sharply, indicating the nasty-looking gash above Ramu's right eye. "Hawa Singh here's not saying anything. Big surprise." She sighs heavily, like a camel assuming a familiar weight. "I don't know how I can ever help you children if you won't help yourselves."

"Hawa . . . Who?"

"Singh," she answers crossly, preoccupied with Ramu, who squirms under her touch. "He was a boxer. Before your time and mine."

She continues cleaning out the gash, stopping to apply more Dettol antiseptic, which fills the air with fumes. "Anyway, out with it," she scolds. "You two are like conjoined twins; you must know something." She glares at me. "And if you care about him, maybe you'll help him out and tell me so I can try doing something about it."

"I'm sorry," I mumble, avoiding Ramu's look, "we've not seen each other much today, so I don't know."

"Hmm . . . You weren't at lunch, Meena, were you?" Sister Gina's eyes narrow. "Something's going on here."

She squints at me for a few moments, searching my face. I have covered the bruises on my wrist and my neck with a long-sleeved sweater over my white *kameez,* but I feel like an open book in front of her, sure that she sees straight through my lie. I stand still, holding my breath, but soon Sister Gina gives a resigned shrug and turns to dispose of some blood-soaked wadding.

Ramu's eyes meet mine. They are filled with fear.

•   •   •

Three days later, trembling in the dark garden, I wait for Ramu. I've been anxious to talk to him alone. Although I have faithfully waited for him to appear at our bench at lunch, he's not turned up. I will find out later it is because Buta came into Ramu's dormitory one night—"he widened his eyes at me and ran his finger across his throat as if to say I'll slit your throat if you talk"—but every time I think of going by myself into the Marigold Garden I turn into a quivering bowl of *phirni.*

But there is nowhere else we have any chance of being alone together, so earlier in the day I sent a note with Jamuna, who attends the same Advanced Mathematics class as Ramu, asking him to meet me tonight.

My breath comes in quick gasps as I look around in wide-eyed terror, expecting Buta to step out of the shadows at any moment and lunge at me. Only when I hear Ramu's voice call out my name does my shaking subside.

"Meena?" he calls again, more urgently, as he steps out into the blackness of the garden.

"Here," I whisper.

"Do you think you should be out here on your own after what happened?" Ramu chastises, his brow furrowing.

"I'm not on my own, you're here," I blurt then fall silent, shy at showing my feelings.

I can feel his reproving look in the shadows of this cloudy, moonless night, but he remains quiet.

"You saved me," I say as I feel him moving closer. He smells exotic, like freshly wet earth after the first monsoon rain. I inhale the scent greedily.

"I . . ." He pauses and shifts uncomfortably. He rubs his nose thoughtfully.

"Did they give you that cut on your eye because of me?" I ask, squinting at him in the darkness. "Sanjay and Buta?"

His voice is tight, tense. "They made Kamal hit me, but he only did it once, and then he ran off."

"Bullies!" I say through gritted teeth.

"I'm glad they made him do it." Ramu grimaces. "If it was Buta and Sanjay, I would look worse."

We are both silent for a moment. I find myself looking over towards the double doors, imagining the door set into the side of the corridor just beyond the janitor's closet where . . .

My imagination stops, words attempting to take over. "I think they were going to—"

"Stop!" he exclaims, as quietly as he can, though it is still loud in the tranquility of the Marigold Garden at night. And close to me, too. He is closer than I realized. "Don't say it," he goes on more quietly, almost pleading. "I can't even bear to think of it."

"Why?" It is a strange question, perhaps, yet pertinent to me.

"*Why?*" he repeats, incredulous.

"Yes, why should it be so terrible for you to think of it? I know no *Dalit* who does not turn servile in the presence of a caste Hindu. I know no Hindu who does not look right through a *Dalit* standing in front of him as if he does not exist. We accept that. No questions asked. I'm just a *Dalit* body." My voice is bitter, even to my own ears.

Suddenly, my stomach churns as a memory invades my mind. I must have been five or six because I remember with a rush that I am wearing the frayed sky blue *kameez* and black *salwar* that was the kindergarten uniform at the Ganga Charitable School for Girls. Men . . . Big men with glittering eyes and *paan*-stained teeth. Their lips were cracked and thirsty-looking. Two, three of them? I can recall being pushed from the small shack where I lived with my mother. The door closed to bar my way back in. Noise from the men: muffled roars that reminded me of bulls fighting. Cries from my *Aai*. Small cries. *Please*.

Ramu's hand touches my arm, snapping me back to the garden.

"Don't say that," he says. "You're not just a *Dalit*."

"I know you," I say urgently. "I know you, Ramu. I saw how afraid you were in Sister Gina's room."

"Afraid? I'm not sc—"

"You're not scared of those boys who are bigger than you," I interrupt. "You were scared I would feel bad because they beat you up for saving me."

I feel his hand on my arm give the slightest of squeezes.

"I know you," I breathe again, reaching up and finding his face. "I feel safe with you. I wa—" my voice sounds strange, higher and squeakier than it usually does. "I want you."

Ramu stiffens, and I instantly regret what I have said. "Say something," I say, embarrassed, as the silence drags painfully on.

"I've only kissed one girl before," Ramu says. His voice sounds small, shy.

"Well, that's one more than me." I giggle. "*Boys*, I mean."

Ramu combs his hair with his fingers, then glances away. "But how many girls have you kissed?" Ramu jokes as he turns his head to face me, his breath on mine.

Suddenly my heart has grown wings and it is hard to feel my hands because Ramu is looking at me, this time with his eyes locked on my mouth.

"Stop talking," I whisper. "Kiss me."

His gaze moves over me in the silver moonlight, intense and piercing. I cannot look away. Then, so slowly I could have easily escaped had I wanted, he leans close and presses his lips to mine. I am not at all ready for the sensation of his mouth on mine—the soft press of his lips, the warmth—I have no idea what a kiss feels like. In Bollywood movies, girls and boys do not kiss on the cinema screen. Lovers embrace, eyes aflutter, breath feverish, and the moment before their lips touch the camera cuts to a wildlife scene straight out of a David Attenborough documentary, with doves cooing and bees flying in and out of the flowers.

No wonder everyone does this so often! Kisses are wonderful. Ramu's lips are soft and full and move over mine with a whisper of sensation that makes my toes curl. If I thought about it, I would not understand what to do. Thank you, *Bhagwan*—my body seems to know. Following my instincts, I wrap my arms around Ramu's shoulders and arch my body closer into his, clinging to him like a lizard to the ceiling on a hot summer night.

The slight movement rakes my nipples over his chest, and even though his flannel shirt and my cotton *kameez* separate our bodies, I feel a sharp zing of current that races from those sensitive points. It is lightning—a fiery need that shoots from my breasts to my belly. I have barely gotten past that amazing sensation when I part my lips at the insistent pressure from his tongue, and the kiss leaps to an entirely new level.

Ramu groans. His hands tighten around my waist and he lifts me, pulling me in closer. The sensation is exquisite. He is hard where I am soft, and his curves fit perfectly into my valleys.

The forceful, hungry, all-consuming pressure of his mouth against mine suddenly ceases. We break apart, both of us breathing heavily in the darkness, our silhouettes shaking slightly amid the shapes of the Marigold Garden, a floral display in varying shades of black and gray.

"What is happening?" Ramu asks between breaths.

"I don't know," I reply, shocked at the wave of desire that ripples through me.

Ramu's head snaps around suddenly as voices echo in the west corridor. Nuns are crossing to go from the chapel to retire to their bedrooms.

"Go now," Ramu whispers breathlessly, "before they catch us."

"But you—" I protest, concerned that he must pass through the west corridor to get back to his dormitory.

"It's okay, *jaan*," he says tenderly, "I will hide and sneak past them." He gives me a little push. "Go, go. I'll be all right."

The confidence in his voice pulls my mind back to how heroic he had seemed when he burst into the janitor's closet and saved me.

"Go," he hisses again, more insistently. "I'll see you in the morning. *Kal subah.*"

"*Acha. Kal subah.* Ramu—," I say, fumbling for words.

"*Kal milenge,*" I hear him echo as I slip quickly through the doors, careful not to make them creak.

I lay awake for hours, my body trembling with unmet needs as I replay our kiss, our embrace, trying to commit every detail of our lovemaking to memory just like we fill out the blue handwriting sampler in Sister Gina's class, copying the sentences over and over in order to learn penmanship. My heart pounds as I wonder what might have happened if we had not been disturbed.

.   .   .

Ramu moves through the crowd towards me. I am in shock—dizzy and excited suddenly, in a way I have not felt in ages. He looks different . . . older. There are tiny creases around his eyes and his walk too, is different from what I remember from all those years ago—it is bold and proud like before, but now his hips and shoulders are thrust forward.

Young Ramu had been an unremarkable-looking boy, I think now, harking back to how he looked in the face-off with Buta and Sanjay. He was of average height, with average-length hair and a neat oval face. He was unremarkable except for those eyes and the look in them. They always showed such purpose, and they still do.

With my heart pounding, I notice how his well-ordered face seems to have grown into itself, along with the lithe frame of his body. I chuckle inwardly at the extra padding around his waist; none of us escapes the vagaries of age, I think. Slightly taller and not overtly handsome, he has become a more rugged and strong-lined version of the young man I had once known. He wears his hair just a little longer, but it still speaks of order and control and, perhaps, a personal barber.

The air in the conference hall smells of perfume and stale coffee. "Ramu," I mumble, feeling all eyes upon me as he extends his hand with a big, warm smile, his eyes bright. "Hello."

I place my hand in his as Ramu's gaze takes in all of me, his eyes finally locking on my face. "You're . . . *you.*" He brings his other hand up to cover mine.

"You're 'you and more,'" I reply awkwardly, my voice a stranger to me. "You've done so well. Excellent speech, by the way." Babble, babble.

Tammy looks back and forth between us, her mouth forming the shape of a perfect zero. "So, you two know each other, huh?" She sniffs.

Still clasping my hand in both of his, Ramu takes me in again and the lingering way he looks at me causes my cheeks to flame. I struggle to meet his gaze, feeling more alive than I have ever felt.

"It's just 'Ram' now," he says, the sound of his deep voice soothing me. "I didn't know you would be here."

"Neither did she," Tammy says, looking pointedly at me.

I glance quickly at Ramu, feeling like the world has just changed from black and white to Technicolor. "I didn't know you would be, either," I say in a daze. "I came at the last minute."

The Vice-Chancellor, having noticed Ram's sudden detour, arrives looking flustered.

Tammy pounces. "Vice-Chancellor, I'm Dr. Tamsin Finch. I'm with the History Department," she says, thrusting out her hand.

"Ah, yes," says the Vice-Chancellor, looking nervously over at Ram, as if afraid of losing track of him. "Lovely to meet you. I would love—"

"If I could just take up one minute of your time . . ." Looping his arm into hers, Tammy leads the Vice-Chancellor away, while I marvel at my friend's adroitness.

12
Meena

With Tammy and the Vice-Chancellor gone, silence surrounds me and Ram. Thoughts whirl through my head like a flock of panicked birds.

Those powerful hands continue to hold mine for a moment longer, then Ramu finally releases my hands from his grip. My hands feel bereft and cold without his warmth, but they still tingle pleasantly. I resist the urge to press my hands against my lips and cheeks.

I feel the stares of the room—of my colleagues trying hard to pretend they aren't looking, their eyes skimming surreptitiously past shoulders, peering over long sips of champagne. Do they think I am acting above my station? My old feeling of being an outcast—an unclean *Dalit*—returns, suffusing me with embarrassment and shame.

If Ramu notices the looks, he doesn't show it. "Do you work here?" he asks, cutting through my inner tempest.

"Um . . . ? Yes. Sorry . . . Yes, I do. Sort of." Get it together, Meena, I scold myself. "I'm a temp . . . kind of. But I'm hoping to make it permanent, or longer-term, at least." I raise my eyebrows, grinning, my old cheekiness returning. "So, if you could put in a word with the Vice-Chancellor for me?"

Ram bows slightly. "My pleasure, madam." He looks around with a strange look on his face. "And is, um . . . ?"

". . . Bhavesh." The name sticks in my throat.

". . . Bhavesh. Yes, is Bhavesh here?" So he knows about Bhavesh, the man who stole me away from him. What must he think? That we have had a happy life all this time?

"No, he's at home with our daughter, Maya." *Perhaps cleaning the wall.* I try not to wince.

"A daughter?" he says, tilting his head in thought. "Wow. I'll bet she's both beautiful and a handful."

I laugh, relaxing into my pet subject. "She's an angel. An angel whose parents spoil her too much." I reach into my purse to show him a photo. "Are you . . . in town for long?"

"Yes. We have a new venture in San Francisco, one that will need a lot of my attention for . . . Well, a few months, at least. I will come and go a little. I like to think that New York can't do without me, but much of my focus will be here."

"Well, that's lovely." *Lovely? LOVELY! What the hell is 'lovely?'*

"Maybe we cou—"

"Ah, Ram!" the Vice-Chancellor interrupts, striding towards us with two glasses of champagne in his hand and handing one to Ramu.

Too soon, I think, plastering a look of respect on my face. I discreetly put the photo of Maya back in my purse. "I apologize, I got a little waylaid."

Just behind the Vice-Chancellor, Tammy pouts apologetically.

"That's okay, Jim," Ramu says smoothly, taking a sip from the champagne glass. "I've just bumped into an old friend, here. This is Meena. We . . ." I notice his pause, "knew each other as teenagers."

The Vice-Chancellor squints at me. Sensing his discomfort at not knowing who I am, I step forward to shake his hand. "Meena Rawat, Vice-Chancellor. We've not met."

"Please, call me Jim. You're . . . ?"

"English Department, cataloging."

"Ah, yes," the Vice-Chancellor says, recovering his poise. "I haven't had a chance to come down and see you yet. How are things going?"

"As always, not enough time to do the job we need to do," I reply with a slight grimace. "But I'm sure we're not the only ones."

"Ah, well, I promise I'll be over in the next few weeks. We'll have a proper chat about how things are going and what you need." The Vice-Chancellor's Adam's apple bobs in agitation, but his voice is kind.

I blow out a breath. "That would be great."

"Excuse me," he says, turning to Ramu. "Sorry, but we'd better . . ."

Ramu nods and looks apologetically at me. "We've got board members, I'm afraid."

"Sounds painful." I execute an elegant shrug.

Ramu laughs heartily at my little sally. I like that laugh—it is infectious, deep and rumbling. Ramu cocks his head towards me and fixes me with an intense stare. "At least now I know where to find you."

I nod and imagine that he shares a faint smile with me as he turns to follow the Vice-Chancellor to a private room into which the board members have retreated. Does he mean it, or did he just throw it out there because it sounded like something he should say? Will he now vanish from my life for another decade?

Tammy's sharp tone interrupts my thoughts. "Right, young lady," she says, "you'd better talk. I want to know all about you and the handsome millionaire. The words 'dark' and 'horse' do not begin to cover it!"

• • •

Summer 2002
Grace Mercy Children's Home

During morning classes, Ramu refuses to look at me. I try again and again to catch his eye, but he proves rather clever at avoiding my gaze. Finally, as if by coincidence, our eyes meet. He looks away sharply, making my insides roil.

What is, at first, fear of rejection and lost friendship has become a virtual rage by lunchtime. *Kutta, Kamina!* Who does he think he is, some Romeo who can put his lips on mine one day and then pretend I don't exist the next? *Yes,* he saved me. He stopped Buta and Sanjay from . . . *from* . . . It is still unbearable for me to think about what they had been planning to do—just the word itself makes me feel sick. But it still does not give Ramu the right to blank me like this. *He does not have the right!*

What makes him think he is so special? It is obvious he came from some small wealth before arriving in Grace Mercy. In the end, though, Ramu is just a *Dalit* like me—the lowest of people. Ah, maybe that is it; maybe that is why he kissed me—so he could reject me. So he, a *Dalit*, can feel better than at least one other person.

I storm back into the dormitory. My foul mood has quickened my usually dawdling feet, and I have beaten most of the other girls, despite taking the longer route to avoid west corridor and Marigold Garden. I stop short after bursting through the dormitory door. There is Roopa, sitting on her bed, with a belligerent look on her face. It appears that she has been waiting for me.

I have hardly seen Roopa since the events three days earlier. The nasty bitch was lying low, perhaps worried that some news of what happened would get back to the nuns. Even 'Princess' Roopa could find herself in deep trouble.

I remember talking to Ramu about Roopa after the Marigold Garden incident. "Nobody's sure about it, but everyone thinks Roopa is a Brahmin. Have you seen how she gets away with getting two cups of the sweet-milk tea, or how she makes crude jokes about the nuns' sexuality and the other girls just laugh?" I thought I was talking idly, but even I could hear the wonder in my voice. "I think someone pays Grace Mercy a lot of money for the nuns to keep Roopa here. Although, as she has never received visitors and almost never leaves the orphanage, it is hard to know how they might have any idea about her treatment here. Hmmm."

I can tell Ramu doesn't share my avid curiosity about Princess Roopa when he turns to me and says, grinning, "She's her own kind of Untouchable, is what I think."

As I have gotten older, Sister Gina has occasionally, in unguarded moments, let me in on a few of the realities of the orphanage's existence. Any orphan who spends more than the briefest amount of time at Grace Mercy understands that things are often tight, especially when we are overcrowded, which is almost the normal state of affairs now. Last month, Sister Gina told me that the money received from local religious authorities is not even enough to keep the Sisters themselves. "Some comes from generous locals," she said, adjusting her glasses on her nose, "and a little from 'cottage industry' by the orphans." (The girls in Sister Agnes' home science and sewing class produce cotton doilies with hand-crocheted lace edging and the boys in Mister Naveen's candle-making class manufacture *agarbattis*.)

The rest, I learn, comprises of *'pashchatap'* donations—remorse or 'guilt' money—from the relatives of the children, orphans or other unwanted children who end up at the home.

"*Pashchatap*," Sister Gina said, "is the most precarious income, especially as most of it comes from just a few donors. And yet it is the income which makes all the difference for the existence of the home."

Looking at how Roopa gets her way in about everything, she must be the subject of one of Grace Mercy's largest *pashchatap* payments. *That nasty, spoiled bitch*, I think bitterly after the attack, *the entire existence of Grace Mercy is resting on her—not that she ever acts like she knows or cares.*

I am startled when I see her. She is sitting on her bed with a book open in front of her, but I think she is only pretending to read. I ignore her as usual and go to stack my textbooks under my own bed. I mutter a soft curse under my breath. My brain is jammed with fear and fury at finding her in the room.

"Meena," Roopa says while I am rummaging under my bed, looking for my math textbook. Her voice sounds awkward, tremulous even. I continue to ignore her, finally locating the elusive textbook, wedging it under my arm and straightening up from under the bed.

"*Meena*," she says more loudly, her voice harsh, scraping the air. My name sounds jagged with unfamiliarity in her mouth. She either addresses me as '*Dalit*,' or 'Oi, you!'

"I have nothing to say to you, Roopa." My voice sounds distant, icy. I am careful not to look at her.

"Meena, about that day," Roopa continues, with a scowl on her face. "I had no idea that, you know, Buta and Sanjay would—"

I explode with rage, flames of heat coursing through my body. "Would *what*, Roopa? That your boyfriend would try to rape me?"

"He's not my—" she splutters.

"What a prince he is," I shout, balling up my fists. "What a prince for Princess Roopa. How romantic."

Spittle flies from my mouth, sending Roopa to back up against the wall behind her bed. I am triumphant; now she fears me.

"And then you held me down again, Roopa; don't think I don't remember. That's how brave you were. Such a heroine." I move towards her.

"B-but . . . I tried to stop them," Roopa protests in a squeak, her eyes wide with surprise.

"And we wouldn't even have been there if you hadn't decided to punish me—for what . . . ?" I thump my forehead with my hand. "For forgetting to put a stupid wristband on! What were you planning to do to me, anyway, that needed Sanjay and Buta there, huh?" Tears are streaming red-hot down my cheeks.

Roopa plasters herself against the crumbling wall.

Stamping my foot, I scream, "I forgot to put on a stupid wristband! A STUPID wristband!"

Roopa stares at me, openmouthed, frozen. Suddenly, the unfamiliar sight of the *Brahmin* 'Princess' looking meek and dwindled steals the edge from my rage. I feel deflated, like a shrunken helium balloon.

The blood rushes to my head and then away. I spin away from Roopa and storm out of the dormitory as several of the other girls arrive back. Dirty tears streak down my face and, embarrassed, I bow my head as I race past them.

"Wow, Roopa," I hear Ganga ask excitedly, "what did you say to the dumb *Chamar*?"

Roopa's reply echoes down the corridor. "Shut up, will you?"

• • •

"So come on, then," says Tammy, her voice full of justified truculence, "you've kept me waiting long enough."

Even though Tammy's apartment is closer, she has insisted that I be dropped off first so she can quiz me. I could not stay at the dinner after seeing Ramu—I had run out, my coat swinging. Tammy had followed me outside, and caught me trying to find a cab.

Shrinking into the corner of the cab, I wish I had been fast enough to make up something suitably shallow and deflecting, and maybe summoned up the courage to hang around for one more drink, helping to cement whatever story I had come up with. But it is too late now for lies and half-truths to be enough to fool Tammy; I am going to have to be truthful, to some extent. How to start? How to tell the truth without sounding like I am spinning some absurd story?

I can tell from Tammy's glare that the limits of her patience and understanding of avoiding my past have been reached. The more aggressive side of Tammy's curiosity is taking over—the way she is biting her nubby fingernails (something she is trying to quit doing) at my stubborn silence. I pat Tammy's hand, knowing she probably made herself look like some pushy, crazy person to the new Vice-Chancellor.

"Meena!" Tammy's cross voice cuts through the rattle of the cab as it jerks to a halt at a traffic light.

"All right, there's . . ." I swallow hard, searching for the right words. "I haven't told you much of my life before America. Ram—Ramu, as I knew him then—he's a part of that."

Tammy leans forward in her seat.

"You heard him talk about *Dalits* tonight?" My voice is hesitant.

Tammy nods.

I moisten my lips before continuing. "I am *Dalit,* too. Or, I was. I married Bhavesh, who is of a higher caste, the *Kshatriya,* so I am elevated by association. But . . ."

"So, you're like the servant's daughter who marries the lord of the manor," Tammy simpers indulgently. "Except, you're still a servant's daughter at heart, and all the other servants and the lord's family still treat you that way."

I look at my friend, incredulous. "No, not really. In fact, not at all." I frown, my voice growing harsh. "Don't Jane Austen me, Tammy."

Tammy looks suitably abashed and pats my hand. "Sorry, I don't mean to offend."

I clear my throat. "I'm also an orphan. Like Ramu."

Tammy's eyes widen. "And you met in the orphanage he spoke about?"

"Yes."

"Wow," breathes Tammy. "Your life is like a film."

"It really isn't," I say sharply, hitting a button. The side window slides down halfway. I drink in the air as rays of glaring streetlights flicker through the cab windows. "It would be a really crappy, boring film if it were."

Tammy's voice is warm, sympathetic, and inviting. "Did you love him once, when you were in the orphanage together?"

• • •

"Sister Gina told me you were crying," Ramu says, watching my face closely.

"I wish Sister Gina would mind her own business," I reply tartly. I twist to look him in the face. "Are you happy, then?" I ask bitterly. "Got what you wanted?"

"What?" Ramu looks genuinely confused.

We are outside on the little bench, our usual lunchtime sanctuary. I fled there for refuge after my outburst in the dormitory, partly hoping Ramu would appear through the dining hall doors. When I heard the heavy metallic scraping of the doors opening, I did not know whether I wanted to touch him or tear into him.

"Why would I want you to cry?" Ramu asks. I stare at the ground until Ramu breaks the silence. "I—"

"You're the *one thing*, Ramu," I interrupt. "You're the one good thing in this place. How many good things did you think I had before you came?"

"That's why . . ." He trails off and looks at me with his brow furrowed, an odd mixture of surprise and fear stretching his oval, studious face.

"*Why* what?" I say, infuriated. "Why you can kiss me last night and ignore me this morning?"

"I wasn't ignoring you." He looks even more bewildered.

"Yes, you were. Don't lie, Ramu." I slap my hand against the bench.

His voice is placating. "I was . . . trying not to look at you for a while."

"And there's a difference?" I respond sharply.

His hands, which he has been folding endlessly over one another, come to a halt. He reaches out towards my arm, but after a second, thinks better of it and drops his hand back again.

"I wanted to see if I could do it . . . Not look at you." He coughs nervously.

"Why?" I ask, even more aggravated. Anger coils through me.

"It was hard. And even when I don't look at you, your face is still there in front of me. My mind puts it there." He folds his arms and holds my gaze.

My thumping heart steps up a notch. "What are you talking about, Ramu? You're not making sense. You don't kiss someone and ignore them." My face burns.

"You do if you think it will be too hard."

"Too hard?" I blink with confusion.

"To love someone in here."

"What do you mean? Plenty of the boys and girls have . . . *things.* They just keep it from the nuns. And the nuns know—they just want you to keep it out of sight. And, you know . . . not do anything too silly."

Ramu reaches out again and takes my hand. I try to pull it away, but his grip is firm. He presses my hand against his cheek. My throat clenches. The air feels still and silent, like the dark, stuffy space underneath a blanket.

"But the others—their 'things' are nothing. They change who they want every other week. I'm talking about loving someone. Oh, Meena, like I think I love you. But . . . It's impossible in here," he whispers, closing his eyes. When I look sideways at him, I see he is stroking his nose slowly.

•   •   •

I creep through the front door, careful to close it inch by inch so it does not creak. The sky is full of ink and speckled light. The moon hangs overhead and watches me, its face never blinking. I give a hushed salutation to the Moon God. "Chandra, *namaskar*, help me get in quietly so I'm not stuck with having to explain."

Outside, the oak trees rustle, though there is no wind. They whisper my name in the same longing tones, as though they are familiar with my sorrow, my fear of being an outcast again, of not belonging anywhere.

A bird may escape a cage built of hate, of the desire for power. But a cage built of need? Of love's darkness?

Silent as a cat, I make my way into Maya's room to sleep, maneuvering gingerly between familiar pieces of furniture, banging my knee a couple of times in the process. On my way, I note that the kitchen wall has been washed. All the same, there will be a large mark on the wall for all to see, at least until the stain is painted over. As I place my hand on the cold doorknob to Maya's room and turn it gently, my fingers feel sweaty. An ocean heaves and crashes inside my chest.

13
Meena

Fall 2014

Fremont, California

In the morning, while the sun makes its way from the garden to flash like a torch with dazzling rays on the kitchen counter, Bhavesh remains silent as I fix breakfast for him and Maya. For once, he is not scolding me, repeating the same things over and over again.

I entertain the possibility he might have felt bad about throwing his dinner the way he did. Bhavesh is not usually one for remorse, yet he has, occasionally, been known to show it. He never says it and never admits to it, yet I have seen it there. A memory sears at me now from when Maya was just born and Bhavesh called his mother excitedly. From the way Bhavesh's Adam's apple bobbed up and down in his throat, I could tell the conversation had not gone as he expected. "Is it because I'm a *Dalit*?" I had asked quietly. Bhavesh grimaced. "It's nothing," he had mumbled before turning away.

I stay out of his way, but without trying to make it *look* like I am staying out of his way. I skillfully dice the Thai chilies he likes and fold them into an egg white omelet and onto his plate. Then I fix a huge, fluffy pancake smothered in syrup for Maya. It is a careful dance, and Maya twirls and sings and 'mommy's' and 'daddy's' her way through the middle of it, happy and oblivious.

My head is buzzing with all the thoughts and emotions the previous night has stirred up. Remembering how Ramu's eyes flashed as they met mine, searching, dark, full of secrets—I drop a serving spoon into the frying pan with a loud crash and Bhavesh scowls at me across the table. I force myself to concentrate on menial tasks that are usually automatic for me—brewing the two cups of coffee I barely taste, cutting Maya's peanut butter and jelly sandwich into triangles just like she likes it—and once I have gotten Maya ready for school and drop her off, only half-listening to her chatter, I turn on the radio as I make my way to work to drown out my thoughts, then turn it off again, the grating voices annoying me further.

Over and over my conversation with Ramu repeats itself, my body prickling at the insane mantra that caught me in a loop of inanity.

Well, that's . . . lovely.

Why the bloody hell did I say that? If there was a 'weakest reply of the year' award, I would have it in the bag. I'm hot with embarrassment. *What on earth must he think of me? That I am some vacuous housewife with no thoughts left inside my head to find something interesting to say, that is what.*

Well, that's . . . lovely.

"Oh, stop it," I admonish myself, turning the radio back on. "No point in being an obsessive over-analyzer." It is a fault I have developed as an adult. In fact, it is most likely a fault I started to develop after falling for a boy the first time, which makes Ram Nayak the cause of both ends of my misery.

Kutta. Dog.

As I get out of my car and walk into the university, I am overwhelmed with a wave of tenderness. Ram Nayak, *Ramu*, had not left me in all these years since the orphanage, and now I have a chance to . . . what? I search my mind for an answer but come up empty.

. . .

An email from Ramu awaits me, sent at just before four in the morning.

My fingers trembling, I pause before clicking on it. Then, with a pit in my stomach from what this might lead to—or what it might mean— I read:

Dear Meena,

It was so good to see you at the university dinner tonight. And strange, as well; don't you think? I can't think of a less private way to meet the oldest and dearest of friends for the first time in years.

I would like to do it properly. We must have so much to tell each other, and it seems a shame to waste an opportunity to at least touch base again.

Please let me know now if you can make dinner or lunch sometime soon. I should be able to make it any time you choose; that's one benefit of being the boss!

Ram

I read the message three times. A short message and to the point. Was it a businessman's message or a friend's message?

Thoughts jostle in my mind. But we are only people who used to know each other; we were more than just friends at one time, yes, but that was a long time ago. Were we just two orphans who got along? All this time later, what do the feelings of two teenagers even mean, if anything?

I examine the email again, word by word. For all my thoughts in the car this morning, and despite the email's friendly, almost familiar tone, a man I do not know wrote them. A man who has had so much happen since I knew him. From a poor *Dalit* orphan to a millionaire; how much must he have changed to make his life the way it is now?

Yet, despite the smart suit and the fact that a grown man had stood before me on the stage last night, my feeling of intimacy with him was undeniable. I, better than anyone else in the room, knew exactly what he meant because I had known the boy before he became the man. The boy who, without all those fancy clothes and impressive speeches, was from Grace Mercy Children's Home.

Throughout the day, as I mindlessly work through my tasks of tracking and indexing documents into electronic format according to University specifications, the email sits silently on my screen. It is a constant presence, a ticking clock, adding second after second to the time since I read it, and I have chosen not to make a reply.

Tick, tick.

I fumble at the computer keys; I should just get rid of the thing, be decisive: out of sight, out of mind, or at least out of my inbox.

I have just minimized my inbox when I hear my office phone, with its annoying electronic ring, cut through my thoughts.

Now in a foul mood from my mind wandering to and fro all morning, I answer abruptly, "Archiving, how can I help?"

"You can help by coming to dinner with me."

Ramu!

"Ramu," I reply, trying to keep my voice steady. I clear my throat. "How did you get this number?"

"Bullying and intimidation."

"What?" I laugh, caught off guard.

"I'm kidding. I just asked really nicely so I could call an old friend who seems to be ignoring my emails."

"I only got it this morning. I hadn't . . ."

"Hadn't what?" His voice is demanding.

"Decided," I admit, a faint chuckle in my voice.

"Come on," Ramu says persuasively, "it's just a tiny spot of dinner. It would be so good to catch up. Our lives are so different since we last knew each other, it will be fun. The stories I bet we could tell each other."

My heart quickens at the thought of spending time with Ramu. "I think the multi-millionaire's stories might prove more interesting than the suburban housewife's."

I hear him chortle and my chest feels like it is too small to contain all the things knocking around inside it. Heart, lungs, a surge of excitement like the sound of a gunshot to a runner. "I don't believe that for a minute."

"This sounds like a sales pitch, Ramu," I tease.

I can imagine him straightening up and adjusting his tie as he says with an amusing touch of pomposity, "Selling is all about helping people to realize what they want."

I laugh. Damn him. "I don't know when yet. Can I email you later today? I'm meeting a friend for lunch right now."

"The one from last night?"

"Yes, Tammy."

"Yeah, her. The Vice-Chancellor looked in shock after talking to her."

"Uh-huh. She's a . . . force of nature."

There is a pause on the other end of the phone like Ramu is about to add something, but all he says is, "Great, I'll wait to hear from you then." He sounds formal.

"Okay," I try to sound indifferent.

Ramu's voice drops softly. "Nice to hear your voice."

I take a breath, stammering. "Is it the same voice?"

Ramu's voice is hoarse when he finally speaks. "Almost, I think."

. . .

When I arrive at lunch, Tammy is face down on the table. After a minute, she sits up. Hair disheveled, mouth lolling open, her head propped in both hands, she groans loudly.

"This is why I don't like to drink much," I tell my friend, setting a glass of ice water and two aspirin in front of her. Tammy sits up groggily, feeling around on the table for her glasses.

Tammy mimics me in a nasal tone. "This is why I meh-meh-meeeeh!"

As an afterthought, I take out a packet of saltines from my bag and push it towards Tammy. Tammy ignores the insult of the saltines but drinks the water with the aspirin in small, truculent sips. "Very grown up. You know, I'd have sympathy for you if it wasn't—"

"If you say the word 'self-inflicted,' so help me, I won't be responsible for my actions." Exhaling loudly, Tammy puts her glasses on her nose and glares at me.

"Well?" I pointedly cross my arms over my chest.

"Have you ladies decided yet?" a young woman in a flowery apron demands. From the annoyance in her voice, I deduce the waitress has already floated by once or twice and assumed Tammy to be unconscious.

"Coffee!" Tammy pronounces without hesitation, placing her elbows on the surface of the table.

"Me too, please," I say, breaking into a mischievous grin as I browse the menu. "And . . . Let's see, what's really greasy?"

"Ah," Tammy complains, with an exaggerated shake of her head. "You—you—There aren't words for the type of person you are."

"I'm joking." I chuckle. "I'll just have a Caesar salad. Tammy?"

"Coffee is just fine," Tammy replies, waving a dismissive hand at the waitress who sniffs unsympathetically and stomps her dissatisfied way back to the kitchen.

"Are you really still that bad?" I ask, cocking my head and searching Tammy's face. "It's past midday." I gesture to the sun streaming into the cafeteria through the windows.

"I may have overindulged," Tammy admits, her voice sheepish, "but my body has always hated me." She grimaces. "Never lets me get away with stuff like this. I'm good to it, most of the time, so you would think every now and then it would let me have a little fun without crippling me afterwards." She shrugs. "Honestly, my entire morning's work . . . It's not even half an hour's worth on a normal day." She shakes her head. "Ridiculous."

"I guess it's expected the night after a dinner," I say, nobly. "You're probably not the only member of staff under-performing today."

Tammy grins, her face merry. "Well, that depends on whether your boss is a tee-totaling work bot called 'Addy.' She's been giving me the evil eye all morning. Probably hexing me, the witch."

I laugh. "Which is she, a robot or a witch?"

Tammy starts to laugh, but the pain makes her cringe. She rubs her head. "Oh, those are just two of the many names I've come up with over the years. Just got to last until the old witch retires at the end of the academic year, then I'm a shoo-in for her job. Unless God sends a happy aneurism before then. I could write to Santa."

"Tammy, you're wicked!" I laugh out loud, unable to contain myself.

"I know, too far," Tammy says, then her mouth puckers as if she's bitten into a sour plum. She rubs her head tenderly. "It's just that it feels like she's sending an aneurysm to me right now."

"She?"

"Oh, for sure God's a 'she.' Don't you think?" Tammy's face is bright with confidence.

In the middle of my laugh, I realize I have not thought about Ramu Nayak at all. If only I could have Tammy twenty-four seven. "I can't say I've had much chance to think about it," I continue wryly. "But the thing I always hear is that God must be a man, else why would He give women periods and childbirth to cope with?"

"Ah," Tammy replies, shaking a finger in the air, "but did you see what God attached to the front of a man's body?"

I put a hand to my mouth.

"I know, right? Hilarious!" Tammy is grinning from ear to ear. "You don't play that cruel a joke on your own gender!"

Tears of laughter are coursing down my cheeks through my blush.

"Stop it," Tammy says, cupping her hands across her mouth, trying to muffle her laughter. "You'll set me off, too. And I don't think my head can take it." She raises her coffee mug to her mouth and looks at me squarely. "So, what's new in Meena's world today, then?"

And that is when the penny drops, so to speak. Tammy is not going to ask about Ramu unless I bring it up. She is going to let me decide whether to say anything.

I feel a small wave of appreciation towards my friend, who has been waiting for me to mention the proverbial elephant in the room—or 'millionaire in the room,' I grin inwardly. My brain whirs like a wind-up toy; Tammy's thoughtfulness almost makes me want to tell her everything. I want to lay it all down and see if my friend thinks I should go out to dinner with this man.

But maybe I know what Tammy's answer will be, and I do not need any stronger voices in my head. Just for now, perhaps I need to keep it to myself. I busy myself with brushing the hair off my forehead and say nothing.

14
Meena

Fall 2014
San Francisco, California

I try to still the butterflies fluttering rampantly in my stomach. As I struggle with the buttons on my black fitted jersey dress—I did not want to wear anything too revealing, and this dress is business-like but elegant and flattering on me—I wonder how many butterflies are for the lies I told my husband and how many for my impending meeting with Ramu.

The dinner at the university had been one thing—a work engagement—but this was quite another. The mark on the wall had been a reminder of why I had—seemingly—gotten away with going. Perhaps in Bhavesh's mind, it was a case of *all's fair*—that I could be forgiven for acting out that once, considering his over-the-top reaction to a slightly cooled dinner.

The fact that he had painted the wall over during the following weekend suggested that he wanted to move past it quickly. In Bhavesh's mind, I suspected, once the stain was gone, the event could be forgotten. *Yes,* that was a very 'Bhavesh' way of thinking, I said under my breath as I put on my new chili-pepper-red coat.

I had not meant to buy it, but when I saw it hanging in the boutique's window near Maya's school, I could not resist it. Something about the red coat—like a *Deghi* chili with its saucy military cut, its pleated back and belt—reminded me of Grace Mercy orphanage and the time I had spent with Ramu. I squeeze my eyes shut against the barrage of memories, and yet I felt something thick and hot welling up in me like lava.

"This evening I'm putting in some extra hours," I tell Bhavesh when I call him at three in the afternoon, pinching the skin between my forefinger and my thumb so I do not sound nervous. As I utter the words as casually as I can, I see two students, both looking like they had just walked out of a medieval castle, linking arms as they walk around the corner into the Humanities building. A rain-dampened sun struggles from the clouds to frame them in its hesitant light.

I hear his offhand assent, knowing what he is thinking: more dollars for his pocket on payday. I grimace at the thought I will have to dip into the small amount of money I have been putting away the past few months. (I had started squirreling away some housekeeping money Bhavesh gives me every month in a secret account.)

Later I will tell Ramu that the lying had come easily, almost scarily so. But that is because almost all of my life is, to some extent or other, a lie. I live my life projecting to everybody else the things I think they need to see and hear. Bhavesh, Maya, my colleagues . . . even Tammy; all of them see a lie or, at least, one part of the greater lie that is Meena Rawat. All of them, to some extent or another, interact with a woman whose thoughts are almost always vetted before being given.

Maybe everyone is a little like this, with a slightly altered version of themselves that they give to the world. Yet I think most lives are not as extreme as mine in this respect. Sometimes I wonder if I know who the real 'me' is any more. Whoever that person is, she is hidden behind many layers of pretense.

So, with years of practice behind me and knowing that the best lies in my house are those which disrupt normality as little as possible, I came back to pick up Maya and make dinner before 'returning to work.' And now I *have* returned to work, parking the car and using university facilities to change into something a little less work-like. I give myself a nod of approval in front of the mirror before catching a bus for the few miles to the Ritz Carlton Hotel. As the bus lurches onto the main road, I wonder at how the date of his birthday had just popped up in my mind after all these years.

I had wished him a 'Happy Birthday' in the email I had sent in response to his dinner invitation, and his response sounded familiar and comforting, like he, too, had missed the calm comfort of our conversations.

. . .

The huge entrance to the Ritz Carlton dwarfs me as I walk beneath the porte-cochere, just like the Grecian-styled buildings in Washington D.C. Bhavesh and I had visited soon after moving to the States. I had been struck by their majesty and the power they'd emanated.

I feel a thread of anxiety running through me as I pass throngs of well-dressed men in fine suits and women in gorgeous dresses and black high heels, and I almost stumble as I make my way through the plush lobby, with its expensive wood paneling, to the dining room. I could never belong here, even after all these years in the United States.

I stop. Why would Ramu, of all the places we could go to fill in the gaps of the intervening years, choose here? The thoughts go around and around in my brain like the bullocks they used in the village to turn the water wheel, but after a moment I force myself to move forward.

In the distance, as I approach, I can see Ramu standing in the restaurant doorway with a bouquet of white roses. He is dressed in a gray, expensive-looking suit. With the top button of his shirt undone and his lavender tie a little loose, there is something effortless about his appearance, like he has come straight from wherever he spent his working day. Yet, I think with a pounding heart as I walk up to him, he looks none the worse for it.

"Ramu," I breathe, touching his arm. Ramu's head pivots, and as his eyes meet mine, there is a flicker, a tiny moment of something that might be uncertainty, perhaps even vulnerability. But his look is almost instantly obliterated by a captivating, confident grin.

"Meena," Ramu says softly. There's a faint note of unsurety in his voice. "I'm so glad you could come."

I cannot really believe I am here, either. It seems so surreal—two Grace Mercy orphans standing at the entrance to a restaurant at the San Francisco Ritz Carlton.

Ramu suddenly remembers the bouquet in his hands and thrusts the flowers forward. "Here," he says. "I just thought I should bring something."

"I haven't brought you anything," I say, taking them.

"You brought yourself," Ramu replies, turning to lead me into the restaurant. He turns and winks. "Much better than flowers."

I blush, smiling. He takes me by the elbow to guide me, sending an unexpected thrill through my body.

I feel a wave of relief when a waiter leads us to a secluded table, well away from the entrance and any windows. It's absurd, really. Who do I think is going to see us? And, on the off chance that someone I know is at the Ritz Carlton, who would think to mention it to Bhavesh?

It is dinner, I admonish myself. That is all. Dinner with an old friend.

The waiter is back to us straight away, laying down menus. I get the impression from his solicitous manner and the way he is laboring tableside to fill our glasses with sparkling water that this waiter has served Ram Nayak here before.

"Are you staying here?" I blurt.

"Yes," he admits, looking so serious that I want to burst into giggles. "Do you think me lazy? I made you come all this way when I only had to come down the stairs."

"And yet you didn't even have time to do your shirt up," I joke, then cringe, unsure why I said it.

"I apologize," Ramu says, fumbling with the buttons. "I didn't just have to dash down from my room, that wasn't quite true. I've only just gotten back from work. I didn't have time to run upstairs."

"I'm sorry," I say, embarrassed. "I don't even know why I said that. You look . . . great. I'm just . . . "

"Nervous?" He raises an eyebrow, his eyes dancing at me.

"Yes, I suppose I am." I play with the snowy damask napkin on the table, keeping my eyes downcast.

Ramu reaches across the table, his fingers briefly twining with mine. His tone is conspiratorial. "Me, too."

I hide a slight tremble of the lips. The feeling of his strong, lean fingers on mine has set up a little chorus of longing inside me. "Surely Ram Nayak, uber-successful businessman, doesn't get nervous?"

"Depends upon who I'm having dinner with," says Ramu lightly.

"Well," I say, recovering my poise a little and flashing him a cheeky grin, "we suburban housewives are quite scary."

"You're more than just a housewife, Meena," Ramu says slowly. "You work at the university, for one thing." He sits back and takes me in, giving a gratified sigh. "Just look at you," he says admiringly.

"Not as far as you." He tries to wave my compliment away, picking up the menu and pretending to study it but I press the point. "No, I mean it. You did all you said you would do and more." I look at him across the table, gazing at him in appreciation.

He raises his eyebrows in seemingly reluctant acceptance of my praise. "To us, eh? The *Dalits* of Grace Mercy."

My face darkens briefly, but Ramu appears not to notice as the waiter returns to take our drinks order.

"I'll just have water, please," I say firmly.

Ramu frowns in disappointment. "You won't make me drink alone, will you? That's cruel."

"Then don't drink," I retort with a wry grin.

Ramu laughs. "*That* would be crueler."

I laugh and turn fetchingly to the waiter. "One small glass of your house red, please," I say coquettishly. "I'm driving."

"Bring a bottle of the Opus One from Napa Valley, please," Ramu says authoritatively, "and I'll make sure the lady drinks responsibly."

I pretend to give him an admonishing glare, then we both pick up the menus, relaxing slightly. I lean back in my chair. Music floats from a baby grand piano tucked into a shadowy corner, subtle enough to add to the intimate ambiance without drowning out the pleasant buzz of laughter and conversation.

"I loved your speech at the university," I say after a moment, not wanting the silence to rise to a level of discomfort.

"I had no idea you were in the audience," Ramu replies, his eyes glinting, "but I guess you were probably the best person in that room to get what I was trying to say."

As I nod, Ramu's cellphone, which he had placed on the table begins to vibrate. We both glance at it, but Ramu checks it quickly, then silences it before turning back to me.

"I hardly ever do stuff like that. I just, I don't know . . . I'm more into doing things than talking about doing things. You would think that maybe I could slow down now, you know—job done, got to where I wanted to get. But I've just got to keep going. Not sure I would know how to stop." His expression is bleak as he says this. Words jostle in my mouth—it's okay, I want to reassure him, you have achieved your dreams, but then the waiter arrives to take our dinner orders and the moment has passed.

"Sounds exhausting," I say flippantly. "But you were always a doer."

Ramu stares past me at the other diners. "It didn't feel like that in the orphanage. I was restrained there." His voice has changed, grown dark like it never was before. "Not that I regret my time in Grace Mercy."

I look up, surprised. "No?"

He grimaces slightly. "Of course, I would rather have had my parents. But I'm glad now that my uncle left me there. I think it made the difference in who I am and how I look at the world." He takes a deep breath and a half-smile flits across his face.

I shake my head despairingly. "Apart from you, Grace Mercy was— ah, what's that American word—yes, it just *sucked* for me." I give a short, mirthless laugh at my Americanism, my complete acculturation into my adoptive country.

His eyes crinkle at the corners as he says kindly, "You were there so much longer than me, for so long before I came there." He glances away, as if more interested in the little drama playing out at the surrounding tables. I notice that he is not meeting my eyes. "And after I left."

"Still, I'm surprised to hear you say that," I narrow my eyes at him. "Some terrible things happened there, to both of us, but the worst of it to you." I frown.

Ramu's phone vibrates again, this time consistently. He sighs, looking blindly up to heaven. "Why didn't I switch the damn thing off?" He glowers at it.

"It's okay," I say. "Please . . ."

With a scowl, he grabs his phone. He holds up his index finger. "Just this one, I promise, so I can tell them to go away." He moves a discreet distance away to speak.

"Yeah, it's Ram."

I try to distract myself by looking around the half-empty restaurant, but I cannot keep my eyes off him. He rubs his nose thoughtfully. I want to say, *There you are! You haven't changed at all!* I feel an exquisite burst of joy in my belly.

The conversation looks involved. Ramu's posture is tense and his face grim as he seems to repeat something over and over again.

The waiter has just appeared with the wine when Ramu returns, looking pre-occupied. As he settles into his seat, Ramu politely relieves him of the bottle.

"Everything okay?" I ask after the waiter leaves.

Ramu coughs out a little laugh. "No . . . and yes. Everything is not okay, but that is just the usual state of affairs. You start a technology company in the States, but before you know it, you're arguing zoning rights in Ecuador." His tone is exasperated.

I chuckle. I lean back in my chair and give him a knowing look. "You love it, I can tell."

He nods back in rueful agreement. "I love it, you're right." He holds the cellphone up in his right hand. "But the phone is going off. I apologize."

We fall quiet as the waiter returns to take our orders. When he leaves, Ramu pours more wine into my glass, the light dancing off the spinning liquid.

I put my hand up to push the bottle away. "No more, please. If I get a DUI, then Bhavesh—"

Ramu finishes for me. "—will know you were here."

I look away, the heat burning through me. I feel slightly sick. What am I doing here? A middle-aged married woman, sitting with a man I should not be with.

Sensing my discomfort, Ramu breaks through the silence. "Tell me about your life," he says, his eyes looking straight into mine with genuine curiosity. "What do you enjoy doing?"

"You mean with the husband who doesn't know I'm here?" I ask bitterly.

"Yes," he says smoothly, taking a sip of wine, "with him."

"Well," I say, staring at the table while I gather my jumbled thoughts into a coherent response. "I guess I'm lucky, like you said. Married a *Kshatriya*, moved to America. I get to work at the university." I laugh humorlessly. "An orphan *Dalit's* dream."

Ramu frowns slightly at my mocking tone. "And a daughter?"

I soften at the mention of Maya, my defenses falling away. "Yes, a daughter." My voice becomes proud. "An American girl, with no caste."

Feeling a sudden wave of sadness, I grow silent and take a long sip of my wine.

Ramu leans back on his forearms and studies me. "What's her name?" he asks me warm and inviting.

My eyes go soft, thinking of eight-year-old Maya this morning, wearing a blue hooded parka and the ripped denim jeans she'd fallen in love with at Target. "Can we get those Mommy?" she'd asked, her eyes incandescent with eagerness, a little lisp in her voice. I had groaned inwardly—I could never resist my daughter when she looked like that. "Maya."

"Ah, yes, you said the other night." He sits back in his chair. "A beautiful name," he says reflectively. I beam as I pull out the picture of Maya I had wanted to show him at the Vice-Chancellor's dinner and pass it to him. "She's a beautiful little girl," he says softly, his eyes locking with mine.

I warm up to my favorite subject, brimming with pride and love. "You wouldn't believe how beautiful. Everything good that could come from me rolled up into this little eight-year-old body." I talk animatedly, my curly black hair rippling over my shoulders. "I spoil her rotten—we both do, really. She hasn't been ruined by us yet, though, so she's just full of all this excitement and enthusiasm, where every stupid thing is wonderful to her."

I see how my words make Ramu's eyes sparkle. He leans forward. "Do you have—" I begin to ask, but he shakes his head with a glint of sadness.

"No," he says, with a faint, delicate shadow of melancholy. "I was married, but it wasn't the time for children. Then there was no marriage." He exhales sharply. "So probably for the best."

"I'm sorry," I say, sitting very still, disturbed by the hot flush of jealousy that courses through me at the mention of a wife. I wipe my lips on a napkin, then ask, "Who was she, if you don't mind?" The napkin muffles my voice.

"Her name is Jane. We met at the university in New York," he says quietly. "It only lasted a couple of years." His regret is palpable.

Ramu drains his glass of wine in one clean gulp. His shirt is still partially unbuttoned. I can see the hollow of his neck—the tanned, taut skin below.

Before I can find something to say, he frowns heavily and continues, "My fault. I had a world to conquer, while all she wanted was to earn comfortably and start a family."

I continue to gaze at him, trying to figure out what kind of husband he was. "Still," he says, pouring some more wine, the confident tone returning. He unrolls his napkin and his lips curve in a dazzling smile. "No regrets, eh?"

15
Meena

Fall 2014
San Francisco, California

Our food comes—a mushroom and truffle risotto for me and a chicken tikka masala for him, with a shared Caesar salad that he had insisted on ordering—and the conversation falters. It surprised me when he ordered a curry; I liked no Indian food that was not homemade. It had come with what the menu labeled a *'chapatti'*—otherwise known as *rotis*. A memory appears so clearly in my head I can smell it. Burnt *rotis* and *daal* without *garam masala* from my time at the orphanage—but this wheat flatbread is nothing like that. It is hot off the griddle, puffed to its maximum, with a pat of ghee simmering in the center.

I watch Ramu's face carefully. "Ah, this is my comfort food," he says, tone bright.

I realize how hungry I am with the first mouthful of delicious risotto, but I do my best not to scoff it down in an unladylike manner. I glance up at Ramu several times during my first few mouthfuls, and eventually, he takes the bait.

"What are you thinking, Meena?" he asks, his eyes softening when he looks at me. "I can see a question in your eyes."

"You can see a question in my eyes?" I repeat, feigning indignation.

He reaches out and touches my cheek lightly. "Yes, I can. Or something you want to say. Just say it."

At his touch, my breathing speeds up like I am some teenager coming face-to-face with her crush. I put my fork down for a moment, thinking about how to better phrase my question. After a considered pause I say in a low tone, "I'm wondering who you are, Ram Nayak."

He sits back in his chair, surprised. "I'm me," he answers, stumbling over his words. "I thought you would understand that better than anyone."

"Why?" I snap. My tone is sharp, but I do not care. I stop eating and place the fork next to my plate. "You're not the young boy I knew, Ramu. We haven't known each other for years. I'm not the girl you knew."

A sick sort of feeling twists in my heart. Perhaps it is because all I can see between us right now is distance. And whatever I had been telling myself, it is a distance I had not truly been expecting or prepared for.

He puts his fork down. "No, of course," he answers with a guarded expression. "We all grow up. And we change. But we don't lose everything of who we were." His tone is measured. "You know, almost everyone I meet now treats me like 'Nayak' is actually my middle name, and my last name is 'Fortune 500 CEO'" He gives a short, mirthless laugh. "You even made a joke about that yourself, earlier on."

"It must be tough," I answer, my voice laced with bitterness. "Is that why you asked me here tonight? Because nobody understands you?" The heat of my temper fizzles like water on a hot *tava*.

The longer I gaze across the table at this man I used to know so well, the more the years apart seem like a yawning chasm, an unbridgeable gulf. It is not just the millions he has made. My stomach sinking, the question arises in my mind: What could his life and mine possibly have in common now?

I realize that my words have left him silent for a while. Finally, he says in a calm, reasonable voice, "I asked you to dinner because I saw you for the first time in years, and that one minute was not enough to satisfy all the times I had thought about you—where you were, what you were doing." He exhales slowly, giving me a look. "And yes, also because I wanted to talk to someone who knew me, even if it was another me from years ago." He blinks and raises his eyebrows. "Is that so bad?"

I push my meal away as I feel tears coming and stand up to go.

"Meena, please . . . Wait!" He jumps up from his chair and reaches out a hand to restrain me.

"I'm sorry," I say, scrambling in my embroidered sack bag for my wallet. "I'm sorry, Ramu, I can't do this."

He looks at me pleadingly. "Do what, Meena?" I've never seen his eyes so dark, so intense with concern.

"Look at you and look at me," I cry in a whisper, my voice as hushed as I can keep it. "My daughter is the only thing that keeps me in my life, and that by a fingernail." A stupid sob escapes me. "I'm . . . I'm *nothing*. That's what I am. Nothing! Still a *Dalit*, no matter who I'm married to. And you're . . . you're *amazing*. With or without all your money. You're who you were meant to be. But I just don't know that person anymore, and I'm not sure I can." My voice cracks and I clench my jaw tight.

Out of the corner of my eye I see the waiter staring at us.

"Who I was meant to be?" Ramu blurts, fists by his side. "What's that, Meena? Lonely? No family? Working because the moment I stop, I don't know who else I am?" A tortured look flashes across his face.

I look at him, eyes bright with tears I will not let fall.

"Please, stay," he says, trying to stop me again, but I place the bills I had been planning to use for bumping up my wage packet on the table and leave without my roses.

• • •

I walk some of the way from the Ritz Carlton to the university as I can't bear the thought of waiting for a bus in sight of the building, imagining Ramu looking down on me from his room. Or, worse, coming after me. Would that be worse? Yes *and* no, I think pensively.

It goes over and over in my mind. Ramu had made an effort to see me tonight. Emailing me, getting ahold of my number, bringing flowers. How many people ever made an effort for me now? No one. Maybe Tammy, occasionally, in little ways. And Maya, in ways that were sweet. But the effort he had made was the exact reason I could not see him, I muttered under my breath. It was a reminder of everything my life was not, everything I couldn't have.

I was supposed to be having dinner with a friend, catching up with an old acquaintance, and you weren't meant to storm out of dinners like that, I scolded myself. It was rude. Besides, I thought, my heels clicking angrily on the pavement, dinner with the man who had once been a boy I'd called Ramu, could never have been 'just dinner.' For him, perhaps, I thought, walking even faster in my distress. Never for me.

16
Meena

Fall 2014
Hayward, California
What is wrong with me? Upon arriving at work, I turn on my computer as quickly as possible.

About a minute later, the jumped-up pile of aging circuitry opens multiple inboxes . . . very, very slowly. Why? Why was it doing that? Why would it think I wanted more than one inbox open? I slapped my forehead—apart from the obvious multiple-clicking thing, it would not let me check my inbox until I shut down the two rogue iterations of the email application, each of which closed so slowly that I wondered whether somewhere within the archaic innards of my work computer there was a 'Lullaby' application, written to sing the other applications to sleep before they could shut down.

But now, finally, I am looking at my inbox, and there is no message from Ramu.

Really, I think again, *what the hell did I expect?* The queasy feeling that has been in my stomach since I awoke this morning rumbles on. I was so desperate to see a message from him. Embarrassingly so. It is embarrassing that I wanted so much to see an email from him.

Even if the message had been along the lines of "Well, screw you," it would still have been preferable to nothing. *Damn it,* I think, yanking my hair from its high ponytail this morning, letting my curls fall in waves around my flushed face. He has turned me into a misogynist's stereotype—the erratic, overly emotional woman who does not know what she wants.

I sink further into my office chair, and for the rest of the morning I move robotically through my workload. At lunchtime I shake my head to clear it and go meet my friend in the cafeteria.

"Come on then, quiet one," teases Tammy, brushing her blond hair back with her short, stubby fingernails. "What's on your mind?"

"Huh?" I ask, my fork pushing a piece of lettuce around my plate.

I look up from my half-eaten salad to find Tammy watching me. "You're far away today. About as far away as I wish my ex would stay."

"Todd?"

"Yes. Creepy, obsessive, no-life Todd. I can't believe I let that man anywhere near my vagina."

I can feel myself blushing furiously. I look around, but the other diners, mostly college students, are busy eating, talking or laughing with each other. "I didn't think you had seen him for ages," I say, trying to turn the conversation away from myself. "I thought he was leaving you alone now."

"I saw him in the Seven-Eleven the other night," Tammy squirms in her seat.

"Was he following you?" I sit back, mouth open in shock.

"No, he was with a girl. And I mean, *'a girl.'* No way she was out of her teens. I'd be surprised if she was even out of school." Tammy laughs—a contemptuous bark.

I stare at her. "So he wasn't following you, then?"

"Well . . . *no,*" says Tammy. "I mean, he just totally blanked me, like I wasn't even there."

I lean forward, my eyes wide with curiosity.

"I know," Tammy groans, squeezing her eyes shut. "I sound like one of those people who gets what she wants, then doesn't want it."

It's okay, I think wryly to myself, *there's a lot of that going around.*

"It's good that he's moved on to someone that isn't me, though I wondered if that girl knew what she was getting into, you know?" Tammy gives a sad, rueful look. "But . . . I don't know, it still hurts to be blanked."

I lower my voice, giving my friend a sympathetic look. "When you're single and he's not, you mean?" I ask.

"Yeah . . ." Tammy flinches slightly. "And when I'm old and she's young. So very, very young."

"Come on, Tammy," I say, grasping her hand and scowling at her, "you're not old! You're what, thirty-two?"

Tammy's shoulders slump. "I'm thirty-three next month, with ovaries that are shriveling up more each day. It's all right for men, isn't it? No hurry to get on with things."

Resentment swirls in my chest, hot and heavy. Yes, the unfairness of it all, the freedom that Ramu has to dine with whom he wants without having to lie about it. The possibilities that lie in his future. I frown, ashamed of myself. Envy, that ugliest of emotions.

"But for a woman," Tammy continues, her tone bitter, "even nature makes you pay for taking the time to make something of yourself." Tammy is quiet for a moment, but then shakes her head. "Whoa, self-pity alert!" Tammy says. She smacks her forehead. "I believe we were talking about your melancholy, not mine," she gently chides.

Damn it. My thoughts are racing and I can feel my cheeks turning warm. I have not had time to figure out if I want to discuss this with Tammy. But who else *is* there to discuss it with?

"I went for dinner with Ram," I say, my voice low.

Tammy's eyes widen. "Ram Nayak, Fortune 500 CEO?"

I give her an ironic look, hearing Ramu's echo. "Yes, that Ram."

"Just the two of you?" Tammy's eyes nearly pop out of her head.

I sigh, a guilty sound. "Just the two of us."

"Does . . . ?" Tammy raises a questioning eyebrow at me. "Does Bhavesh know?"

"It wasn't like that," I say. I can feel my cheeks growing hot with embarrassment. "It was just dinner with an old friend."

Tammy looks at me quizzically for a moment, as if weighing whether to press on. "But does Bhavesh know?"

"No," I say eventually, meeting Tammy's eyes. "He wouldn't understand."

"No," Tammy agrees, nodding her head vigorously. "I don't expect he would."

"What's that supposed to mean?" I demand.

Tammy holds up a hand to placate me. "I mean, your husband is . . ." she clears her throat, "*traditional.*" The muffled sunlight of early October gleams through the windows like gold tissue through grey gauze.

Tactfully put. I know what she means; I cannot deny it. I give a small shrug.

Tammy pauses, choosing her words carefully. "I've only met him once, but . . ."

I nod. "It really was just dinner, but all the same." Feminine laughter rings in the air, and a chair squeaks as a person shifts his position.

"So," Tammy says brightly, her eyes inquisitive, "how was your dinner with the multi-millionaire? I trust he didn't ask to split the check?"

"I walked out during the main course," I mumble, not meeting Tammy's eyes.

Tammy gasps. "Why? What did he do?"

I shift awkwardly in my seat. "Nothing, really. It was me."

Tammy puts a hand across the table. I take it, swallowing hard before replying, "I wasn't ready for the stark comparison of our lives. Just for . . . all of it, really. I shouldn't have gone."

Tammy tries to soften her words with a smile. "Perhaps for the best, then." She pats my hand. "Has he called you since?"

My brain feels stiff and cramped. "I was so disheartened when there was no email from him this morning. Stupid girl." My eyes start to become glassy, despite my best efforts.

"Do you think he . . . ?" Tammy asks, tenderly rubbing my hand. "You know, was he . . . ?"

"I don't know." I hang my head. "I think he was after old times as much as anything else."

• • •

Winter 2003
Grace Mercy Children's Home
The shutters are closed in the mother superior's office—never a good sign—and six people are already in the office, making it cramped once I hear the click of the door behind me.

The mother superior, an almost unflappable woman, looks unusually troubled. Sister Gina always looks troubled, but today there is a droop to her shoulders, a horrid paleness in her face that makes it look white as a sheet. My heart slams in my chest at the sight of three police officers. *Hai Bhagwan, please.* One of them smirks at me as I come in. My skin crawls, and it makes me shrink inside myself. Ramu just stands there, next to the police officers, all bigger than him, his fists hanging like dead weights from his arms, his expression flinty. Except for his eyes, which glitter with fear.

One of the policemen, chubbier than the other two and with a different insignia on his arm—Head Constable—produces a flyer. My heart hammers in my throat. An icy, bottomless feeling settles inside me. Any small hopes I was still harboring of this not being about what I thought it was leave.

• • •

"Kanshi Ram?" I ask, looking at the flyer Ramu has pulled from his pants pocket. He had placed it in my hand after looking around with narrowed eyes, his ears pricked even though, as always, it is just the two of us having lunch on our bench in the courtyard. Today's lunch was smaller than usual, and we have both been making our small portions of rice last.

"He's a *Dalit* intellectual," Ramu replies, waving his index finger excitedly. "An activist."

"Uh-huh," I reply. I raise my eyebrows as if to say, *so what?*

Ramu flashes me a no-teeth smile. "He speaks about equality for *Dalits,* about bringing the ways they have in the big cities, like Delhi, down here. And more."

"He's coming here?" I ask, one eyebrow raised curiously as I read the flyer. I look up at Ramu. His eyes are sparkling.

"We should go!" he exclaims, his smile curling further, like spreading oil.

• • •

"Come in," the mother superior calls out as a knock resounds through the room. We stand staring silently at each other, my heart in my throat.

"Ah," the chubby policeman says as a girl walks in, her step easy and jaunty. "Roopa, is it?"

Roopa keeps her face turned from me, refusing to meet my eyes.

"Yes, sir," Roopa replies. "I'm . . . I'm Roopa." There are spots of bright red color on her cheeks.

"Don't be shy, girl," the chubby policeman says cheerfully, gently patting her arm. "You have nothing to fear here." The last rays of the afternoon sun filter through a broken shutter and glint on the worn brown linoleum.

"I am Head Constable Chekavar," he continues, removing his hat to reveal a sweaty, balding pate. He holds the flyer up to Roopa. "You found this flyer, no?" Roopa gives a small, shy nod, and he says loudly, "Speak up, please, Roopa. We all need to hear you."

"Yes, sir. I found it." Roopa's voice rings with a self-righteousness I can see rising from her pores like sulfur gas.

The shutter moves, stirred by a rare breeze, and the shadows dip and swerve against the bookshelves like frightened bats. I divert my gaze for a moment, alighting briefly on the statue of Jesus dying on the cross as he frowns down at us.

The mother superior stares into the dim air beyond our shoulders, her mouth a thin, pained line. Sister Gina is in silhouette, her head bent as if it's too heavy for her neck to hold up. "And where, may I ask, did you find the flyer?"

Roopa points to me, her voice strong and clear. "In her things!"

· · ·

Once the orphans of Grace Mercy get to a certain age, the nuns encourage us to spend more time away from the home, looking forward to the day when we can hopefully make our way in the world. Although the kind nuns don't wish to throw anyone out on the street, they must prioritize the intake of younger orphans over the retention of older ones.

Buta and Kamal request special permission from Sister Gina to go do research for the history paper at the internet café at New Market in the evening. Granted. Roopa and five girls request special permission from Sister Gina to go watch the Hindi movie "Chalte Chalte" at Alankar Cinema this Sunday. Granted.

So, it is not too hard for the both of us to find excuses to be out on the evening of the rally but, as it will run later than we are usually out on the streets of Kalanpur, we plan to return separately, and we each prepare different excuses for our lateness.

Although the market square is busy, it is far from packed—to our disappointment.

Ramu turns to me and says, "Hmmm, that's odd. The venues for Kanshi Ram's rallies usually over-spill, sometimes with those outside relaying messages passed through the crowd to hear what's being said."

Mustachioed police officers with polished bamboo batons and machine-guns in their hands make their presence quietly known. They fan out with an eerie precision, stationing themselves near exits, appearing to stare through us from behind mirrored glasses. My stomach plunges like an elevator out of control.

And yet, that small knot of fear doesn't stop my mounting excitement. Not only am I with Ramu, but for the first in my life, I am with a great throng of like-minded people. An icy, hollow feeling settles inside me as I remember how my *Aai* and I have been treated in the country of our birth, *as garbage,* because we are Untouchable. And like all memories from my childhood, it blows the raging hole in my gut open . . . the upper caste man who spat at my Aai when she tried to get water from the tap, the ache in my mouth when there is no more rice pudding with raisins and almonds—a-once-a-year-treat—at the orphanage for us, my stomach sour with hunger like it may turn in on itself. I swallow back bile that is trying to rise up into my throat.

Kanshi Ram is not even on the hastily erected wooden stage, yet the atmosphere in the marketplace is already electric. Festive white and orange posters displaying Kanshi Ram's picture adorn a small platform to which a party worker has added a microphone and public address system. A sign behind the stage reads: KALANPUR WELLCOMES BAHUJAN LEADR KANSHI RAM!

. . .

"But it's just a flyer," I blurt angrily, panicked at what the policemen might do. "I haven't broken any law."

Head Constable Chekavar inches so close I can smell the rankness of his breath and body, like rotten eggs. "The flyers were all over town—"

"It was me," Ramu interrupts, wobbling his head solemnly. "I gave her the flyer."

Chekavar spins towards Ramu, almost as if he had expected the interruption. "And where did you get it?" Chekavar asks, his eyes alight. "At the rally?"

Ramu nods, eyes to the floor.

"So, you're an activist, are you?" Chekavar asks, shaking his index finger like a fussy schoolteacher. "Have you joined Kanshi Ram's movement?"

Ramu looks up at him. "No, sir," he stutters, his face shiny with sweat. "I promise. I'm just a student."

"I'm just a student," mimics the policeman. "The first refuge of the belligerent. You're a dirty activist, that's what you are. A trouble-maker." He adjusts the belt barely holding in his fat belly, the rolls spilling over his too-tight khaki trousers. "We'll be having none of that in my city."

He turns to the mother superior. "Was he out on the night of the rally?" The mother superior looks to Sister Gina, who reluctantly shrugs her affirmation. Then he swings back to Meena. "And her?"

"I told you it was just me," Ramu says, his voice quivering. He lifts his palms in the air, his fingers splayed.

"You shut up, you rotten *Chamar!*" the head constable spits. "You're in enough trouble as it is."

Sister Gina's eyes are wide and feverish. A small, new muscle jumps in her jaw.

"Our older students are often out in the evening," the mother superior says, her voice uneven as if she's climbed a long hill. "They aren't our prisoners."

"Well," Head Constable Chekavar says, "this might be the problem. If you kept better control of your students, maybe they wouldn't attend illegal gatherings." He shakes the leaflet in the air, "or keep this filthy literature." He wags his finger at the mother superior warningly. "We shall be paying more regular visits to Grace Mercy in the future." I see one of the other policemen flash a brief, hungry grin.

Head Constable Chekavar stands with his legs apart, his cheeks ballooned in rage as he looks menacingly at me. I try to hold his gaze in defiance, but his mostly calm and reasonable-sounding manner that hints at something terribly dangerous beneath the surface terrifies me.

Once my gaze hits the floor, Head Constable Chekavar turns back to Ramu, letting the leaflet fall to the floor. He unbuckles his belt with a sigh. "Let's get this over with."

"No, *Nahi!*" I cry, starting towards Ramu. "You can't!" One of the other policemen, a bald man with a thin scar running from the corner of his left eye to the corner of his mouth, grabs me and twists my hands behind my back. "This isn't fair, we did nothing wrong!"

I catch a sharp look from Ramu. I can feel his fear in the salt taste in my own mouth. But it is clear that Ramu has been the Head Constable's target all along, even though the flyer was mine. I feel I am in a dark twisting tunnel, which presses in on me, its walls musty-smelling like old socks, gagging me until my chest is about to burst open.

· · ·

"I won't tell you how we are all born to be equal, or about how an oppressive society, an archaic system, has been breaking our county's laws for over half a century."

Kanshi Ram is a powerfully built man of less than medium height, with thick, straight white hair almost to his shoulders. He wears a white kurta pajama and when he walks to the microphone, I can see that he is wearing white sandals, the front of the sandals narrowing down to thin strips which curve up like the ends of a proud warrior's mustache.

He holds up his hands to the crowd and says with a smile like a caress, "If you are here, you already know this."

The market square had filled up late, a flood of people pouring in during the minutes preceding Kanshi Ram's arrival on stage. There had been one group, burly looking *goondas* in heavy, black coats with *lathis* in their hands, who had obviously come to cause trouble. They were likely non-*Dalits* hoping to make a scene by heckling the speaker so that the police might intervene and break up the rally before it could even begin. They were ejected from the square by vigilant party workers to a chorus of cheering from the rest of the crowd. Ramu and I had joined in with the cheers—and now the mood of the crowd shifts; it is jubilantly giddy.

"No, I am here to tell you 'how.' How all of you, by positive action and the sheer force of numbers, will help to make the change that must come." He pauses dramatically to make sure the attention of the crowd is focused on him.

It is hard to see Kanshi *Saheb* now, as we are caught in the press, other bodies closing all around us. The sun is high in a sky of molten silver. The mud-brown walls of the houses surrounding the square throw back the heat, and the smell of dung and buttermilk cling to the heavy, humid air.

Ramu cranes his neck to see the stage, but I have no chance. It does not matter, because Ramu's hand is in my hand, his chest pressing against my back, hot and solid, and Kanshi Ram's words seem distant as heat blooms in my cheeks. My wide-open heart drums in my chest.

"The Hindu traditions are our enemy, but they are not our worst enemy," Kanshi Ram continues, his voice gaining strength. The crowd leans forward, rapt.

"Localization: *this* is the thing that defeats the cause of the *Dalit*. Uttar Pradesh does not care what they say in New Delhi or Bangalore. And even if they do care, they never hear about it." The silent shadows of two circling kite hawks slide down the walls of the whitewashed houses and skitter over the assembled crowd.

"The thing that keeps the *Dalit* man in his place is inaction. We are abused, we are discriminated against, and yet only the abused and the abuser know of it." An appreciative murmur swells through the throng. Since the start of the speech, the palpable tension in the crowd, the excitement, has only grown.

More people arrive, and the space in our little section of the crowd becomes scarcer. Ram glances at me anxiously, a pulse beating erratically in his throat as men are pushed closer and closer to me. He leans towards me until I can smell the clean fragrance of Cinthol soap on his skin. He eyes me warily, then wraps his arm around me and holds me close as if to shield me.

"The things done in a village are almost never reported outside that village . . . so there it stays." Roars of agreement go up in the crowd with every sentence that sounds out from the public-address system.

Closer and closer the crowd pushes us until my body is pressed hard against his. Fireworks burst in my heart and I find it hard to breathe.

Kanshi Ram leans in closer to the microphone and continues, "You are a blessed generation, especially the youngest of you in the crowd, for you have the power to change things. The new multimedia, the social sites, are a gateway to the rest of the world. Spread the word, let them know about everything that happens to you, about all the things you see. Let the world look upon them with disgust, let the other castes feel shame for once."

"Feel shame, feel shame," someone shouts and the crowd groans happily in assent.

"We can do it," Ramu breathes into my ear. I gasp. Fire blazes across my skin and down my belly. "There's an internet café right here in New Market. We can make an account and keep a record of things, make posts when we have enough money to buy some time in the café."

I pull away slightly, look at that sparkle in his eyes. I have never felt this way before, every fiber of my being alive, and . . . belonging. Excitement buzzes like an electric current inside me. Excitement at the heat that swirls between my legs, excitement at the wild abandon he inspires inside me, excitement at how safe I feel by his side.

• • •

This is all my fault.

My chest heaves. I am overcome with guilt for getting Ramu into trouble, worse even than the repulsive feeling of the bald policeman with the scar squeezing my breast as he manhandles me from the room.

"Stay there," he says, pushing me down onto a bench outside the mother superior's office. "If you move, then you'll get the same as him. Stay there and listen to what happens to *Chamars* who get ideas above their station." He grins wickedly and walks away from me to disappear into the shuttered office. I pant as if I have run a mile. All of me is pulsing with sick, sick guilt.

I rub my pinched nipple, struck by how non-*Dalits* are repulsed by being near an Untouchable, and yet have no problem manhandling, even sexually assaulting them. A memory crawls to the surface of my mind like a fat worm after rain. It was the same in the cleaner's closet when Roopa would have stood by and let me be violated by a boy she apparently wanted to date.

Their stupid rules make no sense. I shrug—a painful, heavy-hearted shrug—because it's such a 'Ramu' thing to think. *Mr. Reason.*

The door opens again and Roopa appears outside in the hallway, escorted from the office by the same policeman who had groped me moments before. For Roopa, he is all nods and courtesy. The door closes behind her and I watch woodenly as the *Brahmin* orphan walks off, her head down as it had been in the office. Anger turns inside me like a broken spear tip. But she stops halfway and stands there for maybe ten seconds, several yards away and with her back to me. Then she turns around and walks a few paces back toward me.

"Why?" I croak as Roopa turns and looks at me fiercely. "We do nothing to you. I thought . . . I thought we were okay."

Roopa's nostrils quiver like an overwrought buffalo's. A smile like a crack in old plaster slowly finds its way onto her face. Broader and broader it becomes, then she cups a hand to her ear and strains her neck in the direction of the mother superior's office. The first crack of the Head Constable's belt sounds in the still air, followed by Ramu's cry. Roopa keeps looking at me, her hand raised to her mouth in mock surprise.

"Okay?" she says at last. "You're a fucking *Chamar.*"

She laughs, a mocking, hysterical laugh and walks away as the belt sounds out a second time, Ramu's answering cry a knife through my heart.

17
Meena

Fall 2014
Hayward, California
I walk back to my office and wake up my computer, thinking of all the work I need to get done to make up for a morning spent daydreaming and checking my email . . . Work which now isn't going to get done, apparently, as there is an email from Ram Nayak in my inbox.

Wednesday, October 1st, 2014. 12:24 (PST)
Dear Meena,
I have been wrestling much of last night and all morning about whether to write this email to you. Not because I am upset about last night. Or, if I am upset, it is with myself. I was wrapped up in my own feelings about seeing you again after so long and in no way appreciative of how you might have felt. For that, I apologize.
You're right, I don't know you anymore. And I suppose you don't know me, either. Perhaps this is a good reason to go our separate ways and not to look back.
But if my life between now and when we last met has taught me anything, it's that action is always the better path when compared to inaction. It is almost always harder to do than not to do, but the hardest things in life bring the greatest reward.
Stillness is death, and we are not dead yet.

There I go again, talking about hardship when seeing you is much easier for me, though maybe not as easy as you might think. All the same, I would like to see you again, to try dinner or a drink, or whatever form seeing you again might take.

I know that this is probably difficult for you, and to ask is selfish of me, but all I can do is apologize.

I am at the Ritz Carlton for 3 more nights, then I must return to New York for a few days. Come and find me. Not for old times' sake, but for the sake of now.

Ram

. . .

I think of little other than Ramu's e-mail all afternoon. I barely hear Maya calling me as I help strap her into the car.

"Mommy, listen," Maya says stridently, "can I have a pony?"

"A real pony?" I respond automatically.

"Uh-huh, a real one." Maya crows clapping her hands.

Startled, I nearly drop my car keys. "Daddy just got you a puppy."

Maya chortles with wicked glee at the mention of the little Shih Tzu puppy that Bhavesh had bought her, giving into his daughter's wishes with a minimum of resistance.

"We still need a name for him," I continue, shaking an admonishing finger at Maya. "He's just going to think his name is 'Dog.' I still don't see what's wrong with 'Jadoo,' a good Indian name."

Maya screws up her face.

"Or, 'Peanut?'" I persist as I get into the driving seat and latch my seat belt on.

There is silence in the back, aside from the imaginary sound of Maya's brain strategizing. I stifle a laugh.

Finally, Maya speaks up in a considering tone. "If I have a pony, he can be called 'Jadoo.'"

I sigh as I start the engine. "Maybe when you're older."

"You always say that," Maya pouts.

I slow down the car and take a deep breath. "What?"

Maya's voice is petulant. "'When you're older.' Everything is 'when you're older.'"

I lift arched eyebrows conspiratorially into the rearview mirror. "Well, just think about how great it's going to be when you're older."

Maya's grin fills me with warmth like summer rain in Kalanpur. "Can you and daddy do anything you want?"

"Well . . . not *anything*." I frown. "The problem with getting older is that you get more responsibility. Even if you get what you want, you don't have the time to enjoy it. Then you just don't bother getting what you want in the first place."

Maya looks confused.

"Anyway," I continue, checking the mirrors and dragging away from the curb, "these are not things you should worry about at the age of eight."

Maya's brow furrows in concentration, then her face lights up. "Eloise has a pony."

I raise my eyebrows. "Isn't Eloise the girl with a banker for a father?"

Maya shrugs. "It's called 'Cloppity.'"

I grimace and mutter under my breath, "She should call it 'Money Pit.'"

"What Mommy?"

I wink at Maya. "Nothing, sweetie."

Maya is silent, then says, "I love you, Mommy."

My heart twists painfully. "I love you too, sweetie."

"I love Daddy, too." Maya shakes her head vigorously back and forth.

"I know you do, my baby," I say. Then, in a spirit of mischief, I turn to Maya, eyes glinting wickedly. "I tell you what, why don't you ask Daddy about that pony? I think that will probably make his night."

· · ·

The acrid smell of burned *rotis* fills the kitchen. I was thinking about Ramu while Maya was talking to Bhavesh about ponies. Usually, I would have paid attention to what Maya was saying, as I took pleasure from watching my husband squirm, and he squirmed best in hard conversations with his daughter. *Daddy is Santa an Indian, like you and Mommy? Where do babies come from? How does a hen lay eggs?*

Meeting Ramu the previous night had become a series of snapshot memories and half-remembered snippets of conversation jostling inside me all morning. I stare with unfocused eyes out of the kitchen window as I remember the dinner, as one might remember a beautiful dream, with wonder and resignation and deep regret for what could never be.

I am as dry as the Gobi desert, as hot as the sun that paints mirages across the sand dunes. And in my heart, there is a stirring like the terrible sandstorm that blows from the desert in the summer months. So little. And yet, for my starved heart, so much. These brief memories and my angry exit—which makes me cringe every time I remember it. My lungs hurt when I try to breathe. *What does he want from me? Why now?*

Anguish stings the back of my throat. Anguish and shame. I should not want to allow that man anywhere near me. Ramu abandoned me in the ever-deteriorating surroundings of the Grace Mercy orphanage, where my options had been starvation, life as a nun or marriage to the only man who offered. I feel dizzy, off-balance like I am being thrust back in time.

And there it is, burnt *rotis*. I had been inspired to make *rotis* after having the *chapatti* at the Ritz Carlton the other night, which had pulled me down memory lane in the powerful way that smell and taste can. Everything about that night had pulled me down memory lane—a dark and poorly lit alleyway, so it turned out, with terrifying monsters lurking in the shadows.

In fact, looking at the other two pots, I realize that everything is burned. Dinner is quickly becoming a disaster. Bhavesh comes from the lounge, finally having escaped his daughter and the need to find different ways to dance around the word 'No.' (No, Maya, we can't color the puppy's hair purple. No, not Daddy's either.)

"Is dinner ready?" he asks impatiently. Then he sniffs the air. "Smells burned."

My eyes flip down to the food. *Very* burned.

"What have you been doing, dammit?" he demands, catching the meaning of my despondent look.

"I . . . got distracted." The words come out scratchy and hoarse, almost inaudible.

"By what? What in here could distract you, you stupid woman?" Bhavesh waves his fingers impatiently in front of my face.

Outside the window, the sky turns violet as night approaches, and a flickering yellow lamplight shines in the neighbor's yard, attracting a swarm of insects. "I don't know."

Bhavesh scowls at me. "You don't know? How can you not know what you are distracted by? That is so dumb. Why do you act like an illiterate *Dalit?*" he snarls.

"I'm not . . . illiterate," I hear myself stutter, pressing my fingers to my temples. His words are like bullets exploding in my head. "I'm sorry, okay," I blurt, folding my hands together like a clove. "The food will still be fine."

Bhavesh strides over, picks up the pot of burned *daal* and slams it down so I have to pull my hand back fast.

"It won't; look at it, it's ruined. I thought if I married a *Dalit,* the least she could do is clean and cook." He yells so loudly it is physical, like a blow to my chest. "You're terrible at both." He crosses to the sink and dumps the food into it. "So," he thumps his fist on the counter. "I suppose we must go hungry."

There is a small noise from the corner, like a strangled sob. We both look over to see Maya standing in the doorway watching the argument, her face in a pout, on the verge of breaking and bringing forth tears.

"Stop it," I hiss at Bhavesh. "You're upsetting her."

"*I'm* upsetting her?" He looks like he's seething, but he lowers his voice. "Right," he says to me with a fierce growl. "Bedroom, *now.*"

My legs are trembling. *Burning his dinner! Stupid, stupid, stupid.* "Go to your room, Maya," I say as kindly as I can, but Bhavesh pushes me aside and guides Maya away. I can see the familiar anger boiling in him, and I know I should not have criticized him over Maya, which is always a flash point for him. My mind races to find the best way to apologize before he arrives in the bedroom. Terror thuds out-of-rhythm in my chest. I take a shaky breath. It will be all right; he will not dare do anything with Maya in the house.

"I'm sorry," I say beseechingly as he comes into the room, crossing it in three angry strides and with the strength and fierceness of an enraged bull. "I didn't mean—"

A hand is at my throat before I see it coming. Then the flat of his palm on my face, snapping off the stream of words. I gasp, and then I am shoved onto the bed. Bhavesh crouches over me, his breath sour, hand grasping my neck. "Don't you ever say I'm upsetting my daughter. *You* upset her, you fucking bitch."

I gag as his clutch grows tighter, trapping my words of apology.

"You fucking *Dalit* whore, that's all you are. How dare you speak to me that way? You should know your place." His voice is chill and black, like the inside of a coalmine in Jharkhand.

He grabs a handful of my hair and pulls me up to a sitting position near the end of the bed. With his free hand, he undoes his belt and trousers. His penis is hard when it emerges, and he forces my mouth down onto it. "This is what your mouth is good for," he says. "This. Not telling me what to do."

He rams himself hard into my mouth, again and again. I gag, then cry out in shock and panic.

"Quiet!" Bhavesh's voice commands me from above. "You sound like a pig."

When he mercifully ejaculates quickly, the horrible, warm goo slides straight down my throat. He forces my head up to face him while he stands glaring at me, though I keep my eyes averted. Then he pulls his trousers up and buckles his belt.

His voice is calm, leisurely, reasonable. "Well, I suppose I will have to get takeout, then."

18
Meena

Winter 2003
Grace Mercy Children's Home
Head Constable Chekavar is still buckling his belt as he steps out of the door. He casts a cold, careless look at me as I shrink into the bench outside the mother superior's office. The policeman who squeezed my breast follows behind, his expression predictably smug. I want to leap to Ramu's side, but I cannot move. My feet are like stone, as if I have become a statue nailed to the wooden slats of the bench.

I want time to freeze right there, to stretch on forever. Because when Ramu comes from the mother superior's office, I will have to see the terrible results of my mistake. It should have been *me* under the policeman's belt; I am the fool who kept the flyer and kept it where Roopa could find it. It was my mistake, and Ramu paid for it.

But what makes me feel most sick inside is that for all my remorse as the Head Constable had removed his belt, there had been a small part of me that was relieved it would not be coming down on *my* back. I can barely imagine the pain of it, my bladder weakening at the mere thought. What a coward. What a terrible girlfriend. I do not deserve someone like Ramu.

When he appears, he is supported by Sister Gina and the aging mother superior who half-carry him, half-walk him outside into the dim light of the evening streaming into the open corridor. The last fragments of light from the setting sun have turned the sky gray and forbidding; it is chilly, with a cool breeze blowing. The evening air, foggy now, wraps itself around me like a damp, mildewed shawl. I cannot see, I cannot breathe.

"Meena!" Sister Gina calls sharply, beckoning to me with an impatient scowl to take over from the mother superior. Ramu's eyes are half closed, and he looks on the verge of passing out.

Sister Gina's command shocks me into action and I run to Ramu's side, pulling his right arm over my shoulders. We move him into the nurse's station, which also doubles as Sister Gina's office.

When I joined Grace Mercy, Sister Gina had been timid and soft spoken, the meekest of the nuns running the orphanage. But the years have changed Sister Gina. Some of that softness is gone—years of service to God and to the children have brought tired circles under her eyes and strain lines around her mouth—but she has also gained influence and position within the home. She is now second only to the mother superior, and with each passing month she takes on more responsibility.

We help Ramu onto the ancient examination table under the careful, frowning watch of Sister Gina, who is now Head Nurse, too, having spent years teaching herself medicine and learning on the job. The examination table sways worryingly under his weight.

Sister Gina turns and positions a floating arm lamp. I cry out in shock at the welts on his body. His breathing is shallow and labored, and dark bruises perforate his shoulder blades and back.

"Meena!" Sister Gina clicks her tongue at me in annoyance. "Maybe you should wait back in the dormitory."

"No!" I plead, swiping away my tears. "It's okay, I'm sorry. Please, let me stay."

Sister Gina nods, her expression softening. "Then you can help." She crosses to a cupboard, taking out an enamel bowl. The mother superior who has been standing silently all this time, half-fills the bowl Sister Gina hands her with water and a paper bag containing cotton wool. "I've been making this last," Sister Gina says of the cotton wool— sorrow moving like smoke-shadow over her face, "but I have a feeling we get through the rest of it today. Take some cotton wool and start using the water to clean his wounds."

I do as I am told. There is a hospital smell in the air of disinfectant and fear. Another day, seeing Ramu with his shirt off would stir up a cacophony of confusing feelings. But right now, I cannot think past the lump in my throat the size of China.

Ramu shudders at my first touch, his sharp intake of breath making me pull back with trembling fingers, but he quickly settles under the gentle strokes I make across his shoulders.

I start at his shoulders, while Sister Gina begins near the small of Ramu's back.

"How can they do this?" I whisper to her as we slowly work our way towards each other across Ramu's body once the mother superior has gone off to supervise dinner in the dining hall. "We broke no laws."

Sister glances at me, her intense concentration at dabbing the wounds softening for a moment before returning to her task.

"We are *Dalit*," I go on more stridently, "and we are already lower than them in every way that matters. Why did they have to beat him?"

Sister Gina's tone is abrupt. "Because you did something that scares them. You sought to change the position they hold over you."

"But," I burst out, "they are policemen. They enforce the law, and we broke no law."

"You're right," replies Sister Gina, her eyes opaque as stormy water. "They couldn't arrest you. And they didn't. They acted like bullies instead."

"The mother superior should have stopped them," I complain.

Sister Gina looks sharply at me and I brace myself for a rebuke, but she frowns instead. "She cannot, Meena. I think you know that."

Having wiped the blood and dirt away as well as we can, we use what cotton wool is left to apply antiseptic to Ramu's wounds. He lets out a gasp as we start, but quickly settles again, still without saying a word.

"They will beat a *Dalit* boy," I say and the burn of tears starts again at the back of my eyes, "but they cannot beat a nun." I pause, looking at Ramu's back, imagining him listening to us through the haze of pain he must have felt. "They only beat him because they did not want to beat me, at least not with a belt like that. It was my flyer."

"But they knew he went," Sister Gina says. Her face has gone blank, like a room where someone switched off the light. "And they are not stupid men. They could see that his pain would be your pain." Slats of light fall across the floor from the moon on the other side of the window. "And, as for us nuns standing up to policemen . . . Well, there are plenty of non-violent ways for them to hurt this home." A frown crinkles Sister Gina's forehead. "As hard as you think your life is, Meena, and I will agree it can be, you will one day understand how it is to make decisions that affect the lives of others. Perhaps that will be for your own children." Her mouth turns upwards briefly, the faintest ghost of a smile. "A part of me hopes that it might be here with us nuns, if you so choose, and if fate allows it."

I blink as I look up, startled. I didn't know Sister Gina felt that way. Sister Gina turns to leave the room. "Please, Sister. I'll be silent. And besides, it's not fair to leave Ramu all alone," I cry. I can tell Sister Gina is not happy about it, but she reluctantly agrees.

Once she is gone, I walk around the table, crouching before Ramu and taking his hand. For a while, I just watch him as he lies there with his eyes closed. His expression appears troubled. I refuse to think about how he looked shirtless. Even covered in bruises, the memory of those wide shoulders makes my body tingle. I can feel a blush rising as I remember how his shoulders felt under my fingers when we kissed—firm, yielding and hot. *Hai Bhagwan! Is there no end to this madness?*

Although my heart is drumming in my chest, I put a cheerful grin on my face when he finally opens his eyes. Bleary-eyed, his voice strained, he stammers thickly, "I wish I could wake up to your face every day."

Gooseflesh dances up and down my spine. "And I wish I could fall asleep next to you," I say, the breath hiccupping in my throat.

He gives an involuntary shiver. "I'm cold," he says, his teeth chattering.

I look around Sister Gina's room—there is a high white bed with all her large embroidered pillows neatly arranged against the bedpost and a utility closet in the corner that I fervently hope contains some blankets. I find a single blanket, thicker than the ones in the dormitories, which I place over him.

"I'm still cold," Ramu says hoarsely, his voice muffled under the blanket.

"I'm sorry, *jaan*," I say softly, "there are no more blankets." With a tingling in my chest, I climb into the bed and lie facing him under the blanket.

"What are you doing?" he croaks. He looks closely at my face.

"I just want to keep you warm," I answer brightly.

"We . . . you . . . shouldn't."

"Shh," I reply, placing a hand lightly on his chest. The sweetest ache burns in my heart, hot thrumming gushes through my veins.

I rub his chest and arms, careful to avoid his cut and bruised shoulders and back. Ramu's breath grows more ragged until he bursts out, "Meena—"

I gently kiss his cheek.

"Meena!" he whispers, pulling back as much as the space and his weakened state will allow. "You don't have to."

"I'm not," I say clearly. Joy and tenderness and fierce hope kindle inside me like a prayer lamp. "This is . . ."

I lean up and kiss him softly on his mouth.

He moves his mouth, trying to protest again, but the sounds become gasps. Finally, his voice drifts up to me. "Are you sure?"

"Yes."

19
Meena

Fall 2014
San Francisco, California

The rain is still light as I step from the bus one stop away from the Ritz Carlton. I heard on the radio that a storm is blowing in from the Pacific on this cold, wintry night. It is the front end of the storm but the wind is already up, driving rain onto every inch of my exposed skin. Cold water soaks through the bodice and sleeves of my dress, chilling my skin and turning the once bright emerald cambric dark. It is not a new dress, but it is one of my favorites—a brilliant green like the color of spring with a pink rose embroidered on the front. It is not my warmest, but I couldn't resist it and now, I regret it.

Getting off the bus one stop away from the hotel seems like a silly decision once I am dashing through the wind-blown rain trying not to get soaked. I might as well have stayed in my work clothes for all that I will be presentable when I arrive at the hotel. But I need these extra minutes to compose myself—maybe to change my mind, though I know in my heart that such a thing will not happen. My path is set. I am going to meet Ram Nayak again.

An image of blotting paper keeps coming into my mind. At Grace Mercy, we would use whatever writing materials were available. When we obtained a few fountain pens to practice our handwriting, there were few, so the children had to take turns. Sometimes, if I pressed too hard, the ink would flow too fast from the pen, creating small puddles dripping as I brought the pen from the paper. I would use blotting paper to soak up the ink, which appeared to drink the blue ink we used from the page. Just one tiny dab and the color would spread rapidly across the paper, transforming this once clean, perfect thing in a matter of moments.

Tonight is a little like that, I muse to myself as I pull my silvery-beige, hand-embroidered pashmina shawl tighter around my shoulders. It is my one and only pashmina, and it was a wedding gift from one of Bhavesh's rich aunts. Once I step into the Ritz Carlton, my life will be forever blotted, and I will carry that stain around with me. The one thing I had over Bhavesh, my moral superiority, would be forever tarnished. And yet, irrespective, I am on my way to see the only man, I think with a touch of irony, who could be said to have ever blotted my paper.

I can still remember it clearly, even though it was more than a decade ago. My hand on him as we lay on the rickety examination table, feeling how that most private and mysterious part of his body responded. I had loved it, knowing—one of the few things I knew about intimacy—that his response was beyond his will. Ramu was such a cerebral and serious person. For just my hand to evoke such a reaction, beyond any thought or control, had been so exciting, taking my breath away as I lay panting afterwards.

Our hearts slammed against each other and found the same beat. It had taken all my willpower—my own blood on fire and racing through every part of my body—to be gentle with him. But, it was my gentleness—and, later, his—that truly took my breath away. That made it so different to anything I had experienced in my marriage since. Even in those rare times when Bhavesh was considerate towards me in the bedroom, he had never come close to how that teenage boy had made me feel, even though that teenage boy had left my virginity intact.

As I walk into the reception with heavy steps, I am even more keenly aware than the last time that I am bringing down the tone of the place. Water drips from almost every inch of my person and onto the hotel's marble floors and plush rugs. And the rain hasn't done my hair any favors, either. I feel sordid, even though I have made no decisions about what I want to pass between myself and Ram Nayak tonight.

The concierge, a dapper gentleman with a clean-shaven face and shrewd, observant eyes gives me a sympathetic look.

"I'm here to see Ram Nayak," I say, realizing that I do not know his room number. The hotel is huge, but the concierge obviously memorizes where his Fortune 500 CEOs are staying. *Of course,* I think with a sinking feeling, *Ramu is probably in one of the suites they don't have too many of. Somewhere near the top, and with a name rather than a number.*

"Whom shall I say is calling?" the concierge asks with a raised eyebrow as he picks up the handset.

The memory flashes through the deafening drumbeat of rain, the clap of thunder as the storm roars outside—the e-mail I wrote to Ramu the day after Bhavesh forced himself on me.

Wednesday, October 1st, 2014. 16:52 (PST)
Dearest Ram. Or should I say 'Ramu,' because however hard I try, I can't escape my past, and I wonder if it is the same for you.

I want to see you again, too—to hell with all the reasons that I shouldn't. I can't explain why I want to see you, but have only a desire for all my sadness and pain to go away. Perhaps you can help with that.

I don't know when I can get to your hotel, but I will be there, somehow.

-Meena

"Um . . ." I pause, trying not to give him what Tammy fondly calls my lost-child look. "Meena."

A wave of uncertainty floats in my stomach—I realize the 'um' makes me sound like I am making it up, like maybe I should have added 'Smith' afterwards. Maybe I should have thought of a fake name. The idea seems so clichéd, though isn't meeting a man other than my husband at a hotel like that?

I glance over towards the restaurant, wondering if the concierge knows of the scene I caused earlier in the week. *Perhaps I am on some blacklist.* I feel a film of sweat breaking out on my face, *and he is on the line to hotel security.* I suddenly realize I am trembling. Waiting in the lobby of an extravagant hotel for a man, and a man I barely know. My chest heaves with panic, and the blood pounding in my ears seems to mock my bravado with derisive laughter. And yet, once he was everything . . .

Maya. *Why are you in my head, daughter? Please.* My brain feels like it is unraveling, too many fractured thoughts racing through it at once. My mind is scoured with loathing at Bhavesh and the desire to have a better life, yet I am weighted down with the full, chill burden of loyalty to my husband.

"Mr. Nayak? There is a Meena here to see you. Certainly; straight away." The concierge hurries out from behind the desk and, for a moment, I think my paranoid fears really are about to come true, that I am to be escorted from the premises, Ramu having changed his mind.

"If madam would follow me," the concierge says, his hands clasped to his chest.

He guides me to the elevator, a quiet corner where I can hear the thick, faltering beat of my heart. The concierge inserts a key card and presses the number 9.

"If madam continues to the ninth floor, Mr. Nayak will meet you there," he says with a courtly bow.

"Thank you." I say, trying to keep a wooden face. I notice distractedly how clammy my hands are.

As the elevator door closes, I suddenly wonder why Ramu did not come down and meet me. Is he ashamed of me? Is he attempting to be discreet?

Sensation sparkles across my skin as I wonder what it would be like to touch him again, to run my fingertips across his skin and feel his touch in return, just like how his hand had found its way to the place between my legs on that examination table. He had been so gentle, stroking me softly, sometimes almost tickling me. I squeeze my eyes shut as the memories sideswipe me. But gentle though he had been, the effect on every other part of my body had been violent, and I had moaned with it. Twice he'd shushed me, his sharp reprimand betrayed with a husky giggle which had brought an unwitting smile to his bruised face.

I am brought abruptly from my reverie as the elevator doors jerk open to Ramu standing before me—no jacket, still failing to wear a tie properly. He says nothing, but his face brightens and he holds out a hand, which I take, my heart in my throat. The moment our fingers touch, the whirling maelstrom in my mind stops, that confusing jumble of thoughts shrinking down to a single point; the feel of his skin against mine. My hand in his, so long ago, running from the janitor's closet; my hand in his walking into the market square where we would hear Kanshi Ram speak. (We had never lit social media alight with accounts of our treatment; the Head Constable had seen to our desire to become activists, if that's what it ever was.)

My heart flutters as Ramu guides me forward. The main room of the suite is so large I think my whole house might just fit inside it. Far beyond the windows, I can see the lights of distant ships sheltering from the storm in the bay.

I feel a whoosh of emptiness as Ramu lets go of my hand to take my wet coat. His hands are a soft touch on my shoulders, but the weight of his fingers are like brands on my skin. Then he moves to the built-in bar to fix us a drink.

"I did not know," he says, speaking at last, his deep voice cracking, "if you would come." His eyes are molten with heat. "Even when you sent your email, I didn't dare hope it could be true. I didn't want to say before, to scare you away, but I've thought of you so much over the years, Meena."

I feel a ripple of anger and hurt lying just below the surface—like the molten rock below the mantle—beneath a veneer of longing.

"So where were you?" I cry, my voice unsteady, sounding tiny in the vast space of the dimly lit suite. His expression falters and he stops fixing the drinks before turning to face me, his dark eyes puzzled.

"I was here," he answers eventually, a sudden pained flush on his face that shows me the question has hit home. "In America."

"But you left me in that place," I say despairingly. "All alone."

When I had walked out on dinner, it had felt good to hurl words at him, to see their effect, however embarrassed I had become afterwards. It is not that way now, though neither do I regret my question. It is, I realize, necessary. In some ways, it is more important than the physical contact I have been imagining since arranging to meet him again.

If I only leave the Ritz Carlton with answers to one or two of the questions I have, it will have been worth it. Bodies, lust, whatever these physical things that could happen between us tonight are, they do not provide answers, and how can we take on any new history if we do not talk of what came before?

"It was the plan," he replies, but his voice is wistful.

"It was *your* plan, Ramu," I cry sharply, sounding pitiful to myself. I take a deep breath and force myself to calm down. "You left me there."

I feel his hand on my cheek, and tears smart my eyes. "You're right," he says. "I did, and I am sorry."

Those words should have been enough to silence me. But I cannot give up. My head snaps back round, my face flushed in sudden anger. "Why?"

"Because I am selfish," he replies, his dark eyes mournful. "That's what it took to get me here; only selfish men get to where I am."

"Was it worth it?" I hiss, even more angry now in my abandonment from the one person I ever loved, aside from Maya. I wave arms at the vast room we are in. "To have all this?"

He does not answer, his eyes fixing instead on the mark on my neck, not yet faded from my husband's assault. Ramu moves to touch me, but I step back beyond his reach.

"What's that?" Ramu asks sharply, his finger pointing to the bruise.

"You have no right!" I shout, my breath coming in gasps and my voice wobbly as it always is just before I cry. "You have no right to ask that." I launch myself at him, beating my fists against his chest. "You have no right," I sob, continuing to strike him.

His face crumbles but he stays still, not trying to restrain my blows. My misery engulfs me and my rage wears itself out like a toddler nearing the end of a tantrum. I hit Ramu again with less force than before, my anger dissipating in my tears. Ramu does not lift a finger to stop me, but he says softly, "I am so sorry, Meena."

Still sobbing, I rest my head against his chest, my voice muffled by his shirt. "I just want you to take me to bed," I say, all my doubts fleeing in a single, shining moment of clarity.

Ramu gently loosens my grip on his shirt and leads me into the master bedroom. There in the grainy darkness we stand facing each other, two silhouettes of longing. It is as if we are teenagers again, neither of us sure how to begin. Yet, when our mouths finally come together, there is no awkward mashing of teeth, our mouths fitting together like missing pieces in a jigsaw puzzle.

How have I lived without this? How have I lived without him? Ramu is part of me, wrapped around me like blazing sunshine and pouring summer rain, my breath and my blood, my every thought.

His lips trace my throat and find my collarbones on an indrawn breath. He drags fire across my flesh, taking me to the edge of a chasm, pushing me toward it. His mouth dips lower.

"Undress me," I say in a desperate plea. I fall back onto the bed, and the plush brown coverlet is soft against my arms. "I want to feel your hands taking off my clothes," I say urgently, in a voice I never use and could never imagine using with Bhavesh. I clamp his head closer and push myself into his mouth.

He stands above me, tearing off his tie and shirt in one fluid motion. His wild eyes search mine. Heat blooms in my cheeks and my wide-open heart drums in my chest. Ramu had never been tall, but he had been muscular where so many boys his age were thin or wiry. His shoulders are still broad, his body filled in the way it never was with Grace Mercy's strict rations. I can tell, even in the dim light and with him standing above me.

Ramu slips onto the bed beside me and with a tender hand leans over to caress the small of my back, where all the nerves in my body suddenly converge, where he finds the springy ends of my curls and tangles his fingers in them.

"You are beautiful," he breathes, gathering my hair, my face, gathering all of me as he gently pulls my clothes away. A semblance of sense creeps back into my head. Then it flies right out into the darkness of the night, because Ramu claims my lips with such force, the world goes up in flames around me.

He sucks in a breath, then pulls back just the slightest bit, looking at my naked form. In the darkness, I cannot see his expression. Shame and mortification battle within me as his gaze rakes my body. A tight band constricts my chest, stopping my breath. What if he isn't attracted to me anymore?

"I can't see you," he finally says, moving closer and snaring his onyx eyes with mine. "Not properly. Do you mind if I turn the lights up a little?"

I hesitate, the memory of Bhavesh's voice insistent in my ear, his breath hot and fetid. *Why haven't you used the vanilla perfume I bought you? You smell like a bloody Chamar, like those cheap Indian flowers!*

Or, *why can't you control your eating? Bloody hell, stop the junk food. Your thighs have become fat, like loose elastic.*

"Only if you want to," Ramu adds, his tone casual and light.

"You may not want me when the lights come on," I stammer.

Even in the pale moonlight filtering from the windows, I can see his eyes widen, then narrow. He reaches out and touches my cheek gently. He presses his thumb to my lips. "I know I'll want you more." His voice is fierce with longing.

Later, much later, we sit on the dark purple velvet couch in the lounge, our fingers intertwined as we watch San Francisco's lights silently for a while, the ribbon of cars moving like a necklace over the bridge. I give a wry smile at our wavering reflections in the floor-to-ceiling glass windows. I remember how Ramu's touch, always so tender, so possessive, is imprinted into my soul, his lingering hands transforming me not into the old, familiar Meena, but into a wild and magical woman.

I am floating on a gossamer-pink, candy-cane cloud when I feel Ramu run his fingers through my hair.

"Ever since the day I met you at the VC dinner, I've imagined making love to you . . . again. I've imagined being inside you, fantasized about how you would feel around me." His fingers stroke my cheek. "You've driven me completely insane with lust these past few weeks." He pulls me down on the rug and guides me on top of him to make love again. It is longer the second time, less needful and more loving, like the misty rain back home that falls softly but floods the river.

20
Meena

Fall 2014

Fremont, California

With an affair, everyone seems to concentrate on the betrayal, the guilt. Yet I do not feel guilty. I have lived in the shadows most of my life; it is from years of conditioning that I have learned to repress my emotions with Bhavesh. But, now, the mundane things of everyday life—getting Maya up and dressed, taking a trip to the grocery store, folding the washing—with the memory of Ramu's touch, of feeling him inside me, makes me ponder and explore the shape of this new woman I am becoming.

Who is this Meena who looks out from the mirror with a smile in her eyes when she thinks nobody is watching? When before there was a slump in my shoulders now there is a lilt in my walk. For the first time since my marriage, I loosen my grip a little on the pain I have been holding onto desperately, a raft in my sea of stormy isolation.

Halfway through the next day—Saturday—my memory of the previous night is already breaking up, like a poor television signal. It is becoming indistinct, more a series of grainy snapshots or fleeting moments than a full event. Yet, every time the memories invade, my heart kicks to life in my chest. I cannot speak. I want to be back in Ramu's arms again, even though I know I cannot. Not yet, at least.

And that is when it hits me: I am truly 'that woman,' the one having the affair. How did it happen, and so quickly? All I had hoped for was some sort of closure, but as we had lain there talking idly afterwards, with Ramu licking the chili sauce off my fingers (we had ordered room service after our marathon make-out session), Ramu mentioned that he would be out of town for a few days. "*Jaan,* I have to go to New York on business for three or four days. Will you promise to miss me?" He gently brushed a long tendril of hair from my brow, before lowering his dark head to kiss my trembling lips—and all I had been able to think of was seeing him again. My heart chants mournfully, *Ramu, Ramu, when will I see you again?*

I have to give Bhavesh credit: he feels guilty for what he has done, and, in his own clumsy, repressed way, he is trying to make amends. He has been different since forcing himself on me the other night; he has mostly kept to himself, something that worked to my advantage in arranging my meeting with Ramu.

On Saturday morning, once again donning his role as 'family man,' he makes breakfast, meaning he goes out early for bagels. As I once confided to Tammy, in a rare tell-it-all moment, Bhavesh does not cook. *Amma* made sure of that. For a woman who denounced her son when he married a *Dalit* girl, my mother-in-law still appears to have plenty of influence over the person he is.

Bhavesh was the younger of two boys in a small family. He had lived in the shadow of his older brother with little weight of expectation upon him until his brother had died in a motorcycle accident. Then all of *Amma's* attention had fallen on Bhavesh.

I don't know very much about my mother-in-law, except that she was capable of both spoiling and terrorizing her son at the same time. I had, of course, never met her and it was likely I never would. That was something to be thankful for.

No, *Amma's* son had not and *would never* learn to cook, no matter if he was halfway across the world and estranged from her. He has a wife for that, even if the wife is a no-good, *roti*-burning *Dalit*.

Bhavesh does not apologize. Instead, all morning he jumps in to help with household tasks—drying the dishes I wash, putting them away, even asking if I need his help in chopping the onions for the chicken curry I am making—the tasks that are not truly beneath him. He is never usually tactile with me—though he is with his daughter, forever stroking Maya's hair, planting little kisses on her forehead, or beckoning her over to sit on his knee—but this day, he even occasionally touches me in passing. Nothing erotic, just light, familiar touches that coming from Bhavesh, are more an act of control than affection. They are on the arms, the fingers, even one on the shoulder, and it is only by the force of my will that I do not cringe each time. A frosty knife twists in my gut every time he comes near. He repulses me; he did so before he attacked me. But it is not just the attack, I realize, that makes his touch so hard to bear. It is the fact that he is not Ramu.

In India, people would talk about *Dalits* being Untouchable, but for me it now feels that my husband is the one who should not be touched. It is as if that touch will wash away Ramu's presence from my body, erasing the feeling he has left me with. It feels like the *Kshatriya,* not the *Dalit,* makes me unclean.

I catch Bhavesh surreptitiously averting his eyes from looking at the marks on my neck. They are almost gone now, and my voice is back to normal. It is no coincidence that he avoided me while the consequence of his violence could still so plainly be heard when I spoke. Did that amount to guilt? I do not think so. Inside me, the cynicism pulses like a live creature.

After lunch, Bhavesh decides that we should take a family trip to the zoo. Maya applauds with joyful hands, turning to Bhavesh with worshipful eyes. "Yes, zoo, Daddy, zoo!" I look at them both, keeping my face expressionless. Though I do not particularly feel like playing happy family in public, I suppose it cannot be any worse than being trapped in the house with my now overly attentive husband.

The previous evening's storm has passed, having died away in the small hours of the morning, and it is a bleak day, the sky like smudged kajal. Maya wears a purple paisley scarf. "Purple is my favorite color, Mommy," she announces to me, preening with animated delight as she checks her reflection in the mirror on her dressing table. I wind a grey pashmina stole around my neck, too, though I would have to do so even if it had been warmer. I notice Bhavesh takes a long glance at my scarf as we are about to leave.

I have had years of practice with being pleasant to my husband—or pleasant enough not to draw his attention—so it is not too hard for me to bear the journey next to him in the second-hand Chevy we own. The morning had been worse, as I tried to hold onto my memories of Ramu, every conversation with either Bhavesh or Maya allowing more of those memories to escape. By the time we leave for the zoo, I have tried to push them into oblivion, with little success. The smell of Ramu's sweat, like no one else's. His broad shoulders firm under my fingers. Oh, what foolishness is this?

Perhaps most men who had assaulted their wife in the way he had would watch their spouse's reactions more closely and would not dare believe they were so easily forgiven. Yet, Bhavesh can carry on fairly normally, taking my affirmations and replies to idle conversation—*Shall I turn right here? Yes, Bhavesh. Did you pack water bottles? Yes, they're in the trunk*—at face value, not assuming my genuine feelings to be colored by the sexual violence I had endured from him just a few nights before.

As I watch the Asian rhinos—magnificent beasts which are found in India, though only in the northern swamps and not down in Uttar Pradesh, where Bhavesh and I hail from—I feel my insides slipping away as if they are on a greased slide. I cannot stop thinking about coincidence.

Bhavesh has been violent to me before, though the incidents have been minor, and I had suffered worse when living in the orphanage. Does the fact that this most recent and extreme of incidents has coincided with Ramu coming back into my life mean something?

But, even before I saw Ramu, I had been changing, feeling more disconnected from my life, less able to just accept it. Inside my heart it feels wet, like new rain.

"That is an Asian rhino, Maya," Bhavesh says. "They come from where you are from . . . India."

I study my knuckles. Maya doesn't come from India, though I am not about to correct him. Maya comes from America. She was born in America; she belongs here, and that is important. As the daughter of a *Kshatriya,* Maya would be unlikely to face the stigma in India that I had.

All the same, I do not want my daughter to go to a country that can treat its people in such a way, even if it is a land of heritage for her.

Bhavesh once told me he does not think of himself as American, even though he has an American passport. We have made a good life here, have benefitted from the opportunities the country has to offer, yet Bhavesh would never consider himself to be even partly American. *I am Indian still*, he had said, proud as a Hindu idol. He nodded his head with emphasis. And there are many ways in which I cannot help but agree with that.

So what am I? Where do I belong? Am I American? There are Americans who would listen to my accent and give me a resounding 'no.' Those Americans were, in my experience, relatively few, at least in my part of California. The irony is that, if I went back to India, most people I spoke to would probably accuse me of having a very 'American' accent. In some ways, this orphan girl still does not belong anywhere. I shiver slightly. Months later, I will think back on this epiphany, in telling Ramu how I felt.

My soul is seething within me like a bleating goat waiting to be sacrificed on *Eid*. I do kind of *want* to be American, but I know that a part of my heart is still in India, despite the harsh treatment I received as a *Dalit* child there. It is the land of my birth, the land where my mother's remains still lie in the earth. And I wonder about Ramu, too, who has also made a home in the United States. He made his fortune here, but does he think of himself as American or Indian? Or, perhaps, neither?

"What is India like?" Maya asks as we walk away from the rhinos.

"It is a beautiful country," Bhavesh replies. "A proud country with a rich history, one that goes back so much further than anything here."

"I want to go to India," Maya says.

"One day, my princess," Bhavesh says lightly, "one day."

He glances over at me, and I quickly nod my agreement. "Yes, Maya, you'll get to see it one day."

21
Meena

Fall 2014
Hayward, California

I cannot get to work fast enough on Monday morning. I suddenly notice a police car moving into the lane behind me, flashing its lights. *Oh, no, Bhavesh is going to kill me,* I think in a panic. I got a parking ticket once, and that was not a happy day. "Why can't you be careful where you park?" Bhavesh had yelled, his voice flying around like pots and pans.

The cop car races up behind, then pulls around me and speeds off. The sharp pain building in my chest recedes, and my heart thumps again as I wonder whether there will be an email from Ramu waiting for me.

I glide towards my tiny office as if on little wheels. For the first time in months, I am full of energy. I no longer feel untethered from the universe, and I do not want it to end. I try to be patient with my work computer, but I fail. While I am waiting for it to restart, the computer having crashed on the first go, Tammy waltzes in.

"Hey, girlfriend!" Tammy says, attempting to sound younger and 'hipper' than she is. (In fact, the sad thing is that Tammy has actually been heard to say the word 'hip.') Tammy had been away towards the end of the previous week and across the weekend. She looks tanned, relaxed and happy. She was visiting a friend in LA, and they had planned to spend a day at Disneyland. My heart fills with affection as I look at her.

My desktop loads up and I beam at my friend, while inside I reprimand myself for wishing Tammy away, so I can get on and open my email. "How was your weekend?" I ask, forcing enthusiasm into my voice.

"A-mazing, uh-huh!" The 'uh-huh' is a poor attempt to do a Mickey Mouse–style laugh, but I love her for trying. "But I'll tell you all about it at lunch, yeah? You up for it?"

I nod and my lips quirk upwards. "It's good to see you, Tammy; I've missed you and our lunches." I know my tone is wistful. Although, in some ways, the timing of her trip was good, I imagine the lunches would have been harder in the couple of days after Bhavesh had forced himself upon me.

As much as my friend is usually a breath of fresh air, there are also times when the contrasts in our lives are glaring. Tammy has no husband, and right now she has no boyfriend, but it is more than that. Freedom and respect are a given in Tammy's life, single or not. They are something she can take as a given and be rightfully aggrieved of if someone impinges upon that.

Sometimes, for me, it is a hard thing to be around. My life with Bhavesh has been so much better than the life I could have expected to have in Kalanpur, yet that same differentness I felt as an Untouchable orphan in Grace Mercy sometimes finds me here, too—and that is most often when I am with Tammy. There is no fear in Tammy. None. Sometimes when I hear Tammy talk of one dating disaster after another, her eyes big and shiny and blue as a cloudless sky, her laughter loud and unencumbered, I want the *Dalit* women at home to have what she has. And I want it so badly it makes tears burn in my eyes.

"How was your weekend?" Tammy asks, her voice inquisitive.

My eye is drawn to the email shortcut on my monitor. "Good," I say distractedly. *I slept with a man who wasn't my husband.* "Family trip to the zoo."

"Nice," Tammy says, backing out of the door. "Well, we'll catch up at lunch."

I hover with the mouse pointer. *Vanilla Meena,* that's who I have always been. Safe, ho hum. Until now.

Conflicting feelings war within me. My breath comes in quick gasps as I turn my full attention to my computer screen. How unfair that I should feel guilty for wanting a man I had loved so long ago and was denied having—by life, by family, and even by the man himself. But what I am doing is so extraordinarily selfish—there is no escaping that. How can I ever justify what I am doing to my daughter?

Ramu is just a man I knew for less than two years a decade ago. He can walk away any time he wants and decide not to return my messages. *I* am the one with everything to lose.

But thinking about him in that way seems like a betrayal to the man who has taken more than one beating for me, whose wounds I once cleaned, whose back still bears those scars.

Perhaps I should run and hide from all of it and live out the rest of my at least bearable life along the path of least resistance, and *not* double-click that email icon just yet. But I will have to open his email at some point . . .

Thursday, October 2, 2014. 00:31 (EDT)
My Meena,
You left a few hours ago, and I could not sleep. I see you lying beneath me on the hotel bed, I see you above me on the rug. I see you standing next to me looking out over San Francisco. I see you giving that shy smile and I don't want anyone else seeing that special smile but me. I have no right to say that, but I say it anyway. You are like a ghost, haunting me.

I know you won't see this until Monday, and I wonder about all the things you will be doing until then. I have to be up in about four hours to get ready for New York.

My Meena. Is that too forward? I wish it was so. I wish you were mine. I've had everything too much my own way these last few years. An occasional disappointment is a healthy thing for every life, but not in this. I need you.

Stop haunting me. Or don't. Actually, don't.

• • •

Thursday, October 2, 2014. 16:57 (EDT)

This ghost woman has followed me to New York. I'm supposed to be preparing for a meeting with the board members of an international investment company, and instead I'm writing this email to you.

This ghost just won't leave me alone.

I go to a meeting and she always places herself just behind the person who is speaking. I see confusion, and sometimes worry in the faces of many of these people. 'Why is Ram Nayak not listening to me?' 'Am I boring him?' 'Gee, how rude! How did he ever get to run a Fortune 500 company?'

Luckily, it's occurred to me I have come to the home of the Ghostbusters, so I might see if I can buy one of those proton packs. Possibly a uniform. But then that sounds a little like dress up.

I hope you're laughing. I'm imagining you laughing.

Thursday, October 2, 2014. 20:14 (EDT)

Hi Meena,

It's been a busy day, partly to make up for yesterday's very unproductive one. I just re-read the last email I sent you and cringed a little.

I think you've turned me into a boy again.

But I don't have you. Not in the way I wish I did. That sounds selfish, but it's true. I will fly back tomorrow. Let me know when I can see you. I need to see you.

Your Ram

I read the emails three times over. I feel mushy and wet, like a pile of leaves after they have been rained on. When I read his words I can feel him in the room, I can smell his scent, like English Leather, wholesome and earthy and reassuring.

I had beat him with my fists for his selfishness, for the way he had abandoned me to chase down his dreams, leaving me to a life that had ended with a husband I cannot stand. But now I can see my own selfishness. What will happen to Maya if I continue seeing Ramu and Bhavesh finds out? Thoughts twist like snakes through my brain.

22
Ram

Fall 2014
Manhattan, New York

I close my laptop and cross to the window of my hotel room, looking out over the heated city of Manhattan as it lies around me in the darkness. In the dark only the gray outline of the thin, tall buildings of Manhattan are visible against a moonlit sky. I pull off my tie and run my fingers through my graying hair. Women are such a distraction, I know that. Ultimately, that's why my marriage hadn't worked, and why every attempt at even the most casual relationship before or after that had failed. I do not need a woman in my life.

But Meena is not *just* a woman. Not in that sense. She is different. She is . . . I cannot quite say what she is, cannot put into words the why of it. *Yes,* it is because of Grace Mercy—that shared experience no one else could ever really get. *Yes,* it is also because she was the first woman—girl, really—I ever loved. But it is something else, as well.

It is fate that has brought us together, although I am usually careful of not ascribing supernatural causes to things. What I believe in is seizing opportunities—as opportunities do not last forever. Whatever this is with Meena, meeting her now is like a door that has somehow opened for me. I already missed one chance to spend my life with her, and I have an eye on the possibility that the door will slam shut once more.

It feels . . . right, that we should be given another chance, now that I have made something of myself, now that we are no longer poor *Dalits* in Kalanpur.

Yes, Meena is a door that closed once and has opened to me again. An opportunity to be seized. But I should be careful. She is a married woman with a child and might scare easily. If the door closes and she is lost to me again . . .

For all the things that have gone my way in the last decade or so, for all the surety I have about who I am and the way I live my life, a part of me is still a worrier, like I always was.

• • •

Spring 1999
Kalanpur, Uttar Pradesh

I was always a serious boy, something that intensified after I lost my parents. Mother used to tell me I worried too much, that the world would be the same whether I worried about it or not. She told me that worrying only changed the worrier.

"Listen to your mother, Ramu," Father would say, nodding his head with emphasis. "She is the wisest person I know."

But the serious boy, the worrier, was only a part of who the young Ramu Nayak was. The rest of me was a dreamer.

As a younger boy, I dreamed of fighting monsters, imagining them emerging from the landscape, climbing over a nearby building, or cresting a distant hill. Sometimes, I would imagine soldiers turning up to fight them, and sometimes I would fight the monsters myself.

My parents were happy to let their boy run around making explosion noises in public, not to mention the odd sounds the monsters made. I was their only child—a miracle, they would tell me; I had taken a long time to come along, and they could never make me a brother or sister. As a result, I think they spoiled me a little.

By the time I was approaching my teens, the worrier had grown fangs. Before then, I had worried about external things, like the world's dangers, or what might come and disrupt the happy life I had with my parents. Now there were no more pretend monsters just over the hill, but life was teaching me that there were plenty of real ones lurking in plain sight.

The daydreaming did not stop, though, and I continued to use my imagination. Now my dreams were about who I was going to be as a man. The incredible things I might do . . . race car driver, Bollywood movie star, fast-jet pilot and military sniper all took their turns. Being me, I worried about this. I liked to imagine I was a NASCAR driver but, what if my car tumbled down the front stretch, flipping eight or nine times before rolling to a stop? Or, if Bollywood rejected me because I was too short or too dark or a *Dalit*? I pictured myself flying the world's first delta-winged bomber and in the next moment, I was engulfed in flames from anti-aircraft fire.

Then I met Uncle Nihal.

Uncle Nihal lived in New Delhi, which made him cool before I even met him. He was also rich, owning a leather goods factory and employing many staff—even non-*Dalits*.

Nihal was welcomed into our home like a king. He embraced his younger brother—my father—heartily and showed deferent respect to Mother. His own wife passed away several years back, and his children were already into adulthood, so he came alone to visit.

After we ate a special meal of squash curry fragrant with cloves, cinnamon and cumin; spiced fish *pakoras* and fluffy *chappatis*, Uncle Nihal slipped off alone into the garden to smoke. My family home was not typical of other *Dalit* homes in the city—ours was a two-bedroom *pukka* house built with mortar and baked bricks, with a separate kitchen, and a heavy carved door leading out into a good-sized garden, while most *Dalits* in Kalanpur lived in tumbling, decrepit mud houses with thatched roofs in a small cluster of dwellings, far away from caste Hindu homes. Few *Dalits* lived as well as us—Father was a street sweeper, Mother a cleaner, and, as I got older, school friends pointed out how strange this was.

With Mother and Father busy in the kitchen, washing the dirty dishes and putting them away, I sneaked out to join the uncle I had never met before. Nihal was most of the way through his cigarette, blowing out smoke while wearing a contented expression, and he didn't notice me straight away. I watched in silence, noting that he looked older than

Father, though it was hard to tell how much. He had sharp little black eyes that were buried beneath a monster bush of eyebrows, and a big white moustache hid his mouth. His skin was hard and weathered. *Probably like the leather he makes in his factory,* I thought.

Turning and spotting me, Nihal beckoned me over. "How old are you?" he asked kindly.

"Thirteen, Uncle," I replied, keeping my tone deferential.

He took a last drag on his cigarette and dropped it to the ground. "And do you know what you want to be? You will be a man before you know it."

"Father says I can join him as a sweeper," I replied. I sounded defensive; the question blind-sided me.

A brief flash of annoyance crossed my uncle's face. "And is that what you would like to do?"

I shrugged. There are things I wanted to be, but I was already old enough to know that these ambitions would seem absurd for a *Dalit* child.

Nihal crushed the cigarette stub under his heel and searched my face. "Sit down, boy, let us talk."

I nodded and steered myself to the concrete bench that sat at the base of the *gullar* tree in our garden. Nihal sat down beside me and stretched out his legs in front of him.

"I haven't seen you since you were . . . three, perhaps? I am a busy man and do not see you all as much as I would like, but I love your father—and your mother. We are, however, different people. I am a hard man."

A solid muscular man, Uncle Nihal seemed to loom over me even though he wasn't much taller than me and he was smaller than Father. I locked eyes with him and mumbled, "Yes, Uncle." Some of my doubt must have shown on my face, as my uncle chuckled.

"Coming down here relaxes me, makes me nicer. It also makes me realize I should see you all more often, especially as I get older. Your father and mother are . . . relaxed people. They do not have ambition, and that is okay . . . for them." He leaned in closer to me.

"You give us money, don't you?" I suddenly blurted.

Uncle Nihal looked surprised, but recovered quickly. His face grew somber. "They have mentioned this to you?"

I looked up at him, massaging my nose thoughtfully. "No. I didn't know for sure, not until today."

"I . . ." He made friendly flapping gestures with his hands. "Help."

I gave him a quick, uneasy grin. "But you said you were a hard man. I think helping us makes you a good man."

Nihal beamed like a lighthouse. "Your father is the only person who brings this out in me. Not even my children see much of my generosity; I want them to fight for what they have in life, not be lazy." He sighed and rubbed his eyes. "Your father and mother are not lazy, Ramu; it's important you know this. They are . . . gentle people. There is a difference." He looked at me, his eyes narrowed.

I nodded respectfully with a quizzical look, not quite understanding.

"Would you promise not to mention what you know to them?" Nihal asked lightly. "Even gentle people have their pride."

I folded my hands together. "Yes, I promise." The sky was bright, the air balmy and mild.

My uncle broke the silence. "I asked whether you knew what you wanted to be." His gaze on me moved like a prison searchlight. "I have a sense you are perhaps a little like me."

I wondered if he noticed how I swelled with pride and quickly asked, "How did you get your leather factory, uncle?"

"Well," he said, stroking the ends of his moustache carefully, "the full story is too long for right now, young Ramu. But, I decided I didn't want to be any of the things non-*Dalits*—and *Dalits*—were telling me I could be. I wanted to make the most of myself. New Delhi was the place I could do that. Leather was the medium. It was ironic, though that wasn't why I did it." He shifted his position on the bench as the broad, slanting rays of sunlight shone through the leaves of the old *gullar* tree.

"As a *Dalit*," he continued, his voice grave, "I can dispose of dead animals, even cows. For the other castes, that is fine while I am dragging away rotting corpses for them. But I knew that if I tried to make actual money out of that down here, well, it would attract the wrong attention and somebody would have to 'put me in my place.'" A small breeze blew around us and I could see Mother in the kitchen, mopping her brow with the end of her plain, cotton sari.

"In Delhi, no one cared how rich I got. There, being a *Dalit* worked for me. Dead cows were easy to obtain, especially if people didn't know why I wanted them." He gave me a small, conspiratorial grin. "Sometimes they paid me to take them away, even though they were providing me with the raw materials I needed."

That made me chortle. He was making being a *Dalit*, the lowest caste, the only ones fit for handling the remains of the holy animals, work to his advantage. It was his poor status that had helped to make him rich in a way that would have been more difficult for non-*Dalits*. I wanted to clap my hands in admiration.

"That way," Nihal said, rubbing his fleshy hands together. His eyes shone and his breath smelled of tea. "I could grow my business quickly. I was employing many staff before I knew it."

"I like it," I said, bobbing my head up and down. "I want to do something clever like that one day."

"I thought you might." My uncle smiled and patted my shoulder.

. . .

I am at Teterboro Airport early on Monday morning, before Meena will even be at work. Still, I check my email before getting on my private jet bound for San Francisco. I have always used Teterboro whenever possible. Just a quick trip across the Hudson and Hackensack rivers into New Jersey, it is convenient for Manhattan. Since I am going to be spending more time in San Francisco now, the airport is ideal.

As the jet engines work hard following takeoff, humming away as they push the plane further into the sky, I think for the first time in years about the possibility of something going wrong on a plane. I hated flying the first few times I did it. My first flight to America had been my first flight anywhere. It had been the beginning of my dream, yet all I could think about was how I hadn't wanted to die before I made my dream happen.

It is a little like that now, as the jet breaks the cloud base. I listen to the change of pitch of the engine, trying to tell if there is anything wrong.

I am not scared the way I had been as an eighteen-year-old, flying for the first time, but I still think about how sad it would be if I never saw Meena again. I want to so much.

I think about the emails I had sent her, whether they are good enough to be the last thing she reads from me. With that thought, I get out my laptop and start trying to write something better. Silly, really. I have not worried about anything like this for years. This is what one woman is doing to me. Making me ridiculous. Making me like that worrying boy I once knew.

I like it.

23
Ram

Winter 2002
Kalanpur, Uttar Pradesh

Before Uncle Nihal left to return to Delhi, he bought us a car. It was second-hand and only a little 800cc run-around Maruti, but it was a *car*. I had seen cars around the streets of Kalanpur every day, and I had even traveled in one when my classmate—a non-*Dalit* and the local *Zamindar's* son—gave me a lift home from school (we had stayed after classes ended because he needed my help on a math quiz), but there was something quite different about our family owning one; no *Dalit* in our town owned a car and only a few owned bicycles.

The first time I was alone with it was when Father parked it in front of our house. He secured it with a triple padlock to the steering wheel under the yellow light of the 40-watt street bulb. Attached to a loose socket and swinging in the light breeze, it threw a furtive shadow over the slightly dented Maruti. In the darkness of the night, I ran a hand gently and reverently across almost every surface, inside and out: the pastel-gray bodywork, the chrome-like trim, the frayed leather seats, the doors, the glass, the steering wheel, the dashboard, the magic hiding underneath the hood.

The other kids in the village were only allowed to look and smell the car's wonderful fragrance from afar. Many times I would have to act as a bodyguard and shoo the village kids away—they were considered too dirty to get close to our prized possession. I was glad Uncle had bought it for us, but I also wished my parents could have been able to buy such a thing. The shame of accepting such an enormous gift flooded my head with thick crimson.

One day, I promised myself, I would be able to go out and just buy a car like that. Or a house. Or even an airplane like the ones I sometimes saw in the sky when my friend and I laid out on a blanket on blistering hot summer nights in the open sugarcane fields.

Uncle Nihal left after just a few days. He did not come by again, and my parents rarely talked about him. But those few days changed my life forever.

· · ·

Life carried on as usual. The car quickly deteriorated—even with the help provided by Uncle Nihal, car maintenance was not high on the list of monthly expenses. Sometimes I cleaned it and, in what was a highly amusing role reversal for them, I more than once complained to my parents about the state they left it in. It is not even like it got used all *that* much because Father once told me he was never completely comfortable driving it.

Still, Uncle Nihal chose well, because, despite the lack of care, the thing kept running. Mostly, we used it to take quick trips out of the city on the weekends. We couldn't manage it every weekend—Father had to supplement his paltry take-home pay from being a street sweeper by providing cheap labor to the Khosla Marriage Tent contractor every other weekend—so the car did not run all the time, often with several weeks between uses, yet the plucky little motor never once failed to start for us.

One Saturday, my parents decided upon a day trip to the neighboring holy city of Haridwar. The old engine clanked to life, the car sputtered, raising clouds of dust, and we were on our way. It was a two-hour drive southeast along National Highway 334. We did it once before when Uncle Nihal was visiting, but I hoped this time it would not be as busy as it was then, with hundreds of pilgrims gathered near the banks to take a dip in the gurgling Ganga river.

Our little section of the NH334 was quieter than usual. In any case, Father was a nervous driver, so we rarely broke fifty-five.

"Come on, Manni," Mother teased, her nickname for my father, whose full name was Manprasad. Mother was wearing her one fancy scarlet *Khadi* cotton silk sari, which she kept for special occasions. Its silver-trimmed border had frayed, and I wowed to myself that one day I would buy her a dozen gold-threaded *Kanjeeveram* silk saris like the upper caste women wore. She looked serene and happy as she glanced at my father. His mouth was set in worried lines—except when he looked at Mother. "The streets will be crowded by the time we get there."

I watched from the back seat as Father raised an eyebrow. "But, at least we will get there."

Mother looked over as a white Ambassador car, paint flaking off in a few places, shot past us. "Did you see how old that man was who just passed us?"

"I have my eyes on the road, *jaan-e-janaana*." Only my father could make his own term of endearment sound like a gentle rebuke. These semi-romantic exchanges made me nauseous in private and embarrassed in public, but later I would remember them fondly and understand how rare and precious they were.

"Anyway, see," my mother pointed, with a thin, grizzled finger into the hot dusty glare of noon, "the turn is coming up."

Father slowed for the turn, changing into a lower gear, but the truck behind us did not. I flew forward and an intense pain burst in my chest. I woke up seconds later, I was told, though at the time I had no idea how long I had been out. It took several moments before I had any idea what had happened. My right cheek was pressed hard against something; I was wedged behind the driver's seat and the back-seat cushion, only able to move my arms and legs a little. I could see my mother's right arm and shoulder in her sari blouse, blood staining its whiteness like a crimson tide. But where the rest of her upper body should be, rising and falling under the precise pleats of her sari, there was a large object. It took several more moments and a wave of nausea before I realized it was the front of a huge vehicle.

"Ramu!" floated Father's voice from somewhere in front of me. "Ramu, are you there?"

"Yes, Father," I answered softly, rubbing my temple where a painful bump was growing larger. I tried to lift my arm towards the direction of the front seat. "Mother?" I cried, desperate with fear.

"Don't look, son. Don't . . ." Father's voice sounded choked, becoming fainter as if he was speaking from a great distance. "Are you . . . hurt?" his voice strained through the smoke-filled air between the front and back seats.

"I think I'm okay, Father." Muffled sounds of shouting came from over my head. "I can't move." Panic filled my lungs.

I could hear Father's voice, so small and tinny now, a thin tearing sound.

"I wanted to keep you close. You were all we had." Pain oozed from my father's voice as he struggled to speak.

I knew I should try and get to Father, but a heaviness filled me and kept me from moving. "Father, I'm scared." I whimpered softly.

"M-me too, s-son." Father gave a last, shuffling cough, like someone walking on dead leaves. "S-so s-orry." I shut my eyes tight and wished that time would double back on itself and give me back my life as it was an hour ago.

Even above the sounds of the angry motor, honking horns, sirens, and the buzzing of flies, I heard the hollow call of a pigeon.

24
Ram

Fall 2014
New York

Dearest Meena,

I am feeling mortal today. In me, at least, success has brought a feeling of immortality. When everything goes right, it's easy to feel that nothing, even death, can come along to spoil your good fortune. That ill health, or the misfortune to be in the wrong place at the wrong time, are things which affect only the unlucky, the unblessed.

Ridiculous. Pompous. The kind of thoughts that deserve to be disproved. And, for the first time in a while, I feel vulnerable.

I wanted to write an email that would let you know how I feel about you, just in case the Nayak plane goes down today. Which, I realize, is a stupid thing to do. But let me try, anyway:

I blame you for making me feel mortal. You are my Achilles Heel. My weak point. You damned woman. Yet, if we don't have a weak point, then what are we? Robots? Gods? Neither is something I desire to be. I am not scared of many things, Meena—despite the theme of this email—but I fear what is left unsaid or undone. Or what could have been said or done better. There is nothing more tragic than something unfinished.

And our love has only just begun again. There is so much I should say.

I stop writing and look out the window. We are probably somewhere over Nebraska, judging by the time. A large part of me does not like this feeling of having something to lose, and the implied mortality it brings with it. However, it is bringing me to a realization that my business, this thing I have grown, which has been a measure of who I am as a man, is not something I am afraid of losing. It never has been. In fact, the wild abandon I have shown in every aspect of my business is, paradoxically, a part of what has brought me success.

People, lives, the events we partake in, the things we build for each other . . .

The greatest pressure I have had as a businessman is the responsibility for those people who work in my businesses—for their jobs and careers, and the families who are relying on that. Yet now I have gotten to where almost all my interests have a life of their own. They are like children who have outgrown the parent. All I would ever have to do is let go of the reins . . .

I go back into the email, hovering for a few moments over the 'send' button. Then the cursor moves, and I hover over the delete button instead. Finally, I just close the draft.

To be continued, I think.

25
Ram

Winter 2002
Grace Mercy Children's Home

I lay in the car for almost two hours, the fear like a big boulder inside my chest. I tried not to look at Mother like Father had instructed, but I was unable to look elsewhere. I wanted to crumple against Mother as in childhood, to let her lead me to bed, to sleep away what had just occurred as though it were a fever dream.

After being sawed out of the squashed wreckage of our little car, everyone would tell me what a 'miracle' it was that I was unharmed. How lucky I was to be alive. No one considered the possibility that, as I lay there unable to move, I might have wanted nothing more than to die with my parents.

But *Brahma* would not let me die that day. First, the side of the car was cut away. Although light flooded into the space and the day's air blew in to cool me, the car still held me fast. It did not want to let me go yet. Next, my rescuers worked with the jaws of life to pry open the roof open above me, moving the rear of the car away a little, finally stopping it from pinning me against the driver's seat. Father's seat.

It was like some twisted, futuristic C-section, like in the movie *An American Cyborg* that I remember seeing at Alankar Cinema with some other boys from my class. The image is like a photograph in my memory, for the young man who emerged was no longer the teenaged boy who had gone in. And yet, as the rescue team worked to maneuver me through the space which had now been opened, I found myself reluctant to leave, hands caressing the back of the seat beyond which my father's body lay.

When I finally slept, it was a sleep full of sounds. My father's voice across a decade and a noisy highway, the sounds of my past and present, my reality and imagination, all mixed up with creaking beds, footsteps, dogs howling, the wailing of ambulance sirens, the drip-drip-drip of the tap in our small tin-roofed house in Kalanpur.

Uncle Nihal had taken so long to come down that my parents were already cremated, and I was a temporary resident in an orphanage before he arrived. I assumed a man with my uncle's responsibilities could not just drop everything, even upon the death of his brother. This is the way the world worked, so he had gotten down to me when he could.

I had heard from my father that Nihal Nand Nayak hated flying with a passion I had heard from my father, and would happily spend days on a train to avoid a few hours on an airplane. Even his own brother's death would not get him into an aircraft, so he instead endured the laborious train journey down from Delhi.

I awaited his arrival patiently, sure that it would herald the start of a new life in the capital city. The idea scared me, and I did not know how the cousins I had never met would take my sudden presence among them.

"How are you, Ramu?" Uncle Nihal said gruffly when he finally arrived. We were sitting on a dilapidated upholstered couch inside the mother superior's office. The mother superior had tactfully left us alone, insisting she had to make her evening rounds. "I could take you back to Delhi with me. Treat you like my own, which you are. But I will not be helping you if I do that." Uncle's gaze was fixed on the bouquet of roses in a vase placed in front of a wooden crucifix hanging over a prie-dieu.

At my look of hurt and betrayal, my Uncle leaned in closer. Watching the Adam's apple in his throat bob up and down as he swallowed, I felt despair squeezing my chest like a pair of burning hands.

He said carefully, "I know you cannot understand this now, boy. I don't expect you to. But I don't have as much to teach you as you might think. This is the best lesson I can give you. This, and a promise."

As I listened to the sounds filtering in from the half-open window, he made the offer of a job at eighteen years of age if I could make my way to New Delhi when the time came. I heard the challenge in his unspoken words: 'Be the man who can make his way across the country to Delhi, and I will know you are ready to work for me.'

Nihal left after making a donation to Grace Mercy large enough to ensure that I would stay as long as I needed to. Then he left his nephew where, less than two years later, I would be cruelly whipped by a policeman's belt.

It was as I lay with Meena on a nurse's examination table, which did not want to support both of us, that marked the third big change in my life—not in the mother superior's office under the lash. We had just explored each other, and I had known for the first time the joy such closeness can bring, the intensity of feeling. I took a deep breath and inhaled her fragrance of soft, light jasmine mixed with the scent of moist earth.

Despite the persistent pain in my back, I felt astonishingly present, both when I was intimate with Meena, and now, afterwards. It was like there was something invisible flowing from inside me into Meena, and from her to me, connecting us in the deepest way two people can be.

Pain had given way to desire, but now desire was giving way to a seething hatred, a desperate need for revenge on small-minded men, who were nothing and would never be more than that. Those tiny, arrogant men in their uniforms. One day . . . *one day.*

But I must be practical, I reminded myself. However much I might want revenge, there were other things I wanted a lot more.

Never again would Ramu Nayak be left as vulnerable as he was today. Those men could do what they wanted to me, with only the tiniest of excuses, and not even the mother superior had been able to stop them. All the police officers had was a flyer, yet they could use it as apparently indisputable evidence of . . . of what? Of attending a legal, organized rally?

Never again would I be a man who could be whipped. I would have what I needed to make sure that cannot happen. Money. Power.

My lips brushed Meena's forehead as we lay next to each other on the examination table. She was the other half of this. I wanted her; I wanted her so much, but if I was ever to truly have her, I must be able to take her away from all of this. Not just from Grace Mercy, not just from Kalanpur, but from poverty, from life as a *Dalit*. I needed to give her more than this beaten, bleeding boy. If I was ever to deserve her, then I must leave her and only return as everything she would need me to be.

I would have to bury this orphan, this Ramu Nayak. Find a better name, for a better man.

26
Ram

Fall 2014

San Francisco, California

"What are you doing?" I ask Meena as we lie in our hotel suite together. I can feel her fingers on my back.

Meena looks up into my face. The light catches her eyes, making them shine. For just a second, she looks so much like that girl from the examination table. The past and the present have been fighting each other since I met her again, but I have not yet had any time to make sense of it.

"I'm learning your scars," she answers. "I didn't get the chance to last time."

"I rarely let anyone see them, but you're welcome to look if you like," I say, making as if to roll over. "After all . . ."

". . . I was there when you got them," Meena finishes for me.

"You were."

"It's okay," she says, moving her hand to stop me. "I will learn them by touch, not sight."

I wink at her over my shoulder. "Might take some time."

"I'm counting on it," Meena replies, putting her fingers back to the task of tracing the smooth lines of skin left after my welts had finally healed.

We could not meet for more than a day after I had returned from New York, which had been frustrating. It had not been possible in the evening, so Meena had rushed to her car during lunch and sped over to the Ritz Carlton. I had been waiting in the lobby for her this time, and we had rushed upstairs like excited teenagers, tearing off our clothes as soon as we got into the suite before almost devouring each other.

Between our excitement and the lack of time—not to mention the daylight filling my hotel suite—it could not have been more different from the other night. And yet all that energy and haste had translated into something almost as amazing. Almost. When we lay down afterwards, it was with laughs and giggles.

"You should be getting back to work soon," I say, then let out a small sound of pleasure as her finger continues to trace its way across my back. There is something in the way she does it which threatens to disable me completely. I wonder if she realizes the effect it is having, how close I am to being at her mercy.

"Are you trying to get rid of me?" she teases. The scent of her body—the smell of airy jasmine and cinnamon cloves—hangs in the air like wisps of the past and hints of the future.

I wrap her in my arms and laugh. "I would have you here every minute if I could. But it is you I am thinking of."

"Did your wife know what the scars were?" she asks.

The question comes from nowhere, and I am a little stunned. In fact, I cannot help but marvel at the way her face betrayed no emotion as she asked it. Was she always capable of that? I do not think so. That is a woman's guile and, I realize, I too often think of her as that girl from years before.

I look away, unable for a moment to hold her gaze. "No. I wouldn't tell her, except to admit that it was a whipping. That much was obvious."

Meena is quiet, and when I look back up, her eyes are unfocused, distant. "I don't even know her name."

"Jane. Jane Pitt. Then Nayak, then Pitt again."

"She hasn't sought you out, since . . . ?"

". . . I made my money? No, not her style."

"You loved her?"

I take a few moments to answer. "I wasn't ready."

"I shouldn't have asked, but—"

"Ask," I say, taking her face lightly in my hand. It looks so small and delicate with my fingers across it. My fingers, my hands, have always been those of a worker—rough, thick, powerful—even though they have done little of the work they were built for. "Always, always ask."

"That wasn't really an answer you gave me just then."

I quirk an eyebrow at her. "I said 'ask.' I didn't say I would answer."

She laughs and shoves me gently. Then she sighs. "How is this going to work?" She leans back on the propped-up pillows, biting down on her pink-stained lip. "It was hard enough today, and I'll be half an hour late from lunch. *At least.* I can't do that too often."

"Well," I say, reaching over and opening a drawer in my bedside table. "I had an idea."

I retrieve a phone, which Meena looks at with more than a little horror.

"Only take it if you want," I say quickly. "It's got my number in it, and I promise I'll never call it. Texts only. And you can get ahold of me whenever you want."

Meena takes the phone and palms it close to her chest. "You *have* been thinking," she breathes.

"Plus," I say, giving her a wolfish grin. "I wasn't planning to stay at the Ritz Carlton indefinitely. I'm looking for an apartment; perhaps somewhere near the university would be good?"

27
Ram

Summer 2003
Grace Mercy Children's Home

Meena was going to be a problem. In the time my back had been healing, I had tried again and again to explain what was on my mind to Meena. The thoughts were streaming through my head, like an endless, jumbled radio broadcast, repeating itself over and over.

Meena was caught up in our love, as was I. But whereas that love fueled my thoughts and plans, driving me to think of the future, it only brought Meena more fully into the now.

She was a lone tree in the center of an island of calm—and I was a kite flitting about in the building winds of an approaching storm, tethered to the tree lest I fly away and become lost at sea. Sooner than I'd like, I'll have to cut the line and just let the kite fly. And for all that she was my rock—or tree—I still worried that what I must do might break her.

Or, just as bad, make her hate me.

It is not like I was in a hurry to leave Meena. Our love was now out in the open and, within reason, tolerated by the nuns. Right now we sat together on our bench, sharing our meager lunch. A glaring, summery heat covered everything like a layer of glass. Meena chattered to me about inconsequential things—*I hate all this math homework-shomework Professor Mehta gives us. What should we do this weekend?*

Should we ask the nuns for permission to go see the new movie Kal Ho Naa Ho? Are you going to play in the Grace Mercy boys' cricket team this summer?—and she snuggled into my shoulder, just for a moment, and I let her. The heat fell on us like a blanket, and soon we would have to go back inside.

The monsters had not gone; I knew that. They were waiting under the bed, in the cupboard. But I did not have to deal with them until it was dark, until the longing to get away from Kalanpur closed like a vise on my internal organs. I had cradled this hope, nurtured it, fed it for three months. The time spent healing had given me the opportunity to save money—which I had earned from my part-time job fixing computers at the cybercafe in the nearby town—money I would need for my plan. Finally, the money was enough, though the trip would have to be one way. If I did not meet with some success at the other end, then I did not know what I would do.

Time to tell Meena.

. . .

Fall 2014
San Francisco, California
"Where shall I meet you?" I ask Meena.

"Forbidden Matter," Meena replies at the other end of the line. Her voice sounds low and husky on the innocuous little cell phone I gave her. Since it is a Tuesday, I know she is standing outside a studio door waiting for Maya's hip-hop class to be dismissed.

I cannot help but laugh. "Huh?"

She is whispering now. I have to strain to listen. "It's an ice cream parlor. Well, it's an ice cream *restaurant*, really." I can picture her putting her lush, kissable lips right on the telephone's mouthpiece, so that the other parents cannot listen. "Tammy's taking me."

"Tammy?" I repeat. I hear the doubt in my own voice. "Should I wait around the corner, then?"

Her voice rings clear. "I'm not ashamed of you, you know."

"But—" I rub my nose thoughtfully. Has she thought this through?

I hear Meena's breathless little giggle on the other end of the line and my heart tugs me towards her. I cradle the mouthpiece closer, wishing I could wrap her in my arms right now. She is playing with me. "I'm going to tell her . . . about us."

I run my fingers distractedly through my hair. I stare blankly out of the Ritz Carlton lobby window at the gray fog settling in thick filmy layers across the city. "You—you think that's wise?"

"None of this is wise, my love." The note in her voice makes her sound older, wistful, like the echoing end of a *raga*. We have been like children, this last couple of weeks since I returned from New York. Meena laughs and teases me, so that my heart is naked and open again, like a house with no curtains.

"But she can be trusted," Meena continues forcefully. "And, anyway, before you came along, we had lunch together several times a week." I can hear voices in the background, kids chattering excitedly as they find their parents. Her voice is knowing when she continues, "She will figure out something is wrong, eventually."

We have only met twice more in the evening since our passionate encounter at the Ritz Carlton. I grabbed a taxi to a few blocks away from the university four times during her lunch break, sometimes going to a restaurant, other times picking up a sandwich and strolling around Golden Gate Park—walking close, but careful not to touch—making the two nights of lovemaking all the sweeter for the waiting. Meena walked beside me lightly, happily, though it seemed with half an eye on who might observe us.

"If you're telling her today, are you sure I should be there?" I joke. "I'm the 'other lunch partner.' It could get messy if she doesn't take it well."

"Man up," Meena says, her voice cheeky and chipper. "Come and face her."

"Man up?" I scoff. Meena giggles, sounding again like she is no older than her daughter.

"So, you didn't answer me. You said we're going somewhere afterwards. Where?" she asks, a breathless little catch to her voice as she breaks off to greet Maya, who has come running up to hug her mother. "Hi, sweetheart. Mommy's just finishing up a call—"

My heart twists painfully as I picture Meena and Maya together. "Somewhere special," I reply. "You will like this."

. . .

We were in the Marigold Garden, our special place. The monsoon was late this year, and the air lay stifling around us, like the time I saw Goldie, Mahadev's cat, indifferently sprawled upon a dying mouse. The lush growth in the garden rots in the heat, the hibiscus a diluted pink. Winged flies burst in the harsh sun, their dying mouths still sticky with dreams of golden honey.

"I don't understand," Meena said, her brow knotted, an unfocused look in her glittering dark eyes. Her face broke my heart. *I* had done that to it. *Fool. Spineless wimp. You should have made her understand weeks—months—ago.*

"I want to give us something better," I said. "I *have* to be something better. For you."

"But can't you be something better here?" Her voice wobbled and emptiness exploded inside my chest.

"*No,*" I said forcefully. "I can't. Not here. I've told you this before."

"No, you haven't!" She shook her head. Her nostrils flared like those of an animal ringed by fire.

Her distress made me shiver despite the heat. "I have, you just never listened." My voice was harsher than I intended.

"I . . . You say a lot of things, Ramu. I love the things you say, but I didn't think you were serious, not about going away."

"I will never break this here," I said, my voice pleading, begging her to understand. "I will never be more than a *Dalit*. I need to go somewhere where I can make my world what it needs to be."

"Sounds good," she said weakly. "When do we leave?" She knew what my reply would be, it was obvious in the way she said it. That broke my heart just a little more.

"It just . . . It's not possible, Meena."

Her face darkened. Meena's face almost never does that. "*Tu chootiya. Chootiya.* Fuck you. Just go if you're too good for me."

She turned to storm away, and I started after her, reaching for her shoulder, but she slapped my hand away.

"Meena, I'll be back for you, I promise, *Ram Kasam*!" A sudden smell of jasmine pervaded the air, mingling with a lingering smell of decay.

Meena reached the door, and I noticed for the first time that Roopa was standing beside it, grinning. I waited for her to say something to Meena, but they ignored each other as Meena stormed past. Instead, Roopa looked smugly at me. I watched as Meena disappeared through the door, then finally acknowledged her presence with a glare.

"Trouble in *Dalit* paradise?" she enquired.

"Why are you still here?" I asked, not in the mood to put up with her *bakwas*, her brand of nonsense. "I thought you were off to marry...," my tone grows more sarcastic, "I mean *live with* your cousin."

Unlike Meena, Roopa's face never so much darkened as became murderous.

"Didn't want you, huh?" I taunted her, wagging my fingers in Roopa's face.

"Watch out, you filthy piece of shit!" she shouted. "I could have another word with Head Constable Chekavar."

Roopa was leaning against the wall, and I rushed at her until my face loomed only about six inches from hers. Her confident look vanished.

"I never thanked you . . . ," I said, one hand pointing toward my back, "for these."

Roopa's eyes darted to the door, assessing how quickly she could escape. It was hot and oppressive in the shadeless garden, and we stood blinking under the glaring sun.

"I mean it," I said menacingly. If I was scaring her, that made me glad. She deserved it. "You did me a favor, one you'll never, ever be able to understand."

The anger that had been simmering under the surface since Meena walked out of the door fired into a red-hot rage. My hands balled into tight fists and I held myself ramrod straight. "And even though you're a cruel, vicious, nasty person with a black heart, and you will never be happy, I'll find you and thank you one day."

"Is that a threat?" Roopa asked, pushing herself hard into the wall in her effort to be away from me. A bountiful bougainvillea vine, sunbaked and lush, clambered up one side of the high retaining wall.

I shook my head slowly from side to side, enjoying her confusion as much as her fear. There was a film of perspiration on her brow and upper lip and the clear afternoon sunlight reflected off her face like a beacon. "I know you don't get it, but you've influenced me, Roopa, almost as much as Meena has. Maybe more; who knows?" I was almost spitting at her. "But she's the one I'm going to miss."

I crossed to the door and opened it, then turned back to her. "Oh, and if you touch Meena when I'm gone, I will come back and kill you." I paused, lowering my voice to a hiss. I bunched my fist and shook it in her face. I moved back to the door. "*That* is a threat," I called back over my shoulder as I headed inside.

28
Ram

Fall 2014
San Francisco, California

"It's not the Ritz Carlton," I say, my brow knotted.

"I know, I know," Meena says enthusiastically. She pushes her long, loose curls back with both hands, the small, delicate features of her face lit up and excited as she looks around with mounting interest at the former-Victorian-converted-multi-level condominium that I am renting in downtown Oakland, on the northern side of Lake Merritt. "No offense to the Ritz Carlton, but that's what makes it so good."

The sitting-room windows open onto a balcony overlooking the lake and, exclaiming at the beauty of the afternoon, Meena steps out. The midday sun has just risen from behind the clouds, and the lake touched by its warm, soft rays shines radiant and glorified. Over the water, the sails of a small boat, taking off from the shore, flash and stir. Meena walks to the balcony's edge, leaning on the bronze railing and staring. I go stand behind her and lean forward, resting my hands on the railing on either side of her, her face next to mine, watching as a happy, laughing couple climb into the boat with a huge picnic hamper. We stay there, silent, spooned together against the railing as the boat shoots out into the broad belt of sunlight and disappears over the happy ripples of water.

"The whole flat would fit in just the lounge of my suite over there. In fact, I think I have cars that are bigger," I grumble.

"Oh, dear," Meena says, turning around to face me with an impish grin spread on her face. "Are you feeling a little cramped?" Her scent fills my lungs. Jasmine, starry skies, dark nights. Hot need cramps in my belly. Just her nearness sends my body into overdrive, but I try to hide my longing with small, meaningless commentary.

"Well . . ." I try to give a noncommittal shrug.

The delicate breeze drifting off the lake winds her hair in intriguing designs. "It's cozy," she points out.

I lower my head and say quietly in her ear, "And, close to your work."

She gives me a faint smile and walks back inside, disengaging the loose clasp of my arms. The entire place is laid out in an open floor plan and, at first glance, it looks almost empty. That was intentional and something I appreciated. I also appreciated the little conveniences that are hidden but spread throughout: the television that lowered down into a disappearing console; the stovetop that did the same; and the refrigerator, dishwasher, and other appliances that were camouflaged by wooden panels. Meena looks at the handcrafted crystal chandelier and traces her fingers along every wooden surface she passes. "I love it," Meena breathes.

My gaze is stuck on her fingers as I watch her caress the edges of a rough-hewn oak sideboard almost lovingly, and I imagine her doing the same to me. I ignore that image; instead, I look at her.

"Well, work means I'm going to be mostly in San Francisco for the next five or six months. If everything goes right, we're going to have a major new software house right in Silicon Valley." I stroke my nose slowly. "So, anyway, it makes sense to have a proper place."

Meena turns one final circle and stops when she faces me. She is wearing ankle-length jeans and a dusty pink, long-sleeved silk blouse with a boat neckline that emphasizes the clean lines of her beautiful neck and her delicate collarbones. She looks good enough to eat. "Would a 'proper place' have been a mansion somewhere had you not been trying to get close to the university?"

I grin and turn to look in a cupboard to see if there are any glasses to get us some water. An absurdly desperate desire to run my fingers over her perfectly curved shoulders has haunted me all night. "It might have been a little bigger. I was in a hurry to get somewhere close to you."

Meena pouts, though not very convincingly. "I feel guilty." She is wearing gold chain drop chandelier earrings with dark blue crystal beads that bring out the glowing richness of her skin.

I fold my arms over my chest and raise my eyebrows at her. "No, you don't."

Her coffee-brown eyes dance. She lifts both shoulders high enough to brush her earlobes. "You're right, I don't. You can slum it with the rest of us mere mortals."

My smile fades as I glance around the bare apartment. An ample wind blows from the east window to the north window, lazily puffing out the pale green chintz curtains of both windows. I will need to furnish it; although, between a new business venture and a mistress, I'm not quite sure when. "It's a palace, really."

Meena nods mutely, and the way she sucks in air tells me she understands.

"You know," I say with a grimace, "before Grace Mercy, I never had it as hard as you probably did. We always lived better than any other *Dalits* I knew. But it wasn't like I was blind—I could see how people lived and the places they lived in—especially once you got out of the city." My mouth twists at the memory of my hard bed at Grace Mercy. It was made with wooden planks and had no mattress on it. For years, I had slept on a teal colored blanket that was so old and frayed it had holes in it.

Words crowd my mouth like gravel. "I felt bad back then. I did. Nothing's changed though, has it? At least it's my own money now," I say with a bitter laugh, "but I'm still spoilt and pampered."

"I know you, Ramu Nand Nayak," Meena replies, coming to stand close to me and giving my hand a squeeze. "I'll bet your company does good things with its money."

My mouth twists. I cannot meet her eyes. "Not enough. And it's just money."

Meena looks up at me, her eyes wide, and I give a self-conscious laugh.

"That sounds terrible." I lean back against the black granite countertop, squinting down my nose. "I didn't mean it like that. We don't give enough as a company—I don't, as an individual." I lift my hands in a hapless gesture. "But it's not the money that's lacking; it's the time to figure out where to put that money. Money on its own helps, but it's like the thing with the finger and the dyke."

Meena stifles a giggle, coloring.

The sight of the blush dancing on her cheeks almost throws me off balance, but I continue. "Bad analogy. I mean, you can throw endless money at a problem, but if there's no thought or effort put into the application of that money, much of it gets wasted." I pause, a familiar weight pressing down on my chest. "Charity, helping those who need it, it's just like business in that respect. People, ideas, talent . . . These are the things that get results." The sunlight dances off the edges of the beveled chandelier, bathing the rich, mahogany walls of the flat in rainbows.

I lift a shoulder, gesticulating with my hands. "Money is like the gas in your car, Meena. Okay, you won't get to work without it, but the gas doesn't operate the vehicle, and it doesn't make the turns that get you where you need to go."

I stop, hearing the pontificating tone of my voice. Meena has a patient look in her eyes, like the looks she once gave a young boy called Ramu as he outlined his plans for world domination. I clear my throat against the embarrassment leapfrogging up my chest. In spite of my success, my wealth, and my material possessions, I feel less worthy of her adoration than that brave, beaten boy had been.

I avoid looking at her eyes. "I'm weak, you know." I say, focusing my gaze on the Versailles chandelier glittering in the bare flat. "I'll always forget myself, sooner or later. I'll forget the value of things and take living like a king for granted."

Meena reaches up on her tippy-toes and gently places a finger on my lips. "Don't, okay?" She scans the apartment. "This place will suit you just fine. It will suit *us* just fine." I groan in agreement and pull her into my arms.

. . .

Fall 2003
Kalanpur, Uttar Pradesh
The cheapest sleeper from Kalanpur to New Delhi was five hundred and eighty-five rupees, leaving me with less than three hundred rupees in my pocket.

Through the murky November morning, the auto-rickshaw bumped and weaved along Kalanpur streets. I sat on my hands to keep warm, speeding past figures draped in shawls huddled around small fires. Grace Mercy to Muzaffar Nagar, the railway station, a half-hour stretch of lurching over a dozen speed bumps, then navigating around the occasional roundabouts clogged with the day's traffic and the occasional contemplative cow. Meena, with a sullen look and a long face, sat next to me. I wanted to hold her hand in mine, but her disapproval settled over me like a sheet of steel. She was at least coming with me to see me off.

At the station it was noisy and chaotic—passengers and beggars and vendors selling samosas and sprouted lentils, patchwork handicrafts, softcover books and posters of smiling babies and snarling American wrestlers. The sun beat down on an empty line of carriages standing sullenly on one side. Coolies jostled and pushed passengers while precariously balancing *tachey* cases on their head. The railway platform overflowed with all kinds of people—withered men whose lips were stained redder than blood with betel juice, exhausted migrant women with glinting bangles and crying infants reclining against battered suitcases and bedrolls, Indian troops with handlebar mustaches curled up the side of their cheeks, and the little girl whose full-length skirt was smeared with dirt—but not enough to hide its vibrant mustard yellow.

Meena and I sipped tea in terracotta cups at Ajni Tea Stall, watching the sleeper roll in, its wagons creaking and clanging as though they were reluctant to come to a halt. It would take me all the way to Hazrat Nizamuddin station in the capital, a journey of about a day and a half from Kalanpur. Excitement revved my heart, and a tingly warmth rose in my chest, but I could not show it because Meena's eyes were dark and stormed with anger.

Looking at the map on the wall in Sister Gina's office the morning after my beating, I realized I had only ever traveled a little over a hundred miles from Kalanpur. New Delhi was more than fifteen hundred miles away, and the route the train would take was likely to be a lot further than that.

"Meena." I put my cup down and looked directly into her eyes. "Please try to understand. I have to do this. Everything I have learned at the orphanage . . ." I paused, studying her through squinted eyes, then continued. "Everything is now going to come down to this one meeting with Uncle. He has been very clever to make a successful business out of one of the dirty jobs *Dalits* are left to do. It still makes him a *Dalit*, though. The world around him is still the same. He lives in Delhi, so perhaps he is not as sneered at and excluded as he would be here, but he is still and always an Untouchable in a caste-based society."

I stopped. Meena was crying silently, her nose watering as much as her eyes. I pulled out a crumpled-up tissue from the back pocket of my jeans and handed it to her, then waited until she blew her nose.

"I'll come back for you, *jaan*. I promise." I pressed a palm to her right shoulder blade. She drew a shaky breath and wiped her cheeks. Finally, she nodded, her expression stoic. "I promise you," I cried urgently.

There were a hundred emotions milling around in my head, but I gave her a quick hug and boarded the train. People were packed into the second-class compartment like gunny bags. I found my sleeper compartment, taking the lower bunk so it would be easier to come and go as I pleased. As the train pulled away, I saw Meena waving. I waved back until she receded from view. My stomach felt as if it had an army of butterflies fighting for room. With a whoosh in my chest, I wondered yet again whether I was the sort of person who my uncle could respect.

A shrill whistle blew, the guard waved his flag; the engine gave out a puff—then another—and the train began to move. Soon the train was clear of the town, with fields of jute and sugarcane passing below me. The uncultivated fields without even grazing cattle gave me a sense of sorrow. One of those fields could belong to the orphanage; children could work the field, grow their own food maybe sell it at market. What a waste!

The train tore along through the day with a deafening roaring of wheels. We passed villages, which comprised clusters of mud-houses, closely packed together in the stink of cow dung and the haze of smoke thick enough to choke out a citywide infestation of flying insects. Near Aligarh Junction, an entire pack of wild dogs chased alongside the train, yelping and jumping back as they get too close. "Good job, boys," I shouted out to them. But I had too little food to throw them a scrap.

A middle-aged man, erect and narrow-shouldered with a round face, a black mustache and bushy eyebrows entered the compartment. He was wearing a grubby white *kurta* and white *dhoti*, powdered with dust. In one hand he carried a stainless-steel tiffin box, a red thermos in the other. I rose from the lower bunk and offered it to him.

"You're kind," the man said, "I don't think anyone would want to see me trying to get up there."

I chuckled politely and climbed to the top bunk, resuming my gaze out the window.

"You going to Delhi?" The man's voice, disembodied and tinny, floated up. The wind groaned outside the compartment, a low monotone. A spattering of rain peppered the compartment window.

"Yes," I replied. I leaned over the side of the bunk and peeked at him.

The tiffin box lay open on his lap and I could see that it contained two fat, brown *gulab jamuns*. The scent of the sweet balls soaked in sugary rosewater syrup and cardamom wafted up to me and made my mouth water with longing. The man shifted his gaze in my direction. "You're quite young to be making such a long ride on your own. I hope you don't mind me saying that?"

"Yes," I said, massaging my nose slowly. "I suppose I am."

"I'll bet there's a story there," the man said, looking up at me and smiling kindly. "I've got *gulab jamun* here, too much for one old man. But just the right amount for two men to share while one of them tells the other his story."

Gulab jamun. The memory of the last time I ate *gulab jamun*, sharing with the girl I would come to love, made me miss Meena terribly, and a lump forced itself into my throat. I pushed it back down and leaned over the side of the bunk, where the man offered his tiffin to me.

I looked at him then dove in, fishing out one with my forefinger and thumb. "Well, I could start with the last time I ate *gulab jamun*."

The man slurped enthusiastically as he threw the glossy dumpling into his mouth.

I told my story between mouthfuls of the *gulab jamun*, its sweet juice running down my chin. I spoke of the orphanage and Meena, of the policemen, and finally what I hoped to achieve from the trip.

As I finished dropping down to stretch my legs a little, the man nodded appreciatively. "I am lucky, it seems; I find you at an important point in your life, on an important trip." The man opened his thermos and offered a cup of steaming milky tea to me. I took the cup he offered and slurped appreciatively. The bunks were lit up, clear as the rainy gray twilight that filled the compartment.

"This is it," I agreed solemnly. "I will know much more about what my life could be in a couple of days' time."

The man sat back, looking satisfied. After a moment, he cocked his head towards me. "You know . . . I don't even know your name."

Before I could answer, the man held up his calloused hand. "Actually, you know what? I think that with all this change in your life, you can be anyone you want to be." He smiled, revealing teeth stained with betel nut. "What would you like me to call you?"

With a jolt, I suddenly knew I could not be 'Ramu' any longer. The boy with the dead parents, an orphan whom policemen feel free to hurt and humiliate.

I straightened my shoulders and took a deep breath. "Just call me Ram."

29
Ram

Fall 2003
New Delhi

Uncle Nihal was kind to my father and to our entire family. He had bought us a house and a car and had evidently given us some small 'allowance' each month. And yet, as I approached what has recently been renamed 'Nayak International' in the Rohini area of New Delhi, my fear of seeing him and speaking to him grew.

A quivering haze covered the evening sky. My auto-rickshaw driver eased his auto slowly forward, honking his horn as he swerved around people, bleating animals, pedal-rickshaws, more people and cars. He helpfully pointed out the housing complexes we passed on our right. "They are dubbed 'DDA flats,'" he told me, after the Delhi Development Authority, which built them. The flats with their acres of yellow stippled walls, their banks of mailboxes, their grassy courtyards with *neem* trees and children's swings contrasted vividly with the bustling industrial town of Nayak, which we were now entering.

Rohini was a relatively new sub-city in the northwest of New Delhi, and Nihal Nayak set up his factory early on. It had been a gamble—he had told me on his last visit to my home—with so little else there at the time, but the rent was cheap, making all the difference in the early days of the business. Now Rohini was one of the most important developing areas of the city, and my uncle's market expanded year after year.

Memories swelled in razor-sharp flashes of lucidity: how Uncle looked when he told me this, twirling the ends of his moustache and turning to wink at me as he sat under the shade of the *pipal* tree in my parents' modest backyard.

The capital city had been an experience for me. With my hand grasped firmly on my three hundred rupees as I disembarked at Hazrat Nizamuddin station, I moved among swirling currents of brown-skinned humanity, lights everywhere and the smell of Delhi—curry, stench from an open sewer, old grease and burning cow dung—in my nostrils. Old Delhi's narrow streets, swarmed with people, cows, bullocks, bullock carts and ancient buildings with sculpted stone lattices still visible behind jury-rigged aluminum siding. They co-existed with New Delhi's gleaming skyscrapers teeming with India's biggest contributors to global capitalism, apartment towers like fists raised triumphantly towards the gods, shopping malls as far as the eyes could see and endless traffic. And people, more people! The vibrant cacophony of smells, noises and clothing made my chest ache by the time the factory finally came into view.

The setting sun lit up the twenty-year-old gray cement building from behind, its fluorescent green and pink walls reaching into the leaden sky like a promise. I wiped sweat from my brow and found a shaded spot at Famous Tea Stall in which to sit, the cool air helping me clear my head. As I sat on a short-legged bench outside the stall, sipping tea from a squat, thick glass, I prepared my speech.

Remember, I thought to myself, *you are not Ramu, his nephew. You are Ram, and you have come to him with a business proposition. You are a product, and you must sell yourself to him.* There was no point in putting it off any longer. I gave a hard sigh and got up on my feet.

The absence of a gate or guard was a surprise, as was the fact that I could walk straight up to the factory and in through the open side of the building with no one asking who I was. The caustic air pinched and scratched the insides of my nose well before I even reached the huge vats of what I later learned were chromium sulfate.

Uncle Nihal had been a well-groomed man the two times I remember meeting him. He was clever and thoughtful, wearing cotton and *khadi* safari suits in summer colors of beige or cream when he visited us. To my mind, he looked like a suave but portly advertisement for Gwalior Suiting. But this was a dirty, smelly place—the air a throat-tightening mix of bad eggs, rotten meat, and acrid ammonia.

I passed by a thin, pockmarked-faced, bare-chested man slamming a long hook into a sheet of hide and dragging it into one of the giant cylinders. With a shock I realized that no matter how much money Uncle Nihal had made, with enough to buy his brother a car and send him money every month, being a *Dalit* was not just about poverty, being spat upon in the street or cleaning up other people's shit for less money that it took to feed a family. You still had to work in the shit. Even if your own hands were not the ones getting dirty, yours was still the smelly business, the business that no one else wanted to do.

I sucked in a monster breath, my abdominal muscles clenching as I remembered how clever I thought Uncle Nihal was to use his Untouchable status to find a way to make money. How I had straightened my spine and puffed out my chest with pride when I made myself the same promise: who I would become, how I would change the world around me to ensure I was not still the stinking rear-end of society. I didn't feel so sure anymore.

As I hurried all the way through the huge tannery which was the size of a tennis court, I got a few stares of *are you sure you're in the right place?* from men tending the enormous wooden drums where the hides tumbled in a blue bath of chemicals. The blue chemicals spilled and splattered all over the floors and the walls and the people who worked with it. I came into a smaller storage shed where animal hides, partly cured, were being cut and treated, and I saw skinny boys feeding skins at high speed into a big press. They wore shorts and flip-flops, and looked like young teenagers. I averted my eyes from them and bit down on my tongue.

Three small container-type buildings made of corrugated steel were stacked in one corner of the storage shed. Another set of wooden steps led up to the top container—the only one sporting windows. My uncle's face peered down at me, and a few moments later he rushed down the steps to meet me.

"Ramu, my boy," he said, opening his arms in greeting, "I had no word that you were coming." He looked older, his face gaunter than before and bearded, but when he spoke, his voice was still the same as years ago—the brown-sugar voice I held onto in my dreams throughout Grace Mercy and throughout the making of the young man I was now.

"I wanted to surprise you, Uncle." I allowed him to fold me into his arms. I noticed his eyes had gone wet. "And it's Ram now."

"Ram . . ." Nihal repeated, looking amused. "Well, you've surprised me. How has it been at . . . ?"

I jutted my chin at him. "Grace Mercy."

He gave me a pleasant nod. "Yes, yes. How has it been at Grace Mercy? Have they taught you well?" Two of the young boys staggered past, carrying an open barrel between them. It must have contained fifty liters and was labeled 'Formic Acid.'

I shoved my fists into the pockets of my trousers, trying to stop myself from squirming. "Yes, the nuns have done their very best with us." The scars on my back began to itch. Perhaps it was the chemicals in the air, seeping through my sweat-soaked shirt.

"Good, good." He stood in front of me and held up his hands. "I'm sorry I haven't been down to see you, like I intended." His voice turned gruff. "*Dhanda*, the business has been good here. But, whether business is good or bad, my presence it still needed . . . only for different reasons." Nihal turned around and shouted to one of the boys, "Moti, go bring us some chai from the stall."

My heart beat erratically, as though I were still that naïve boy in my parents' backyard, balanced on the threshold of adulthood, looking at my uncle with admiring eyes. My foolish heart—it was as though the world had not taught me a hundred bitter lessons since then. "That's okay, Uncle. I understand." A feeling of resentment slowly swirled in my stomach. God, how prickly my back felt, the skin stretched too tightly between my shoulder blades. One hand almost reached round to see if I could scratch it, but I forced myself to stop.

One of Nihal's bushy eyebrows rose up his forehead. "Well, if you're here for that job interview I mentioned—"

"Not quite, Uncle. You told me to wait until I was eighteen, but I'm not there yet." I squared my shoulders.

Nihal cocked his head and continued pleasantly, "Well, seeing as you've come all this way, there is no point in being difficult over just a few months. You've made your way here across most of the country; I think that should be enough to get you through the door." He took a step back and threw up a hand to indicate the steps leading to his office.

A quiet rage simmered within me as I stood before him. I was struggling to hold it in check as I said quietly, "I didn't come for a job, Uncle. I came with a proposal."

After a moment of shock, Uncle Nihal's amused grin returned. "Okay, young Ramu." His eyes softened. "I mean . . . *Ram*. Let's hear it." His voice was indulgent, as if he humored me.

I could feel a muscle jumping nervously in my cheek. "I want you to help me get a scholarship to a university in America."

Several workers in the storage shed glanced over at Nihal's loud, deep-throated laugh. "I wouldn't do that for my own children; what makes you think I'll do it for you?"

I pressed my fingertips into my temples and fell still for a long moment. Then I forced myself to go on. "Because you would be paying for your children to go. You're not paying for me. Any money you spend on my education will be a loan. You'll get it back, with interest. A lot of interest." I was happy that my voice sounded confident and clear.

Nihal's eyes narrowed. "It sounds risky to me." His gaze did not let mine go, but his dark brows dipped in a sharp V. "Giving loans isn't really my business. What makes you think you can get into an American university, let alone make the money to pay me back?" He handed me one of the two glasses of tea that Moti had brought into the shed.

The scars on my back were aflame, but I ignored them. I gulped at my tea, but the hot liquid only fanned the flames in my belly. "Because Grace Mercy did exactly what you said it would, Uncle."

Nihal studied me, his gaze crawling up my face.

"It made a man of me." I cast an involuntary glance around at the storage shed. There was a closeness in the air, a threat of the long, stifling working hours. "A man who wants more than life is going to offer him."

Nihal's little bear-like eyes perked up. "What sort of interest are we talking?"

I gave him a hard look. "I will pay back every rupee you invest in me four times over, within ten years of the start of my degree."

"Or . . . ?"

My brain was like stone—my tongue, too. I tried desperately to think. "Five percent of everything I earn after leaving university, payable to yourself and all who come after you. Until my death."

Nihal held my gaze, seeming to search for something in my eyes. I didn't flinch or look away. One day, I would look back on this moment, feeling like it all hinged on holding his gaze.

My uncle broke into a great big grin, revealing teeth as cracked as they were yellow.

"I like the way you think, Ram."

30
Ram

Winter 2014
San Francisco, California

"He bought her a puppy." The afternoon sun paints the walls of my apartment a gentle gold.

"What?" I ask. I turn on my side to look at her. My gaze roams over the planes and angles of Meena's face and her slightly guarded expression.

"Bhavesh," Meena replies, her forehead creased. "He bought Maya a puppy."

"Oh," I say, unable to think of a better reply. Meena's mind has been somewhere else today—I wonder if it is about the puppy. She is lying naked and glorious on the bed before me, her hair spilling like black water over her bare breasts. This moment should be amazing, as so many moments have been since I found her again. She had a half-day at work but kept it from Bhavesh, so we now have all afternoon together. But . . . I take a calming breath, but it doesn't work.

We made love, and though she moved and moaned, I could feel her distraction like a bad feeling in my stomach. I press my fingers to my eyes and rub. Usually when I make love to Meena, the sheer force of emotion that comes with it drives the passion—the animal side of love-making—to new heights, rather than obliterating it, like it always had with other women. With other girlfriends, I could not wait for them to leave after having sex, but with Meena, I am always checking to see that she is still tucked into my side.

But today my one-sided passion feels sordid. I swallow hard. There is nothing I can say that won't sound paranoid or self-obsessed. So, even though my eyes are burning and my brain blurry, I have kept quiet, hoping for the feeling of wrongness to go away.

Meena turns around to look at me in the eyes. "He feels it, I think. Something wrong."

"You think?" It is a nothing answer. I keep my face carefully blank.

Meena's expression becomes frustrated. Her gaze skitters away from mine. "We had sex last night."

"Was it good?" I blurt, stung. The thought of Bhavesh touching her makes my stomach clench, like there's a rock lodged at the very bottom.

"No," she answers matter-of-factly, tucking a stray curl behind her ear, "though he was more tender than usual."

Meena rises, puts on a silk robe I bought for her, and heads out into the lounge. I find a pair of trunks and put them on before following her into the open-plan lounge and kitchen. I had remembered to pull the blinds and darken the room before Meena had arrived, but a stray ray of sunlight breaks through a gap in the blinds and pokes me in the eye.

I find her coolly drinking a glass of water by the sink. I try to take her emotional pulse, but her face is hidden by a cascading mass of curls. *I could lose her.* The possibility hits me square in the belly, churning to acid in my gut.

"What's the matter?" I ask. I yank the cord, and the blinds snap open, flooding the room with light.

She pushes her mass of curls back with both hands. "The same things that have been the matter for the last few months," she says. She glances over, but only long enough to dip her chin. "I just haven't said it."

"I thought . . ." I close my eyes, inhaling her familiar scent, "things were good."

"They are good, Ramu," she answers evenly. "But they are just this." She waves a hand and her gesture seems to take in the still-bare apartment, the impermanence of our relationship.

Anger rises inside me, silent and swift. "Then leave him," I say shortly.

She rinses out her glass as if she didn't hear me. Frustration burns across my chest and spreads outwards. I can no longer bite down on my impatience. "I mean it, Meena."

I follow her into the lounge area where she stands back from the window, peering down into the small alley, tucked away from the busy streets of downtown Oakland and filled with shops selling antiquarian books and faded theater posters.

"I know we haven't talked about this, *jaan*," I continue, my voice gaining strength, "but I know how I feel. My feelings are as strong as they have always been. It just depends on you."

She turns around. Her head whips up, her eyes blowing wide. "On me? You—you—*asshole!*" Her voice is shaky. "This is all so easy for you."

"Easy? Seeing you go home to him every day?" I sputter for a few seconds before my anger catches wind. "How is that easy, especially when you're telling me about how he fucked you?" I pound my fist on the oak sideboard, rattling the crystal decanter lying on the wooden surface. I feel my face turning red with anger.

"And you think I want that?" she yells back. "To be fucked by him? How like a man to be jealous, rather than to pity me for all the times I must lie there and do my duty to my husband." She shakes her head sadly. The afternoon sun shines through the windows like the flame at the back of a vast baker's oven. "You're a better man than him, Ramu, but not by as much as you think."

The words travel down me like a lightning bolt, pinning my bare feet to the hardwood floor. Her voice softens. "You don't have children; you can't understand."

I fold my arms over my chest, feeling cold despite the inside temperature. "Then take Maya," I say forcefully, after a long pause. I clench my fisted hands to my side.

Meena lifts her shoulders up to her ears. "*Tum nahi samajh saktey.* You don't understand," she says, both her words and tone careful.

I walk up behind Meena, who has turned to look out of the window again. My hand comes up but falls short of the shoulder I want to place it upon.

"Why did you leave?" she asks, her voice hollow, still facing the street.

"Sorry?" I lift a shoulder as if to ask, *What do you mean?*

"Why did you leave me at Grace Mercy?" she says, her expression serious but stony.

Guilt nips at my insides. I lift my hands in a helpless gesture. "I asked you to wait for me."

She whips around, her accusing gaze lasering in on mine. "You knew I wouldn't be able to, not if the chance came." Except for the distant sound of a car honking on a nearby city street and the periodic sounds from the vintage fridge, it is very quiet. I can hear the thud of my heart racing.

"I thought you believed in me." I hang my head.

Her frown deepens, and her eyes flash with something I recognize as despair. "I was a teenaged *Dalit* orphan who was likely to starve to death if I didn't find a decent marriage. Obviously, you don't remember how it felt to scarf down a *roti* with a, a . . . a pickle and feel relief there's something lining your stomach, but I do." Her voice is shaking with anger. She crosses her arms over her chest, her hands fisted so tight her knuckles turn white. She draws a shaky breath and continues, painfully exhaling, "I was *eighteen* when Bhavesh and I married, Ramu. It was a miracle a *Kshatriya* even wanted me, let alone at that age. Without a dowry, I would have been lucky to have found even a *Dalit* who would marry me."

I scrub a hand down my face, noting abstractedly that my anger has dissipated, morphing into sorrow. Her voice cracking, she says, "Bhavesh essentially paid my dowry by gifting it to my aunt and uncle, and he has often reminded me of how not all of the money found its way back to him again." Meena's voice trembles on the edge of anguish. "As far as he is concerned, I am still paying off their debt."

A surge of sadness for what might have been jabs me in the center of the chest. I want to take her into my arms. I want to say, *I'm sorry, please forgive me*, over and over again. But her face is walled off. "But I was going to come back for you," I say instead, "I promised I would."

Meena's eyes are huge and damp as she turns to me, her voice low. "So why did you marry?"

. . .

May 2005
New York

My choice of course at NYU was arrogant. Correct, but arrogant. Uncle Nihal had wanted me to do business, or possibly accounting; then, trying to meet me halfway, business technology. But I wanted to know everything I could about computers.

"Uncle," I argued, "computers are the business of the future. The more you know about a computer, the less you need to know about business."

Of course, Nihal would always bring out the "Whose money is paying for this, anyway?" to which I would reply, "Ultimately, mine." And, as furious as Nihal would seem—as much as I am sure he would like to slap his self-assured, smug, know-it-all little brat nephew—to him, I was a thoroughbred horse, a secret stallion that no one else knew about.

"And anyway, Uncle," I said obsequiously, folding my hands in deference, "you can teach me all that you know before I go."

Nihal's eyes glittered, and he puffed out a laugh devoid of humor, one that said, *I'm on to you, Son.*

Before he could say anything else, I rushed to speak. "The rest I will learn from books when I am there. And experience."

Nihal pressed his lips together and smiled upon me with unusual affection. I felt relief loosening the muscles knotted across my shoulders. I knew he was thinking ahead to the way he would sit years from now, in the purple Delhi twilight, speaking of it all to his sons—and their sons as well. There would be a look of wonder on the youthful faces as he told the story of how he had discovered an up-and-coming computer genius.

Halfway through my spring break at NYU, I sent a letter to Sister Gina enclosing a small donation with news of my good fortune and achievements and asking if Meena could write back to me. I had not meant to put it off that long, but it had taken me more time to settle into a new life in America than I had anticipated. I had answered a dozen Help Wanted signs, but no one wanted to hire a brown, scrawny kid who spoke broken English, until a turbaned Sikh manager at a fast-food restaurant took pity on me. As soon as I got my first month's wages, I was able to move out of my bed at night—a bench at Central Park—and then begin the hunt for cheap college housing. And so, weeks had turned to months, until finally I wrote the letter asking about Meena.

Her reply arrived as I worked hard frying burgers at Wendy's. "Uncle Nihal, see how I am like you, yes?" I had said on one of my few phone calls home. "I am using my lowly position in society—as a student—to make money from the sacred cow in a way that few other people want to. Right?" I had laughed uproariously, enjoying my own wit, but somehow, Nihal had not been amused.

I was running late the morning I received Sister Gina's reply, so I could not read it until I was on my lunch break at work. Halfway through my workday, I could not bear it anymore. I said I had to use the restroom. In the poorly lit men's restroom reeking of industrial-strength cleaner mixed with the stench of urine, I tore open the envelope with shaking fingers.

Ramu, it is wonderful to hear from you. You were always one of our best and brightest students, and it fills my heart with the warmest feeling to think of you in America, studying to do great things. We are so proud of you here.

Thank you so much for your donation. It is much needed and very appreciated. The mother superior passed away during the winter, I am very sad to say. I am the acting mother superior, for now. Although things have been more difficult for us here, we are still going. Yet sometimes we must turn orphans away, as much as it breaks our hearts to do so. The generosity of the community is not what it once was, and a charity which provided our school supplies has turned its attention elsewhere. There have been weeks when we nuns must go hungry so the children may eat. Yet we acknowledge we must feed ourselves, for if we are not here, who will the children have?

With things as they are, we must encourage children to leave and find their way sooner than we once did. With this in mind, I will give you news of Meena, whom I know you asked about. Meena had stayed with us much longer than most, and when she turned eighteen, I had been considering whether we might find a place for her among the nuns here, especially following the death of the mother superior. Fairly or otherwise, I have always favored you two Untouchable children more than many of the others because life has been hard on you in more ways than one.

However, before I could make my decision, Meena was offered the hand in marriage of a Kshatriya man, an offer she accepted, as I'm sure you understand any orphan girl would, especially one of such age and status. I urge you to consider that God has willed it this way. He has smiled on her, and perhaps he has smiled on you in removing a distraction, however lovely, from your path.

Now is your time, Ramu. Please write us again. You will be an inspiration to everyone here.

Acting Mother Superior, Gina.

31
Ram

May 2005
New York

"I have never dunk . . . I mean, *drunk* a-alcohol before, did you know that?"

"Well," the pretty woman said, "seeing as we met about twenty minutes ago, there are probably many things I don't know about you, Ram."

"Thash not really my name." I shook my head at her solemnly.

"You lied to me about your name?" She narrowed her eyes.

"No, not . . ." I realized that the sentence ahead of me had too many difficult words and concepts in it, so I scrapped it and went for another one. "My name ish Ramu."

"Well, that's close enough."

I suddenly thrust a finger skyward. "And yet, a whole other pershun." I may have attracted the attention of some of the other drinkers in the bar.

"So, who is this other person?" She leaned forward, suddenly more interested.

I thought for a moment. "Which one?"

"Let's go for Ramu. Who's Ramu?"

"He's . . ." I stopped. Even through the alcoholic haze that currently threatened to lay me low on the bar's very comfortable—*inviting,*

THE AWAKENING OF MEENA RAWAT

magnetic—black leather sofa, a part of me wanted to hide the shame of my past. But the world began to swim again, and it was either keep talking or give in to the swirling darkness. "He's an orphan. A lowly *Dalit*. The s-son of a street shweeper, with no 'proshpects,' ash you Americans call them. He's a loser . . . b-born into a world of losers."

"Wow," the woman said. "That's tough." Boy, she was pretty, even seen by the dim light in the bar. "And who is Ram?"

"Turns out, he'sh a bit of loser, too." I cleared my throat, rubbing my nose slowly.

She laughed at that. It felt good to make her laugh. "Bad day?"

"Bad day," I agreed. I folded my arms across my chest and tried to hold her gaze.

She looked me up and down. I was still wearing my uniform from the burger place, minus the cap with the little cow on it. "Well, if you lost your job," she said, "no offense, but I think you can do better."

I look down at my uniform for a moment, then at her. The stupid look on my face was replaced with a big, wide grin—I think.

"Thanksh," I say. And that was the last thing about the night I could remember.

· · ·

"It broke my heart, Meena, when I found out that I could no longer have you." I stand stiff and twitchy behind Meena, my fingers clenched into fists by my side. It is close to five and the T.V. glare in the living rooms of other apartments shows against the blue drift of dusk. "I was doing it all for you."

Meena steps closer to the window. Anyone looking up would see her there, above a small antique store. "Not true," she says, as if she does not care anymore. Meena passes a hand over her mouth and shakes her head hard, back and forth like a dog playing with a rag toy. "You were ambitious when I met you, Ram. And, either way, I would have happily remained a poor *Dalit* to be with you." I wince inwardly as I see how her face is locked down like a vault.

"That's easy to say now, Meena, but you know how it was." Guilt compresses me like a vice. I swallow down a sigh. "You know what they did to me. What would our lives have been like after the orphanage? Would you have wanted our children to grow up there, the way things were?"

"Children . . . ?" she whispers, her longing so obvious it is written in the air. "We could have gone to Delhi together," she continues with a wobble in her voice, "and found jobs with your uncle."

The impulse to convince her it was all for her rises inside me like a wave of tsunami, and I bite down on my tongue to hold the wave inside. I rake shaky fingers through my hair.

And yet, now that she says it, I wonder if I *had* used my love for her to drive my own ambition just like she thinks. Had I?

.   .   .

The world existed somewhere between my pillow and about half an inch above my pillow; that's as far as my head wanted to go, even when an unexpected female voice sounded from the other side of the room.

"Was that really the first time you ever drank anything?" she asked.

I tried to move my head, but I could only see a pair of jeans. "Yeah," I said.

"I'm not sure whether to say 'congratulations' or not." I heard a chuckle in her voice.

"What . . . ? Did . . . ?"

"Two very good one-word questions," she replied. "The answer to the first one is 'I took you home, because I couldn't have handled the guilt if you were found floating in the Hudson this morning.' And the second is, 'Ha, ha, ha, don't flatter yourself. And you really weren't in any state, anyway,' even if I had wanted to take advantage of you."

"How did you . . . ?" Bright sunlight plunged like tiny knives into my bleary eyes.

"I'm a student at NYU, too, dumb-ass. It just involved occasionally slapping you and getting you to point the way. I slept the night on the floor because . . . Well, I might have had a few drinks myself, and my dorm felt a long way away last night." She came over and crouched beside me. "I'm Jane, by the way."

"Thanks, Jane," I managed in reply.

She was a little plainer than I remembered, her pale skin almost luminescent in the morning light, and the hair I had thought brown was instead tinged nearly red. But then she smiled, and that smile matched her confident, honest tone perfectly. "You're welcome, Ram."

She dug into her pocket and pulled out a packet of what looked like boiled sweets. Taking one for herself, she also offered one to me. I eyed the thing warily. Food of any sort was not high on my stomach's list of priorities.

"It's okay," Jane said. "It's an herbal hangover sweet." I think my expression must have remained doubtful; maybe it was the very American way she omitted the 'h' in 'herbal' when describing what she was offering me. "I swear by them, honest. If you're not spitting it out and vomiting within the first ten seconds, then you're going to feel like a new man in twenty minutes."

I reached out a hand. "Good sales pitch."

"Well, I am a business major," she said, handing me the sweet. "And this," she held up the packet of sweets, "is going to make me my fortune."

Too late, I had already put it in my mouth. "Sho, you mate it orshelf, then?" I asked around the sweet.

Jane stood up and crossed to the sink. "That's just how you were talking last night."

I rolled over onto my back and stretched. I *did* feel a little better already, though I suspected that had more to do with conversation and concentration than the sweet that had been in my mouth for ten seconds. Still, at least I had passed the 'vomit point.' "Don't remind me."

Jane filled a glass with water. "There's no shame in letting go a little, Ram." She took a drink, then brought it over to me. I sat up in bed a little as I took it.

"I can't allow myself to let go," I said.

"Why not?"

I waved a hand, indicating the room—my life here in New York, which was a luxury even compared to the better parts of my life in India. "All of this, it's too important." I put a hand to my forehead, rubbing the soreness there. "I dread to think how much money I wasted last night."

Jane sat down on the end of my bed. "From what I saw, Ram, not too much. Your tolerance for alcohol isn't there yet."

I gave her a sarcastic smile, but conceded that one to her. I liked this girl and the familiar way she spoke to me, yet the reason for my turning to alcohol last night was coming back into my befuddled head, causing even more pain than the hangover. I closed my eyes, and the memories slammed into me: Grace Mercy with its yellow plaster fallen away to chunks, its roof crusted with mossy growths and a girl who smelled of night-blooming jasmine waving to me in the blazing heat of a railway station.

"College is important for everyone here, Ram," Jane continued. "We're all sacrificing to be here."

"You don't understand," I said. "Where I'm from—"

"I hate that," she interrupted.

I looked at her. "What?"

"I hate people telling me I don't understand, or that my experiences or opinions are worth less because I had an easier upbringing than them." Her face took on an animated look. "You said last night that you were an orphan. And a *Dalit*—which I looked up on your computer just now, hope you don't mind. And, for the record, you look really touchable to me. But, you know what, you didn't choose any of that, just like I didn't choose my upbringing, even if life seems to have dealt me a better hand than it did you. What matters is what I do going forward, because there's not one second of my past that I can change."

. . .

"I can't change that now, Meena. Just like you can't change your marriage or your child. We only have where we are now and the chance fate has given us."

"But sometimes what fate gives us are responsibilities, Ramu." She spears me with a hard gaze, and her mouth settles into a thin line. "Things we can't walk away from. You must get that, like the way you talked about your company and its employees. Well, a child is just one person, but they are also everything." A shrieking comes from a few houses down—children playing in a yard somewhere.

She waves her hands agitatedly, her voice rising. "I couldn't just take Maya from Bhavesh, because if there is one thing I can say about that man, it's that he loves his daughter." Her voice tips into a light yell and her body shakes with what I know is frustration. "She loves him, and she is happy with him."

I step closer to her, resting a supportive hand on her shoulder. "But she loves you, too."

Meena closes her eyes. "Her happiness is more important than mine in every way," she says slowly, as if she's speaking to a child. "More important than ours. And, when I think about these last few months and what I have done—whether or not Maya knows it—then Bhavesh has been a better father to her than I have been a mother." Meena swallows and doubt pushes across her face like a shadow. Outside the windows, the dusk is already deepening into a glowing blue.

Fury fires in my throat, grips me by the gut and overshadows every thought. "So, when Bhavesh forced himself on you, was he being a good father then?" The question comes out in an angry hiss.

Meena shoots me a murderous look. My cheeks burn. No, it wasn't a fair thing to have thrown back at her. She steps away from the window, turning to me with arms defensively crossed in front of her chest. She lets herself fall against the wall, shoulders hitting it with enough force to make her wince.

"All I can see in our future is my daughter getting hurt—that's all I can see in it." Meena speaks into the shadowed silence of the room. "I love being with you, Ramu, but some day we will have to face up to what all of this means." I can see she is blinking back tears. "Things never stay still forever."

My breath catches at the tone of finality in her voice. "Change is the only universal truth," I murmur.

"What?" The sadness in her dark brown eyes is a wave I could drown in.

Outside the window we watch two hawks swoop and skydive against the blue sky. "Someone I used to know said that." I give a small mirthless laugh. "It was one of her favorite sayings. It's a saying, isn't it . . . ? 'The only things that are certain are death and taxes.' But she would say that was bullshit, that the only certain thing was change, and that everything in the universe is always changing, from a microscopic level up to the movement of galaxies."

Meena gives a brief smile then, unexpectedly. "It was your wife who said that, wasn't it?" Her smile is like watching the sun burst through clouds on a rainy day in Kalanpur.

"Yes," I reply wryly.

"Clever woman." Meena tightens the belt on the black silk robe. "I guess she must have been if she was at NYU." If there is jealousy there, she keeps it from her tone. "But I would add that, just like the stars and the planets and the galaxies, things have a habit of coming back around again." Meena walks over to me, puts a hand up to my face and strokes it. I pull her fingers to my lips.

"And, if we're not looking, they smack us right in the back of the head," I say sadly.

She lifts a shoulder. "Yes, sounds right. I know we can't change the past, Ramu, but it's still there." I can see she is chewing her lip. "After all, it made today."

I kiss her hand. "Sometimes, I think it would be nice to just pick one moment and stay in that moment forever."

"Maybe," Meena says after a few moments when all that can be heard is the hum of the fridge and the thrum of traffic in the distance, "that is what the afterlife is like."

32
Ram

Winter 2015
Oakland, California

"Would you like another cup of coffee while you're waiting?" calls a bored voice above me.

I look up from the Purchase Agreement I'm reviewing on my laptop to a tall waitress in a red T-shirt who had seated me on a street-side table for two, while simultaneously tossing down a laminated menu. I check the smartphone watch on my wrist and tap the face twice with my finger.

12:32 p.m.

Damn. Meena is thirty minutes late. She's never late. I peer down at the remains of the coffee in my cup.

"Sir?" The waitress persists with a peevish look on her face that makes no pretense of trying to be friendly. With her blonde hair in a tight, high ponytail, she looks like she's a cheerleader moonlighting as an adult.

"Yes." I nod distractedly. "Could you bring me another cup please with cream and sugar?" I keep my voice pleasant.

"How about if I just bring a pot?" She arches an eyebrow at me and gives the table a quick wipe.

"That's fine." I slip off my glasses and squeeze my nose worriedly. Federico's is overflowing with the noisy lunch crowd, which started arriving fifteen minutes ago. It has been thirty-five minutes and Meena still has not called, has not texted, has not anything. Is she all right? Worried thoughts are buzzing in my brain. Is everything okay with Maya?

I reach for my phone, frowning at the empty screen as a gust of wind sends a few dry leaves spinning around my feet. Pulling up the number for the cellphone I gave Meena, I try again, hoping she will pick up this time.

My muscles wind tightly as the tone rings and rings. The auto-recording kicks in once again: "You have reached 510-226-5555." I wait for the beep, putting several spoons of sugar in my second cup of coffee.

The restaurant is located on a tiny street, a mix of local and tourist shops, a block south of the Marina. It is a gorgeous afternoon, the sun high enough to sit on the roofs of the adjoining buildings like a great open fire warming everything.

As soon as I hang up, my phone shrieks. Ah, finally . . . Meena. My relief is a slow build, wrapping me in warmth like Meena's sleeping body did two evenings ago in my condo. It settles over me like sunshine on naked skin.

But it is my administrative assistant. I groan as I reluctantly take the call.

"Tell Doug we need it . . . He's got to make it happen . . . It's got to be that one, Felicity . . . Alright, give him another thirty-percent to play with, but that's his lot . . . I'll be the judge of what constitutes a 'Money Pit' . . . Look, I gotta go, I'll check back later. Yeah, have some good news for me, okay?"

I brush my fingers through my hair in irritation as I scan the café and the street outside for Meena. I finish the call just as a heavy-set woman approaches my table, seeming vaguely familiar. She is easily five-ten, with blue eyes hidden under thick, blond eyebrows and a leathery, suntanned face crowded with freckles that are dimmed under a layer of makeup. Her mane of frizzy blond hair is cut short and the baggy black pantsuit she wears looks like it comes from a thrift store. "Tammy?" I say rising to my feet to greet her, suddenly remembering who she is from the Vice-Chancellor's dinner, which now seems like a lifetime ago. I hide my stab of uneasiness with a cheerful wave.

"Ram Nayak, Fortune 500 CEO," she replies with a drawl.

Embarrassed, I give a small laugh, trying not to be irritated. "Ram will do." I look at her expectantly, but she gives me a long, watchful look, saying nothing.

I break the silence and pull out the chair opposite mine. "I'm due to meet Meena here any moment," I say, my tone formal, "if you would like to join us?"

Tammy hesitates, wringing her pudgy hands together. "That's why I'm here. Um . . . " She clears her throat. "She's not coming."

"Not coming?" I scowl in puzzlement.

"Her husband turned up to take her to lunch." She emphasizes "husband" with a look of disdain on her face.

"Bhavesh?" My voice tightens before I speak.

"Meena texted as if we were meeting for lunch." Tammy holds up her phone and I notice her chipped nail polish, a five-and-dime shade of light brown.

I scan it quickly, stiffening as I read the words.

Hey, honey. Can't make our lunch at Federico's as Bhavesh has surprised me, which is nice of him. We'll do it next week, instead.

As I stare at the words, my mouth dry, Tammy continues in a faltering voice, "It's just that Meena and I weren't planning to have lunch at Federico's today, so I knew the message was off." She smiles wryly, showing a smudge of pink lipstick on her teeth. "Although we still manage to have lunch together occasionally, I'm lucky if it is now once a fortnight." Her voice trails off and she gives me a lopsided grin, like she has lemon in her mouth.

Her face flashes pity as I take a deep breath and pass her phone back to her.

I clear my throat, trying to regain my composure. I arrange my features into an expression of polite interest, even though I want Tammy to leave so that I can strategize what to do next. "Thank you for coming; you're a good friend to her."

She ignores my obvious attempt to be alone and plops down on the chair. "Maybe it's not my business, but where do you see this all going?" She watches me with a guarded expression.

Shocked, I look off to a space above her head and hold on to my pleasant façade. "It's . . . complicated."

Tammy snorts at my textbook evasive reply. Her expression seems to say, *Honestly, it's like I'm dealing with a couple of kids here.* She raises her eyebrows at me.

"It probably wasn't any less complicated a few months ago, and I doubt it'll be better in six months' time. But her husband will find out, if he hasn't already." There's a long pause, then she says curtly, "You kinda need to figure out an answer to that question." She has gone bright pink but for the white area around her flaring nostrils, which stands out like a rash.

I automatically stand as Tammy rises to her feet. She gives me a blinding grin, then steps around the table and stands on tiptoe to plant a kiss on my cheek. I grin back in shock.

"Just checking one off the bucket list," she says with a wink, miming a check in the air. "Kiss a millionaire . . . Check!"

She takes a few steps, then stops and turns back. "And, a bit of 'Affairs 101' for you. I wouldn't stay here long. If Bhavesh has seen her phone, he might find a way to swing by."

33
Bhavesh

Winter 2015
Fremont, California

> *Recipient's name:* Sarla Devi Rawat
> *Amount of money order:* $500
> *Address of recipient:* Plot No. 15, Khairabad, Sitapur District, Uttar Pradesh

I might not have thought too much about a restaurant receipt in Meena's coat pocket, except to think the stupid woman needed to stop spoiling herself all the time. You do not see me going out to a restaurant or café for lunch every day. It is an event if I even manage to grab a sandwich.

Sometimes I swear that woman thinks she is better than she is, like she really belongs among those professionals, those 'ladies-who-do-lunch.' Well, she is wrong about that, in more ways than one.

Maybe because I am stuck at the bank, filling out this new demand draft form for the money I send to my mother twice a month—I should change banks again, it would serve them right, the stupid tellers that are here—but suddenly, *Amma* pops into my head. It is as *Amma* says: Meena should just stay at home and behave like a proper wife.

The university job seemed like a good idea at first, to have the extra income. My imports could go up and down a little and suffer some seasonal differences, but now we were too used to extra money that we did not really need.

And what if they promoted her or extended the contract again? I would have a fight on my hands to get her to quit then. I should not even have to be thinking this way, but that was America for you. Too soft with its women. So many women with the sort of attitude that would not be tolerated back home. Still, this is what happens when you move to another country; you must accept their ways, even the ones that make no sense.

And America *has* been good to us, but still, you must not forget who you are or where you come from. My wife sometimes needs reminding of that. Of who we are, who *she* is. Sometimes I wonder how different things might have been if I had listened to my mother, if I had gone with her head, rather than my heart.

. . .

February 2005
Sitapur, Uttar Pradesh
I approach the address where they are waiting for me, accompanied by some brother of my friend who has arranged this—or maybe cousin, or uncle; I don't know or care. The whole thing is dumb, really, just a picture. As *Amma* says, pictures can fool a man, especially if a man is a fool.

It had all started only as a way to spite my mother. "There is a suitable *Kshatriya* girl in the neighboring town whom I have decided you will marry," *Amma* had said over dinner, casually deciding my fate as she was deciding what *sabzi* to cook for dinner that night.

When I had asked to see her photograph, *Amma* had held out a hand, cutting off my half-formed protests, saying instead, "*Bas*, Bhavesh, I have decided. The girl is suitable and they are giving a sizable dowry." *Amma* is determined to control every part of her son's life. Her *only* son's life. Which, of course, is at the heart of the problem.

Maybe things would have been different if I had not been left fatherless at nine years old. My father, Mohan, died of a heart attack, and by the way she spoke of him afterwards, *Amma* thought this extremely lazy of him. "*Hai Bhagwan*! Your good-for-nothing-father," she would go on and on to me and my brother, her chest heaving, her face flushed, "always drinking and staying out late! I told him not to. Of course he was going to have a heart attack." I privately thought that my poor suffering father's heart had reached its nag limit, but at *Amma*'s outburst, I would bite my lip and look down.

As a young boy, I sometimes thought there needed to be a god of overbearing mothers, as the position would easily have belonged to mine, who already seemed to think she had divine authority. "I have heard the Goddess," *Amma* would say, turning a scowling face on me and my brother, Utpal and holding our hands as she walked us to the Shastri Vidyalaya Middle School. "Both of you boys, study hard, get good jobs and marry good *Kshatriya* girls who will give me strong sons. No bad company or loose girls for you. Otherwise you will die early like your father did," hissed *Amma*.

"Who are loose girls, *Amma*?" I wanted to ask, but before I could say anything, we turned into a gravel road which wound through fields of mustard flowers and ponds filled with mosquitoes, taking us westward to where we could see the school's locked iron gates.

My brother Utpal could do no wrong in my *Amma*'s eyes until the fucking lotus had gone and died, too—in a motorcycle accident. Of all the crappy things my camel's-backside of an older brother had done to me, dying was by far the worst. He had been the golden boy. "Ah, Utpal, my son," *Amma* would say, bestowing one of her rare smiles on him when he showed her his report card, and Utpal would grin on one side of his mouth, slurping on the fat *gulab jamun Amma* fed him with her own hands, while belittling me out of the other side. Oh, how he used to laugh at 'stupid little Bhavesh.'

It would have been nice to be able to say something like, 'Ha, look who went and let down *Amma* now,' once my brother was dead. And yet, if *Narak* has a window to this world, then Utpal is probably looking up from Hell and still laughing at stupid Bhavesh's lot in life.

I tried my best to become at least an adequate replacement for the family's lost future. I had even started my own export business for motor parts, but *Amma*'s deep discontent was never far from the surface. "*Amma*, I got a new contract today with Chrysler Corporation," I said excitedly, bringing her fresh goat meat from the market to cook for dinner so that we could celebrate my news. "Oh, if your dear brother was still alive," *Amma* said, releasing a sigh so deep I knew it carried the full weight of her heart, "Together you could have doubled the sales, put a shining *tikka* on the Rawat name—"

It was like my childhood replaying itself. I would laugh if I were not so angry.

The one area where I might make it up to her was in attracting a good match for marriage. *Amma* was already putting the word out for a suitable bride for me, but it soon became clear that even in this, her only remaining son was going to disappoint her. I wanted a pretty wife, not the dark, fat *Kshatriya* girl she had chosen for me because, "She is from our *samaj* and her father is giving me twelve cows and a new Indica car," *Amma* said to me, her voice cold and crackling like snakeskin.

"But . . . but *Amma*," I stammered. "Why do we need a car? I thought you liked my Hero Honda scooter." *Amma* looked at me, her face expressionless, and I could feel myself shrinking. Disappointment worked in me like a poison. If I couldn't please her no matter what I did, it occurred to me that I might at least have this one thing for myself. A wife is something you get stuck with for the rest of your life, so I wanted her to be *my* wife.

Amma's face when I refused the match she had finally settled on for me was one of fury and outrage. Then my friend—a vendor, actually—had shown me a picture of this *Dalit* girl whom he was thinking of going to see. I gave the picture a cursory glance, thinking it would repulse me. This girl was unclean, the lowliest of the low. This was what I had been brought up believing. I waited for disgust to break over me like a flood wave, but I found my gaze held by her unexpected beauty.

They hold me at the door for a moment, which is irritating. Just let me get on and meet the girl in the flesh, I think, for the picture must surely have flattered her. I want to see the dispiriting reality and be done with this foolishness.

A *Dalit* girl. The word is delicious in my mind, delicious where it should be dirty. The idea of taking a wife from the lowest of classes moves me inside like a warm sponge on a cold day. It is sordid, I know. What will she be like, a young *Dalit* woman? I have known only *Kshatriya* women. How different will she be to talk to, to touch, to be inside her? The thought excites me like the hot, dry wind that blows from the desert of Rajasthan in the summer, though I am half-expecting to be hurriedly exiting again as soon as good manners allow.

I understand the hold up, annoying though it is. In the world of brides and matchmaking, presentation is everything, and almost all will rest on the moment I walk through the door. Then, it is happening; they—Gopi, a short dark man with streaks of grey about his ears, a gentle paunch, wearing a crumpled cotton *dhoti* and a frayed blue shirt, and his wife, a plain-looking woman, bulging, round eyes, thin lips and a mouth that never smiles, in a pomegranate-red silk sari with a modest gold border—are beckoning me in.

I am unprepared for the beautiful sight that awaits me, and I can feel my face giving away my feelings as the room politely holds its breath, waiting for me to speak.

The cramped drawing room has little furniture except for a tired block-printed brown sofa, a low wooden table, two wicker *moras*, an ancient-looking bronze flower vase mounted on a stool in a corner, and a large-sized framed photo of Dr. Ambedkar on one wall along with pictures of Lord Krishna and Lord Rama. The white walls need color, every window needs covering, and the floor needs a carpet. I am not a rich man when compared with many other families from where I grew up, but it is still clear that, dressed in a brown poly blend suit by Gwalior Suiting, I am by far the wealthiest present today.

The girl is standing in the doorway from the kitchen holding a plastic tray with teacups, a pot of steaming milk-tea, and a chipped china plate with Parle Glucose biscuits. She wears a simple sari, her arms are bare, and her makeup is minimal. They have made her up as best as they can, yet compared to the potential brides I have met with *Amma* in the preceding few months—wearing pink or orange *Benarasi* saris glittering with zari thread, arms heaped with gleaming gold bangles, hooped earrings so large they knock against their cheeks—she is perhaps the most naturally beautiful creature I have ever seen.

Her skin is only a tone or two lighter than my own, but it is light enough to be rare in Uttar Pradesh. Rarer still among *Dalits*, I suppose. The uncle is notably darker than his niece, I observe. But, though fair brides are prized perhaps more here than in any other part of India—this is the least of what draws me in about her.

Something strange is happening to me with every passing second I look at her. Her unjeweled neck and ears draw attention to the slightly pointed nose, curving and ever-so-slightly off-center, as if broken at some point in her life. The rounded cheeks, the full mouth and slightly pursed lips. A man could kiss those red lips for hours and they would look more luscious for the pounding. The hair itself, thick and shining where it has been tamed around the head in an attempted bun, ultimately dissolves into an ever-frizzier and more untamed mass.

My eyes move down to her small bust. Unlike most other men I have discussed these things with, I have never found the size of a woman's breasts in any way proportional to my level of attraction to her. If anything, it is the opposite for me. Hips, however, are another matter, and she is ample in that regard.

My eyes drift upwards again. She is a small thing, though not the tiniest I have seen. *Good.* I have had too much of big women in my life, both in size and personality. Those bashful eyes finally look up and meet mine, and that is when I know I am truly lost. They are huge, dark pools, her eyes looming large within her face, and those caramel colored irises dominate within them. A man could find eternity in there.

I practiced saying her name to myself before I came. It is not a difficult name, yet still it was important to say it right the first time she hears me speak.

"Meena," I say, her name both awkward and delightful as it leaves my lips. "I am Bhavesh."

I cannot wait to get outside and alone with her, away from the fawning relatives. But once in the garden, my mind is racing, trying to find something to say. With the audience standing and gazing unashamedly at us from beyond the glass doors, we cannot be properly alone—propriety would not allow it, anyway, even with a *Dalit* girl— but, turning our backs to the house, we at least get an illusion of privacy.

I am twenty-four, my own search for a match having first been put behind the search for Utpal's best match, then held up further by my mother's high expectations. But, even though she is younger than me, the girl beside me is too old to be unmarried; soon she will be considered an old maid. *Ah*, I can see from the way she clenches the edge of her sari in her fist that she is nervous. What I should be thinking about, of course, is how to exploit her advanced age in any bargaining that follows, but right now I am too caught up in just looking at her.

"Your photo was lovely," I say, attempting to fill the growing silence, "but now that I see you, I know it was not a trick of the camera."

She blushes, lowering her startled eyes quickly. "But do you not worry about my caste?" she asks, her voice soft but rich. "I am *Dalit* . . . Untouchable. I would pollute you. You would be marrying below yourself."

So beautiful and unaware of it. So unspoiled. Oh, how that makes me want her. "I do not care about caste," I say, meaning it.

. . .

Lying, deceitful, unfaithful, *Dalit* bitch. After all I have done for her, lowering myself to lift her up, giving her a life she could never have hoped to have otherwise. Dirtying myself every time I touched her. Living in this godless country, just so we can live apart from the shame of what we have done.

I look at the receipt again. I almost toss it in the trash, so I nearly overlook the most important detail. Not the place, not the amount of money she'd wasted, but the time. It wasn't a lunchtime receipt, but instead it had been issued at eight-thirty-four on Wednesday night, when she had told me she was working late.

34
Meena

Winter 2015
Hayward, California

"I think he knows," I whisper, my hand to my throat, as Tammy steps into the room, her chest heaving with exertion.

Tammy's office is much the same as mine: tiny, overheated, badly in need of a coat of fresh paint, smelling of Darjeeling tea warmed overly long on a hot plate and dusty old folders, but while mine is housed in a temporary annex building at the rear of the campus grounds, Tammy's is tucked away in a warren of rooms on the second floor in the main campus building. She must have walked rapidly, cutting through the campus grounds to reach my office, and it takes her a minute to get her breathing under control.

Tammy settles a round, black-clad hindquarter on the bottom of my desk, wrinkling the edge of a manila folder titled, 'Project Restoration: Guidelines to create and maintain original cataloging records, including upgrading existing data in compliance with current national standards.'

She squints at me, her round face set in lines of uncharacteristic anxiety. "Yes, I just saw him outside."

My stomach twists.

"It's okay, it's okay," Tammy says, holding up a hand to forestall the panic she must see on my face. "He seemed fine to me, though . . ." and haltingly, she tells me about her encounter with Bhavesh.

"I'd grabbed a sandwich after I met your Ram Nayak and hurried back to the university. I gobbled it down at my desk, then headed over to your office. I wanted to be there when you returned from lunch." The whirring of a lawnmower floats through the afternoon.

"I think it was five minutes before the end of your usual lunch break when I approached the outer door, yet there, leaving it, was Bhavesh. I didn't know whether to look at him or catch his eye—we had met only twice. In fact, I'd had the distinct impression on the second occasion that I was being blanked." She cuts off, thinking she has gone too far, but my face is watchful, knowing.

Tammy continues, "He probably won't even remember me, I thought."

From behind my shuttered window, I can hear the muffled sounds of hundreds of chattering, excited students as they mill around the campus. "And yet, he did, smiling at the point of recognition. He's a handsome man, which somehow annoyed me. I'm not really sure whether I had noticed that before."

What Tammy leaves unsaid, but I can see from the way she narrows her eyes, is that there was something in Bhavesh's polite smile, something she picked up on just before he spoke, that chilled her. Maybe it is imagined, something she projects upon him because of what she knows. I know for certain she has not forgotten how I came to work that time months ago, my neck covered with telltale bruises.

In my mind's eye, I imagine Tammy and my husband together; how they start to see each other. Then, they lock glances: Tammy's poised and watchful as that of a fox and Bhavesh's gaze haughty, his lips thinning with impatience.

"Tammy?"

"Ah, Bhavesh. Meena's husband?"

"Yes. I apologize for interrupting your lunch plans unannounced."

"That's fine, don't be silly," Tammy says with a shrill laugh. *"It's nice of you to come and take your wife out to lunch. I wish I had a man that would do that for me."*

He gives her a smile with closed lips and nods.

"Well, I must get back to work," he says stiffly, *"to put food on the table."*

Then he strides away.

Yes, I can picture how that went.

Tammy laces her hands across her chest, studying me.

I close my eyes, feeling my arms rash beneath my silk blouse. When I open them again, Tammy places her warm hand on mine and gives me a gentle squeeze.

"Okay," she says briskly, pulling up the ratty visitor's chair, "let's think about this. I mean, what did you talk about at lunch?" She gnaws unconsciously at a stubby fingernail.

I shake my head numbly. "I don't know . . . stuff."

"Normal stuff?"

My head is foggy. "Yeah, I guess." I wave my hand agitatedly. "But . . . Well, he just sort of . . . kept looking at me."

Tammy's face bears a peevish look of discontent. "Husbands . . . do that."

"Not mine," I say bluntly. "He hardly ever looks at me."

Tammy nods at me sympathetically, reaching out to pat my hand.

I can feel the treacherous sting of tears behind my eyes. "Oh, Tammy, what am I doing?"

Tammy purses her lips, as if stifling the acerbic response trying to rise in her throat. She arranges her features in a polite mask. "Following your heart," she says gently, her blue eyes softening.

I hang my head, willing the tears not to course down my cheeks. "I'm not allowed to do that." I shift uncomfortably, embarrassed.

Tammy gives me a bewildered look, raising her eyebrows. "Why not? Because of Maya?"

I pause, choosing my words carefully. "Yes, she's a reason, but not the first one."

Tammy looks at me, her eyes widening in surprise.

"Because I'm an Indian woman," I say slowly. "Because I'm a *Dalit* who was blessed by marriage to a *Kshatriya*." I look at her beseechingly. "Do you know what that means?"

Tammy snorts and inclines her head quizzically. "Not the faintest clue. Can it be cleared up with antibiotics?"

"It means I am scum." I cannot hold back my tears any longer and break into a sob. "Bhavesh honored me with marriage," I choke. "He could have married someone of his own caste, someone better, who might even have brought him honor." My breath expels in a rush. "More than this, he brought me to America for a better lifestyle and so our daughter can have the best chance in life."

I grip the edge of my desk. The sound of a toilet flushing from the end of the hallway floats through the crack under my door. "I would be nothing without him, just a street-trash orphan."

I tug at the sleeve of the thin, long-sleeved mustard-colored top I am wearing. Tammy has told me she has always been a little jealous of my style, somewhere between what she would have expected of traditional Indian dress and something more western-formal. "It makes you seem like this effortlessly cool hippy, putting together outfits that shouldn't work, but do," she had once said. Then she had grinned at me. *"Bitch. If you weren't so damn adorable . . ."* I had stuck out my tongue at her and laughed.

"I spent the first eighteen years of my life in rags, Tammy, being either spat at or ignored by most decent people—hunger constantly invading my dreams—and he took me away from all that when he did not have to." I bury my head in my hands, wishing I could silence the motor inside my head.

Anger slashes Tammy's round features. "I'm pretty sure decent people don't spit at other people. Or beat their wives, for that matter."

I shake my head dully. "You don't understand, Tammy." My chest is heaving. I sniff back a giant sob. "In India I am not a person, not in any way that counts."

A frown breaks out on Tammy's face. "That's bullshit, Meena, and you know it."

I feel myself go hot. "Do I?"

"Easy," says Tammy. "I didn't mean to offend you." She raises her palm placatingly.

"When I came here, I was a lower-class Indian woman in a foreign land. I knew my place, which was at home, looking after my husband. Then it was looking after my daughter. I was happy—as happy as I knew how to be." The inside of my mouth puckers as if I have bitten into a hot chili. Tammy's face is a picture of stunned disbelief.

"Then I got a qualification and took the job at the university to better myself. My husband's business was going through a bad patch and Bhavesh thought it was a good idea to have another income, though he never quite put it that way. More like, 'I wish you would contribute, you lazy *Dalit*.'" My accent, softened over the years in America, comes out more fully as I do an impression of my husband. I slow down and try to speak more clearly. "Although, when I got the job here, I think he wished I would do something more . . . womanly, even if it brought in a little less money."

Tammy rolls her eyes.

I shrug. "I'm not sure I can make you understand this, but it's taken me ten years to even begin to wrap my head around the idea of sexism." I pull a face. A brief shout from outside the window like kids guffawing over a joke floats into the room.

"And then I met you," I throw Tammy a quirky grin. Barred light comes through the shutters, filling the modest interior. I reach out and touch her cheek fondly. "And you, damn it, ruined me."

Tammy half-laughs, half-coughs. "Meena, language!" She gives me an amused look. "So, this is all my fault?"

"I'm joking." I stick my tongue out at Tammy then, and shake my head slowly, "But you are a part of what's happened to me these last few years."

"Happened to you?" Tammy shifts in her chair.

I make a wide sweep of my right arm. "I've become more American."

"Call me biased," Tammy says, leaning forward a little, "but I can only think this is a good thing."

I sigh and massage my eyes. "An American woman in a traditional Indian marriage, it just doesn't work. If I can't be his demure little *Dalit* wife, then it just can't work."

I see the frustration in Tammy's face. "It's not his fault . . ." I say. "Don't look at me like that. He will always be an Indian man living in America; he doesn't know any other way."

Tammy shakes her head vigorously and crosses her arms beneath her bosom. "I can't say it's okay, Meena. The way he treats you will never be okay."

I look away. Guilt floods over me like blood in my mouth. I taste it, swallow it whole. "And *I* can't say it's okay anymore. I've tried, but . . ."

"Restless?" she interjects. "Is that what Ram is? Restlessness?"

A big, foolish, sentimental smile spreads itself over my entire face. "Oh, he's so much more than that. But his timing was . . ." I laugh. "Impeccable."

I turn to look at Tammy again. "I keep asking myself what I would have done if Ramu had come back into my life two or three years ago. I never loved Bhavesh, not the way I love Ramu—maybe not at all. But, all the same, I think I was too grateful for my lot in life back then." Tammy's eyes are wide with concentration. She is listening carefully. "Maybe I would have met him for a cup of coffee secretly, but that's as far as I think it could have gone."

Tammy impatiently waves this away. "Then maybe you don't love Ram as much as you think you do."

"He was going to come back for me, you know." My tone sounds wistful even to my ears.

Tammy's voice is high and cracked with surprise. "What?"

"Ram was once he had made his fortune in America." I swallow painfully and give a small nod. "He was going to come back to Kalanpur for me."

Durga Ma in the framed poster hanging over my desk seems to gaze sadly down at me.

I snort derisively and jerk my chin towards Tammy. "Pffft! What orphaned *Dalit* girl could ever believe such a thing once she is old enough to stop believing in fairytales and silly stories?" I sag into my chair, suddenly bone-tired. "That her orphan *Dalit* boyfriend is going to make it rich and come back for her? Who believes such nonsense?" My voice, an octave lower than usual, quavers; I am close to tears.

Tammy comes around the desk and takes my hands in hers. She holds me to her ample bosom, while I finally break, falling into heart-wrenching sobs. Someone knocks on the door behind Tammy, a harsh noise in the small room. "Go away if you know what's good for you," she calls out, her voice strident.

A short, thin, bespectacled man pulls the door open and pokes his head through the opening. It is Drew, one of my team. The poor guy looks about twelve, though he is actually twenty-three and has prematurely thinning hair. Tammy once confided in me that she has thought about trying to ruin him if she ever catches him alone and vulnerable on a work night. I was shocked at the thought, but then I began to see that Drew might appreciate it, and Tammy might even quite enjoy it. Alas, so far, all she has done is terrify him by making lewd suggestions every time he's in the building.

Tammy balls her fists. "Drew, I swear, if you don't get out now and never breathe a word of this to anyone, I am going to start bad sexual rumors about you that will n-e-ver go away!" Her blue eyes flash with anger.

Drew hurriedly closes the door behind him, and we hear the quick patter of his retreating footsteps.

Tammy gently wipes the tears from my eyes and leans back with a solemn expression on her face. "I will not offer my opinion unless you ask for it," she says meekly. A smile begins to form on her lips. "So, do you want it or not?" she demands a minute later.

I laugh and wipe at my tears, too. "Yes," I say, a friendly mocking tone in my voice, "of course I want it."

Tammy's expression is smug. "Thought so. If I were you, I would take your daughter and run. Money talks in this country, Meena, like in most countries. If you take Maya and live with Ram, there's no way he's getting her back, even taking the infidelity into account." I stare at her. I cannot help but flinch at the mention of that word. Tammy pauses then continues. "You're her mother and you're a fit one. All the courts will care about is that you're not crazy or on drugs, and that she's provided for."

"But Bhavesh will be granted some sort of access, and he might try to run to India as soon as he has her." I slap a palm roughly to my forehead. "Oh, God, *Hai Bhagwan,* I can't even believe I have been thinking about this stuff."

"But you have," Tammy says approvingly. "Look," she continues, her blond hair shining like a halo in the afternoon sunlight streaming through the window, "if there was evidence of violence, even an accusation . . . or any doubt about him as a father . . . ?"

"No," I snap. My breath comes unevenly. Tammy looks surprised. "He worships her. I can't do that to him, or to her."

Tammy sits back on her heels, crossing her arms on her chest.

"You know what?" I ask, pressing my fingertips to my temple. "I've been thinking that maybe this isn't all to do with Ram, but that it's about me, too. I said, didn't I, that I don't think I would even have had the affair a few years ago?"

Tammy looks at me with curious and wary eyes. "Uh-huh?"

"Well, what would I do if Ram hadn't turned up? Would I just go on feeling out of place, not really a part of my Indian household, but not part of this country I live in, either?" I speak roughly. "Maybe I need to start thinking about what is important to me outside of men." I drag shaking fingers through my hair. "Who am I? What do I want?"

Tammy rests an elbow on my desk, placing her chin in the palm of her hand. "You know what?" she asks wistfully. "I think you should move in with me." Her voice is dreamy.

I cannot help laughing. "Like some crazy girl's apartment . . . bachelorettes, or something?"

Tammy arches an eyebrow. "Or lesbian lovers. I'm easy."

I hold my sides, laughing so hard I fear I might burst. Only Tammy can turn my tears from sadness to hilarity so quickly. Living with her would be great in another life.

"Either way," Tammy chuckles, getting up as a distant clock chimes five p.m. "I think there's a sitcom in it."

35
Bhavesh

Winter 2015

Hayward, California

It could be anything, I think to myself as I drive to the university. Just dinner with that silly slut friend of hers. Pammy? Tammy? Something like that. I remember meeting her once, and how carelessly she was dressed, in a dingy, colorless, faded cotton skirt and top, her thin blond hair pulled back and twisted in a tight little knot high on her head. Bah!

A sickening chill shoots through my body like an electric shock. The thought of it—the idea of Meena moaning as some other man thrusts himself into her sets my blood boiling. That boiling blood is desperate for an outlet to blow off steam, but it has none, save for the accelerator under my foot.

I am doing fifty-five in a thirty mile-per-hour zone. The lights turn against me at just the wrong moment and I brake hard. *What are you doing? Calm down, you idiot, keep your head. You have a gorgeous daughter who needs her father alive and not in jail.* Maya was the best thing—maybe the *only good thing*—to come out of the decision to marry a *Dalit* and alienate myself not only from my mother, but from everything I knew growing up.

• • •

March 2005
Khairabad, Sitapur District, Uttar Pradesh
I have not been in the family home for over two months. A crow sweeps down from the cloudless sky with a shrill scream. I walk up to the white brick house with careful, muffled steps. Already, it has changed for me. For all the challenges that growing up in that household had brought, it had, nonetheless, been homely. The dust of my history covers this house. This is the house I will always know as *Amma ka ghar*. *Amma*'s house.

Walking in my shiny black shoes across the dusty, sprawling compound, that ashy dust settling around me like a shroud, it doesn't feel like home at all. When I refused her match for me, the row was so great that I stormed out of the house and have not returned since. Along the boundary wall, a soundless lizard leaps to swallow a bug. The looks I receive from Bhagat Singh, the cow-hand, and Pappu, his helper, who deliver the milk from our cows to the local market as I walk up to the house at this early hour are long and disapproving. *Amma* has been letting the servants know all about what a trial her only remaining son has turned out to be.

I am not sure why I have come back to give her the news of my impending marriage. I want, of course, to invite her to the wedding. But, more than anything else, I want to mend the gulf between us. Taking a *Dalit* wife would never be the best way to do that, but she will have to see that the choice is mine. And, it is a test of her love for me—whether she can come to accept it. Because deep down, I *do* love my mother—with an intensity that can be maddening. It is foolishness, but I can't stop myself; I want her love and, hopefully, her respect.

My arrival at the door is met with a stony-faced reaction, but *Amma* quickly disappears into the kitchen at the back of the house to make tea. I sit on the sofa in our main living room and wait for her while a weak sun casts rippling crescents on the wall. She would make even her worst enemy tea, once they had crossed her threshold, and food, too. It took several protests to stop her from preparing me lunch. I want things said and done. Besides, no one other than my mother could insist upon lavishing a person with hospitality yet still make them feel like an inconvenience.

"If you've come to your senses," *Amma* says when she comes back in. She pours sweet, milky tea suffused with ginger, clove, and cardamom from a silver teapot into an earthen cup, then hands it to me. I take the steaming cup, breathe deeply into the aroma, and watch *Amma* as she purses her lips. "I think you're too late. The Varma girl has been promised; we shall have to start our search all over again. I expect I shall be dead before you find a suitable match." She glances at me and clears her throat.

"I've found a wife," I say, stopping her rush of words. I splay my hands out before me, admiring the gold signet ring on my little finger, which had once belonged to my father. *Amma* halts mid-pour over her own cup.

Her face closes, but she recovers her poise quickly enough, asking me warily, "And?"

"Her name is Meena; it is a friends-of-friends-of-an-acquaintance sort of thing." I exhale on the ring.

Amma rolls her eyes, and I look down, polishing the stone on my trousers.

"Sounds . . . Well, I think you know how it sounds." She throws me an accusing look. "Would I at least know of the family? Are they close by, well known?" she asks irritably.

I try to keep my face expressionless as I answer. "No, I don't think you would."

I get up and cross to her, pulling out the photo from my wallet. *Amma* digs out her spectacles from inside her sari blouse and holds the picture at arm's length, squinting and tilting it to catch the light. Her eyes are narrowed and speculative, and I can see her mind is busy making plans.

"Hmm . . ." Her voice is testy. "Those hips could be broader, but not a total loss. I'm not sure who dressed her, but . . ."

"But isn't she pretty, mother?" I whisper.

"I suppose. All you boys worry about is 'pretty.' But, once you are married, it is the least relevant thing." She glares at me, her voice volcanic. "Trust me." She hands the picture back to me forcefully. "So, come on, what else is there to tell about her? How much are they asking?" In the distance there is a somnolent buzz of a tractor on the mustard fields.

"That's the good news; it is quite reasonable."

Amma's face darkens, her cup halfway to her lips. I notice that she looks old suddenly—skin on the face sagging a little, new bags under her eyes since I last saw her. "So, what's wrong with her? Is she lame? Simple, maybe?"

I take my seat again on the low-back sofa, settling far into it to get as much distance as possible while *Amma* takes another sip of tea. "No, no, nothing like that. She's . . . *Dalit*."

Amma chokes on her mouthful of tea, shrieking as scalding liquid lands in her lap. The room is still with the absolute silence of shock. I leap up from the couch, but *Amma* refuses my offer of help. She dabs at the fast-spreading stain with the edge of her sari. Two spots of color rise high on her cheeks.

"Please tell me this is a sick joke, Bhavesh," *Amma* says once she has recovered a little. Her eyes are wide, feverish. "Tell me you are trying to put me in an early grave with your poor sense of humor."

"It's no joke, Mother. She may be *Dalit*, but I love her." I speak slowly, my voice gaining strength with each word.

The next few moments will be clearly etched into my memory for years to come. *Amma* raises herself up. She is not a tall woman, though she is broad and bulky. I am slow to my feet, so for a moment she towers over me, like a raging goddess looking down upon an impudent mortal. I flinch, and when I look at her closely, I can see she is furious.

"Get out!" Her voice scrapes and screeches against the sides of her throat. "Get out of my house!"

I put my hands up. She steps towards me, and I instinctively move backwards, almost falling back into my seat.

"You piece of dung!" she screams, advancing slowly onwards. "How can you stand the smell of a *Dalit* woman? A *Chamar*! You break my heart. Why didn't you die instead of your brother? Why are you all I am left with?"

I expected that, but it still stings. "You will love her when you meet her," I say, holding my hands out in a gesture of peace, "and her caste will not matter once we are married."

"Won't matter? *Won't matter?* It will always matter, you stupid boy!" Her lips are clamped shut and there are thunderbolts in her eyes. "Everyone will know; everyone will find out you've brought the family to its knees. But, even if they didn't, *I* will know. I will know that you polluted our bloodline with sewer trash."

. . .

"Bhavesh," whispers Meena, raising startled eyes to my face. There is a false smile pasted on her face. What is this I am reading in her eyes? Surprise . . . Or fear?

"What are you doing here, husband? Is Maya okay?" She strives to keep her voice normal, but I can see how bloodless her face appears against the dark mesh fabric of her ergonomic chair, how her chest heaves.

"Yes, of course she is okay," I snap. It's hot in this room; I'm sweating into my collar. Rage sears my veins like a poison. But I have to play along. I have to be patient as the matador, waiting to swoop once I know the truth about the receipt. I deliberately make my voice soft. "Can I not come to take my wife out for lunch?" She doesn't answer my question; she just looks at me with wide eyes, but I pretend not to notice.

My attention wanders past Meena's cautious gaze to the open window behind her desk. It is a day in early February; the afternoon light comes at a slow slant through the blinds, making me squint.

I shift on the balls of my feet, cross my arms on my chest, and give her a sidelong glance. "You must take me to one of these places that you and your friend . . ."

"Tammy." There is a frown gouging her forehead.

"Yes . . . That you and your friend Tammy go to." I beam at her.

Her tongue darts out to lick dry lips, then she says quickly, "Um . . . Yes, that would be fun, wouldn't it? If you don't mind, I just need a quick visit to the bathroom before we go."

I nod curtly, and Meena snatches up her bag as she goes to leave her office. "You need your bag to go to the toilet?" I ask, arching an eyebrow.

She flashes me a disarming smile, but I notice that her bottom lip quivers. "If I'm going to lunch with my husband, I want to look my best."

I grab the strap of the bag, gently but firmly pulling it from her shoulder. "You are beautiful enough for me, Meena, and I don't want you to be any more beautiful for the other men."

Her expression is uncertain, worried for a moment, but then she relaxes with a small laugh that sounds more like a cough. "If only I saw what you see when I look in the mirror." She surrenders without any further protest.

I am pulled between a desire to nose around her office and to look through the bag. I am looking for something; I just do not know what it is. I will know it when I see it: it will be another red flag item.

Quickly, I rummage through the bag, but it is a horrible mess—her wallet, a pack of tissue paper, two black Pilot pens, a yellow highlighter, assorted makeup items, drugs (travel–size vials of Advil and Gas-X), a pencil with no eraser, an address-book, a box of Altoids and chewing gum. How can a woman this disorganized be employed in a position where she organizes things? I grimace. It is the same at home. She is always the untidy one.

The office is less cluttered, banal and functional—save for the framed picture of *Durga Ma.*

I give a derisive snort. Meena would never try to put such a picture up at home—she knows I wouldn't like it. My amusement quickly turns to irritation. Is *Durga Ma* the extent of her rebellions here at work? What else is she up to while she disregards her duties at home?

There is the clicking of Meena's heels on the ceramic floor and she steps back in with her phone in one hand.

I force a smile. "How long have you had that old thing for?" I ask, holding out a hand. She hesitates a moment, then passes it to me. Her mouth is opening and closing, but no sound is coming out.

"I'm not sure. Almost two years, perhaps," she says finally.

"We should get you a new one," I say, frowning suddenly. "You've locked it. Why have you locked it?" I ask her coldly. How dare she lock the phone?

"For security. And I have pictures of Maya on there." She watches me warily.

"What's the pattern?" I ask, feeling my face become hard as ice, and she draws a zigzag in the air. A look flashes across Meena's face, clear enough for me to read it: fear.

"If you're going to lock your phone," I say, flinty-eyed with rage, "don't do something so obvious, or what's the point?"

As we leave the office, I browse her phone as she fidgets next to me. I can see her peering over my shoulder. "Hmm," I say, "this is an older operating system." I turn a feral grin on her, noticing how jumpy she is. "My phone is Android, too, but it looks completely different. This is terrible."

It is, of course, a cover. I am checking her call history, then her messages. I see a message sent to Tammy just a couple of minutes before:

Hey, honey. Can't make our lunch at Federico's as Bhavesh has surprised me, which is nice of him. We'll do it next week instead.

Honey? Is this how she speaks to her idiotic American friends? This country is rotting her from the inside out. Still, what can I expect from her? She is only a Dalit, so she is naturally weak and lazy. This country would be bound to corrupt her first, to turn her American. My body is at once hot and cold and shaking, like the time I had gotten malaria just after my father died. I stomp my dissatisfied way through the University grounds. I hope that Maya has more of my sensibilities than hers. My daughter was born in this country, and will sound American, but I will bloody ensure that her heart remains as Indian as it can.

I look again at the text before closing it and handing the phone back to Meena.

Federico's. I try to think if I know where it is. I would love to be able to drive by, but I know so little of restaurants compared to my wife. No, no idea about Federico's. That's okay; I will find out, and once I do, I will choke the lying life out of her, no matter what happens to me after that.

36
Ram

Winter 2015
Oakland, California

"He knows," Meena says on the other end of the line. Her voice is shaking.

"Bhavesh? How?" The floor tilts and rocks, threatens to throw me off. A frost-knife twists in my gut.

"I don't know how, but why else would he come to my work like that?" Her sentences are short, jerky. "He's never done that, Ramu, *never*."

My brain is like stone, my tongue as well. I search for words to calm her. "Okay, that means he suspects, but does it mean he knows?"

"Is there a difference for us, Ramu?" Her voice is a hollow echo.

A heartbeat of silence. I feel a prick of premonition, as though my life is turning like a ship in a storm.

"Ramu?" Meena calls with a catch in her voice.

"I guess." I clamp my lips shut to not let my sigh escape.

"You . . . guess?" Her voice is shrill.

"If he finds out," I say, "if he finds out and you say you can't take Maya from him, then either you lose her, or he makes your life a misery, or he . . . What? Fucking beats you, kills you, because you're an unfaithful *Dalit* whore?" My chest heaves.

On the other end of the line, I can tell she is shocked from the way she catches her breath on a gasp. She did not expect this.

I could call on an army of lawyers, I could fill up a plane with the finest New York has to offer, I think desperately, *and fly them out to San Francisco for as long as I need, but if Meena won't take Maya from her father, what would be the point?* I run agitated fingers through my hair. Outside the big plate-glass window, the weather itself is nervous—sullen gray clouds racing across a slate sky.

"So, what . . ." Meena cries in great gasps. "This is it?"

I feel as if Meena's words are underwater as a rush of memories floods me.

. . .

November 2007
New Jersey
"I never see you, Ram." Jane's voice is petulant.

"But this is . . . This is what we wanted. It's what we went for." I sigh inwardly and drape a tentative hand across her shoulder.

"No," Jane says, "it's what *you* went for. I'm a final year Business Major." Jane glowers at me.

"Fuck you, we made this decision together. It was your idea to invest in the architecture, dammit." My voice comes out harsher than I intend.

"And your idea to invest in the people and roll out the back-end to other businesses, rather than focus on the site." The words are complimentary, but the tone is all accusation.

"And now we've got a model we can take forward. Come on, Jane, this is it. This is our chance, *the* big chance; the sky's the limit." I determinedly keep my tone mild, my expression pleading.

"We, we, we." Jane's tone is peevish.

"Yes, we . . . Always. You're my wife," I tell Jane, putting all the confidence I don't feel into my voice.

"No. You, this was your dream. I just came along for the ride. I just . . . I realized something . . . seeing you up there today. Well, I realized three things." Jane holds up her palm, three fingers pointing upwards.

We are outside the conference center in downtown Las Vegas. It is dark, the air damp and muggy. This is our first expo on scientific computing, and, though it feels like a huge thing, it is the smallest of many steps I am about to take.

"What did you realize?" I ask, the impatience clear in my voice.

"First, that this really is your dream, not mine. I got on board because I wanted to help you, because I loved you." I don't miss her use of the past tense. Her voice gains strength with each word.

"But you're a Business major," I exclaim. "How can you not love this? What we're doing is so clever. I bet there are people in your class who would give everything to stand where we are right now—an idea *and* an opportunity." Excitement turns inside me like a puppy at a picnic.

"You're not listening, Ram," Jane says, leaning back against the wall and pulling out a pack of cigarettes from her pocket.

"You're smoking again?" It's a reprimand at a time when cigarettes aren't the issue.

"I only wanted to be with you, and it's already like we're living two different lives. This is just the start, Ram. You've so far to go. If I don't do this now—" Her voice rings out in the hot, humid night.

I hear her, but I'm still not really listening. "In fact, screw your classmates. Do you know how many people where I come from—"

"Shut up, Ram. Shut up!" I do shut up, partly because Jane is shouting and drawing the attention of other people leaving the center. "I don't care, Ram. I don't care who deserves this opportunity more than me, because I don't want it. I'm doing a Business degree so I can get a nice, safe, boring job in a big building made of steel and glass." She looks at me steadily for a long, full moment. "So I can get a good flat and live a comfortable, average life with someone I love. Hopefully, have some children by the time I'm thirty."

I blink with surprise. She has my full attention at last. "But, we'll get there, Jane. We'll get there."

"When?" Her voice is a whiplash.

Of course, I have no answer to that.

"This is it for you, Ram, and I'm so happy for you. But from here on . . ." She pauses, the air darkening like dying coals around us.

I think frantically, *From here on, I will have to travel, to be on the ground, selling, demonstrating, talking people into what we are offering in a way that no one else really can. It's down to me.*

"I can't come with you, Ram, and I can't wait for you, not when we don't know how long it will take. And I sure as hell can't get in your way." She puts a hand over her face, her fingers splayed. I could see her eyes blink through them.

No, no, no! This is unfair, she can't put me in this position. Why shouldn't I have my passion and my love? "Come on, Jane. Don't do this, don't put yourself on one side and the business on the other. It doesn't have to be this way. Don't make . . ." I try not to hunch my shoulders apologetically.

". . . You choose? I'm not, Ram. I'm saying it's over." Her voice is chilling. Goosebumps dance down my spine.

"No, Jane . . . I love you. You're my . . ." I draw a shaky breath, tug at her sleeve.

"But I don't love you anymore, Ram." Jane stands in front of me, arms crossed, slit-eyed. "I want a divorce."

That stops my pleading, though I don't, *can't* believe her.

"But, for the record," she continues, "I would have expected you to choose the business over me."

"That's not fair." My voice has fallen to a whisper.

Jane takes my hand. "Don't get me wrong, Ram. I'm not saying you don't love me enough. It's not a crime to love your achievements more than people. To put them first."

"Isn't it?" I'm not agreeing with her that I love my dreams more than I love her; but were it true, it would surely make me the lowest type of person.

"No. Maybe it even makes you better." She shrugs. "Or maybe there's no answer, and it just doesn't matter." The ear-splitting wail of an ambulance siren fills the quiet darkness of the night.

I look at her for a long moment, trying to find the words that will make a difference. What comes surprises me, I think, even more than it surprises her. "What happened to the entrepreneur I fell in love with, Jane?" I ask. "What happened to the inventor with the herbal hangover sweet?"

For a moment, it does not seem like Jane is going to reply. Even when she does finally say something, it is not really an answer to my question.

"Don't look back, Ram," she says firmly. "Entrepreneurs never look back."

37
BHAVESH

Summer 2015
Fremont, California
Six months later . . .

It is a weekend morning that drags sluggishly. The air rumbles like a pack of Harley-Davidsons. The Argus that lies discarded on one corner of the overflowing desk predicts that it is going to be a muggy day with possible thunderstorms. Meena has gone to work after leaving Maya at her friend Allison's house. She said something about putting in extra time because of an upcoming project deadline.

I am in my study, ostensibly filling out invoices due at the end of the month from my Indian vendors, but in reality I am enjoying the pot of Darjeeling tea, two-egg omelet and two *parathas* Meena made fresh for me before scuttling out of the door. Long before I was up, she was bustling about in the kitchen, getting my customary Saturday breakfast ready. Chop, chop. Slicing the onions and the green chilies for the omelet *very* finely, just the way I like it, and kneading the dough and rolling it out for the fresh *parathas*. With the first stirrings of wakefulness, about seven in the morning, the familiar aroma of *parathas* being cooked in ghee on a hot *tava* with spicy potato mash wafted into the bedroom, easing me into a hungry alertness.

I am sipping my second cup of tea when the cellphone trills. I glance at the caller ID display and pick it up, frowning heavily.

"*Amma*, is everything okay?"

"Why would you ask that? Can I not call my own son?" Her tone bristles.

After moving to America, my mother and I initially had not spoken for five years. I'd sent a message when Maya was born, along with a contact number, but I hadn't heard anything until two years after that.

She had initiated contact on Utpal's birthday, of all days. No accident there, and no prizes for guessing which son she was *really* missing.

The conversation was jerky, jingling with odd, unfitted facts like a pocketful of nails. I'd mostly just listened, answering carefully when asked questions, enduring the occasional put-down from my mother, and avoiding the subject of Meena entirely. I spoke of Maya, who was already the very center of my existence.

I listened as *Amma* told me she would call again next year, and she disconnected the line with a loud click. My truant heart had felt a wondrous, party-balloon lightness as though I might float up to the ceiling. And that was how it had gone, with my mother calling each year on the day of my brother's death.

Until now. This call was seven or eight months early.

"Today isn't . . . you know. You're early." I can hear the uneasiness in my own voice.

"You may blather, son, but you are at least perceptive. Humor your mother, let me chat a while. How is my granddaughter?"

"She's eight."

"I can count, you fool. I asked how she was. She doesn't smell, does she?"

"Smell?" My eyebrows draw together in a frown.

"Yes, that particular *Chamar* smell."

My mouth is dry. "She's . . . everything."

"Happy?"

"Very happy."

"And very American, I suppose. Not cheerleading, I hope, or whatever it is they do?"

Time for the first lie of the phone call, a familiar ritual. "No. She's clever, though."

"Clever doesn't fetch a good bride price."

"It . . . It doesn't work that way over here, Mother."

"I know, I know."

There is a long pause on the other end of the line. "Mother?"

"Is your wife there?"

A rock lands in my stomach. "Meena?"

"Of course, Meena. You haven't got another one, have you?"

"But, you've never—"

"Well, I am now. It's about time I had a word with her."

Only ten years too late. "She's at work." As soon as I say it, I regret my unguarded words.

"At . . . *work?*" Disapproval hangs on the sound waves thick like sagging rain clouds. "Oh, Bhavesh. Why did you do it? Why did you have to marry a scheming *Dalit* girl and go to the other side of the world?" My mother sighs heavily. "I don't blame her, you know. I almost admire her, trapping a *Kshatriya,* making some idiot boy who should have been a man fall in love with her. It's quite a coup. But why *my* son?"

"Mother . . . " My mouth is sticky with shame.

"I'm dying, Bhavesh. I'll be lucky to make a month."

"I'll come—"

"No! No, you won't. You'll stay there. Even if I have forgiven you, some of your relatives never will." I do not know if I believe that, but then my belief is not really a factor here. Even my teeth ache with shame. "I wish I could say you weren't a disappointment, son, but you are. I love you, but you have dashed all my hopes. Try not to be any more of a disappointment once I am gone."

When I put the phone down, I lean back against the wall.

My mother is dying. I examine this idea cautiously, as one might finger a newly formed scab to test if it's healed underneath. I feel numb. My instinct is to jump on an airplane—relatives be damned—and head straight there. But the feeling, I think, is just that. Instinct. Surely it is not love?

A little sunlight, pale and sickly, trickles into this room full of my mother's disapproval. I should be angry with her; I *am* angry—the way she speaks to me. I probably make as much money as half of this extended 'family' who will apparently never forgive me. She does not talk about that, does she? Granted, wealth in America and wealth in Uttar Pradesh are not of equal value, but all the same.

Amma talks of this great shame I have brought upon them. Yes, I married a *Dalit,* but the ground has not opened up and swallowed anyone. And *I,* more than anyone else, live with the consequences of that choice. The disrespectful wife who thinks she is better than me, who lies about where she has gone at night. Resentment settles on my shoulders like ash on the overcoat of a man standing too close to a burning building.

I stack the half-empty cup of tea on the dinner plate and charge into the kitchen. I put the dirty dishes in the sink with a loud clatter. I am sure about that, the more I think about it. The bitch is lying, either to go and eat dinner with that whore friend of hers, or so she can be with another man.

It feels like a clawed hand is placed around my chest. The thought of her giving herself to another man . . . No wonder so many American women end up cheating on their husbands, when they spend so much time beyond their sight, I think bitterly. But *my* wife? She belongs to me; she is *mine* alone.

My heart thumping, I try to force the thoughts away as I storm back from the kitchen to my office, but they only grow stronger. How long? It could be years, many men. I catch sight of myself in the hallway mirror and slow my stride. I know I am still handsome. Many women would find me attractive. Meena's girlish looks quickly became replaced by something womanlier. But there is still something of the boy about my eyes, even into my thirties.

I am too soft with her, I think, forcing down my panic. She should thank her good fortune every day that I married her, rather than leaving her to shovel shit in some gutter in Kalanpur. I bring my fist down on my desk with a thump that sends the bills flying to the floor. She, an aging *Dalit* girl, got both a *Kshatriya* and a handsome husband. *And* I gave her a beautiful daughter. How dare she make me feel like this?

• • •

I pick up Maya from Tuesday dance practice as what's-her-name and her daughter—Maya's friend—Allison, are away. It was lucky I had remembered, as my wife should have been back to do it. There is still no car in the driveway as we pull up, and the house is quiet and dark.

The early July sun is just beginning to disappear behind the rooftops, and the outside world only just starting to turn grainy, yet the house is already full of gloom as Maya and I enter. I turn on one of the spotlights in the kitchen and dining area, yet its attempt to beat back the darkness is lackluster.

Where is she? Why is she not back? She should be here.

"Where's mommy?" Maya asks, returning from putting her bag away. Still in dance clothes, she begins to practice some moves. Hm . . . A few of these moves are not suitable for an eight-year-old girl. My mother's disapproving voice is in my head. *Arre*, what's wrong with you? Now my granddaughter is going to be one of those shameless *Nachnewalis*?

"At work, *pyaare beti*. I'm sure she will be home soon." I stifle a sigh.

"We should cook dinner together," she says, performing some twirl. "It would be fun."

"Do you have homework?" I ask in a bland-as-oatmeal voice.

Maya stops, the joy of dancing having been interrupted by the mention of the dreaded 'H' word. "Math," she says grumpily.

"Why don't you get it done now? You're always too tired after dinner." I take her firmly by the shoulders and turning her in the direction of the staircase.

Maya looks for a moment as if she is about to argue, but says, "Yes, Daddy," and heads to her room. If Meena had been asking her, I muse, she would have argued. Meena is too soft on her and it annoys me. You don't have to give in to a child all the time to win their love.

Halfway to her room, Maya stops and calls back to me. Her voice is pleading, one I always find so hard to resist. "Can we have takeout pizza tonight, Daddy?"

"We've had takeout too many times recently," I reply, clenching my fists and jamming them by my side, "because your mother is always late."

Maya flinches slightly.

• • •

"Where have you been?" I hiss when Meena slides into the kitchen. Meena jumps; I am in the lounge part of our open-plan living area, sitting in almost total darkness as only one of the low-wattage kitchen spotlights is on.

"Work," she answers stiffly. "It is Friday and there was a point I needed to reach before leaving for the weekend. Since they renewed my contract, the pressure is on." She flips on a switch, flooding the kitchen with bluish florescent light. "Plus, the traffic is always worse if I leave late, and I needed to make a quick stop at the grocery store, as well. Sorry I didn't call."

"I thought the point of your job is that you would be home on time," I snap at her.

"The point of it is earning money." She says shrilly, then cringes, as if regretting her unguarded retort.

"What about having expensive lunches and dinners?" I shoot back, feeling the muscles in my neck tightening. I stand up and come partially into the light.

"What?" Her forehead creases in perplexity.

"What? *What!* How about 'Sorry' or 'I beg your pardon, Husband?' You have no manners anymore, woman. I think it's that friend of yours." My voice rises several decibels. I don't care.

"I just . . . I meant that I wasn't sure what you were talking about."

"Are you stupid?" I demand, a murderous rage filling my throat.

Meena does not answer for a moment; then, with a note of fear in her voice, she asks, "Where is Maya?"

Caution flares over her face like a matchstick flame. It annoys me, sets my blood boiling. And there it is, the same feeling as in the car earlier, the same image in my head of some faceless man—white, long-haired, muscled—driving himself into my wife. Deep, deeper than I could ever go, because this man was never ruled by his mother, never bested over the telephone from half a world away.

"Fuck you," I spit out, shaking my fist in her face.

That faceless redneck—no, he is a surfer and a body-builder as these American heartthrobs always are—elicits noises from her, noises she has never made in ten years of marriage with silly me, who ran away from the mother he could not deal with. Women always get the better of me.

"Bhavesh . . ." Her voice is hushed, her lips trembling.

I step into the light and, seeing the look on my face, Meena takes an involuntary step backwards. My one hand is in my pocket, fingering an unseen receipt. "Do you love me?" I ask from between gritted teeth.

"Yes," she replies after a moment, and I see a look of blank surprise cross her face, followed almost instantaneously by fear.

"Say it," I hiss, grabbing her by the throat and tightening my grip, bringing my face close to hers.

"I love you," she answers quickly, clumsily.

"I'll be in my office," I say icily, releasing her. I walk past her, the receipt slipping out of my pocket. "Call me when dinner is ready."

38
MEENA

Summer 2015
San Francisco, California

Tammy kicks a stone in front of her as she walks along the sidewalk on the street in the Tenderloin neighborhood of the city. Her shoulders are hunched, hands in the pockets of her black pants as she walks quickly, wending her way through panhandlers, the homeless and their shanties and drug-dealing street punks. There is a wind blowing, even though it is mid-July.

"So," she asks, "why the mysterious message, girlfriend? You call in sick and then you want me to meet you at lunchtime . . ." She is scowling, her lips tightly pursed as she looks around the intersection where I have arranged to meet her and makes her last word an expression of disgust. ". . . *Here*."

I get her point. I am standing outside a grocery store with so much ironwork in front of its window that the products on display are barely visible. At the opposite corner is a boarded-up dry cleaner's shop covered in graffiti-decorated plywood.

Yes, I know it's not the best neighborhood, I tell myself, *but it's all I can afford.*

"I wanted you to come and see an apartment with me," I say, leading her around the corner and in front of a dilapidated sandstone apartment building.

"Are you and Bhavesh looking to become downwardly mobile?" Tammy cracks. Then she stops for a moment, making a dramatic gesture of looking to either side of and behind me. "Wait there . . ." she says. "No controlling husband here to look at the apartment with you . . . Are you finally thinking of leaving him?"

The conversation can go no further, as Sadie—the agent I spoke to a previous lunchtime—walks out from under the front marquee. Sadie is every bit as plastic as she had sounded on the telephone, with a fake tan and nails and impossibly thin eyebrows. All the same, I feel jealous of her. For all her saleswoman falseness, I bet she is her own person—a career woman who does what she wants.

She takes us up an elevator which discharges us on the third floor. A gloomy gray-walled hallway carpeted in a dingy indoor-outdoor floor covering leads us to an apartment at the corner of the hallway. Sadie opens the door into a small hardwood-floored living room. Through a quaint archway I can see a queen-sized bed, covered in a floral-designed comforter and pillows, a bureau of drawers, and an overstuffed reading chair in the opposite corner by the bathroom. A kitchenette which is part of the room, has a stove, sink and refrigerator lined up against the wall, with cabinets above.

"As you can see, the apartment comes furnished," Sadie says breezily, holding her arms open wide as if to say 'what a find.'

I exhale for what feels like the first time in hours as I walk on the nubby carpeting with gold and burgundy curlicues like carpet from a movie theatre lobby.

"So, what's going on?" Tammy asks, coming up to stand next to me in the bedroom. She has finally glared at Sadie enough that the agent has suggested she give us a few minutes to walk around on our own and headed out to wait in the corridor. The thought briefly crosses my mind that she might think we are a couple, the two of us, and it is a thought that makes me smile.

"Stop grinning and tell me," Tammy pushes, exasperated.

"I can't do it anymore, Tammy," I say. "I just can't." The weight that had been pressing into the center of my chest all morning finally begins to ease. "I've tried, but life with Bhavesh is impossible and soon it will . . ."

"Explode?" she finishes for me.

I nod. Something like that.

Tammy surprises me, stepping forward and embracing me in a tight hug. If Sadie comes in now, I think it will confirm her suspicions. "I'm proud of you," Tammy says. Then she steps back and looks at me. "With Maya, yeah?"

"Oh, my goodness, yes," I say forcefully. Then, more calmly, "It's not like he's a bad father, but . . ."

"Being a crappy husband is reason enough, Meena, you know this." Tammy wags an impatient finger at me. Then she reaches forward and clasps my hand. "One step at a time, huh?" Her eyes sweep across the living area. "It's not so bad," she says. "You think you'll take it?"

"I'm not thrilled on the area," I say.

"Clearly there are not enough middle-aged men standing on street corners and holding bourbon in brown paper bags," Tammy says with a wry smile. "You know?"

"Screw you," I say with a giggle. "It's all I'll be able to afford." After a moment, my smile fades. "He won't let her go easily." I squeeze her fingers. "Even a few miles across the bay."

39
RAM

Summer 2015
Fremont, California

It is a modern, two-story American suburban house with a stucco exterior and a red Spanish-tile roof in the middle of a row of identical wood-steel-blend tract homes. The lilac tree in the tiny front yard is so heavily laden with blossoms that its boughs graze the ground; the sky above it so blue it looks enameled. A slight breeze rustles the leaves of the tree and I watch fat squirrels darting at play.

The yard has a border of blue delphiniums, yellow-leaved fuchsias, and a climbing rosebush near the mahogany front door. Is Bhavesh responsible for that, or Meena? It feels like another black mark against me that I do not know. I imagine Meena outside pruning on the weekend, remembering how she loved the Marigold Garden at Grace Mercy.

The August afternoon bakes waves of heat from the blacktop as I sit, parked in a rental car under a gigantic oak tree, a little way up on the other side of the street. This is the last place I should be, and it is a selfish thing to do. My presence here could do her so much harm. My throat stings with guilt as though I just ate a cactus.

But it needs to be done, I cannot just fade out of her life with a whimper. For one thing, even though we have been apart for six months and eight days, I do not think Meena wants me to. For another . . . I look down at the laptop resting on my legs. It is closed, not switched on; it does not really need to be, as I can bring every image and most of the text on it to mind.

An Indian man comes out of the house and gets into an SUV parked out front. That must be Bhavesh. I should duck down, even though I am in the overhanging shadow of the tree and probably not too visible, but a kind of morbid curiosity keeps me up, watching.

I have, of course, found what I can of Bhavesh online. It is the way of the world now, that one can be at least curious without it feeling like malign intent. There is not much there, though; almost nothing personal. I have found one solitary picture.

All the hatred I had felt every time I remembered the unexplained purple bruise on Meena's neck isn't there. He is just a man, average height, average build, hair thinning, clothes that could be newer. Where is the monster I had been hoping for?

Within thirty seconds, Bhavesh is in the car and gone. I dial the office on the vehicle's hands-free.

"Felicity . . . ? It's Ram."

The woman on the other end of the line is younger than I am, but she always sounds like she is middle-aged and behaves like she is my mother. It is a professional relationship, which somehow works for us.

"Ram who?" says the crisp female voice on the other end of the line.

"Your boss," I say, my voice both laughing and exasperated.

"No, sorry, you must be mistaken. I don't have a boss, just a man who gets me in on the weekend then disappears when he's got meetings scheduled." Her sigh is so loud it could pierce an eardrum. I can picture her frosty purple fingernails flying over the keyboard of her laptop as she speaks to me. It is as if her cell phone is surgically attached to her ear. She is worth her weight in gold, and her paycheck reflects that.

I sigh. "Just hold my calls for an hour, would you? I'll be back, I promise."

There is a moment of silence on the other end of the line. "It's her, isn't it?"

Just then, the front door of the house opens again. Meena is bringing out the trash. How normal. How charming and homely this scene is. Her hair is up in a topknot, she is wearing an old sweatshirt and jeans, and she looks tired but so exquisite. Longing racks my insides. Oh, how my heart aches for her.

For this.

Not hotel rooms, not even our little fake apartment. But this. Shared life. Normality. Whatever my life has been since that car wreck over twelve years ago, 'normal' has rarely been a part of it.

"Just . . . just hold them, will you?" I grab my laptop from the passenger seat. The door behind Meena is open, and a little figure appears in it. It must be Maya. She is already in a nightgown and robe, even though it is afternoon. Her hair is in pigtails. *Pigtails.* I grin. Maya calls out to her mother, but between the distance and the car windscreen separating them, I cannot hear what it is. Meena turns around. "Go inside Maya. I won't be a minute."

I am a voyeur, sitting there, but who knew that voyeurism could be so painful? I am breathless, as though someone has punched all the air out of my lungs. They both head back into the house, and it takes me another minute to gather myself before I can head up to the door.

"You," she says belligerently as she answers. "What do you want?" It is not the dream reception, but what could I have expected? I shift uneasily. Well, that she might refer to me by name, at least.

"I . . ."

"You can't be here." She is obviously annoyed by my presence, like I have magically—and, of course, unwanted—brought two separate realities together. "You can't be here! You'll ruin everything."

"I have to speak with you," I blurt, before her words steal the last ounce of courage I have mustered.

It seems for a moment like she will shut the door in my face, her hand twitching convulsively as she holds it there. "Go down the side," she says instead, a frown marking her face, "and wait in the playhouse."

"Playhouse?" I ask, not sure I've heard it right.

"Go!" she barks.

I find my way to an unlocked side gate and through to the garden. Various toys, sit-on vehicles and even an empty wading pool litter the space; and there, at the back, is what can only be described as a 'pretty cool' playhouse. Built so that the branches of a tree almost cradle it, like a parent's protective arms, the playhouse is made of wood and sits on a raised platform, reached via a ladder-like flight of steps. There is even what might pass for a veranda at the front of it.

Wishing I did not always have to wear a suit, I climb the steps and open the door, bending to make my way into the cobwebbed interior. A small blackboard is in one corner, and various toys cover the floor, some ragged, some new. To my left is a plastic table with two tiny plastic chairs and a plastic tea set upon it.

So, this is it, I think, placing the laptop down and trying to take a seat without toppling backwards in the tiny chair. Meena has no idea how fitting this is. I stretch my arms over my head. I am filled with power and potency and well-being, with the infinite possibilities this matchstick house spins for me.

She arrives a minute later, stooping through the door with a practiced grace that I had not managed.

"I've got Maya busy in her room for now," Meena blurts out. "She can't see you, okay? She just can't." Her voice is low, fierce. "Bhavesh is visiting a business vendor, then grocery shopping on the way home, so he should be an hour and a half, at least—maybe more." The look on her face is guarded.

I place two plastic cups on the table and mimic pouring cups of tea as she takes the seat opposite me. "Sugar?"

Meena gives me a puzzled look, but her lips quirk in an unexpected smile.

"Nice place," I give her a thumbs-up sign. I am close to her again, the scent of sweet jasmine and Meena filling my nostrils. That familiar scent of pain and loss, of shame and pride makes me almost dizzy.

"Just like all the others around here," she answers modestly, then sits up straighter in the child's chair, "but maybe I appreciate it more than most. We're lucky."

"Yeah, nice house," I agree. "But I actually meant . . ." I flick my eyes to indicate the playhouse surrounding us, closed on every side so it is cozy, intimate. My heart sings. Even the dust, which spins in the thin columns of light allowed by the tree branches, seems to have a festive air.

"The playhouse?" Meena gives a disparaging shrug. "Bhavesh made it for Maya. He was out here every weekend for two months, mostly just scratching his head and looking angry." Her brow is knotted. "I hated it. He was always in such a foul mood when he came in, but you can't argue with the results. It is a playhouse made of love."

Her wry tone makes me chuckle.

"So," she continues, her initial shock appearing to have faded, "I wasn't even expecting to hear from you, let alone have you turn up on the doorstep." She pauses, finally looking up. "Did you know Bhavesh would be out?"

"I . . . saw him leave."

I brace for an explosion, but a look of amusement springs to life on Meena's features. I can see the laughter bubbling in her throat and spilling over in her voice. "Are you stalking me, Ram Nayak?"

"Kind of," I confess, giving her a solemn look. "I needed to speak to you."

"We have phones, nowadays," Meena says irritably. "I still have the one you gave me. Or you could have come to my office, or emailed me to meet, or have done anything except come to my house." She gives a small grimace.

"I . . ." I look at her mutely, feeling uncharacteristically bashful. "I couldn't wait."

Meena nods towards my laptop. "What have you got there?"

The air between us is strange. Not formal or strained, but more like friends. It seems so recent, the last time she lay in my arms, the last time she sat atop me, moving . . . moaning. Yet, in this tiny, almost intimate space, she feels distant to me. Desolation crawls up my spine.

"What happened?" I ask, rubbing the side of my nose.

"Reality," she says with a sigh. The gentlest smile kisses her lips and makes her eyes glow. "I think we did well to suspend it for as long as we did."

We hold each other's gaze across the tiny table for a few moments. There is still love, I realize, despite the space that has grown between us.

"Did you ever communicate with Grace Mercy after leaving?" I ask her. Memories of our time together from an earlier era float like gossamer through my thoughts.

After a moment, after being thrown by what feels like an abrupt change in conversation, Meena looks ashamed. "A few times. Once after we moved here. Bhavesh would not allow it after that. He said I should not dwell on my old life." She gives a derisive huff. "I am an orphan *Dalit* only when it suits him and a *Kshatriya's* wife when it does not. I think he was just worried I would try to send them money. Which I would have." Her tone is defiant.

"Me too," I say. "I tried, but it closed down early in 2008, just as the system that was to make me my first few million was beginning to take big orders." I hurry into speech, knowing I'm speaking too quickly to hide the sting of my words. "By the time I found out, the building was already gone, flattened to make room for ten new luxury homes."

"Sister Gina?" Meena asks, sucking in air. She clasps her hands tightly in her lap.

"I could not trace her," I answer. "And I really tried." I make a face. A residue of melancholy sits on my heart like sand. "I would have saved it. That and more. Because of Sister Gina."

I turn the laptop towards her. On the screen is a picture of a large building. I can tell from Meena's expression that she knows straight away that it is in India.

"What's that?" Meena's eyes light up with curiosity.

I hold her gaze for a long moment. "It's mine. Nihal traveled to Bihar, near the border, to acquire it for me."

"You ask too much of your old uncle," she admonishes me. "Getting an old man to travel all that way."

"It is for a good cause," I reply. I lift up a hand apologetically.

Meena doesn't ask me the obvious question, though the look she turns on me pleads for the answer.

"I was thinking an orphanage, just for *Dalits*. Or, either way, for the most disadvantaged children." I pause for emphasis.

Her eyes light up with excitement. I knew they would. "That's a great idea, Ramu! Good for you."

"I've been putting money into different projects back there for quite a few years now," I say quietly, "but it has always been disorganized. A little here, a little there, just guilt money, really. For my success, for not being able to save Grace Mercy."

Meena gives me a small nod, encouraging me to continue. Bits of sunlight bright as butterflies shine through the wooden slats of the playhouse. "I've had the idea to do something more focused, more fitting like this, for a long time. But with work, six months—even a year—can go by just like that."

"Plus," Meena says, with the wry smile I love, "you've had other distractions for the past six months."

"I thought what I needed to do was set up an organization, something with a budget and staff that could run itself." Meena listens to me raptly. "But . . ."

She throws me a look of confusion. "But what?"

"Then you came along." I give an involuntary grin.

"See," she says, her face clearing, "a distraction."

"No, no, no," I say, reaching across the table towards her face, but I check myself halfway.

I sit back, trying to make myself comfortable in the small child's chair. "I forgot who I was before you came along. And you reminded me of where I came from, who I am." I give a derisive snort. "Business, this country, it's all a distraction. A beautiful one, that has made me very rich." Meena studies me with sharp, unblinking eyes. "But then it made me keep going, on and on, making more money, always in much the same way." I pause and take a deep breath. "I forgot why I was doing it. I threw a few million dollars India's way here and there to pay off my conscience, and I just kept working."

I pick up the laptop and shake it gently. "*This* is why I left. Not just for a better life, but for a better *way*. A better world. I left to get the power to change the world around me. Now I have it and I am still in a country that doesn't need me to change it."

"What are you saying?" Meena asks, a note of caution in her voice.

"I'm saying that if I'm going to do this, then there's no one better to run it on the ground than me. There are plenty of safe pairs of hands to leave the company in here." I run my fingers through my hair, tousling the unruly curls. I'm overdue for a haircut. "And, even if they send it out of business six months after I'm gone, I'm going to arrange an exit that means I'll have more than enough money to run this orphanage far beyond my lifetime."

Meena's hand flies to her mouth. "You're going to leave?"

Her voice is small and gravelly with fear, and it is the best thing I could hear from her.

I look at her directly, my eyes scanning every beloved feature. A shaft of August sun falls on her face and she seems to light the playhouse. "And you too, if you want."

40
MEENA

Summer 2015
Fremont, California

"I was thinking an orphanage," says Ramu from across the small yellow plastic table in Maya's playhouse, "just for Dalits. Or, either way, for the most disadvantaged children."

Joy fills my mouth, sweet as honey. It is a perfect thing for a man like Ramu to do with his money, making sure that children like us get the best start in life. I am touched that Ramu trusts me with this fragile, newfound vision. He watches me anxiously, waiting for my verdict. "That's a great idea, Ramu," I say excitedly. "Good for you."

And I mean it, I am happy for him. Happy, with just a twinge of sadness. Perhaps even a pinch of jealousy. Yet, would I rather have not had those six months together? Would I rather still be oblivious of Ram Nayak and his plans for the future? Of course not, even taking into account the mess it could have made of my life. But—there is a 'but.' A but that I cannot put into words yet and cannot even frame clearly in my mind. The yearning that shoots up from the soles of my feet is like a lancet, striking me in my most secret parts.

But then, that sounds like wishing my daughter away. Instantly, regret slams into my body, sharp as a sword thrust. God, I bite the inside of my cheek, hard, until I can taste blood. How far I have come from being the mother I thought I was.

"*This* is why I left," Ramu says, gently shaking his laptop and the picture of the building that will be his orphanage.

"What are you saying?" My throat clenches. A metallic fog winds itself around me.

"I'm saying that if I'm going to do this, then there's no one better to run it on the ground than me." His face is in shadow, but his eyes shine like mercury. "I'm going to arrange an exit that means I'll have more than enough money to run this orphanage far beyond my lifetime." *Beyond your lifetime. But are you not immortal, my Ramu?*

His words lacerate my skin, nails of rust and ice. "You're going to leave?"

He nods, not taking his eyes off my face.

• • •

I hardly remember Ramu leaving. I have a vague recollection of my response to his proposition. "No!" I whispered fiercely, and then . . . Because I wanted him gone before the floodgates of my tears opened, I summoned up a ghost of a smile from somewhere. "Yes, yes, I'll think about it," I told him, as I closed the front door, the ground buckling up around my feet.

Outside, the sky has coagulated into a steely gray. I am suffocating. Anger explodes in my chest. How dare he put me in this position between a dream come true and my daughter? Fists tightly clenched, I pace up and down the living room. Blood roars in my ears like a tide. *Ram Nayak soon plans not only to leave San Francisco, but to leave the entire continent of America,* says a dull voice as I'm swept away.

I run upstairs. Maya is in her room, lying atop the covers in a nightgown and robe, watching cartoons. I lie down behind my daughter and pull her tighter than a hug should be, though Maya does not complain because she is so absorbed in the cartoon. I nuzzle her, breathe the scent of her hair and the back of her neck, and run the tips of my fingers along the shape of her thin little arms.

So perfect. So innocent. How can I think of leaving you?

• • •

Why couldn't Ramu have just come back? Or, even just have contacted me in time, to have given me the hope that a life together was just around the corner? I would not have married Bhavesh, I would not have . . .

Maya. The thought deflates my rising anger. Maya, my daughter, you are the blessing of a miracle life never told me I would need. When you throw your arms around my neck, offering me a chubby cheek for a kiss, your brown eyes smiling with mischief, I love you so much, I could die for you.

But, sometimes, I feel trapped by you, by Fremont and this suburban life, the commuting and the goddamn cataloguing, the person my life here has made me become, in a country where most women have control over their own lives. I am sinking into quicksand, my mouth filling with mica and grit. *Who am I?* A role player, who plays so many roles that I have lost my own identity amidst all the confusion.

Restlessness gnaws at me. I cannot sit. I walk to the window and fling it open, letting the cool evening air blow over me, lifting before it the fog of my confusion. I cannot help thinking, *If I don't go, then Ramu will do it without me.* It may not make the slightest bit of difference to the orphan *Dalit* children of India whether or not I join him, but an orphanage of this type is where I can belong, where I can most perfectly just be Meena. For a moment my greedy, forgetful heart leaps. This life I have built over the cinders of my passion and my pain, this life where I have redefined happiness as merely existing—how unremarkable it has been. Until today. I close my eyes against the sharp pain of what could be.

The door flies open. Charlie, Maya's little Shih Tzu puppy, comes in, brown tail wagging excitedly, and he makes a meal of getting up on the bed. Without ever taking her eyes from the TV, Maya accepts him next to her and begins idly stroking the top of his head. A great sigh shakes me, all the way to the core of my heart. What I would not give to be Charlie, whose primary concerns in life relate to eating, 'walkies' and urinating on things.

Tears stream from my eyes. "Maya . . ." I say, though my daughter is engrossed in an episode of Coco and her friends. "Oh, Maya."

41
MEENA

Summer 2015
Fremont, California

Still crying silently, I prepare Maya's favorite dinner, *rajma-chawal,* and bring it to her. I wipe my tears and crouch on the bed to watch the animated television series with Maya.

"Don't be sad, Coco," says Coco the Cat's best friend, after announcing she's moving to another state. All the friends break out in tears. "I'll be back for Thanksgiving and Christmas," she reassures them, squeezing their hands. "My grandma lives here, so I have to come visit."

"Do you promise you'll visit me?" a tearful Coco looks at her best friend.

"Yes, I promise."

"A pinky promise?" I guide a spoonful of *rajma-chawal* into Maya's upturned mouth. The light from the screen casts an unearthly glow over her rapt face so she looks heart-catchingly innocent.

"Yes, yes." Best Friend Forever stretches out her hand, and Coco wraps her pinky finger around Best Friend Forever's pinky finger like a loop. Coco smiles wide and looks into Best Friend Forever's eyes, their fingers wrapped around each other. *The End.*

I shut off the T.V., take Maya gently by the shoulders, and turn her so that I can look into her eyes. Her black, wavy hair is tousled and her still chubby cheeks are pink. Her brown eyes are velvet-soft and intent.

"Maya, my *bitiya*," I say urgently, "I want you to listen carefully to what I'm going to tell you. Remember how I told you about the little boy whom nobody loved because they thought he was different from everybody else?"

Maya nods her head, but I can see she is miles away, twirling her fork on the mound of *rajma-chawal* on her plate.

I pull Maya towards me and squeeze her hard. I nibble on Maya's ear like I used to do when she was little.

"I love you, Maya."

Maya launches herself at me, putting her face right up close to mine so that our noses are practically touching. "I love you too, Mommy."

"Do you remember the story of Chetan, who was not allowed to play with the other kids?" I remove the plate of rice and beans from Maya's hands and place it on the bedside table.

Maya turns her earnest brown eyes on me. "Because he had six fingers instead of five?"

"Yes, that's the one!" I scoop up my daughter and cradle her on my lap. I wind my fingers between Maya's little ones, and look down at them, the thin and the chubby together.

"Chetan had six fingers, and so he was different. Other children didn't let him eat with them or play with him and he was so lonely."

"Why didn't his Mommy help him?" Maya looks up at me, a knuckle in her mouth.

"His Mommy died when he was very little, Maya."

"So he had no one?" Maya's eyes are wide with astonishment.

"No."

"Not even a Daddy?"

"No." In the overhead light from the ceiling lamp, her eyes are still and shining, focused on my face.

Maya bites her lip. I can visualize her thoughts running round and round like dogs trapped behind a fence.

"Maya, what if your Mommy went away to help Chetan?" I deliberately make my voice casual.

"No, no. I don't want you to go away," Maya says immediately, snuggling into my arms.

I tuck her head under my chin. "Maya, sometimes people need to go away." I smooth Maya's curls away from her forehead and hug her tighter.

"Like Coco's best friend had to go away?" Maya asks solemnly, her eyes like saucers.

"Yes, like that. You don't want that boy to be forever lonely, without any friends, do you, Maya?" I grip Maya's face on either side of her jaw and turn her chin gently upwards.

Maya's forehead is scrunched in thought.

"Will Daddy also go away?" There is a moment of utter silence and I look deep into Maya's eyes.

"No, *bitiya*."

"And Charlie?"

"No, *bitiya*."

"But who will make *rajma-chawal* for me? Daddy doesn't know how to make *rajma-chawal*." Maya's face crumbles and I can see the tears aren't far away.

"You're my *bitiya*. You're my angel and everything will be all right." I touch Maya's cheeks, then kiss her on the forehead. "I'm always going to be your Mommy, Maya and I'll make sure you're all right. And, when I see you again, Maya, I will have *rajma-chawal* for you."

"Do you promise, Mommy? Pinky promise?" Maya's little face is intense and serious.

"Yes, Maya, *bitiya*. I pinky promise you," I say, using my soft mama voice as I hold her tight.

Charlie leaps between us, his tongue wet and drooling as he tries to break us apart.

Maya wriggles off my lap and jumps off the bed to play with Charlie.

I look at my precious daughter, my heart pounding wildly at the tips of my fingers like a leaping fish.

42
BHAVESH

Summer 2015
Fremont, California

Driving back from Kamal Spices on this unusually warm August evening, I think about India. I grimace. I do not miss the place.

It was hard for several years, with a new wife and learning to run my business from the other end of things. And we were happy then, even though we were poorer in those first few years. We enjoyed the simple things together, like a once-a-month trip to the cinema or ice cream at Ben & Jerry's.

We discovered Muir Beach, a tiny little town with its golden beach, on a quiet Sunday in winter, almost deserted and with one optimistic shop open, selling ice cream. It was not like Baga Beach in Goa, but Meena had been taken with the place and it felt like our own little find. At some point we stopped going.

I search my mind for a reason why we stopped going.

Of course, it was because of *Amma*'s phone calls, which had begun a year or so after my marriage.

"Mother?" I nearly choked on a mouthful of the potato chips I was munching on when I first heard her voice, faraway and unfamiliar.

"What is all that noise, Bhavesh?" *Amma* asked in an annoyed tone.

"I am driving, Mother." My stomach muscles tightened in anticipation.

"But . . . I called your home," she said with an irritable clatter of crockery. I had a sudden vision of her drinking her afternoon chai with freshly made *nimki*.

"I have call forwarding; it sends the call to my mobile phone if I am out." I gritted my teeth and forced myself not to stammer.

"Oh . . . Should you be driving and talking?"

That sounded dangerously like concern for her son's welfare. "It's hands free, so I can speak to you without holding the phone." I blinked.

Silence on the other end for a moment. "These fancy gadgets of yours, Bhavesh, they are nothing. They do not make the man." *Why does she phone only to insult me?* "I wish you would have been more like your brother. He was a good, traditional Indian boy. He did not need 'call forwarding' or 'hands-free.' A good, honest life in the village was enough for him." *Amma* snorted loudly.

"Sometimes, Mother, I don't think you knew Utpal as well as you think." As soon as I said it, I regretted it.

"Well, he didn't run to the other side of the world with a *Dalit* whore, leaving his mother without a son." *Amma* snapped.

"No, he had to die to get away from you." Bitterness made my tone sharp. I waited for the explosion, but the silence on the other end of the phone was more damming. "Don't call her a whore," I said finally, but my voice lacked conviction.

"What else do you call a woman who profits from bringing a respectable man low? You gave her a better life and gave up everything you had, son, and in return you got her body. I wouldn't be surprised if you don't even get much of that anymore, except on her terms."

"Mother . . ." I took one hand off the wheel and rubbed my eyes tiredly.

"Don't be weak, son. All you have left is your place in your own home. I expect you to at least be a man in that." I felt slightly sick, but before I could respond, she hung up.

Can you blame me for wanting to be the man *Amma* would be proud of? Especially when the guilt over abandoning *Amma* became a giant fist squeezing my heart, so it seemed like it would burst.

There were other reasons we stopped going, too, I muse: after that first year or two, and with Maya on the way, the business had needed to take off, and it did. True, things do not always run smoothly, but it is a business, and it has kept us in a comfortable life since then— supplying motor parts to companies that sell them for several times the price.

Somehow that said a lot about America, but you would not catch me complaining. And no, I do not want to go back to the dust and the dirt and the rainy season, to where the poor people are right there in your face, wherever you go, not nicely hidden away. And to the relatives, where there is always at least one with an excuse to look down their nose at you, an aunt or uncle whose son has done some fantastic thing.

Nobody cares here, nobody asks; they all just leave each other alone, which is fine with me. Yes, there are things about the 'American Way' I have never liked, influences on my wife and even my young daughter that are unhealthy. But Maya is happy and Meena just needs . . . *watching*. It is all manageable.

No, nothing to miss in India, nothing except *Amma*.

The news of my mother's illness has been playing on my mind. If what she said was right, *Amma* will soon be dead. "Do not come here," *Amma* had insisted, "None of the relatives have forgiven you for marrying a *Dalit*." Her words were like a slap. The worst part is, I knew it was true. Well, fuck them. Fuck them all. I'll do what I want. *Yes,* I think, turning onto our street, *I'll tell Meena that I'm going to fly out tomorrow, as soon as I get in. About time we put some of that money she has been earning to good use, rather than letting her squander it on dinners she lies about.*

The thought of leaving my useless wife on her own and in charge of Maya for what is likely to be weeks is not appealing, but I have no other choice. I had been toying with the idea of relieving Meena of her debit card and giving her an allowance instead. That was how it was when we were first married, and I do not know why I had let that change. I am too soft, that is why. Still, she would have to be allowed to keep the card, at least until I am back.

I pull up onto the drive and get out, several bags of groceries in hand. Look at me: running errands and running my daughter about while my wife spends all that time at her job, putting things in order, or whatever it is she does. I swear that woman thinks her work is more important than her home. *Things need to change around here . . .*

A suitcase faces me in the hallway when I open the door. I have a surreal moment, as if my wife has somehow tapped into my mind, read my thoughts as I was on the way back from the grocery store and already started packing my suitcase for India. Absurd, of course. I shake my head ruefully.

Meena walks into the hallway, a smile dancing in her eyes, and stops at the sight of me. There is a long moment as we stand there looking at each other, neither speaking. The setting sun pulls a rain cloud over itself like a comforter. She blanches. Her hand flies to her mouth.

She draws in a deep breath, pulls herself tall. "I'm leaving you," she says eventually. The big clock in the hallway, a housewarming gift from the mother of Maya's school friend, strikes three times. I have always hated that damned sound.

"Wh-what?" I drop the shopping bags. It's true. The receipt . . . It's what I thought it was.

Meena bites her lip. "A cab's coming. I'm not taking the car. I've packed some clothes and a few other things."

She is so short in the way she speaks to me, so matter of fact, that it throws me, despite the fear evident in her tight expression. The words crash into me like waves in the ocean and plunge back into it. *How is this possible? I left forty-five minutes ago on a normal weekday. Just a trip to the store. Now my wife says she is leaving.*

"Is it . . . someone else?" My voice quivers with cold hatred.

She holds her body rigidly. "Yes . . . sort of." I notice the stiff angle of Meena's neck. Guilt, sorrow, dismay, defiance—I can't count all the things it conveys.

The hair rises on the back of my neck. "Sort of?"

Her breath comes in agitated puffs. "There is another man. But I'm leaving because I don't love you, Bhavesh. Because I . . . just can't be here anymore."

Horrible, hot anger engulfs me. It is long overdue. Despite the receipt, my suspicions, the jealous thoughts, I had not really believed deep down that my nondescript *Dalit* wife could attract another man. Neither did I think she would expect to survive away from me. *Me, who* had given her everything she had. The cords in my neck are tight with the need to shout, but I deliberately soften my voice. "Get in the kitchen."

"Bhavesh . . ." In the uncertain light, I can see black circles under her raisin brown eyes. She flings her hands up. "You can't, not this time."

"Can't what?" I growl and grab her wrist, twisting it slightly. There's no sound save the slow, deliberate clicking of the big clock in the hallway.

"Okay." She huffs impatiently, as if I am an annoying inconvenience. I let go of her hand and she acquiesces to my command, moving towards the kitchen with rapid steps, rubbing her wrist as she walks.

The puppy tries to follow us into the breakfast nook, nipping at our heels and growling at us, and I have to usher the thing back into the hallway before I can shut the door.

"Where is Maya?" I ask, a frisson of fear in my voice.

Meena says quickly, her voice small and damp. "In her room. I won't try to take her, Bhavesh."

"You are right that you won't," I say coldly as I follow her into the breakfast nook and through to the kitchen. Anger and relief feel like a rabbit running wildly around my rib cage.

I close the door to the hallway. I glare at her across the spillage of muted late afternoon light streaming in from the window. "We keep it down," I say.

"Agreed." She looks relieved.

"Fucking whore," I say, stepping directly in front of her. My finger stabs at the air near her chest. "I should kill you right now."

Meena pales, but keeps her composure. "You won't, though."

"You think? I saw a woman dragged off when I was growing up, never seen again. She wasn't even a *Dalit*."

"You dinosaur!" Meena cries, her face furious and knotted. "This is America. A taxi cab is on its way, and people know where I am and what I'm doing." *I bet one is that Tammy whore*, I think, *egging my wife on. If ever a woman needed a man to keep her in line.* A nuclear heat radiates from my bones. My cheeks quiver with rage.

"And you love your daughter too much to go to jail for me." She tilts her chin at me in defiance.

"How long have you been planning this?" I ask, feeling myself become still.

She smiles, a lopsided, pained smile. "About thirty minutes."

My hands fist into tight balls, my knuckles hard and white. "Who is he? Do I know him?"

"He is someone I knew before you. He . . ." She stops, her voice cracking. "I ran into him about eleven months ago."

"Eleven months! You . . . How?" I sit down on a dark wooden dining chair. It is too much to process. Eleven months. I feel the color drain from my face. How could I not have known?

"He wanted me," she says, a defiant edge to her voice, "and I wasn't going to." The words seem to bubble out of her. "But, do you remember that night you forced your penis into my mouth because I burnt the dinner? The night you nearly choked me with it?"

I slump in the chair, a foul odor like resignation filling my nostrils.

"Your penis forced into my mouth, worse than you would treat some whore. That's what made the difference. I want you to know that." All I can see of Meena's face, of her profile, is stony. Her arms are crossed stiffly on her chest as she leans against the center island.

I feel sick suddenly. I remember the mark of my hand on her cheek, like a brand. I see the hate in her eyes, hard and glittering like diamonds, and I know then there is no hope. I look at the floor and take deep breaths to try to drive it away. "Go then," I roar. "Go, you ungrateful, Untouchable bitch. Go from all I have given you, all I have sacrificed for you. India, my family, my mother, I gave it all up for you." My hands tremble at the injustice.

"I know," Meena says, wincing, then nods toward Maya's bedroom. "But she's the only bit of it I'm grateful for."

"You won't see her," I add quickly and rapidly. I look at her with furious determination.

Meena scurries around the kitchen island and towards Maya's room. "I'm going to say goodbye to her."

I leap straight out of the chair, bouncing on my toes like a boxer. "No, you won't!"

Meena rolls her eyes at me, dismissive, disdainful. The temperature of my blood rises a few degrees again and I grab her arm, tightening my grip on it.

"Ow," she says. "Let me go!"

I glower at her, my eyes like slits. "You're not seeing her."

Meena wriggles, but I keep my grip tight. "Don't be stupid."

She makes a frantic grab for the door handle but fails to break my grip. I start shoving her down the hallway. I am done with her.

"Get out," I say savagely. I gesture to the front door with a grim twist of my wrist. "Get out of my house!"

Meena darts toward Maya's room, but I grab the collar of her blouse and yank open the front door with my other hand.

"I want to say goodbye to my daughter!" she screams, tears rolling down her cheeks. With a final shove, I push her out, sending her stumbling on the path.

Maya appears as I throw Meena's suitcase after her. Maya stares at Meena, then swivels her head to look at me, her lower lip starting to tremble. The puppy zigzags excitedly in front of her, yapping delightedly at the sight of the front door. Charlie loves his evening walks.

Meena clambers to her feet. "Maya, my sweet. Mommy—"

I slam the door in her face.

43
MEENA

I glance at the cheap little twenty-five-dollar phone in my hand, the phone my multi-millionaire lover gave me. A bubble of schoolgirl hysteria expands in my chest. I had lied. No one knew what I was doing, no one was expecting me. I'd called a cab, but that was all. When I had begun to pack, it had been an emotional act. A desperate shoving of clothes and memories into a suitcase—to stem the feelings growing in me, restless and cresting like a storm wave.

I could go to the apartment I have newly leased, but the thought of being with Ramu, of making his dream mine, pulls at me like the moon pulls on the tide. Slow and insistent. It is not the thought of starting out alone that scares me; rather, it is the prospect that, with Ramu, I could change the world a little that excites me so fervently. To provide a safe house to abandoned or abused girls and train them in skills to make them independent—the idea has consumed me like a tornado, so I could not eat or sleep properly since Ramu's visit.

I put my face in my hands as I wait under a gigantic oak tree, a little way up on the other side of the street. When Bhavesh ejected me through the front door, my phone was in the kitchen, my purse in the bedroom. I had not known how I would pay the cab driver, or how I might call Ramu. Then I remembered the phone Ramu had given me.

With everything that happened that afternoon, I had forgotten about my hotline to him, which I had switched off and stored in a 'secret' compartment in my suitcase. Bhavesh never did any packing, so it had seemed like an ideal place to put the phone when the affair ended. I was going to get rid of it—obviously I was.

I never had. It was absurdly sentimental, but letting go of the phone would be like finally letting go of Ramu. I loved its retro LCD display, the way it fit in the palm of my hand. I'd also loved the way he was the only person on the other end of it.

The cab driver doesn't trust me. Greasy hair. Pockmarked face. Bushy eyebrows and a prominent overbite. Behind his wire-rimmed glasses, his eyes go comically wide. "Is this all you have, lady?" he gestures at my single piece of hard-cased Samsonite luggage. I know I must look a sight: kajal smudged on my tear-streaked face, hair wild around my shoulders, my blouse undone and missing two buttons from the scuffle with Bhavesh.

I draw myself to my full five feet two inches and give him my most charming smile. "Yes, I left in a hurry, but I'll take care of you when you drop me off." He looks at me doubtfully but fetches my case and puts it in the back with me, so I can retrieve the phone. I am so relieved when it starts up and finds a signal that I could sing with happiness.

"Meena?" Ramu's voice is small and gravelly with disbelief.

"Ramu, are you at the apartment?" My heart gives a great, hurtful lurch, as though it were trying to leap out of my body to meet him.

"Yes, where are you? Are you okay?" His words come in a rush.

"I'm outside. I've left him, Ramu. I've left Bhavesh." Relief forces my eyes shut.

"That's . . ." His voice cracks. "I'm coming down."

"Ramu." Under my fingertips, the phone has sprouted fragile, magical wings.

"Yes?"

"Bring some cash."

•   •   •

A rectangle of quivering evening light covers us as we hold each other. He does not ask questions and we do not go to bed, despite the way we both ache for the other one after almost seven months apart. Instead, we sit on the long bay window seat in our little living room. It really is *ours* now. The evening moon floats like a thin cucumber slice in a lemonade sky.

I cry, great, wracking sobs laboring like stones from my heaving breast for Maya. How is it possible to be so happy and relieved, so free, and at the same time to feel such loss? Time passes, the room turning to gray and then falling into darkness like a shroud, and Ramu asks the question.

"Maya is staying with him?" He reaches over to smooth my ruffled hair.

I let out a breath, my chest shuddering. "Yes. She belongs here."

"But . . ." He pauses, giving me an appraising look. He runs agitated fingers through his hair.

"But she will hate me?" I finish his sentence for him. My breath is a solid thing, stuck like a bone in my throat.

It is a valid point and one which has crossed my mind. That Bhavesh might poison Maya's young mind against me.

"It doesn't matter." A moan rises from my throat.

"Doesn't matter?" He raises his eyebrows so high they disappear under the hair that has fallen on his forehead.

"It matters to me, of course. Just the thought of it hurts so much, like I might drown in it. But *I* don't matter. I don't have to be the most important thing in her life. It's okay if she hates me, as long as she is happy." I squeeze my eyes shut. Grief pulses inside my head as constant as a cloud of black flies.

Ramu draws me close to him and puts my head on his chest. He kisses my head gently, his breath like a web on summer grass. It quells my doubts.

I take a deep, shaky breath. "When are we going?" I ask.

"To India?" He tips my face up and looks at me searchingly. "When do you want to go?"

The thought of going back to India, to the scent of spices and dust, surges inside me like a wave. I clutch at the collar of his shirt. "As soon as we can."

．　．　．

"I am leaving the country on Saturday, Bhavesh," I say over the telephone. I can hear a squeaky, high-pitched note in my voice. I clear my throat.

"Leaving with your millionaire, Nayak?" Bhavesh asks roughly.

"You've been busy, huh? Who did you talk to, Tammy?" My heart speeds like a racecar in my chest and my hands shake uncontrollably.

"Your aunt." Bhavesh snorts.

My body is heavy with resentment. "Were you asking her for your money back?"

A tunnel of silence stretches between us. The air is full of unspoken words, a vicious silence, like the moments before a bridge collapses. I should be careful, I realize. Insults won't get me anywhere.

I wait for my heart to slow down. "I want to see Maya before I go."

"Where are you going?" His voice is cold and heavy.

I hesitate, not wanting to tell him.

"India. Bihar." I stammer a little.

"Why there?" Bhavesh asks, contempt dripping from his voice like cream.

"We are going to start an orphanage." I exhale slowly.

He laughs, a laugh like a hyena. "*Kitne stupid ho tum!* How fucking pathetic, abandoning your daughter for a bunch of worthless rat children you don't even know."

I swallow, pushing back several possible retorts from my mind. "Can I please see her before I go?"

"No." My heart plunges as the line cuts off with a click. The air rushes from my lungs.

．　．　．

"Bitch!" Tammy says, never one to mince her words. "Leaving me for a millionaire. You're a cliché, Meena, I want you to know that. Straight out of an E. L. James novel."

"Who?" I ask, not hiding my confusion.

"*Fifty Shades of Grey?*" My face remains blank and Tammy rolls her eyes. "Never mind. Let's just say that some people will do *a lot* to hang around with a millionaire."

I reach over and touch my friend's hand, a rare sardonic smile finding its way onto my face. "I would still leave with him, even if he was only a millionaire."

Tammy grins back. "A Bhavesh-free life suits you, Meena. You're . . . *blooming* already."

My smile fades. "But a Maya-free one doesn't."

"You know my opinion on that." Tammy wags a finger in my face, her voice fierce.

"I can't do it," I reply. My mouth feels full of sawdust. "I . . . If you could see him with her, and her with him, you'd get it. He is the best father, but just a really shitty husband. For me, at least."

There is silence between us for a moment, Tammy still looking unconvinced.

"I . . . Look, there's something I need to ask of you, and I'm not sure you'll like it. I want you to look out for my daughter, try to make sure she remembers me." I hold my breath, my hands clasped tight.

Tammy's expression is a kind one, but the words are what I expected. "How am I supposed to do that? I'm fairly sure your husband hates me."

I shake my head helplessly. "I don't know, but . . . given time. Maybe."

• • •

San Francisco
Summer 2015

It is a hot August morning with a slight breeze when Ramu and I head out from our apartment to leave the country. This trip is just a preliminary one, as Ramu estimates his departure from the business will take a few months to achieve properly. But it is still the start of the dream.

And yet, I feel bittersweet as we get into the chauffeured car and begin the drive out to San Francisco International Airport. Our route takes us through busy areas of the city which I know I will miss. The symphony hall passes by on the right. For years, I have had an unspoken desire safely locked in a dark box to spend a night there and hear the orchestra.

"What are you thinking?" Ramu squeezes my hand and brings me back to the present.

"Oh, silly thoughts," I answer ruefully, thinking about the likely lack of symphony halls in the remote parts of Bihar.

He looks at me over the top of his gold wire-rimmed glasses with a languid smile. None of this has seemed real, these last five days that have gone by like caterpillars do. It has been like a kind of limbo. It has not been like the affair we carried on for several months, flying past in a blur, nor has it been like living together in a pretend marriage.

I returned to the house—using my spare key—in the day when I knew Maya would be at school and Bhavesh at work to retrieve my phone and passport. Once inside, I glanced around the house I'd shared with Bhavesh for ten years, feeling like a stranger in it, all the while darting furtive glances over my shoulder, feeling I would get caught any minute. In spite of the warm sunlight streaming in through the garden window, I felt cold and uncomfortable.

I continued to work—and the commute had been easier—although my five-days' notice had not been received well by my department head. I said goodbye to Tammy in a tear-filled lunch on Friday, yet all of it has been like holding in a long, protracted breath before doing the crazy life-changing thing we are about to do.

"Thoughts for another life," I add. This, *this* seems real, despite the chauffeur and the dream-like, muted cyan sky lying beyond the car's tinted windows.

Another life . . . One that is fading further with every mile the car covers as it whizzes south along the freeway. Sorrow and guilt tears through my heart. A life where I could still live with my daughter. It is the hardest thing I have ever had to do, to leave Maya behind. To not know if and when I will see her again. How many times in the last few days have I run the other scenario through my mind? Of snatching

Maya, of using all of Ramu's money and influence to play the system and hopefully keep her from Bhavesh.

I make a small, agitated sound; my chest feels as if someone is squeezing it with an iron fist. Maybe I should not leave my daughter with a man who could treat his wife in such a way. I have thought about that, too. Because it was not the memory of how many times his fingers brushed Maya's hair, or squeezed her hand when they went out together, or the way he's always buying her toys, even the puppy she wanted. Nor is it the way he always wants to educate her, how he becomes his little girl's own personal tour guide on a day out at the zoo, admirable though this attitude might be between a traditional Indian man and his daughter.

No, it is simply because Fremont is the best place for Maya right now, and to take her away from her father would break her little heart as much as her mother's leaving will.

As we turn back inland a little, that last stretch towards the airport, I crane my neck desperately to take one last glimpse down towards the end of the bay. I cannot really see Fremont from where I am. The gray morning is like a huge lead-coated balloon, everything outside an indefinite haze. But I can imagine it, the cookie-cutter, beige house where my eight-year-old daughter, who I have never wanted to hurt, whose world I have wanted to keep innocent and magical forever, is waking up on her first weekend without her mother.

44

BHAVESH

"Get up, *pyaare beti*. Get up."

Maya rolls over, her eyes blinking in the first rays of the sun entering the room through the shutters. It is the weekend; usually she is the one waking her parents up, not the other way around.

"I mean it, Maya," I say again, my voice insistent. "*Please,* get up."

The crackle in my voice wakes her up. "What is it, Daddy?"

"We're going on a trip."

"Are we going to see Mommy?" Maya's voice is chirpy and high-pitched with excitement.

"Yes, yes we are, my sweet. As long as we hurry."

"Goodie." That has woken her, and she sits up as I hand her some clothes. "No wash, Daddy?"

"No time, sweet."

I can see Maya's brain whirring: she may have been awoken early, but this is turning out to be a good day already. No wash *and* she is going to get to see Mommy, who she has missed so much all week.

"Will Mommy be coming home today, Daddy?" Maya's face is so intense with feeling I have to look away.

I stop, crouching down in front of her. "I tell you what; why don't you ask her that when you see her?"

.   .   .

MEENA

Ramu, out of habit, tried to book us in business class. I felt that the extra fifteen thousand or so dollars was not quite in the spirit of the trip. Guilt flitted darkly over his features when I gently pointed this out to him. We have compromised with 'Economy Plus,' which was *only* about eighteen hundred more than regular economy.

Sometimes the numbers in Ramu's life make my head spin. You would think millionaires would be a little . . . *sensible* with their money, if not downright tight. How else do you amass so much of it? But not Ramu, apparently.

"Boarding hasn't begun yet," Ramu says, looking at the board inside the terminal. "Are you okay with the luggage while I make a quick pit-stop?" He blinks at me patiently.

"Sure." I will have to get him to stop referring to going to the bathroom as a 'pit-stop.' Not the time for a racing metaphor, I think ruefully.

I chortle to myself, a far-away look on my face. *Damn,* I am going to be an interfering . . . Well, *mistress,* I suppose. I was never that way with Bhavesh, who had taken any attempt to interfere in his well-being as some sort of insult to his manhood. But with Ramu, I am getting an ever-growing instinct to look after him, to make sure he is safe and properly presented to the world.

Maybe I am getting old. Or, more likely, maybe I am missing the little girl who has always been the victim of my motherly interfering before now. My heart feels like one of those towels *Aai* wrung before she hung it out to dry.

"Mommy!" I shudder as a bolt runs through me like an electric shock. The call is distant, muffled within the insidious cacophony of the airport terminal. Though it could be any little girl, it is as if I have just conjured up my daughter up with a mere thought.

"Mommy!" The second shout cannot be ignored. I turn, my heart smashing against my ribs. Maya comes running up to me, big brown eyes that mirror her confusion, her long dark hair a tangled brunette bird's nest, gnawing at her lower lip as she launches herself into my outstretched arms. Bhavesh is a little behind her and out of breath. I gather Maya, lifting her.

"Maya, Maya," I say over and over, tears falling to smear over smooth, eight-year-old skin. My tongue is thick with thankfulness. Bhavesh catches up, a murderous look on his face.

"You brought her," I say, surprised and grateful. "You brought her to say goodbye."

"No, Mommy," Maya says, drawing back and fixing me with a serious look. "We came to make you stay."

I shoot Bhavesh a glance, and he returns my look with a cold, hard glance. "We came to give you one last chance," he says frostily. "One last chance to come to your senses and return home, where you belong."

"Please, Mommy," says Maya, "I'm so sad without you there." Then she buries her face against my skin again. I breathe in her scent, her hair smelling of Suave Watermelon Kids shampoo.

I look past her at Bhavesh. My body is pierced with needles of fire, rage against Bhavesh for using his daughter in this way and my powerlessness in his hands. His lips are pressed into a thin white line. What I see in his face is the same expectation he has had throughout all our married life: that he will get his own way.

I put Maya down and crouch so that only she can hear what I have to say. "Maya, sweet girl, I need you to listen to me now. Remember what I am going to say." I pause, waiting for my daughter to wipe a tear away. "Are you ready?"

Maya nods, her face intense and shiny. All around us people whisk by.

I capture Maya's hands between both of my own palms and look deep into my daughter's limpid brown eyes. "I love you more than anything in the world. My going does not mean that I love you any less. You understand?" I ask softly.

I can see Maya feels the weight of my words even through her despair. Tears well in her eyes, but she does not avert her gaze. She inclines her head as if to say, "Yes, Mommy, I understand."

Outside the airport terminal window a jet airliner roars off, taking away. "I'm leaving because sometimes things have to change, or they become bad. Sometimes people can't live together anymore, and that's Mommy and Daddy. Daddy loves you and will look after you, and you will see me again." I put a hand to the side of her face and press my daughter's face to my chest. I have a single second to convey my love to her, as fiercely as I can, before a menacing shadow falls over us.

I look up to find Bhavesh towering over me. "What are you telling her?" he snaps.

I stand up, clasping Maya's shoulder for support—otherwise, I would surely collapse, my heart is so heavy. "That I love her, and that you love her."

His forehead creases in furrows. "So, you're coming home, then?"

"*No*, Bhavesh." I speak forcefully, the words falling from me as distinct as chiseled stone.

"You will burn in hell for this," he seethes, pulling Maya around to stand behind him. Maya whimpers. His icy words fall like hail, piercing my skin, and penetrating the floor. "I will make sure your daughter knows you for the selfish, deceitful whore you are."

I become aware of someone standing nearby; Ramu has returned, stealthy as a tiger, and places himself just a few feet behind me. Bhavesh sees him.

"Does it make you feel good," Bhavesh spits at him, "taking a mother from her daughter?"

Ramu meets Bhavesh's seething gaze calmly, levelly. Suddenly, it as if the airport has faded away; we are back in a dining hall in Grace Mercy Children's Home, boys of a higher caste tormenting Ramu and me for washing and putting away our dishes too early—so we could get to class in time—before they washed their own. I remember how that ended: the hotheaded boy Ramu beat senseless another boy who stupidly laid a hand on his Meena. The look of horror on Mahadev's face as he pulled Ramu off the boy had been almost worth the month-long detention Ramu was given as punishment.

I take a step forward to plant myself between them.

"Maya is welcome to come along, too" says Ramu. His voice is measured, but taunting.

Ramu hardly seems to move when Bhavesh charges past me and the punch comes at him, twisting his body just enough for Bhavesh to go sailing past, then lose his balance and stumble to his knees.

Instinctively, I grab my daughter to shield her. I squeeze her to my belly and press my palm to her ear.

"That's the free one," Ramu says, his hands bunched into fists like a boxer about to enter a ring, "and you missed. No more free ones."

"You don't get to say her name!" Bhavesh bellows. Around us people are murmuring, looking at us with raised eyebrows. My skin prickles from the hundred eyes that watch us. "You don't get to say my daughter's name! You are taking her mother away."

Ramu wavers, and reproach flits across his face. He looks at the floor beside Bhavesh. "Get up, man," he says. "Take your daughter home. This isn't the place." A cracked tiredness runs through his voice.

Bhavesh gets to his feet, batting away an offered hand. "I don't want to touch you," he says. "*Chamar*, you scum. All your money, your shiny suit, none of it can mask the stench that comes off you. You sicken me." He staggers over towards Maya and yanks her away from me. I lunge at Maya, but it's too late. "Take her, then. She's just a used up, second-hand *Dalit*. I have what I want from her." Spittle sprays from his mouth like venom.

I watch Bhavesh. For all that Ramu disgusts him, he is happy to put his face just inches from the '*chamar* scum.' Ramu does not flinch, and Bhavesh wisely keeps his fists by his side this time.

"I've already had what I want from her," says Bhavesh. A nasty grin begins to widen his mouth. "Again . . . and again . . . and again."

Maya's lips quiver. She can hear all of this. I find myself looking down at my daughter as she watches her father abusing Ramu and, in turn, abusing me. It is as it has always been, the higher caste putting down the lower one.

The announcement for our flight's boarding gate begins over the airport's speaker system and I look back at Bhavesh, a thought forming, a feeling that I had assumed now beginning to change.

"And she's not even that good," Bhavesh says. "Most of the time she just sounds like a pig."

I edge myself and Maya away from the pair of them, the sensation of moving almost dreamlike as we start to melt into the flow of people who are nervously moving past Bhavesh and Ramu. *He loves his daughter, but if Maya stays with Bhavesh,* I think to myself, *then she will grow up exposed to the same venom, the same rhetoric.* I know it; he won't be able to help himself.

"Do you make the pig noises, too, eh? Two *Dalit* pigs rolling around in the filth."

I do not see Ramu's reaction to this latest insult, as I am already pushing Maya at a fast walk towards the gate. The thought of my daughter one day speaking Bhavesh's prejudiced views is too much for me.

"Mommy?" Maya says, belatedly realizing that we are moving away from them.

"Maya, *pyaari beti*, you're coming with me. Is that okay?" I ask, my back tight with a feeling like pins and needles, waiting for the inevitable shout. It still hasn't happened.

"Coming?"

"To India, with me and Ramu?"

Maya nods her head, her tearful face crumbling like soggy soda crackers.

That is all the reassurance I need, and we are almost running as I see the shuttle for the main terminal pulling in ahead of us, its doors opening and passengers spilling out.

"Eh! Eh! What are you doing?" Bhavesh's shout cuts across the busy hall and I glance back to see him starting to pursue us. Ramu looks bewildered for a moment, then gives chase.

Ahead, passengers are boarding the shuttle back to departures. "Run, Maya," I say, "or we'll miss the train!"

My daughter looks confused and my heart is breaking for her, but she does as she is told and, in that moment, I have never felt more strongly that I am doing the right thing. We make the train, pushing past the stragglers, and I turn to see Bhavesh running—huffing and puffing in pursuit. He waves his fist and mouths something, though I can't tell if sound is coming out. The stronger and the more athletic Ramu is gaining on him.

"Stop!" Bhavesh shouts, only a few feet from the doors as they begin to bleep a warning that they are about to close. Suddenly, Ramu shoulders past Bhavesh at a sprint and leaps through the doors as they shut.

The carriage is busy enough that Ramu nearly knocks an elderly woman over and everyone turns to look as Bhavesh reaches the doors, which have just shut him out. He bangs against them.

"You bitch!" he shouts, the words mostly muffled by the glass, though I can read them on his lips. "Give me my daughter you filthy *Dalit* whore—"

He carries on, but the train begins to pull away.

"Hi Maya," Ramu says, smiling down at her. Then he looks at me. "Maya's coming, then?"

All I can do is numbly shrug my affirmation.

"She hasn't got her passport with her by any chance?"

I shake my head, the enormity of what I have just done sinking in. "She doesn't even have . . . a passport."

Ramu pulls out his phone. "Okay, no biggie. I've got people, we can sort this."

"Really?" I say, hope leaping in my chest as he pulls up a number and calls it.

Ramu's returning look is only half-reassuring. "You think he'll flag down airport security or the police?"

"Probably," I reply, but at the same moment Ramu's phone connects him with someone.

"Congressman Larry!" he says with a businessman's exaggerated joviality. "How would you like a cheap and quick way to pay back that five-million-dollar favor you owe me? I need a passport for a little girl."

EPILOGUE
Meena

Fall 2030
Sonoma, California

When I pull up at the end of the dusty trail in the rental car, Maya is still speaking to Bhavesh up on the small, sloping piece of land he rents to keep his goats on. I look at my watch and run my hand across my eyes. We will miss our flight if we do not get moving, so I am going to have to go up there and get Maya . . . And, *dammit*, see Bhavesh.

Vineyards stretch away on either side as I walk up the path to where the pair of them are talking near the gate. Several small trees cover my approach and I stop, unashamedly eavesdropping as I strain to listen to their conversation.

"Eh, I like it here, Maya, it's quiet."

"I know, Dad," Maya replies with that calm, measured voice of hers, "I'm just saying that you need to get out more. You could still meet someone," she says with a brittle laugh. "It's not too late, you know."

My twenty-four-year-old daughter sounds like the parent as she speaks, and a small flush of self-satisfaction and pride washes through me.

"I've got my goats," he replies with forced joviality. "What more do I need, eh? There's Anisha and Suraj and Maya."

Maya laughs. "She's definitely the naughtiest."

"I know," Bhavesh agrees. "Did I ever tell you that *Amma* raised cows?"

"No," Maya says, although I know for a fact that he has, several times.

The mention of Bhavesh's mother is enough for me. I take a deep breath and stride out from under the tree to break things up.

"Mommy!" Maya says as they notice me.

Bhavesh scowls automatically, although he quickly forces a smile back into its place. "Is it that time already?" he asks.

"I'm afraid so," I say, smiling pleasantly to him. I only saw Bhavesh the first day we arrived and exchanged barely a dozen words with him. It is always this way when I bring Maya to visit. "Rush hour is starting, so we need to leave plenty of time to get there and return the car, otherwise we'll risk missing the flight."

"I've got the night shift at work, so I need to head back and get ready, anyway," Bhavesh says, a little like he is giving permission for me to bring the visit to an end.

"Do you like it?" I ask about his security guard job without thinking. I wince inwardly, waiting for a snippy reply, but the import business had once been everything to him and I still cannot get my head around him working for a boss.

"It's quiet," Bhavesh mumbles, but that is all I get, which is probably for the best. He never argues with me in front of Maya anymore, so I guess she may have saved me from a more defensive reply. "Until next year," he says, turning to Maya, and he hugs his daughter goodbye.

•   •   •

Twenty-hour hours later, we are back in Himachal Pradesh where the monsoon season is finally beginning to break up. From my vantage point in the orphanage's kitchen, crouched as it is in the low-lying Shivalik foothills, I can finally see the white-capped range. The view of the distant mountains that Maya sketches from her favorite perch—a covered veranda with a railing hanging on the brink of a precipice—is the best it has been since the start of the rainy season.

I bustle out onto the veranda bearing a heavy silver tray with three bone china cups of tea.

"Darjeeling, just how you like it," I say gently. "Ramu brought some back from the town."

"Thanks, Mom," she says, giving me a sidelong grateful look as she adjusts the *pallav* of her sari to bring the cup to her lips. If I was twenty years younger, we could be twins drinking Darjeeling tea in handloom saris.

Ramu appears on the veranda, dressed in an old-fashioned *kurta* and gold-rimmed glasses, his hair newly washed. How I love this about him—not a hair out of place, so suave and well-groomed. Not like Bhavesh, who looked like a grizzly bear in the mornings.

We sit in the still air, silent except for the clanging of yak bells, as a lone Sherpa farmer moves his herd on the sides of the mountains, gazing at the first splendid view in months. It has been worth the wait. Over to the left, twisty pines cover a landscape of snow-clad slopes. The ink-blue Shivalik ranges of the Himalayan foothills rising in the distance are touched by mist and the golden rays of the sun. Specks of yellow and brown flash across the valley as a flock of mynas take flight, their flutter tinkling the row of little brass bells hanging from the eaves.

"Hmm, good news! I've been reviewing the numbers. The business we launched years ago is showing an exceedingly tidy profit." Ramu says, slurping his tea around the word 'profit.' His delighted gaze bounces between Maya and me.

I am pulled back by a memory some ten years ago. Ramu sitting on this red cushion—with an ethnic elephant motif on its cover—on this dark-stained wicker chair, contemplating the stupendous view as he does now.

"I want to run something by the two of you," he had said to Maya and me as he cleared his throat and lifted his chin. "I've been thinking." I remember him pulling at his nose and rubbing it slowly.

I had rolled my eyes in Maya's direction, who grinned discreetly. "What have I told you about this 'thinking,' my love?" I had said, turning back to Ramu. "Always trouble."

He playfully leaned over and flicked my shoulder. "It is the driving to town that does it. It is like meditation."

I punched him on the arm. "It should be like watching the road. This is why I never let you drive the school bus."

Ramu sat up straight in his chair, animated. "I think we should start up a business."

"You don't think maybe the orphanage is enough to occupy us?" I asked with mock outrage.

Ram removed his glasses and polished them on the edge of his linen *kurta*. "I mean . . . more like making the orphanage into a business."

"You're right," Maya piped up, a clear note of irony in her voice, "make those little monsters earn their keep." We could hear in the distance the chiming of a metal gong and the excited chattering voices of children as they ran out of their classrooms. Five years since beginning the orphanage we were at capacity, turning away new children every week.

Ramu ran his fingers through his hair and gave us a reprimanding look.

"I used to be good at this sort of thing." He shook his head mournfully. "I was the master of the pitch."

I put a hand on his knee. "Well, we *are* a tough audience." I gave him a quick kiss on the cheek. Maya looked away. "Go on, my love."

Ramu grabbed the arms of the chair and leaned forward, his elbows on his knees and his hands clasped under his square chin. "I was thinking how we have always been good with teaching I.T. skills. It's so important, such a good way for a *Dalit* child to get a job where no one cares about their caste or where they have come from."

His enthusiasm was catching. "Do you really think it would work?"

"I don't think we have taken it far enough." His eyes struck us like a patch of searing sunlight, his voice intense. "I want to set up a website and software production company and have the children run it when they are old enough." He paused, looking reflectively at Maya. "With my help, of course."

He raised his arm and pointed out across the fields, stubbled with what remained of that year's crop of maize—thin, yellow stalks jutting out of the powdery brown soil—where the light was showing the first signs of waning. "And this is the clever part. For those good enough, we send them out into the world with a little start-up capital—maybe a 'pay-it-back-when-you-can' loan—and get them to do the same. Get as many orphan *Dalits* out there as possible, owning tech businesses, with disposable income and their own measure of . . ." he said grandly, "power."

Maya looked at him searchingly, intently listening.

"You know?" he prompted, his voice clear and confident, like how he sounded when pitching to investors. His eyes sparkled. "The power to make the world the way they want it to be."

A shrill ear-piercing sound rings through the corridors of the Nayak-Dalit Boys and Girls School and punctures my reverie, pulling me back to the present as *Masterji,* the school headmaster, shakes the traditional brass bell with an ornate wooden handle. There is only a momentary lapse prior to the thunderous sound of feet hammering on the stairs of the new three-story building adjacent to the lawn where we now sit.

I turn and look at Ramu, who is still going over the accounts. His hair is shot through with silver streaks and just in these last few years, crow's feet have appeared around his eyes, accentuated when he is deep in thought. My gaze roams over the planes and angles of Ramu's face— oh, how he still makes my heart dance. Often, he looks tired by this point in the day, yet he is always up early and never shies from taking on the most physical of jobs around the place.

Six-year-old Savita, her braided black hair flying in a long braid behind her, comes running out onto the veranda in a faded blue *salwar-kameez, chappals* worn thin. She skids to a halt in front of Maya, turning worshipful eyes on her.

"Miss Maya," she says commandingly with her hands on her waist.

"Dance class!" Maya exclaims, peeking a look at her wristwatch, a silver dial on a thin silver strap, and leaps up from her seat. "I am so sorry. Tell the others I will be two minutes getting changed."

She squeezes Savita's thin shoulders and lightly pats my back as she moves towards the main building, which doubles as an assembly and concert hall. She stops for a moment, raises her face with a bright, affectionate look, then turns back to lean down and kiss Ramu on the forehead.

"Most Glorious One, it was a wonderful idea then and now," she says, a fond note in her voice. Then she goes off to earn her keep, too.

ACKNOWLEDGMENTS

To my mom, Inderjit Kaur Ahuja, who gave me the gift of life and of storytelling.

To my husband, Tony Judge, thank you for your support in every way, and for giving me space to chase my dream. I simply would not be here without you.

To my son, Amaraj Judge for always being willing to brainstorm story ideas, plot problems, and pacing issues. You are my sounding board, my spring board, my story board.

To my daughter, Ghena Judge, for believing in me, and for pushing me to keep striving. Your unflagging encouragement of my writing healed the sting of a mountain of rejection and kept me going.

To my Dad, Joginder Singh Ahuja, your gentle cheerleading is imperative and your love is even more so. Penning Meena and Ram's story was hard labor and many hours of research. My path to publication was riddled with frustration and tears. But my writing journey was buoyed by the incredible generosity and support of so many people I could never name them all or ever thank them enough. But I'm going to try, anyway:

Thank you to Nikhil Shah for being my first beta reader, and for your insightful critique of the manuscript that led to the current version that someone else fell in love with.

Thank you to Margo Perin, my earliest editor, for teaching me how to write a saleable novel.

Thank you to my copy editor, Rain von Schwartzwalder, who went beyond the scope of her hire to point out mistakes and typos and suggest edits to make the prose better.

Thank you to my writing cohorts at Hedgebrook—Susan Bockus, Kathi Hansen, Gretchen Frances, Shala Erlich, and Emily Uecker—for their invaluable feedback. Special thanks to our incredible instructor, Samantha Chang; you made me see the hot issues in the manuscript, which has made *all* the difference.

Thank you to the memoir coach, Tammy Coia, and my Baja sisterhood of writers—with a special nod to Susan Simister—for your careful, kind and honest read of the manuscript, and for being my champions.

To my friend and writing coach Teresa Burns Gunther who inspires me with her words and her spirit. Thank you for holding my hand every week. My amazing Thursday writing group—Caroline Wang, Maniyka Veena, Paula Terzian, among others—whose strong writing voices rally me on.

Thank you to all the subscribers of my blog, and my well-wishers—you know who you are—too many to name, who repeatedly cheered me on, and kept asking when my next novel was coming out.

And lastly and most importantly, to each and every one of you for taking the time to read my words, to you I give thanks from the bottom of my heart. Without you all these people would have supported me for naught.

I love hearing from readers, so if you'd like to get in touch, you'll find me at:

http://thebrownneighbor.com

or visit me on
Twitter (@brownneighbor) or
Facebook (@AnoopJudgeAuthor)

ABOUT THE AUTHOR

Born and raised in New Delhi, Anoop Judge now resides in California. She is married with two nearly grown and fully admirable children, but she's also a recovering litigator, a former TV presenter, and a blogger. She is the author of two books *Law: What's It All About & How To Get In* (Twenty-Twenty Media), and the novel *The Rummy Club*, which won the 2015 Beverly Hills Book Award and received three other awards.

Her essays and short stories have appeared in *Down in the Dirt* magazine, in *Rigorous* journal, in *Scarlet Leaf Review*, in *Moon* magazine, and in *Litbreak* magazine.

An excerpt from this novel initially published in Green Hills Literary Lantern was nominated for the Pushcart Prize in 2019.

Most of her work can be found online at:
http://www.thebrownneighbor.com

NOTE FROM THE AUTHOR

Word-of-mouth is crucial for any author to succeed. If you enjoyed *The Awakening of Meena Rawat*, please leave a review online—anywhere you are able. Even if it's just a sentence or two. It would make all the difference and would be very much appreciated.

Thanks!
Anoop Judge

CPSIA information can be obtained
at www.ICGtesting.com
Printed in the USA
BVHW071155180521
607630BV00003B/195